MW01152294

THE
LIGHT
OF
LIFE

ALSO BY EDWARD W. ROBERTSON

THE CYCLE OF ARAWN

The White Tree
The Great Rift
The Black Star

THE CYCLE OF GALAND

The Red Sea
The Silver Thief
The Wound of the World
The Light of Life

THE BREAKERS SERIES

Breakers
Melt Down
Knifepoint
Reapers
Cut Off
Captives
Relapse
Blackout

REBEL STARS

Rebel
Outlaw
Traitor
Ronin

THE
LIGHT
OF
LIFE

THE CYCLE OF GALAND, BOOK 4

EDWARD W. ROBERTSON

Copyright © 2017 Edward W. Robertson

All rights reserved.

Cover illustration by Miguel Coimbra.
Additional work by Stephanie Mooney.
Maps by Jared Blando.

ISBN: 1546397892
ISBN-13: 978-1546397892

To Vonnegut, an early inspiration.

Mallon and Gask.

The Collen Basin and other lands.

EDWARD W. ROBERTSON

1

Dante clasped hands with his foe, ears ringing with the beat of his heart. On the white, bone-like surface of the ground, Gladdic gazed up at him, eyes shining with tears. Beside Dante, Naran looked thunderstruck and Volo looked ill, but Blays' shock was already being replaced by understanding.

And condemnation.

Gladdic tilted his weathered face to the clouds, as if seeking the gods behind them. He held the stump of his right arm close to his chest. Dante tightened his arm and helped the old man to his feet.

"I want nothing more than to leave this life and step into the beyond." Gladdic's voice was husky, as if he was announcing the death of a dear friend. "Even so, I will help you fight what has been unleashed. But I believe our fight will be in vain."

Dante tried to smile, but his mouth wouldn't do more than twitch. "You'd be surprised how much you can accomplish when you don't know that you're not supposed to be able to do it."

"This belief explains much about your behavior."

"I'm sorry." Naran's reddened face swiveled between them. "I don't understand what is happening."

"That's because you're in possession of a working sense of

right and wrong," Blays said. "What's *happening* is that Dante is proposing an alliance. With Gladdic. Not Gladdic of Yorton, friendly baker. But this Gladdic, the most unfriendly butcher."

This left Naran too flummoxed to speak.

Spears of guilt ran up Dante's spine. "You don't know what you're talking about."

Blays snorted. "You're doing that thing where you throw away every principle you've ever had because you think it'll provide you the slightest advantage in getting what you want."

"We've stumbled into something we don't understand. We can't afford to make rash decisions right now."

"And the decision to befriend a mass-murdering lunatic is reasoned and logical?"

"You saw what we fought back there. He was trying to destroy it—and we stopped him."

"'He' being the same person who has also repeatedly tried to destroy our allies from existing. Based on Gladdic's history of judgment, he was probably trying to stop that big fellow back there from declaring world peace."

"You are more correct than you know," Gladdic said. "But this 'world peace' would be the peace of eternal slavery."

Blays turned on him with the full fury of his scorn. "He's going to enslave us all, is he? Then why have you spent the last year trying to colonize the Plagued Islands and exterminate the Collen Basin? Driven mad by the impending end of the world, no doubt?"

"It was thought that the Eiden Rane remained in his prison. Unbeknownst to my former ally the Drakebane, who ruled these lands, the rebels of Tanar Atain have been working to release him so that he might destroy the Drakebane for them."

"This is exactly why we need his help." Dante glanced in the direction where they'd fled from the being Gladdic called the Eiden Rane—the White Lich—but the ghoulish landscape was currently empty. "He knows a whole hell of a lot that we don't. Fire destroys, but it can also illuminate. We need to see what it can show us."

"Right." Blays swung back toward Gladdic. "Where did you come by all this knowledge? Reading books? Speaking to people?"

The cadaverous man nodded. "In large part."

"Excellent. Then we will also go read these books, and speak to these people, freeing us up to kill you now."

"As you wish."

"We came here expecting to kill him," Dante said. "So to you, any action that *doesn't* involve killing him is the most foolish act since the last time you forgot to eat breakfast. But new information has come to light. Information that changes everything. Our plans have to change with it."

"Let me give it some thought." Blays wrapped his hand around the hilt of his sword. "On closer consideration, I'm pretty sure it's still a great idea."

"If we slay him now, we have no idea how long it'll take to learn about the Eiden Rane. Because whatever it is, the Drakebane's last act here was to try to destroy it. And when that failed, he was so terrified of it that he's abandoning his homeland altogether."

Blays' sword arm relaxed, the tension moving from it to his face. As he made a rare struggle for words, Naran surged forward, shoving Gladdic to the ground. The priest attempted to catch himself with his right arm; the impact of his stump against the stony surface made him gasp.

Naran drew his saber and jabbed it into the hollow of Gladdic's throat. "You murdered my captain. My oldest friend. My savior. In return, I send you to the Tilted Cabin that rests at the bottom of the sea!"

"Make it quick." Gladdic's gaze had shifted past Naran to the south. "After, you will want to run."

Dante wrenched his eyes away from the unfolding execution and to the southern horizon, beyond which they'd last seen the White Lich. There, a pair of dark shapes loped swiftly through the upthrust field of bony growths. The creatures had the length and height of wolves, but they were as slender as ferrets and as graceful as Galladese fishing-cats.

Dante's mouth dried out. "What are those?"

"His scouts," Gladdic said. "Although such a term understates their danger. They are more than a match for armed men. And their skin is hardened against the blades of the Odo Sein."

"Thanks for the warning," Blays said. "Got a boat we can use while you stay here and bravely hold them off?"

"Yes. It is beyond the labyrinth."

"Perfect. Don't worry, we'll *definitely* send help."

"The *labyrinth*?" Dante grabbed the priest's intact arm. "I don't know why you're willing to help us after everything that's happened. But if you want us to get out of here, then show us the way."

Again, Gladdic looked up at the clouds. A look of deep yearning creased the corners of his eyes. Coming from any other priest, Dante would have assumed he was beseeching the gods for aid, but he felt abruptly certain that Gladdic was wishing to die.

Gladdic's shoulders sank. "As you wish."

He loped forward, moving easily despite the grievous wound that had claimed his right arm. Naran bared his teeth and followed. Blays spewed profanity. Volo, normally as free with her opinions as a crow, ran along as if in a trance, still stunned by the understanding of what her rebel movement had done in releasing the Eiden Rane.

Dante held the rear, keeping one eye on the creatures as they pursued the five of them across the field of white spikes and red pools. He had utterly exhausted himself in the battle against the White Lich. The others were battered themselves—and Gladdic had just said the animal scouts were hardened against the nether-fueled Odo Sein blades they carried. There would be no more arguments between them. Not until they were out of this place and into safety—or whatever passed for it these days.

Gladdic weaved through a field of rocky protrusions streaked with iron rust. Beyond the next ridge, the ground leveled out in a plateau standing a hundred feet above the swamps below. Gusts of wind snapped at their clothes. A blank wall of rock rose from the end of the plateau, broken by a single opening just large enough for a single person to squeeze through. If Dante'd had any power remaining, he might have etched a staircase twenty feet up to the top of the short cliff, but as it was, there was no way forward but through the door.

Outside it, Gladdic opened his palm and whispered to himself. Pure white light blossomed from his grasp. He entered and the others followed. Inside, their breathing echoed from the tight tunnel walls. It smelled damp, shot through with the scent of aquatic life and lingering decay.

The tunnel forked. Gladdic glanced down each branch before continuing to the left. He'd hardly gotten ten feet before the labyrinth forked again. This time, the priest continued to the right, hardly breaking stride.

"You have this memorized?" Dante said.

Gladdic shook his white-haired head. At the next branch, he came to a stop. "Look into the nether. Where you find it, go the opposite."

"Why? Because you think it's a sign of evil?"

"Because down that path, things have died." The priest moved onward into the gloom, sandals scattering a pile of small bones. "The Drakebane betrayed me. He and his people will have departed, taking their boats with them. Yet we hid another canoe for just such a situation as ours. If it remains, you may employ it."

Blays grunted. "How gracious of you to bravely use us to save yourself."

"Just as you always have, you mistake me. This is not about my own life."

"So after devoting your golden years to murdering heretics, your enemies, and especially us, you suddenly want to save our skins?"

"Correct. For I believe you are the only ones who might slow the White Lich's progress."

"*Slow* him? Don't you mean stop him?"

Gladdic made a creaking noise that might have been a laugh. "You scatter words like bait on the surface of a lake, but I use each one as I mean it. To slow him is the best that you can hope."

Blays was quiet for a moment. "If you don't think we can kill him, then what's the point?"

"To allow the world a few more months of innocence before it is consumed."

At the next intersection, Gladdic took the right path, only to stop a few feet into it, murmur something under his breath, and backtrack. Down a side tunnel, Dante thought he heard breathing in the darkness. He told himself it was merely an echo.

Light shined ahead. After the black halls of the labyrinth, it burned like white-hot metal, yet it was nothing more than the overcast sunlight of the day. They stopped outside the exit to let their eyes adjust. The land before them ramped down to the rust-colored waters of the deepest swamp. At the boundary, a large canoe waited beside the white bank.

"That is my vessel," Gladdic said.

Blays strode forward. "I don't care if it's the boat waiting to ferry Lyle's blessed ghost up to Double Heaven. We're taking it."

As elsewhere in the Wound, the ground was scattered with

spindly, tree-like white structures ranging from two to eight feet tall. Before, Dante had taken them for a bizarre form of stalagmite. After hearing Gladdic's claim about the overflow of nether in the Wound, however, it looked as though the earth was sprouting bones.

These provided decent cover, yet the way ahead looked quiet and clear. Dante jogged after Blays. Halfway toward the boat, two shadows darted along the shore, far too agile for their size. Long claws sent grit scattering across the ground. The creatures came to a stop directly in front of the canoe.

Both had the height of a full-grown wolf—perhaps closer to that of a mule—but now that they were closer, Dante saw why they had appeared so slender: rather than animals of living flesh, the two creatures were made of naked bone, the same as when he reanimated a rat to scout for him. Rather than being white or yellowed, these bones were black.

He reached toward them with his mind. "They've been reinforced somehow. Like the swamp dragons. They'll be toughened against our swords."

Blays drew his Odo Sein blades. Purple-black nether shot along their lengths, swirling like lightning. "Bad move on their part. That only means it'll hurt more."

"The Eiden Rane has forged these animals into weapons," Gladdic said. "Don't let arrogance blind you to their danger."

Blays rolled his eyes and advanced, angling to the right of the two undead beasts that were cutting them off from the canoe. Dante drew his sword, jerking at the twitch from deep inside his spine. Nether flowed along the steel. He moved to Blays' left flank. Wordlessly, Naran unsheathed the sword he'd looted from one of the fallen knights and closed ranks.

"Look out!" Volo pointed uphill. There, two more of the creatures had appeared on the ridge. They held position, as still as statues, before springing downhill with frightening speed.

"Quickly now." Blays bent his knees. "Before they catch us in the back."

He charged the nearer of the first pair of animals. It skipped to its right. Dante pressed forward, driving it back toward Blays. Naran cried out, throwing himself toward Dante. Dante had only turned his back to the other beast for the briefest moment, but it had closed the distance between them with a single bound. Naran smacked into his side, driving him to the ground the instant before the animal soared over him. It reached for him with its scything claws, inches away.

At the shore, Blays swiped at the first of the creatures with both swords. It dodged most of his attacks like it was made of smoke. The few strikes that connected made a dull thwacking noise. Volo stuck close to Gladdic, brandishing her short, heavy-handled dagger. From her posture, she seemed to understand it would do little good against the bony monsters.

Stiff from their battle with the White Lich, Dante shoved himself to his feet. The beast that had flung itself at him had already come about and was lashing at Naran with its claws, skipping from side to side with the twitchiness of a wasp. Naran shuffled forward and took a backhand swipe at its neck. The creature tucked its front paws beneath it, the sword chipping into its shoulder blade as it rolled toward him.

As soon as it got its feet beneath it, it exploded toward Naran. The captain fell back, hacking at the animal's face and landing a glancing blow on its bony cheek, sending up a puff of bone powder. The creature sailed forward, plowing into Naran's shoulder. He collapsed under its unholy strength.

Dante was already charging forward, slamming his nether-wrapped blade into the beast's springy, naked spine. The blow landed with a dry crack, jolting up Dante's arm. A black chip spun away. The undead creature lashed out at Dante, claws gouging his forearm, and bounded backward.

Naran hauled himself to his feet. He was bleeding from three parallel slashes across his left shoulder. "Are we so much as hurting them?"

"Try for their joints," Dante said. "They don't bleed, but we can whittle them down."

Dazzling light spewed to his left. Gladdic faced down both of the animals that were charging from uphill, blasting them with streams of ether like symmetrical storms of lightning. Shadows steamed and sizzled away from the creatures' bones, but still they ran on, leaping from rock to rock. Gladdic stood firm, sheltering Volo behind him, showing no intention of trying to run. He didn't look scared. Just a little bit sad, as if hearing of the death of an old lover he hadn't spoken to since he was young.

The ether flared so brightly Dante had to shield his eyes. The lead creature tossed its head and peeled to the side. The second dropped into a crouch and sprung, claws reaching for the old man.

Shadows swept to Gladdic's hands. He planted his feet and sent a flood of nether coursing toward the oncoming monster. It disappeared into a cloud of darkness, crying out with a metallic, trumpet-like squall. Gladdic dropped to the side, kneeling in his plain gray robe. The creature tumbled past him, emerging from the shadows, clawing out to all sides to try to arrest its skid. Sections of its black bone had been scoured white.

An object bounced downhill toward Dante. It landed a few feet away: a severed bony paw, claws gnarled tight. The ankle, however, was all wrong. Rather than being slender, it was wide. Knobby. If anything, it looked like a vertebrae.

Naran called out in defiance, blocking a swipe of a claw with his sword. Dante ran to join him. They stood shoulder to shoulder, fending off one attack after another, but the creature was so quick they rarely had the chance to counter. To Dante's right, Blays was holding his own against the other scout that had cut them off from the boat. Inch by inch, he pushed his opponent toward the shore, but other than a few white chips cut out from its bones, the construct had suffered little appreciable damage.

Dante frowned, examining the one he and Naran were doing their best to contain. As a whole, its skeleton looked like no other animal he'd seen — but that was because no such creature existed. Rather, it had been forged from the bones of several different animals: the paws and claws of bears; the spine of some great cat; the strong snout and fangs of a massive wolf.

As far as he knew, such a thing should be impossible. When he reanimated a dead creature, he could only do so because the nether in the animal was already in sympathy with every other part of itself. Cobbling together multiple pieces from other animals, even of the same species, shouldn't result in anything more than an inert jumble of bones.

The beast drove forward, pushing him and Naran back in a frantic scrabble. Light and darkness shimmered where Gladdic did battle with the other pair, but the energies were already dimming. Gladdic had spent most of his powers fighting the White Lich. Soon, they'd be left with no sorcery whatsoever.

As Dante and Naran battled the monster back, Dante examined its long, sinuous spine. The vertebrae in its ankle couldn't be a mere artistic quirk. Not when the nethereal trace — the dark soul of the body — was contained somewhere within the spine, a fact Dante had only revealed during their trip to and the battle at the Wound of the World. Physically, the creature's spine showed no signs of irregularity. Frowning, Dante delved into the nether. The shadows within its vertebrae seemed normal as well.

After another exchange, the beast skipped back, favoring its front left paw. Naran pressed in on it, seeking to exploit their advantage. The beast tightened its fleshless jaws in something eerily like a smile and reversed course toward Naran. He thrust forth his sword. It clipped through the animal's ribs, sending chips of bone to all sides as the whirling nether discharged itself, but the beast kept onward, clawing at Naran's arm. He cried out and dropped his blade.

Before Dante could close on them, the animal raised its other paw high into the air and smashed its claws down through Naran's chest. Naran collapsed in a gout of blood.

The creature opened its jaws to crush the captain's skull. Dante hammered his blade into the side of its head, sending small cracks webbing from its eye socket. The animal whirled away.

As it dashed past him, Dante offered a clumsy swipe at its backside. The strike wouldn't do more than annoy the creature, yet it jerked its hips away as if he were about to plunge his weapon into its heart. As it flashed past, he got his first good look at its tail. Rather than being the typical streamlined extension of the spine that you saw in rats and dogs and so forth, the tailbones of the amalgamated beast were a short jumble of delicate bones that appeared taken from the ankles, feet, and toes.

"The tails!" Dante yelled. "Hit them in the tails!"

He sprinted after the retreating beast. It broke into a headlong run, opening ground between itself and him. Along the shore, Blays battered at his foe, pushing it toward the water until it was obliged to turn ninety degrees and break into a gallop in an attempt to peel away from the banks.

As soon as it pivoted, Blays flicked his sword at its backside. The nethereal blade bit into the monster's tail, sending small bones flying in all directions. The animal arched its back and tumbled into its component bones. Nether flowed away and vanished into nothing.

"As usual," Blays said, "when all else fails, stab them in the ass."

Up the slope, Gladdic had already reduced one of the beasts into a mangled heap that was currently dragging itself away through the crooked white pillars. The priest sent a savage blast of nether toward the remaining creature's tail, followed right after by a strike of ether. The twin forces pummeled into the animal's hindquarters and blasted the beast apart.

Dante jogged after his opponent, giving Blays the chance to catch up. The construct stared at them with its eyeless pits, then turned around and scampered up the hillside as fast as it could.

Dante sheathed his sword and ran back to Naran. The captain lay on his back, blood streaming from deep slashes that ran from his chest to his gut. His breathing was rapid and shallow, blood leaking from the corners of his mouth. He blinked continuously. Wary of depleting even another drop of his own trace, Dante reached for the ether. A pinprick of light appeared on his finger, then faded slowly to nothing, like a ship's lantern carried off into the night. He'd spent all of it earlier, too.

"Naran." Blays flung himself down beside the captain, grabbing his shoulder. "You're going to be all right, do you hear me?"

Naran rolled his eyes to take in Blays. A cold shudder ran down Dante's body. He grabbed at the nether around him, trying to force some last shreds to his command, but it slipped from his grasp like mist.

Volo ran up beside them, teary-eyed. Gladdic walked along in her wake. The priest gazed down on the dying man as if deciding which slice of beef to toss into the pan. He braced his hand on his thigh and lowered himself to his knees. A halo of clear light coalesced around his hands. The glow stretched into beams, shaping a cage of light around Naran's body. The cage contracted around the captain's chest wound, filling the gashes with a substance like sunshine reflecting from calm water.

The ether dimmed to a translucent, gelatinous state. The gashes grew opaque, vague hints of striation within them, then coalesced into ghostly muscle and skin. The outer layers hardened until the organs and bone beneath them were little more than murky shapes. After another moment, and his skin was unbroken beneath the long slashes cut through his jabat.

Naran coughed, spewing blood. He inhaled with a long gasp, then bucked upright, slapping his palms on the stony ground.

"He will live," Gladdic declared. "We should go."

Dante and Blays pulled Naran to his feet. Gladdic walked to the canoe and settled in its rear. Volo untied its lines and produced a pair of paddles. Bracing the shaky captain's arms over their shoulders, Dante and Blays helped him totter to the canoe and climb inside. They followed him in and shoved off, Volo taking the lead, Blays paddling behind her.

"How did you know to strike them in the tails?" Gladdic asked, his voice barely more than a monotone.

"They were composed of several different animals," Dante said. "That shouldn't have been possible. Not unless some higher magic was holding them together. When I saw a vertebrae where it shouldn't be, that made me think of traces."

"Traces?"

"The deep nether left behind by death. It's housed in the spine. I figured the lich might have found some way to mix up multiple skeletons and fuse them together using their traces, but their spines looked to be from a single animal. But the tails weren't—they were all jumbled up."

"Cunningly wrought. In seeking to destroy them, one would seek the head. The neck. Perhaps the ribcage. The tail, however, would be the last place one would think to strike."

"Fascinating," Blays said. "Now that you've cracked this mystery, how about you two geniuses put your big brains toward getting us away from this hideous place that keeps trying to kill us?"

Volo consulted with Gladdic regarding their current location and the closest alternative that might not be so full of the Eiden Rane's horrors. No matter how hard they paddled, the white bulge of the Wound loomed behind them, ruling over the top of the pale, ghastly trees, as if it meant to follow them to the ends of the earth.

2

"There's nothing on me, is there?" Blays turned in a half circle, tugging at his tunic for a better look at his back. "No spiders? Or ticks? Or spider-ticks that can build webs inside you and suck your organs dry like flies?"

Dante eyed him. "Why would you be worried about parasites? Everything in this place is dead."

"First of all, it's always a good time to be worried about parasites. Second, we just escaped from a guy who murdered several Andrac like they were mice in his pantry while assailing us with hundreds of not-zombies. Then he capped off the day by harrying us with skeletal monsters whose existence you thought to be impossible until the moment they started clawing you to bits. Forgive me for being concerned the lich might have planted something smaller on us."

"There are no vermin on you."

"I'm more worried about there being vermin *in* me. You use nasty things to spy on people all the time. You think that bastard can't do the same?"

Suddenly alarmed, Dante tucked into the nether, running a quick check of the shadows within Blays to confirm he wasn't harboring anything alien. When nothing showed up in Blays, Dante made a quick pass of the others and their surroundings on the small island where they'd finally tucked in after hours of paddling through the swamp.

"I don't see anything." Dante raised an eyebrow at Gladdic. "Do you?"

The priest shook his head. "Nothing."

"Then we're free of him," Blays said. "So that means I'm safe to shout, as loudly as I can, *why are we still traveling with someone who tried to slaughter the entire Collen Basin?*"

His words hung and died in the still, damp air.

Stiff and sore from the day's exertions, Dante seated himself on a white rock. "You just saw why."

"Because something strange and disturbing just came out of nowhere to muck up our plans? What else is new?"

"We've never seen anything like this before. We can't throw away our resources just because we don't like how they smell."

"'Resources'? Is that your new word for 'bloodthirsty maniac'? Have you forgotten the cave in Collen? The one we found after we drove him out of the city?"

"I never will," Dante said softly. "But we're the ones who stopped him and the Drakebane from destroying the White Lich. I'm afraid that if we don't learn what this thing is and what it intends to do, what we saw in the cavern will be seen all across this land."

Blays stared at him, then spread his arms at Naran. "Surely *you* don't think this is a good idea."

Naran seated himself on the ground. His face, normally a glowingly sun-burnished brown, was still ashen from the encounter with the lich's scouts. "I hate him like I hate hell. But I wouldn't be poised to offer you an opinion if he hadn't healed me this very day."

"Right. So one life saved, a few tens of thousands to go."

Dante ran his hands through his tangled hair. "The rulers of Tanar Atain were so terrified of this thing that the Drakebane's family spent decades organizing a takeover of Mallon in case they had to run from it. Volo, your friends in the Righteous Monsoon meant to use the White Lich to overthrow the Drakebane. Did they understand exactly what they were unleashing?"

The girl darted a look at him, her dark Tanarian eyes haunted and burning, then stared out into the swamp. "They told us the Eiden Rane was the only thing that had ever beaten the Knights of Odo Sein. That he'd protect us with one hand and smash the Drakebane with the other. But some of the others, those who came from the outer swamps, they said the Eiden Rane was a monster. That he'd devour us, too. We laughed at them. But we were wrong."

Blays scoffed. "How do you know that? Because he was trying to kill us? Did you forget the part where Gladdic and his pals had been trying to murder the lich with Star-Eaters? Maybe he was pissed off and mistook us for his enemies."

"No," Gladdic said. "He will take this land. He will kill those who live here—or turn them into the Blighted, the half-mad people who hide in the water. And once the swamps are his, he will devour one land after another. Just as he attempted to do an age ago. That is what we were fighting to stop."

"And congratulations on the bang-up job. Even if you're telling the truth, and for once in your miserable life you're trying to do the right thing, do you really think that undoes everything *else* you've done?"

"Do you believe I followed the Drakebane into battle at the Wound because I sought redemption?" Gladdic laughed raspily, full of bitter mirth. "Why would I want redemption when I had only ever done that which was holy?"

Blays' hand curled into a fist. "Tell that to the Colleners."

The priest grimaced, his face going dark. "I have failed to stop the Eiden Rane. I have been betrayed by the Drakebane. I have seen my beloved city swallowed by his insurrection. Everything I have fought for has been I lie, and everything I held has been lost. But *none* of this is a more wretched torture than your self--righteous harangues. Choose what to do with me and be damned!"

"He's right," Dante said. "Time to choose. You can kill him now. Or we can use his knowledge and abilities to see if we can stop what's been unleashed on the swamp. It's your call."

Blays scrunched his blond eyebrows together. "You're serious? This is my decision?"

"Yours and Naran's."

"This is one of your ploys. A clever way to pressure me to give in so you can feel like we all agreed to it, keeping your conscience clean."

"Okay, then *I'll* decide."

Blays swore and turned to Naran. "Just say the word."

"I want nothing more than revenge." Face downcast, Naran closed his eyes. "But then I think about the joy that lit up Captain Twill's face whenever we came to a new port. She loved seeing new places. The stranger the better. I think she would have liked Tanar Atain very much. If what Gladdic says is true—that this land is under siege—Twill would not have wanted to see it destroyed in her name."

He placed his hand on the ground, as if needing to steady himself. Blays worked his jaw, looking ready to spit. In a violent lunge, he picked up a rock bigger than his head. He screamed, the muscles of his arms bulging, and shot-putted the rock into the water with a titanic splash.

He took three deep breaths, shoulders heaving, then turned around, face perfectly calm. "Very well, we've reached a consensus. Gladdic, if you'd be so kind as to brief us as to the Eiden Rane situation?"

The priest regarded Blays quizzically, then made a thoughtful noise. He paced deliberately about the small and mostly bare island. "There are many stories regarding the Eiden Rane. As with all such situations, most of these stories are rife with superstition and groaning with ignorance. Strip these falsehoods away, and we are left with certain stark truths: the White Lich was a great sorcerer. Drunk on his own arrogance, he crossed a line he wasn't meant to cross. And for all the vast power this granted him, surely the gods cursed him, for..."

Gladdic stopped pacing. He stared into the bare white trees as if he were listening for a distant whistle. He muttered to himself, then shook his head hard.

"Ignore what I, in my arrogance, have declared as fact," he said. "I was not there to see these events myself. So how may I claim perfect wisdom over what was and what wasn't?" He smiled sneeringly—this seemed to be aimed at himself—then made to fold his arms. Seeing the stump of his right elbow, he blinked in surprise.

Still looking at the wound, which he'd smoothed over with ether, he went on. "Three different stories are commonly told of the White Lich. The first is the story told in the court of the Drakebane. The court's priests and historians tell that the Eiden Rane began his existence as a sorcerer named Bade, in the ancient capital of Godo Hadein. Bade soon acquitted himself as perhaps the most powerful talent of his generation, yet due to a renegade quality within his nature, he often found himself in opposition to the emperor's politics. As a consequence of his intransigence—some of which, the history claims, amounted to a hair's breadth from treason—when it came time for promotions and honors, Bade was regularly neglected, attaining a station equivalent to the head priest of a small chapel.

"In time, the emperor fell sick. The disease was unknown; none of his sorcerers could diagnose its cause, nor cure its effects. Day by day, he wasted away from the vile corruption within his veins. In desperation, he summoned Bade to him and made a vow: if Bade could cure his sickness, the emperor would make him high priest of the land.

"Bade bent his powers to the task, yet was unable to reverse the disease. He ventured into the deep swamps to meditate. In the darkest night, a ball of light appeared from the trees. It whispered to him with promises of its own: the light of life could save the emperor. It beckoned him onward, warning him that the swamps ahead were full of demons. Just as the light had foretold, the demons assailed Bade from all sides, but with each attack, he turned them back with the might of his sorcery.

"Mile on mile, they ventured into the wilds. At last, the light stopped before a cavern. Bade entered. Within, he found another light of such purity that his eyes overflowed with tears; so holy was its glow that he nearly turned back, believing he was too mean a creature to touch it. Yet he picked it up and departed the cave. The being that had guided him to the cavern praised him for his strength and bravery, then worried aloud that the light within would be wasted on a dying old man rather than a sorcerer of such grandeur. For whoever received the light would spend eternity with it.

"Hearing these words, Bade remembered all of the times he had been overlooked. And he used the light upon himself.

"When he returned to Godo Hadein, he came to the emperor, making many false efforts to cure him. The emperor soon died. And that is when Bade revealed the power the light had imbued him with. He seized Godo Hadein, then the empire. For years, he ruled with an iron fist. His power was untouchable. It was during this time that his enemies, working in secret, created the Odo Sein, the only force capable of neutralizing Bade's great power.

"When they were ready, they marched on Bade's redoubt. Yet even they could not destroy him. They could only seal him within the Riya Lase, the Iron Prison. And there it was that, just as the glowing guide had promised him, Bade would spend eternity with his forbidden light."

Gladdic fell silent. Dante's eyebrows were lifted so high they felt in danger of disappearing up his scalp. "Does that remind you of anything?"

Gladdic smiled wryly. "A garbled version of your northern heresy."

"You mean the heresy your entire faith is founded on?"

"A heresy which our faith corrects, while yours, unable to cope with the betrayal of your dark lord, continues to worship a devil as your first god."

"Will you two shut up and tell us what this means?" Blays said.

"Arawn had a 'forbidden light' of his own," Dante said. "But instead of keeping it from the lowly humans like the other gods wanted, he smuggled it to Carvahal, his half-brother, to bring down to earth and kindle the fire for humanity. But in his vanity, Carvahal locked Arawn away in the starry vault so he'd get all the credit for himself."

"So what are you saying? The Tanarians are filthy plagiarists?"

"Exactly. If so, I don't think much of this story can be true. Most likely, it's propaganda ginned up by the Drakebane Dynasty to cover their own crimes by dressing them up in the legitimacy of our faith."

"There is another option," Gladdic said. "Perhaps *our* faiths are stolen from *them*."

"Ha ha."

"You position yourself as such a liberal truth-seeker. Yet you reject out of hand the possibility your chosen faith might not be the oldest?"

Dante drew himself up. "How long ago did Bade rule?"

"This history places the date eight hundred years in the past."

"Then we know our stories are older. In the lands of Weslee, their faith is also a branch of Narashtovik's—and they've been cut off from us for a thousand years."

Gladdic waved his intact hand. "I would not place so much importance on the date in the Tanarians' story. It is almost surely false. Their lords have outlawed writing among the commoners so that they might have control of their history, which they see as a tool to be altered whenever it will support their present needs."

Blays' mouth fell open. "Well *that* violates everything I believe in."

"It is very brave of you to denounce the rulers' policies when none of its supporters are here to hear you. However, the Drakebane's lineage does not exert such measures for the sake of mere power. They do so in order to throw down the Eiden Rane whenever he manifests."

"He's just popping up all the time, is he? Then what's the big deal this time?"

"The Drakebane Dynasty has dedicated itself—and in many ways, all of Tanar Atain—to keeping the White Lich contained. That is why the Emperor maintains the Odo Sein; that is why he places such demands and taxes on his subjects; that is why all of the country is trained to think of itself as a singular body, with each person belonging to a specific part where it is their responsibility to execute specific duties.

"In normal times," Gladdic continued, "the Drakebane's knights keep close watch on the tomb and the lands that surround it. Whenever the Eiden Rane stirs, he is met with a vast host, and is neutralized before he can muster but a portion of his awful strength. This time, however, the rebels undermined us, assisting him so that he might emerge ahead of schedule. The desperation of our situation can be seen in the fact that rather than gathering his forces to try to reclaim the capital, the Drakebane struck here instead, meaning to spend the last of his

THE LIGHT OF LIFE

strength attempting to return the Eiden Rane to his vault."

Blays pursed his lips. "I don't know if you've noticed this, but our friend Dante here spends more time reading than he does breathing. If there's been a world-saving battle against the White Lich, and it's been going on for centuries, why hasn't he ever heard of it?"

"For the same reason that so little else is known of Tanar Atain. Such information is not allowed to pass beyond the borders." Gladdic waited for more questions. When none came, he resumed pacing. "If the first story I have told you is the province of the Drakebanes, you will feel no surprise to learn that those among the Righteous Monsoon tell a different story.

"Long ago, when time was fluid, and the weights of justice bobbed like seeds on the tide, people lived in splintered tribes. Life was war and war was life. Suffering was one's second skin. Silver—yes, even gold—flowed from the mines like glittering wine, but rather than passing to those who were good, who would use it to feed those who hungered and heal those who fell ill, it was hoarded by kings and tyrants, who spent it on axes and pikes, raising more armies to prosecute more wars. And so Suffering became a god in itself.

"In their desperation, the people prayed to the gods, sacrificing what little they had in vain hope of relief. The gods made sport of their strife; if ever they intervened, it was only to prevent the mortals from giving up all hope and lying down in despair.

"Yet Unu, Mother of Islands, grew wrathful at her peers' contempt for their mortal toys. She came before Endek, the swamp wizard, and she breathed the mists of the morning into his lungs, and poured the light of the righteous into his ears. Then Endek doubled in height; then Endek's powers grew sixty-fold; and Unu sent Endek forth into the mortal lands.

"He slew the kings. Butchered the tyrants. Blasted with fire the mercenaries who robbed and raped the weak. None could so much as scratch his skin. Within a year and a day, the land had been purged, and lay at peace. Those who hungered were given food. Those who wasted of illness were given medicine. All stood equal before the measures. They shed the skin of suffering. In time, their peace was so complete they quit their tasks to lounge in freedom. Time itself mattered not; they quit their hour-glasses and calendars. And then, at last, secure in their golden age, they quit their sacrifices. Their offerings. Their prayers.

"An outcry grew among the gods. Not only had they lost the sport of watching the people suffer, but they had lost all love and duty from their worshippers. Coming together, they assembled a great host and descended on Endek, Champion of Unu. They battled him from the coast to the darkest marsh. From the northern hills to the southern rift. So great was Endek's sorcery that even the combined might of the gods couldn't destroy him — but they *could* imprison him. Hence they sheathed him in cold iron, inscribing the words of their curses upon the faces of his prison, such that his strength was made nothing.

"With Endek gone, some who had lived in his peace fell into corruption, pillaging their neighbors. Pillaging became conquering, and then the clash of armies. Within a year minus a day, the land had fallen back into darkness and strife, and people again suffocated within their suffering.

"For all of the centuries, whenever Endek the Eiden Rane has attempted to escape his bonds, he has been beaten back. Yet among the Righteous Monsoon, it is told that if he can be released for good, he will restore them to their golden age." Gladdic bowed his head to Volo. "Do I represent your faith fairly?"

"That's what they told us," Volo said. "But they never said nothing about the way he *looks* at you. Like you're just a crop for his harvest."

"So the Eiden Rane was sent by the only good god to usher in a golden age of perfect peace?" Dante said. "That sounds even more like propaganda than the Drakebane's version."

Gladdic gave a small shrug. "At one time, I thought the same."

"But not anymore?"

"After the treason I have witnessed on this day, I believe *all* might be lies."

"There's one place the stories are in accordance," Naran said. "In both cases, the lich's power has come from a source of light."

"The natural assumption is that this refers to the ether." Gladdic adjusted his gray robes, which had been soiled with blood and dirt during the fighting and escape. "The final story of the Eiden Rane's origin is not told in any courts. In fact, it in itself has many different versions. But each one repeats the same common themes: that long ago, a sorcerer and his wife lived with their children at the edge of the known swamp. One day, the sorcerer's wife fell ill. Over the following days, their children did as well. Though well-versed in the healing arts, the sorcerer could do nothing to reverse their worsening condition.

"In fear for their lives, he passed into the unknown swamp. There, he sold his soul for the power to save his wife and children. Yet when he returned to his house, all of his family had perished.

"Their deaths, in conjunction with the deal he struck, drove him mad. Over the next few years, children started to go missing from the villages in the hills. The village elders warned the bereaved parents to leave the matter be. In time, however, their grief proved too much. They assembled a war band and hastened into the swamps, following a trail left by the most recent of the vanished children—a trail that led them directly to the sorcerer's home.

"There, they found their children had been turned into pale, vicious demons. In their horror, the villagers slew the changed youths, then burned down the sorcerer's abode. This goaded the sorcerer and his demons into laying waste to the hills. The villagers had sorcerers of their own, however, and quickly, a hellacious battle ensued. Yet the hill-people could never destroy the sorcerer — for in the bargain he had struck in the swamp, he had been given a new body, and left his old form with the demon with whom he'd done his deal. Unless the old body was destroyed, the White Lich could never die.

"Hill by hill, the people were pushed back. At last, with no hope of defeating the White Lich, they enacted the only plan that could stop him from poisoning the whole world: they destroyed their own lands, slagging them into a melted and poisonous miasma through which not even the Eiden Rane could cross. Later, the lich was imprisoned. Yet the hills remained forever tainted."

Dante scratched the side of his jaw. "You're talking about the Hell-Painted Hills. But that's not the story the Alebolgians tell. They say the hills were invaded by a plague of enormous pale locusts."

Gladdic favored him with a disdainful look. "Where did you encounter such a version? The high courts of Cavana?"

"Lady Vita of Osedo. She's educated and well-traveled."

"That is precisely your problem. On such matters, you cannot trust the tales of the nobility. What do they have to fear of what lurks in the wilds? They will warp the story to whatever suits their fancy. Rather, you must speak to the peasants. It is they who are exposed to the monsters of the outlands. They are the ones who must face the terrors of the wilds. That's why *they* must remember the *truth*."

Blays flicked a pebble into the water. "I'm glad we've had this talk. I feel much safer knowing that we're basing our battle plan on state propaganda and peasants' fairy tales."

"Some day you will learn that scorn is no replacement for wisdom."

"Before or after the day when you learn that you're going straight to hell?"

"On that front, you might not have long to wait." The old man's face twisted in something that could have been a grimace or a smile. "I give the third story special credence for reasons we have already discussed: it has never been coopted by would-be despots and warped into a shape that bolsters their cause. I believe it may contain basic truths about the Eiden Rane—including how he might be defeated."

"You must not think it's *all* true," Dante said. "It claims the White Lich can't be destroyed. But you and the Drakebane were trying to do just that, weren't you?"

"The Drakebane believed that the lich's time in captivity will have significantly weakened him. It was thought that, with the Odo Sein present to dispel the enemy's sorcery, they and the Andrac might be able to cut him down and bring him to his final death. But we underestimated the aid the Monsoon had provided him. You are aware of the Blighted?"

"If I knew anything about these matters, you'd be too busy tending to the Blays-shaped sword wound in your throat to answer our questions."

Gladdic stared at him a moment, then puffed his cheeks with wry laughter. "When the Eiden Rane emerges from his prison, he is relatively weak. To restore his power, he draws humans to him and drinks some vital essence within them. This corrupting process also enslaves them to his will. The resulting product is known as the Blighted—the pale people who hide beneath the water. The rebels had already smuggled many souls to him before today, hadn't they, girl?"

Volo's jaw trembled. "They were captives. Taken from the Drakebane's soldiers. They said they were being taken to a prison in the deep swamps where the Drakebane couldn't turn them free."

"Some were soldiers, yes. But they needed more bodies than that. Many were innocent villagers whose deaths your leaders then blamed on us. It is amusing the crimes a good man will commit when he is convinced that he is the savior, and that his enemies are devils."

"I expect you could write several books on that one," Blays said.

"So the White Lich is more powerful than you anticipated he'd be at this stage," Dante rattled off, doing his best to wrestle the conversation back into a productive arena. "How then do we stand against him?"

Gladdic gave one of his shrugs. "We do not. To fight him directly would be to shed our blood on his altar."

"To fight him *directly*? There's an alternative?"

"The key lies in the third story of his creation. The villagers of the hills were unable to destroy the Eiden Rane because they were fighting his avatar rather than his true form: the body he abandoned to become the lich. You might dismiss this story as a 'fairy tale,' yet for all the Drakebane Dynasty's strength and preparation, they have never been able to finally destroy the Eiden Rane."

Blays squinted. "The Drakebane Dynasty does a lot of sister-marrying, do they?"

Gladdic gave him a disgusted look. "Why would you reach such foul assumptions?"

"Say you're right, and the only way to kill this fellow is to kill his original body. If the Drakebanes have spent hundreds of years trying to kill his *new* body, they must be completely gods damned inbred."

"I am not the first to suggest a search for his original body. Previous attempts have never been able to so much as prove its existence. The Drakebane believed that I was wrong, and that even if I *was* right, we would not have time to track his first body down."

Dante stood from the rock he'd been seated on. "That's your proposal? Find and destroy this first body?"

Gladdic nodded once. "We have no allies to draw on, no armies to summon. We lack the strength to battle the White Lich himself. The same might not be true of his frail mortal heart."

"What happens if we can't stop him?"

"Then he will convert more and more Tanarians into the Blighted, expanding both his army and his personal power with each step. Once this nation is fully under his sway, he will take the next, and each after it in turn. That has always been his goal."

To the west, the sun was nearly extinguished behind the clouds and leafless white trees. The others looked tired. Anxious. Dante had no doubts that he looked as bad. That might have been the only thing they all had in common. He was a former Mallisher, but had spent the last half of his life as a priest in Narashtovik. Blays had also come from Mallon, but had the look of a Collener, and now split his days between Narashtovik and Pocket Cove. Naran was a merchant and sometimes-pirate descended from those in the far south. Volo was a young woman from these forbidden swamps—just yesterday an eager rebel, she seemed to have wholly turned on her former cause.

And Gladdic, an old man from the highest echelons of the Bresselian priesthood, who Dante would joyfully have murdered just a few hours earlier—and who now claimed to be fighting against an evil far greater than anything Gladdic himself had ever dreamed of.

It was a very odd group. But it had the potential to be a very effective one.

"We could walk away, and hope you're wrong about his goals," Dante said. "But you could also be wrong about the extent of the lich's power. Which means we might have the strength to stop him."

"And if he is right," Naran said bitterly, "then no one else will have a second chance."

Volo nodded. Blays tilted back his head, then did the same.

For a moment, Dante wished they'd insisted on leaving. "Okay then. How do we find the lich's mortal body?"

Gladdic gave a small, sinewy smile. "It was my hope that you might provide answers to that."

"Until ten minutes ago, I didn't know he *had* a mortal body. If you're depending on me for answers, then we could save ourselves a lot of trouble by stabbing ourselves right now and sparing the lich the hassle."

"Perhaps you already possess knowledge, yet are unaware. Tell me the details of your encounter with the lich."

Dante launched into as comprehensive an account of their battle as he could provide. The others pitched in with observations of their own. Gladdic showed no emotion until the end, when Dante described how he had yanked up the solid iron ground and trapped the White Lich inside it.

"Now that was a clever solution." Gladdic frowned at him. "How have you learned to command the earth like that?"

"Wouldn't you like to know," Dante said. "It didn't imprison him for long, though. He'd gotten free by the time we'd escaped."

"The walls of the Riya Lase are treated with great magic. Mundane iron would only hold him for a short time."

"Why iron?"

"I do not know. But its need here is why none is to be found elsewhere in Tanar Atain." Gladdic swayed, then seemed to swoon, seating himself heavily on the bare ground. Dante took a step toward him, fearing his injury had finally overwhelmed him, but the old man pressed his gnarled hand to his face, shaking his head slowly. "Nothing you have told me is of any use. Even if the first body is real, we will have no more chance of finding it than any of the others who have tried."

Blays gawked at Dante, then at the old man. "*You* suggested it! Why couldn't you have given up this fast when you were putting thousands of people to death in the Collen Basin?"

"You think this is sudden? I have spent months thinking on this matter. I have dissected and discarded every way in which I might find the Eiden Rane's first form. In my delusion, I thought your encounter with him would provide the solution."

"You son of a bitch. Were all your promises of help just a trick to get us to ferry you away from danger?"

"Why does the mind betray us so? Why does it ever lift our hopes only to torture us anew?" Gladdic's eyes went wide with shock. "We assume the gods gave us consciousness as a gift. But what if it was punishment?"

Blays moved his hand to the hilt of his sword. "Then I'll be happy to rescind your sentence."

"I was wrong to let my delusions infect you as well. Flee from here. Flee, and hide, and live out however few days are left to be lived."

Dante gritted his teeth. "Will you stop your stupid *whining*? You might have run out of options, but you're looking at the kings of bad ideas. We haven't even *started* to get dumb yet."

"Correct." Blays dropped his hand from his weapon, smiling a little as he walked about the island. "Shall we start being stupid? Do you suppose the White Lich ever goes back to visit his first body?"

"Why would he do that? To say hello? To gossip about his latest plans to swallow up the world? Returning would only leave him vulnerable to being followed."

"He's got to keep it locked up somewhere, right? If your heart was a separate entity from your body, you wouldn't let it just wander around unsupervised."

"But if it's still in some sense mortal, it would need food and water. Someone must be caring for it."

"Or some*thing*." Blays pursed his lips. "If all the body needs is the occasional sip and nibble, it would only require a servant or two. Are the Blighted competent enough to handle something like that?"

After a moment, Gladdic realized he was being asked a question. "The Blighted retain enough intelligence to perform such a task. And their loyalty to the Eiden Rane is perfect. They would never betray him, nor fail to do their duty."

"So this whole thing could be operating out of a single shanty in the middle of nowhere."

"Meaning it could take us years to find," Dante said. "And considering the Drakebane's people have been looking for *centuries*, I wouldn't count on us finding it through traditional means."

Blays sniffed, wiping his nose with the back of his hand. He paused then, staring at whatever he'd smeared onto his hand as if it held great secrets. "The lich bleeds."

"I don't remember that. And I got an awfully close look at him as he was pounding us all into the ground."

"All right, he doesn't bleed *blood*, but when you cut him, his wounds exude a substance us non-liches might equate with blood."

"That white liquid." Dante drew back his head. "You think we can track it."

"Assuming it's got any connection to his first body — and, just as a reminder, assuming that this first body even exists — it'd be slightly easier than searching every square inch of swamp."

"Easy enough to find out. Suppose we've got any of his blood left on our swords?"

Gladdic had been sitting cross-legged, head bowed and shoulders slumped. Now, he lifted his chin, eyes gleaming faintly. "What do you mean? Are you hounds, that his blood might lead you to his other body?"

Dante laughed. "You don't know about blood tracking? What kind of a sorcerer are you?"

"It's very easy to be as learned as you when you belong to an institution of heathenous warlocks. When one must learn on one's own, every step is a struggle."

"You're the reason people in Mallon can't learn the nether in the first place!"

"I'm but a drop amongst the ocean. Even if I favored permitting the study of the shadows, if I were to express such beliefs, my reward would be my execution."

"*Do* you favor letting your people learn the nether?"

Gladdic's eyes tracked across the landscape. "I no longer know what I believe — and it no longer matters. Bressel has fallen to the Drakebane's conspiracy, and is under his law now."

Blays tipped back his head. "Can we discuss Bressel's theological policy *after* we heroically save Tanar Atain?"

"All of the blood in your body shares a nethereal connection to itself," Dante said, spreading his hands as if to trace a net. "If you have one drop of someone's blood, you can follow the nether in it to the rest of it. We're talking about doing the same to the White Lich. Everyone, check your weapons."

They drew their swords, the Odo Sein blades circled with sinuous patterns of nether. Seeing no stains on his weapon, Dante delved into the nether, searching for specks of it glommed onto the steel, but found nothing out of place. He inspected the others' swords to similar results.

"But we cut him," Naran said. "All of us saw it."

Dante pressed his knuckles to his forehead. "It isn't the same blood that you and I have. It could have boiled away. Melted into the ether. Or maybe our swords drank it up. Doesn't matter, really."

"It surely does," Gladdic said. "If the blood is unstable, then even if we were to acquire a fresh sample, it would vanish before we were able to use it to locate the prime body."

Dante swore, sensing the whole idea was about to go up in smoke. But there was an obvious test. He set his blade against the pad of his left pinky finger—gently; even a touch of the Odo Sein weapon was enough to open a deep cut—spilling blood onto the steel. He withdrew his wounded hand. The blood rested on the steel. Dante continued to watch. At last, the droplets started to shrink. Within a minute, they had vanished completely, absorbed by the whirling nether of the sword.

"That's a relief," Blays said. "If we can be reasonably sure the lich's blood doesn't just spontaneously disappear, then our only problems are everything *else* that's wrong with this plan."

Volo tossed a small rock to herself. "Like how to get blood out of the Eiden Rane without getting added to the Blighted?"

"I propose one of *you* fights him. A good knock on the nose should have him bleeding like any other man."

"All right," Dante said. "Then you can hold the jar under him."

Gladdic made a murmuring sound. "We will have to find another way. To fight him directly would mean death."

They tossed forth one idea after another, only for each one to be battered down. The sun died away, leaving them in the perfect stillness of the lifeless night, the only motion the twinkle of the stars overhead. In the middle of their discussion, Dante realized Volo was snoring.

"That looks like the best idea anyone's had all day." Blays stretched his arms over his head. "What say we figure out how to stop the unspeakable darkness once we're not so damn tired?"

They drew up a watch schedule. Before bedding down, Blays took Dante with him to make a quick check of the island's perimeter.

Blays weaved through the pale trees, dropping his voice about as far as it would go. "Are we really going to do this?"

"Stop the mad sorcerer from turning everyone in Tanar Atain into living zombies?"

"You know what I mean."

Dante was quiet for a moment. "We'll work with him until the threat is under control. Then we'll see he gets the justice he deserves."

"You swear to me?"

"You've got my word."

Blays nodded, looking satisfied. "Also, it's your responsibility to make sure he doesn't murder us in our sleep."

They finished their circuit of the island, then rejoined the others in the center, where the spindly trees were just dense enough to conceal them. Dante took first watch, but even when his turn was done, he slept lightly, keeping hold of the nether like it was a dagger under his pillow, jerking awake at every flicker of shadows, real or imagined. Once, he woke to the sound of Gladdic muttering to himself, but the old man was dead asleep.

Dante awoke with a start. He felt as though he'd been asleep for some time; to the east, the first hints of light shaded the sky in dark gray. Volo was gone—she had last watch—but so was Gladdic.

Dante stood, gazing into the darkness, a cold sweat clamming his skin. He walked quickly to the water's edge. The swamp of the Go Kaza was as silent as ever. Dante drew his antler-handled knife, ready to lay open the back of his arm, and moved through the trees.

Ahead, Gladdic crouched by the water's edge, washing what remained of his right arm. He'd healed the stump until it was as smooth as sanded wood. Seeing Dante, he rushed to tuck his stump against his chest and cover it with his robes. He stopped himself, mouth crooked in contempt.

Absurdly, Dante felt a twinge of guilt. "Did you try to regrow it?"

"It would likely have been too late."

"But that wasn't worth finding out?"

"Better to leave it as it is. So that I will always be reminded of the price of self-deceit."

"Alternately, you could write yourself a note on the matter." Dante motioned to the water. "All clear?"

"I would not make that assumption at this time. Yet sleep has aided my clarity of mind. I know a way to get the Eiden Rane's blood. I will send the Andrac to assault him."

"They'll be able to last long enough to escape?"

"If they strike with surprise, and flee as soon as their claws are bloodied? Perhaps."

Dante rubbed grit from the corner of his eye. "Why don't we create a whole army of demons? Rip him apart with sheer numbers?"

"'We'?"

"I figured out how to make them for myself. That's how we were able to learn how to destroy them."

"I wondered." Gladdic sounded as if they were discussing an inn he used to favor on his travels but which had closed up shop twenty years ago. "Each time you raise an Andrac, it takes something from within you. Something that is slow to recover. Even a sorcerer of vast power may control no more than a handful at a time. After my expenditure yesterday, I won't be able to summon more than one or two for some time."

"Could I create enough to destroy him?"

The priest looked him up and down. "Perhaps if we had been working in concert at the moment of his release. Now, he will already be too strong. Especially as we lack the Odo Sein's ability to neuter his sorcery."

"What if we could do it? But you fear him too much to try?"

"If you believe that, then I can guarantee that you do not fear him enough."

46

They ate dried fish for breakfast, which Dante was getting extremely sick of, and loaded into the canoe. Volo struck northeast, back in the direction of the Wound. It was warmer than the day before, more humid, and sweat soon slipped down the back of her neck. Blays took up the other paddle, speeding them along through the lifeless and phantasmagoric reaches of the swamp.

Taking in the bony white trees and blood red water, Dante glanced back at Gladdic. "How did you ever get involved here in the first place? Pursuing the Andrac?"

"Correct."

"How'd you hear about them? We had to dig through the archives of both Narashtovik and Collen. Even then, they barely had more than a few scraps of information."

"Gashen's blood," Gladdic muttered. "I knew the Collen Basin maintained hidden archives. Where do they keep them?"

"In Mallish temples," Blays said. "Better go burn them down."

"I ask only from curiosity. The Collen Basin means nothing to me now. It was under the Drakebane's advice that I sought to purify it."

Dante grunted. "To clear it out, you mean? Suppose he wanted to secure a safe place for his people to move to in case the White Lich broke free?"

"It would have been much less costly and messy. Yet when that plan fell through, he executed his plan in Bressel instead. As for the Andrac, I located the information I required within the lore of the Shrouded Hand."

"The Shrouded Hand?"

"The institution that even now has spies in Narashtovik. Don't tell me you were unaware?"

"That's a matter for my chief of espionage. Anyway, we were a little more concerned with rooting out spies from the Gaskan Empire to care about Mallon."

"And what of the decade since your war with Gask?" Gladdic

rolled back his eyes. "How can someone as oblivious as you have defeated me?"

Blays shrugged. "The gods must think you're a jerk, and seek to help us."

"I expect they do believe that of me. But if you believe they care anything for *you*, I can only pray they will wait to punish you for your hubris until after we're done working together." Gladdic moved on while Blays was still mid-snort. "The Shrouded Hand keeps watch on all of the heretics that surround Mallon. Gask. Narashtovik. The Collen Basin. And lands far beyond these. Additionally, they keep records of your atrocities, and the dark magics through which you discharge them."

Dante perked up his ears. "You catalogue our abilities? I thought studying the nether was the sort of thing that earned your body a burial in Whetton and your head a grave in Bressel."

"Its study is banished from all common use, yes. Only those who prove themselves beyond corruption are allowed access to the forbidden materials of the Hand." Gladdic laughed raucously, the sound hanging in the damp air. "An 'incorruptible person'! What a contradiction of terms. Since such people do not exist, the Hand's rules guarantee that it is staffed by those who are happy to *lie* about being beyond corruption. Hence their insistence on purity only makes them more impure."

"Pretty ironic, all right. Why do they study us? So you can hone your ability to fight our sorcerers?"

"That is a part of it. Another part is so that we will be aware of what your corruption looks like before it can taint us. Regardless, we wander from the original question. Within the Hand's records were accounts of invincible demons from the swamps of Tanar Atain. Through deft negotiations, I acquired an audience with one of the Drakebane's secretaries, and then with the Drakebane himself. We struck a bargain. He was allowed access to certain resources in Bressel. Things that seemed harmless at the time, but were vital to his coup. And I was allowed access to his priests.

"They had forgotten how to give life to the Andrac themselves. Even their stories of the demons' origin were confused — some said they were created to wage war on the Eiden Rane, while others claimed they were the *soldiers* of the Eiden Rane. Yet from their disparate lore and tales, I was able to scrape the grime from the window of truth and reveal the lost secrets of how the Andrac were made."

"You should be very proud of yourself," Blays said. "It isn't often you get to take a piece of scholarship and turn it into a war crime."

"Condemn me as you will. Yet it is through these efforts that I came to know the Drakebane, and to assist him against the White Lich. If not for my quest, you would already be dead by the lich's cold hands."

They glided onward. The clouds held position overhead, muting the sun. Dante kept his eyes on the water. While they were still at least three miles away from the Wound, a pale face broke the surface, staring angrily. Dante cried out and struck it down with a lash of nether.

He leaned over the gunwale, hunting for more. "The White Lich makes the Blighted. Can he can see through their eyes?"

Behind him, he felt Gladdic extend his perception into the nether in the water. "It is possible."

"Don't you think that might have been a good thing to mention before we blundered into his enormous spy network?"

"It is possible."

Blays thrust out his arm toward another Blighted snarling at them from the water. "He *looks* unpleasant, but you suppose he'd warm up if we invited him over for tea?"

He was only halfway through his words by the time Dante and Gladdic had each flung a sorcerous bolt, one nether and one ether. They crashed into the Blighted, sending blood hissing into the water. The body keeled over backwards and landed with a foamy crash. Blays and Volo paddled hard, bringing them up against the flank of an island.

Dante swiveled his head, watching for any disruption of the water's surface. "There's only going to be more of them the closer we get to the Wound. If just one of them signals the White Lich, he'll be waiting for us."

Gladdic rubbed his hand up and down his jaw. "I should have expected him to move this quickly. Yet if we don't press on now, he will only have more time to strengthen himself."

"You said this will only work if we have the element of surprise. What's the point of pressing on if we're doomed to fail?"

"Because there remains a chance that we won't!" Gladdic pounded his fist on his thigh, but rather than punctuating his defiance, the gesture seemed to deflate it. "Why are we ever compelled to lie to ourselves? If we attempt to sneak forward, we will surely be caught; if we slaughter every Blighted we see, we will only declare ourselves more loudly. There is no winning. We might as well wage war on the sky."

They were all silent for a moment. Softly, Volo said, "Maybe we should leave. So what if he takes Tanar Atain? The Monsoon already owns the country. And the Eiden Rane owns the Monsoon."

"There is no land to where we might flee that—"

"He won't come to and gut us like perch. Yeah, I get that. What I don't get is if it's all so inevitable, why not go enjoy whatever time we got left?"

"We could sail the seas," Naran mused. "They are much larger than the earthly world. Let him try to catch us when we travel with the winds."

Blays shot them all a look of contempt. "Haven't any of you ever burgled a manor before? Or been forbidden from seeing a nobleman's daughter? You don't come to the front door dressed a s *yourself*. Gladdic, these Blighted things, just how smart are they?"

"They can obey simple commands, but they are barely capable of wielding weapons."

"So most of them are as dumb as a wet shoe?"

"If your shoe possessed a primal desire to separate you from your limbs."

"Right. Then all Dante has to do is disguise us."

"With illusions?" Dante said.

"With your world-renowned dressmaking skills. Although yes, it might be a little bit faster to snap your fingers and make us look like a log."

"We'd have to travel at a most un-log-like speed. I won't be able to sustain the illusion for too long."

Gladdic moved his finger across the air as if underlining invisible words. "Then I will forge the Andrac now. It has no need for air, and may travel along beneath us."

"How will you find the traces out here?"

"Why, I suppose that I shall look for them."

The priest instructed them to move on. Volo and Blays steered them through the small rocky islands and the grasping white branches of half-submerged trees. Dante's heart beat steadily as he searched the surroundings for any glimpse of ripples or pale faces.

"There." Gladdic pointed to an island to port. "Let us make landfall."

They pulled up beside the island. Debarking from a canoe onto higher ground wasn't the easiest task in the world, but Gladdic stepped out as lightly as a sailor a third of his age. Whispering to himself under his breath, he bent over, passing his hand a few inches above the ground. He made an irregular circuit, then came to a stop.

He bowed his head. Light shined from his left hand, then winked off. The air around him darkened as if the sun was falling into an eclipse. Nether dashed about like angry black wasps. These slowed, dancing gracefully, then converged on a single point and disappeared. While Dante was still trying to figure out what in the world Gladdic was doing, a tube of shadows coalesced eight feet above the ground, extended horizontally, and unfurled into an Andrac.

The Star-Eater opened its mouth and hissed like water poured on embers. Within its throat, light shined like purest ether.

"How did you know where the traces were?" Dante said. "And for that matter, how did you illuminate them?"

Gladdic cranked his head around. "How do *you* do it?"

"With a hell of a lot more difficulty than that!"

The old man smiled smugly. "Perhaps I shall tell you that when you tell me the secrets of how you have learned to fight them."

"So you can figure out how to make it so I can't kill them?"

"Such knowledge might also aid our plight against the Eiden Rane."

"We'll see about that if we can't find the prime body." Across from them, the towering demon flexed its claws. It looked potent enough, but compared to the staggering power of the lich, it no longer felt so fearsome. "How loyal are they? Will it really challenge the Eiden Rane by itself?"

Gladdic regarded the demon with a strange mixture of sadness, pride, and some deeper emotion that might have been regret. "They exist to challenge. To fight. To shed blood, and kill what they can. For isn't that the essence of the nether that shapes it?"

"Not in the slightest."

"But isn't —"

"Whatever it is, you're both wrong," Blays said. "Now can we get on our way?"

Volo edged back a step. "It isn't getting in the boat with us, right?"

Gladdic motioned to the demon. It cocked its head. Still gesturing, Gladdic said, "Follow beneath the boat. Do not be seen. Soon, you will face a great foe."

The Andrac grinned, flashing its long fangs, and waded into the water, which it barely seemed to disturb. It vanished beneath the surface without so much as a bubble. Dante stared after it for a moment, struck by the strangeness of working alongside one of the very monsters he and Blays had shed so much blood and sweat learning to combat.

He shook his head and looked up from the water. Nether lay everywhere in great heaps. He had the sudden conviction that if the swamp were to dry up, it would reveal a bed of solid bones. He called the shadows to him, wrapping his arms in darkness. He drew them wide and laid them over the canoe, blacking out their sight. As he stretched the nether further, shaping it into the appearance of a toppled white tree trunk, it thinned out, giving them a shaded but clear view of their surroundings. They could see out, but the Blighted wouldn't be able to see in.

"We are now officially a tree," Dante declared. "Let's hope the Blighted don't have the brains to wonder why a tree is cruising about like a hungry fish."

They struck away from the island, continuing toward the Wound. Dante could feel the condensed nether of the Andrac shadowing them from below. More than once, he imagined the demon launching itself from the depths and grabbing hold of their canoe, crushing it to splinters and drowning them in the waters.

"We will conceal ourselves a short way from the Wound," Gladdic said. "The Andrac will go forth and make its strike. Should it survive the encounter, I believe it will be able to retreat swiftly enough to escape. With this vessel, we will be able to out-pace any but the White Lich himself, and as he is still building his strength, I doubt he would pursue us alone."

"Let's hope so," Blays said. "Either way, I'll be paddling away like I've stolen something. That'll be a hard one for me to imagine, but I'm willing to make the effort."

Two white faces appeared ahead. The Blighted stared at the passing "log" with mild annoyance, which seemed to be the least hostile expression they could muster, then swam onward, keeping no more than their eyes above the surface.

Volo headed down what turned out to be a sort of box canyon of rock and scattered bones. As she backed up, Dante kept both eyes open for a trap. They were soon speeding along again. A white hill appeared above the ghostly trees, looming like the lost shell of an enormous sea creature. The first time they'd come to it, Dante hadn't had any idea what was lurking inside it. Seeing it now, he felt a cold sweat rise from his skin.

A quarter mile from the rise of the Wound, Gladdic motioned them into the lee of an island. The Andrac surfaced beside them, head lifted in an arrogant tilt. Gladdic leaned over the side of the canoe and whispered instructions. The demon bowed its head, turned away, and swam toward the high white hill, leaving barely a ripple behind it.

Dante nicked the back of his arm, keeping the nether at hand. Blays loosened his swords in their sheaths. Gladdic had gone perfectly still, preparing himself to receive the ether.

They waited in silence for twenty minutes. Without apparent provocation, the priest frowned, the creases around his eyes and mouth deepening by the minute.

"What's wrong?" Dante craned his neck toward the Wound. "Can you see through its eyes?"

Gladdic held up a hand for silence. He moved his mouth as if speaking, then swayed back, wincing. "The Wound is empty.

The White Lich has gone."

EDWARD W. ROBERTSON

3

"He's gone?" Blays said. "Like *gone*-gone?"

The priest nodded. "The Andrac and I share a bond. The connection is dim, but the message is clear. The lich is no longer present in this place."

"Typical. He heard we were coming and dashed off like a coward."

Dante tugged the end of his nose. "The demon hasn't been gone more than half an hour. That wouldn't be nearly long enough to search the whole place."

"Our bond is not subtle enough for the Andrac to explain," Gladdic said. "But I assure you, its confidence is complete."

"Either that or it's been bewitched by the Eiden Rane and is luring us into a trap."

Dante hadn't meant this as more than grumbling, but to his consternation, Gladdic gave the idea serious thought. "If such a thing had happened, I believe I would have felt a change in our connection."

"Well, tell the Andrac to keep looking."

The priest nodded. They didn't talk much over the next fifteen minutes. Then Gladdic raised a salt-and-pepper eyebrow at Dante. "The Andrac is insistent that our quarry is gone. You may hang back here if you wish, but I am going in to investigate for myself."

Anger flared in Dante's chest. "Is that your attempt to manipulate me?"

"Are you so ruled by your ego that you think this is about *you*? Young girl, I require passage to the Wound, if you please."

Volo glanced between them. "Well? In or out?"

Dante clenched his teeth. "Take us to the Wound."

Volo and Blays paddled them onward. Though it was beginning to sap his strength, Dante maintained the illusion of the log around them. The white shell of the Wound climbed higher and higher. Near its base, bodies floated lazily in the red water, but rather than being Blighted, they were Tanarians in their tunic-like jabats. Some were dressed in the colors of the Monsoon, but others wore the green and white of the Drakebane's men.

Volo scowled at the ones that bobbed too close to the canoe, shoving them away with her paddle. She guided them to a low shelf of white stone and dropped the twine-wrapped rock that served as the vessel's anchor. Dante dispelled the illusion of the log. With the haze of nether stripped away, the overcast light felt incredibly bright.

Blays peered into a rocky canyon. "Unless any of you has a thing for being murdered alone, I suggest we go in together."

Gladdic stepped onto the white stone with a look of visceral disgust. "This place is unholy. A mockery of life."

"Welcome home!"

The priest snorted. Dante climbed out of the canoe, reaching into the nether. It waited thickly, but didn't feel particularly disturbed. Gladdic strode forward, his dirty robes flowing about him. Naran glanced back at the canoe as if in longing.

They entered the canyon. A naked Blighted lay on the ground, his bare back gashed open. Blays gave him a preemptory stab in the back of the neck. The body didn't so much as twitch. Their group continued to the end of the little canyon, which opened into a stretch of the reddish pools and shrub-like mineral projections that made up most of the heart of the Wound.

A towering dark shape flowed out in front of them. Dante startled and grabbed for the nether, but it was only the Star-Eater, baring its teeth at Gladdic in frustration. The demon gestured with the fluidity of the shadows of clouds, then turned and loped onward. Gladdic followed it at a jog that seemed too sprightly for his advanced years. Then again, a deep connection to the nether or ether seemed to stretch out a person's life. Cally had made it well beyond a hundred years and might well have lived for decades more. The Keeper had known Cally in their youth, and she was still going strong. Dante might be able to expect another century of life for himself.

Assuming he wasn't devoured by an evil Tanarian demigod first.

The landscape was speckled with a few bodies of both Blighted and humans, but without any living people in it, it looked almost unbearably stark—even more so, in its way, than the upper heights of the Woduns, which at least looked like it belonged to the world around it.

The five of them came to a ridge overlooking the bowl-shaped valley where they'd fought the White Lich. They hunkered behind cover, surveying the slopes and the central mound that held the wreckage of the iron prison of the Riya Lase. The bodies were more plentiful than ever, but not a one of them stirred.

Volo swept back her dark hair, retying it behind her head. "If he's not here, then where'd he go?"

Gladdic's eyes were hooded. "It is difficult to say."

"You're some kind of monster-person, aren't you? If you don't even know how to get to the Eiden Rane, why should we keep you around?"

The old priest glanced at her sharply, lips pressed into a thin line. He laughed once through his nose. "Tanarian bluntness is as bracing as the strike of a cane. Under less trying circumstances, I might have come to like it." He considered the valley. A low wind picked up, hissing monotonously through the coral-like structures jutting from the ground. "With any luck, the lich has taken the Monsoon to crush the nearest settlement of Drakebane loyalists."

"That's your hope?" Blays said. "That he's off slaughtering civilians? Are you even *trying* to not be hated?"

"The alternative is that he endeavors to release one of his lieutenants."

"Er, he has lieutenants now?"

"Over the centuries, numerous sorcerers have been sent to destroy the Eiden Rane. All who fought him were thought to be slain. But the Drakebane believes that not all of them are dead — rather, that the lich bound some of them to him as his servants."

"We're fighting an entire order of liches now? Quick question, will anyone fault me if I decide it's surrendering time?"

"If the Drakebane's theory is true, however, I don't think the lich will seek to free his underlings just yet. He will wait until he has strengthened himself, and his servant-sorcerers will have no chance of overthrowing him."

Dante got up from behind cover and walked slowly downhill. "Can you track his footprints with the ether?"

Gladdic rubbed his jaw, which had started to sprout white stubble. "Let us find out."

They headed toward the central mound, wary for ambushes even though the Star-Eater had already checked the area. As they neared the heart of the Wound, Gladdic slowed, bending closer to the ground. They climbed the slope, passing the corpses of several mangled Odo Sein. Dead for not quite a day, most were stiff, limbs twisted tight as they bucked against their death, but a few had already begun to relax into the final surrender to their fate.

At the top, the ruins of the giant iron hexagon that had enclosed the lich lay in rusting silence.

Gladdic circled the grounds, then stopped and rested his left hand across his navel. "I see nothing. The traces of passage only last so long."

Dante blinked against a gust of wind. "Maybe they regrouped elsewhere in the Wound before striking out. The tracks would be fresher there."

"Perhaps. But the longer we spend searching, the more any tracks will fade."

Lacking any better ideas, they advanced toward the southern reaches of the Wound where the Monsoon had made their landing. By the time they got to the low-lying shore, Gladdic still hadn't found a single ethereal track.

Gladdic screwed up his face and spat on the gritty white rock. "Damn this grimstone. It is too solid for feet to leave their marks upon. Even bare dirt would have betrayed their passage."

"That's what this stuff is?" Dante ran his hand over the ground, which felt like something between sandstone and bone. "Grimstone?"

"As I told you. Where nether concentrates beyond what is natural, the earth grows as if it were a living thing."

"Could this have been the first source of life?"

"I suppose so. As long as you are willing to denounce every story told in your precious *Cycle*."

"Not necessarily. The gods could have employed this process to create us."

"Yet all mention of it was dropped from the tale of creation? Your beliefs ride you like a knight rides his horse, spurring you on to gather the justifications they eat as fodder!"

Naran stared out at the wind-rippled swamp. "People might

not leave tracks on bare rock. But they can leave them on water. When *The Sword of the South* has been on the hunt for other vessels, we found some of them by the refuse they dumped in the water — and the birds and fish that came to eat it."

"There aren't exactly many animals around here to be drawn to their spoor," Dante said. "Then again, there isn't much in the way of currents, either. You suppose they were stupid enough to cast their trash behind them as they went?"

"If they are sailing out to fight, the members of the Monsoon might have dumped unnecessary weight. Besides, for the humans among them, everyone eats."

"And shits," Blays said. "Don't forget shits."

Gladdic sent the Andrac off into the nearby waters. Volo fidgeted, glanced at the others, then ran west along the thin shelf of rock protruding from the base of the Wound.

"Hey!" Dante yelled. "Where the hell do you think you're going?"

She stopped and turned, fists balled at her sides. "This is right near where we left my canoe."

"So what? We've got a perfectly good one right here."

"But it's my way-boat. I'm supposed to go with it until one of us dies!"

The look on her face was so anguished that Dante was almost ready to let her go look for it. Instead, he shook his head. "It's too dangerous. The lich is gone, but we don't know he took all of the Blighted with him."

Blays rattled his sheathed swords. "I'll go with her. Won't be long. I know how impatient you get."

He jogged after her, brooking no argument. Volo beamed at him. The two of them disappeared around a bend to the north. Dante cursed under his breath. The Andrac was back in minutes, silently insistent it had found something. Dante gritted his teeth and gazed west. Just as he was about ready to go after the others, a canoe swept around the bend of grimstone. Volo sat in the front, grinning like the sun, eyes wet with tears.

She pulled up beside them. "Thank you for waiting. If I'd lost it for good, I don't know what I'd have done with myself."

Dante didn't suggest that she might have simply christened the newer vessel as her replacement way-boat. They transferred their things to her canoe, then paddled around the southern face of the mounded white hills. The demon showed them to a large portion of yellow rinds bobbing against the side of a rock.

"Great," Blays said. "As long as they're intent on feasting their way across the entire swamp, we'll be on them in no time."

Without explaining what he was doing in case he was wrong, Dante scooped up some of the rinds, squeezing out what little liquid was to be had from one of them. He plunged into the nether in the pulp, holding it in his mind. The resulting signal was slow to come; when at last it did arrive in his head, the pressure it created was so slight that it sometimes disappeared altogether.

He pointed to the south. "I think they went that way."

Blays cocked his head. "The fruit told you that, did it?"

"I'm tracing the nether in this part of it to the nether in the rest of it. Now let's get a move on before the rest of it ceases to be fruit and enacts its new life as sewage."

Gladdic made a noise of dissent. "How will we avoid being spotted by the Blighted? Will you disguise us as a log all the while we pursue the Eiden Rane?"

"Do you have a better idea?"

"Do you think one cannot object to a fault unless one also has a solution?"

"Lyle's balls, you idiots." Blays paddled them about, heading back toward land. "This place is loaded with dead people. And what are dead people?"

"An often-overlooked source of meat?" Dante said.

"Close! Dead people are humanity's fruit. Once they drop to the ground, you can take whatever you like from them. The Monsoon are the lich's buddies, right? Pop us into their uniforms, and the Blighted will just think we're allies trying to catch up with the others."

They scrambled ashore and made their way to the closest battlefield, where there were more than enough dead Monsoon for their purposes. They shucked off their nondescript jabats and replaced them with the colors of the rebellion.

Gladdic's legs extended from the base of the tunic like white staves of gnarled wood. He held his heavy gray priest's robe out before him. "When I donned my robes, I always thought I would die in them." He cast the garment to the ground. "Perhaps I did."

They returned to shore and clambered into the canoe. Volo and Blays paddled hard to the south. A few minutes later, Naran pointed out a scrap of white fabric idling on the surface. It had the look of a bandage. Not long after that, they found another one. A little beyond that, and they nearly plowed into a bandaged corpse floating facedown in the water.

The link to the fruit rind dimmed, fluttering like a tatter-winged butterfly. Within a few hours of travel, it died altogether. By that point, however, they had the enemy's general course—assuming the Eiden Rane was traveling with them, which Dante wasn't sure of but Gladdic insisted was almost certainly the case—and had passed by several other bits of debris cast aside by the living humans traveling with the army. All they had to do was catch up before the enemy changed course.

Yet as soon as the fruit rind's connection gave out, so did the trail of garbage. As time wore on, Dante scanned the waters to all sides, sourness growing in his stomach.

"We've lost the trail," he said. "They must have changed direction. We should backtrack to the last refuse we saw. We can paddle in concentric circles until we locate another sign."

Blays furrowed his brow. "You think the best way to catch up to our foes is to sail around in circles?"

"We'll lose some ground at first, but we don't have a choice. It's better than losing them altogether."

Gladdic was as still as a stump. "We will keep going forward."

"We've made a mistake. Typically, you don't solve a mistake by continuing to make it twice as hard."

"Although that would explain a lot about him," Blays said.

"I have become an expert in losing faith." Gladdic gestured to the south. "And I tell you that now is not the time to give up."

Spite gathered in the back of Dante's skull. "I'd have thought that a complete lack of evidence is a great reason to lose faith, but your complete lack of evidence has convinced me otherwise. On we go."

Volo shrugged and paddled onward. Around them, the growth stopped being rocks that looked like trees and started being actual trees again, albeit ghostly white ones. The water remained empty of any spoor. Gladdic sat with his eyes forward and glazed, looking like a boy who'd been dragged to the temple sermon when the year's first good snow was busy falling outside.

"You see that?" Volo pointed ahead. "Because if you don't, you're all even older than you look."

A hundred feet ahead, light shimmered on the water. At first Dante thought it was a patch of oil, or an illusion, but it only strengthened, defining itself into a ribbon that weaved through the many small islands that humped from the water like the bleached shells of turtles.

Gladdic allowed himself a smile. "Their path is revealed in ether."

"Let me guess," Dante said. "Just as Taim told you it would be?"

"Taim doesn't speak to me. Does Arawn speak to you?"

"Only to tell Dante what a disappointment he is," Blays said. "How *did* you know it'd be here?"

"I don't believe the Eiden Rane expected pursuit." Gladdic ducked under a branch. "After so long in the prison of the Riya Lase, his hunger for his old power will be immense. He will head straight to his feeding."

Back on the hunt, Volo and Blays paddled with renewed purpose. When their arms wore out, they switched with Naran and Dante. They entered the ruins they'd passed through on the way to the Wound, crumbling walls and foundations lying among the rubble of themselves. Dante now understood why they'd been abandoned — if it was abandonment that had destroyed them, and not the wrath of the Eiden Rane.

The trees changed too, slim orange things that braided together at the trunk like the ropes of warships, the leaves slender and black. Grotesque as they were, after the otherworldly and unstirring forests around the Wound, they were an oddly welcome sight.

After the deadness of the Wound, every swoop of a dragonfly or ripple of a breaching fish made Dante jerk his head around to make sure they weren't about to be attacked. Mortals didn't have the focus to watch everything around them, did they? There was so much happening at any given time that you could only pay attention to a tiny sliver of it. Dante was abruptly discombobulated by the idea that this was true of all facets of life — that for all his wisdom, all his acuity, he was actually seeing no more than a single fly as it bumbled about, while being blind to the wondrous forest that the fly lived within.

For miles, the brightness of the trail held steady. As the afternoon wore on, the partial sunlight seemed to diminish it. And when dusk neared, and the daylight waned, the trail was fainter than ever.

Dante peered down at the ribbon of ether as it passed beneath their bow. "Is the path fading?"

"They outpace us," Gladdic said.

"They're traveling with a small army. They should be as slow as their fattest oarsman."

"Their oarsmen are Blighted. While they aren't physically quick, they are tireless. If we wish to catch them, we must be the same."

Blays swore. "Easy for you to say, One-Arm. *You* don't have to paddle."

"We might not have the endurance of the half-undead," Dante said. "But we do have the cheating powers of humans. Paddle hard enough to wear yourself out within ten or fifteen minutes. Let me know when you're starting to flag."

"The sign will be that I'm calling you a gods damn slavedriver."

The bugs were starting to get to them, and before they carried on, Volo passed around the red paste the Tanarians used to ward off the worst of the bites. This done, Blays and Volo dug into the water, arms flexing as they pulled themselves forward. The canoe sliced along fast enough to ruffle Dante's hair. Blays and Volo were soon breathing hard, the collars and underarms of their jabats darkening with sweat.

They continued on until they were red-faced, then Dante and Naran spelled them. The ribbon of ether seemed to steady out. They swapped rowing duties again, then a third time. Night fell, the air awash with the chirp of bugs and frogs. The trail shined like melted stars, lighting the underside of the forest canopy.

Before Blays and Volo took their next shift, Dante sent the nether into their muscles, washing away most of their tiredness, and tended to the blisters forming on their hands. When it was their turn, he did the same for himself and Naran. They covered mile after mile, the trail getting a little stronger by the hour.

When the nether grew less effective at taking away their exhaustion, they slowed at last, three of them snoring in the boat while one paddled onward at a slow but sustainable pace. Whenever Dante woke, Gladdic was seated in the same position in the stern, his eyes sunken pits within the crags of his face, which in the glow of the ether looked as white as something left in water for too long. He gazed into the ethereal pathway like it was a scroll unfurling before him. One filled with secrets that had been lost for ages.

By morning, they were ready to restart their frantic pace. The landscape flew past them, easing from the warped orange trees surrounding the greater Wound of the World and back into the typical swamp of Tanar Atain. Which meant that it was also once more full of awful creatures, to say nothing of the schools of flesh-eating ziki oko swimming under the surface.

It also made for an abundance of insects. With the trail growing brighter, Dante slew a trio of dragonflies and reanimated them. He directed one a half mile ahead to make sure they weren't about to run into anything nasty, then sent the other two whirring high above the canopy, scouting for the enemy flotilla.

"A disgusting process," Gladdic commented. "Taking life and subverting it into parody of itself."

Dante pulled back from the insects' sight. "Do you give yourself fifty lashes in penance whenever you wear a buckskin? Or eat a rasher of bacon? The insects are just a tool. Nothing more."

By early afternoon, the ethereal path was glowing so hard Blays muttered that you could cook by it. A group of animals screamed from the trees. Volo swore to herself and angled away from the yelping creatures. A few minutes later, she swung around a stand of mangroves growing in a semi-circle. Inside the circle, wooden cages hung from the branches, suspended a few feet over the slack water. They were painted red and filled with human bones. In any other realm it would have looked like a scene of gruesome torture, but in Tanar Atain, it was a cemetery.

"I know this place," Volo said. "It's for the village of Raga Don. They breed combfish here. Rip out the ribs and give them a good boil, and you've got the best comb you'll ever find."

Dante reached for the gunwale of the canoe. "Could this village be what the lich is coming for?"

"Stands to reason," Blays said. "You don't get a mane of hair like his without a quality fish-comb."

"Which way is it from here?"

Volo did some thinking, then pointed several degrees to the right of the path the ether was currently displaying. "That way. Not far."

Dante shifted his vision to his dragonflies, diverting two of them in the direction Volo had indicated, one soaring high and the second skimming beneath the canopy. The upper dragonfly veered toward a clearing. Like most Tanarian settlements, it was roughly circular, with a few outer islands raised for paddies and the thickly-growing stands of banana trees. In the center, a long pier supported dozens of rafts bearing small shacks. People tended to the fish pens and worked beneath tarps that kept off the worst of the sun.

"Found the village," Dante said. "But I'm not seeing any rampaging hordes."

Naran pressed his finger to his upper lip. "Is there any chance the lich is merely passing by?"

"Even if he is, we have to warn them," Blays said. "Tell them to get somewhere safe."

"Precisely where might be 'safe'?" Gladdic gestured to their surroundings. "All of this will soon be his. Death is the safest place they can be."

"We should sweep in and kill them ourselves, then? Is that your solution to everything?"

"We'll warn them first," Dante said. "Then finish tracking

down the White Lich."

They abandoned the trail and made way for Raga Don, paddling hard. Dante kept one dragonfly circling above the settlement while the other two searched in the direction the ethereal path had been taking. While their canoe was still a mile out, the circling dragonfly spotted movement within the trees beyond the broad round clearing that held the village.

Dante sent the insect in for a closer look. Seated in the canoe, his eyes flew open. "The White Lich—he's right outside the town. And so is his army."

He took the dragonfly lower. The lich's forces were spread across scores of canoes, most of them filled with half-naked Blighted who paddled forward with crude, heavy strokes. The canoes near the back of the armada were crewed with members of the Righteous Monsoon, who remained in possession of their humanity, at least for the moment.

The Eiden Rane sat on a white chair atop a platform mounted across two canoes. His long white halberd lay across his knees. Next to his immense bulk—ten feet tall, with the build of a blacksmith—the Blighted crew looked as scrawny as toddlers. His skin and clothes were the blue-white of mountain snow that had never melted. While his clothing looked solid enough, his skin was semi-translucent, and glowed from within like some variant of ether. His eyes cycled between every shade of blue. His face was beardless and looked to have been carved from ice. His features were foreign, the corners of his eyes and mouth stretching too far to the sides, his nose a thick wedge dividing his face.

"We're too far away to warn them, aren't we?" Blays said. "Please tell me he's just there to challenge them to a friendly game of Run."

The canoes were already spreading out to circle the village, sticking to the cover of the trees. Dante punched his thigh. "He's surrounding them. Total ambush. We have to move fast."

Gladdic pressed his lips into a tight line. "You can't save them now."

"But we can set the Andrac on him before the fighting's over."

The priest smiled grimly. "You have no mind for sentimentality, do you? No wonder you make for a challenging foe."

Uncertain if that was something to be proud of, Dante motioned them onward. The Star-Eater slid through the water beneath them, a disturbance of nether that felt wrong to be a part of. As the Eiden Rane's forces circled Raga Don, Dante racked his mind for a way to warn the villagers, but they were too far away for him to do something like write a message in the sky. Anyway, thanks to the policies of their former emperor, the Tanarians were completely illiterate.

Through the dragonfly's limited hearing, he heard a man cry out from the trees ringing the settlement. A figure appeared in a simple canoe, paddling hard toward the low-lying gate set into the underwater nets that surrounded the village in order to keep out the flesh-eating ziki oko. A pair of workers glanced at him from the outer paddies. As he continued to shout, two canoes of Monsoon soldiers emerged from the trees and swung about. Archers stood and loosed arrows. These slashed down around the lone boatman, sending up gouts of water. The second volley struck him down, slumping him over his gunwale. His canoe drifted to a stop.

The two paddy farmers jumped in their canoe and paddled like mad toward the town dock, hollering as they went. People spilled from their house-rafts, staring at the incoming boat, then ducked back inside their homes. Some emerged with short bone-tipped spears or compact bows, the arrowheads hewn from high-quality Tanarian glass. Others carried small children, running to the northern edge of the docks.

There, as in most Tanarian settlements, Raga Don had a single tower for defense. Built from mud bricks, it was thirty feet tall, bearing many narrow windows and a single door of reinforced wood. As citizens piled into it, archers pulled canoes from the water and flipped them over on the docks around the tower, taking cover behind the hulls.

Canoes full of Blighted emerged from all sides of the forest. Seeing the pale, manic faces, some of the villagers wailed. The archers on the dock let fly with a few exploratory arrows, but the Blighted didn't change course. They reached the outer nets and hacked through them.

Arrows flew thickly. The Blighted swung about and converged on the far end of the dock, leaping out without concern for their boats. Carrying spears, hatchets, and clubs, they raced from raft to raft, dragging dozens of people out from hiding. Clubs rose and fell, stilling the captives' kicking legs. The Blighted bound them and tossed them in a heap on the dock.

A contingent of Blighted pulled away from the captives and ran pell-mell toward the tower, forcing the archers who'd been harassing them to lock themselves inside the fort. The Blighted reached the door and pounded on it with hatchets, clubs, and bare fists, screaming thinly, their faces warped with hate and frustration, looking mad enough to chew their way through the door.

Archers leaned from the upper windows and took what shots they could. The Blighted fell one after another, hardly scratching the banded door. Heartened, the defenders yelled battle cries and redoubled their fire.

The Eiden Rane's boat approached the end of the dock. He stepped forth, glaive held in his left hand, the tails of his white cape flapping behind him. Both ether and nether churned around his right hand, the shadows flowing like turbid water, the ether like light split by a prism. An arrow arced toward him. It struck his chest and broke in three pieces.

Those that followed fell away just as harmlessly. The lich stopped twenty feet from the tower and raised his right hand. Without so much as a twitch in his expression, he sent nether streaming toward the door. The door jerked, then ripped itself apart, vomiting shattered boards and twisted iron across the dock.

The Blighted bared their teeth and charged inside.

The fighting was over within three minutes. The Blighted marched the surviving defenders outside, packing them into a tight mass. Many of the villagers were bloody and in pain, but few appeared to have serious wounds.

"I don't understand," Dante said. "They're not killing the villagers."

Gladdic nodded. "He would not waste good lives."

Through the dragonfly's eyes, Dante watched as the Eiden Rane gazed impassively at the prisoners.

"You did not understand what you fought, or you would not have resisted." The lich's voice had a metallic ring, as though he were speaking through a giant stovepipe. "Worry not. Now, I bestow you with understanding." He swiveled his craggy head to the Blighted. "You may take your tenth."

The Blighted arched their backs in pleasure, eyes overflowing with hurt and gratitude. They swarmed forward, grabbing one out of every ten villagers and dragging them screaming from the pile of bound people. The Blighted ripped and clawed at their prey, digging their bare fingers into bellies, gnashing at necks and hands. The victims erupted with screams, their pain turning their voices inhuman.

Blood spattered across the dock. Bits of flesh rolled and bounced. The Blighted didn't even seem to be eating: just rending and chewing, shredding and destroying, strips of skin dribbling from their mouths and falling down their chests.

"What's happening out there?" Blays said. "You look like

you're watching hell."

"I might be." Shakily, Dante turned to Gladdic. "Send the Andrac to the edge of the forest."

The old priest lowered his gaze to the water. Dante could feel the density of the demon's nether slipping forward, lost in the murk. It soon passed from range of his senses. In the village, the dock was slick with blood and scattered with chunks, but Dante made himself keep watching. Anything he could learn from the savagery could be vital.

The Blighted slowed, calming from their mad and frenzied scrabbling. The wrath and pain on their faces seemed momentarily eased. The White Lich gestured to them to move back. They wandered away with the sluggishness of those who had feasted too much the night before. Some of them dragged severed arms or disembodied rib cages behind them.

The White Lich approached the remaining villagers. Some bucked and wriggled at their bonds, trying to roll away, even if it meant falling into the swamp and drowning. The lich made a flicking gesture. Nethereal bonds locked them all in place.

"Right now, you fear." He leaned closer. "You should relish it. In another minute, you won't be able to experience that feeling ever again."

He lifted his finger, a dot of purest ether circling its tip, then seemed to think better, taking a heavy step forward. "Do you understand the cruelty of the state the gods have condemned you to? In crafting you, they have made you more than the animals, but so much less than the divine; in result, you lack both the conviction of the beasts and the invulnerability of the immortals. Your existence is one of fear and frailty, with just enough of the divine spark to understand that you have been cheated, but lacking both the wisdom and the courage to know what to *do* about it.

"You would have gone to your graves in ignorance—only to

serve your creators again in their heavens and hells, never to understand *why* you owe them for the misery they have filled you with like water in a glass, nor how to escape it."

The lich parted his lips in a snarl, his teeth glinting. "But I have seen the shape of their plans. I have mapped a chart of its evil — and the path to tear it all down. Fear me, if you think fear will help you. But I am your salvation. And together, we will destroy those who have cheated you."

He lifted the index finger of his right hand, the other fingers curled. Ether gleamed on his fingertip, as bright as a candle. Then a bonfire. Then the sun. Dante tried to shield his eyes with his hand, but the sight was inside his mind. He made himself watch, eyes streaming from the glare. A strange, tendriled fog formed around the piles of frightened people. It lifted and snaked toward the lich.

The people gasped, arching themselves like strung bows. As they sputtered, more fog spilled from their mouths, cohering into tight lines and probing toward the lich, who thrust back his shoulders. The tendrils flashed with pinpricks of light, intensifying like the rising of a white sun. The people began to scream.

They bucked and thrashed. Their skin grayed, marbling with red lines. The tendrils unspooled faster and faster, rushing at the lich and meeting his skin with erratic pulses of light. He closed his eyes, shuddering as the power entered his body.

Dante swallowed. "Send in the Andrac."

"You are certain?" Gladdic said. "We have but one — "

"He's turning them. He thinks he's safe."

Gladdic turned away, a vague scowl overtaking his face as he bent to directing the Andrac. "It will be done."

"What do you mean, he's 'turning them'?" Volo said.

Dante swore under his breath. "Into something else. Something that isn't alive."

"Where you're from, you say 'turning' instead of 'killing'? So you would say 'Please turn that snake for me before it bites me'?"

"Some people might say that."

"Like who?" Blays said. "You, when you're lying to a young woman about what's happening, presumably because it's so gruesome that we're about to find out if an Andrac can soil itself?"

Volo thrust out her jaw. "I carry dead people around every corner of the swamp. I'm alone the whole time. I don't need you to protect me from the truth."

"He's sucking the soul from them," Dante said. "Or a vital essence of some kind. It's about as pleasant-looking as it sounds."

Blays nodded. "Well can we make him *not* do that?"

Dante watched as the people thrashed so hard they split the skin on their knees and elbows. They bucked a final time, then stilled. Their skin paled from the marbled gray to a sickly white. So far, the Eiden Rane had only targeted a quarter of the prisoners, and the others stared at the bodies with bulging eyes.

A dead man's eyes fluttered open. He tipped back his head and gasped, his face twisting with rage. Around him, the others shuddered and awakened.

Becoming the Blighted.

"I'm not kidding," Blays said. "If he's massacring them, *can* we stop him?"

Gladdic shifted, adjusting his unfamiliar jabat. "We would only add our corpses to theirs. This village must be sacrificed in order for the others like it to be saved."

"'It must be sacrificed.' Neat way to wash your hands of it."

"You speak wisely. To reject the responsibility of what we do is to deceive ourselves into thinking we bear no guilt for it. So I will rephrase: *we* must sacrifice this village, and be stained for our decision."

On the dock, the lich swayed, lowering himself to one knee.

The last of the tendrils of light curled around him like tame snakes, settling into his body with a final white pulse. Head bowed, he took a deep breath through his nostrils. The newly-formed Blighted turned as one to stare at him. He gestured vaguely, motioning them to join the others.

"How close is the demon?" Dante said.

"It is within the clearing. Your orders?" Gladdic raised a white eyebrow. Dante couldn't tell if there was anything ironic in it.

"Send it in."

Dante guided the watching dragonfly higher, giving him a better vantage of the field. The Eiden Rane remained kneeling. Blue veins twinkled under the surface of his skin. The Blighted old and new watched him with curiosity. Still locked in place, some of the survivors moaned or cried, but most were silent, making no attempt to move. Dante had seen people's passive re-action to coming death a hundred times before, but he still didn't understand why they didn't struggle against their fate. Was it the instinct of a lizard batted about by a cat, hoping that by play-ing dead, its tormenter would lose interest?

Or was the surrender of hopelessness even more powerful than the will to live?

A black figure surged from the edge of the dock, barely dis-turbing the water as it vaulted onto the boards. The Andrac flexed its claws and leaped at the White Lich, grinning with a wickedness Dante had once thought was born from an evil love of the slaughter, but now understood was the thrill of combat and the testing of mettle.

The Eiden Rane's ever-changing eyes seemed foggy, as if he was watching a scene within another realm. He had set down his halberd while Blighting the captives. He cast forth an arm in warding. The Star-Eater raked its claws across the lich's forearm. Nearly silver in color, glowing liquid stuck to its claws and oozed from the three gashes.

"It has the blood!" Dante tried to jump to his feet in celebration; the canoe rocked violently beneath him and he promptly reseated himself. "Tell it to get out!"

Gladdic closed his eyes, brow crinkling. On the dock, the Andrac struck again, pushing the lich back a step. "It ignores me. It believes it can win."

The Star-Eater brought its bloody claws to its mouth, licking them clean with a pointed black tongue. Dante's heart beat hard, sweat squeezing from his skin. The White Lich drove a fist at the demon, which took the blow square in the chest but barely rocked back. Wisps of nether peeled away from the Andrac's body, but it was already reaching forward, inserting its claws through the lich's guard and jabbing them into his stomach.

The strike would have gutted a mortal man. Possibly cut him right in half. The demon's claws sank no more than half an inch into the White Lich's belly before coming to a sudden stop.

The Blighted widened their eyes in hate and swarmed forward, grabbing up the weapons they'd dropped so they could murder their share of the villagers with their bare hands. As the lich and the demon traded blows, spilling a bit of nether and a few small spatters of iridescent white blood, the lich began to react faster, blinking repeatedly as clarity returned to his eyes. A point of ether glared from his finger.

"Get it out of there!" Dante grabbed Gladdic's shoulder. "The lich is about to tear it apart!"

Gladdic grimaced and nodded shortly. Sweat stood up across his brow. On the dock, the first of the Blighted reached the Andrac, hacking at it with hatchets and spears that didn't so much as scratch its shadowy body. It ignored them, launching a second flurry of attacks at the lich, who blocked whatever he couldn't dodge, leaving a few shallow scratches across his arms.

The Eiden Rane narrowed his eyes, battering down another attack, then pushed his right palm forward. A beam of eye-watering ether lashed between him and the Andrac's chest. Nether boiled away in dark clouds. A fist-sized hole opened through the demon's body.

The Andrac's mouth widened, showing the star burning within its throat. It toppled backward from the edge of the dock and sliced into the murky waters.

Dante punched the side of the canoe, skinning his knuckles. "He's killed it!"

"No." Gladdic's voice was calm. "My link to it remains alive. But the Andrac is wounded. It may need our help escaping."

Blays squinted. "The thing we sent in to prevent us from getting our asses kicked by the big evil bastard now needs us to go fight the big bastard ourselves?"

"We will not engage the lich unless we are very desperate or very stupid."

"We have to go in," Dante said. "This could be our only chance to get what we need."

Blays swore and picked up a paddle. The canoe sped through the trees, already within a half mile of the settlement. Dante pulled two dragonflies toward them to make sure the way ahead was clear of Blighted or Monsoon pickets.

The third dragonfly kept watch over the dock. A transparent cube of light appeared around the White Lich, condensing into his hands. He blasted at the water with lances of ether, following the Andrac's path away from him. Steam spread over the water with the suddenness of a marine fog rolling in from the sea. A beam of ether ripped into the side of a raft-house, planks and splinters cartwheeling through the air.

The lich clenched his fist and ceased his assault; the demon had put too much space and cover between them. The blue-white figure conjured a ball of ether, sending it winging over the low rooftops. It steadied six feet above the water, streaming toward the trees. Tracking the Andrac's position.

The Blighted threw themselves into their canoes and paddled crazily after the ball of light. Monsoon soldiers joined the chase, keeping a bubble of space between themselves and the Blighted. Rowers brought the lich's personal vessel before him. He stepped into it with no obvious haste. His soldiers pushed off, paddling hard to catch up with the others.

"The bad news," Dante said, "is that their whole damn army's after the Andrac. Including the Eiden Rane."

Naran ducked his head, angling for a better view through the trees. "What is the good news?"

"Who said there's any good news?"

He directed Volo to the right, veering them away from a Monsoon canoe keeping watch on the woods. The trees thinned before them. Rain began to pelt the foliage as they reached the open water of the settlement. The ball of light—and, presumably, the Andrac—had already cleared the fish nets, and was streaking toward them. The enemy canoes were strung out behind the light, the closest lagging it by a hundred yards. The White Lich hadn't yet reached the fish nets, but he'd caught up to the back ranks of the Blighted.

Volo and Blays swung the canoe about, keeping them just inside the treeline. The ball of ether lined toward them. Suddenly concerned the lich might notice them, and convert the harmless light into something most harmful, Dante called to the nether, feeding it the blood from his skinned knuckles. He sent a bolt of it hurtling toward the glowing ball. The two forces impacted with a burst of black and white motes. When these cleared, the ball was still trailing forward. Frowning, Dante hit it harder, knocking it apart.

The Andrac emerged from the water an arm's reach from the boat, making everyone but Gladdic and Blays jump. Its claws shook as it reached for the boat. Its body, normally pitch black, appeared hazy in spots, especially around the wound in its chest, which hadn't seemed to have healed at all.

"It needs inside," Gladdic said. "It is too weakened to travel on its own."

Before Dante could object, the demon was hauling itself up the side of the boat. Though it was massive enough to capsize the canoe, they barely swayed. It crouched in the stern, folding its limbs to take up far less space than seemed possible.

Blays drove his paddle into the water, pulling them away from the oncoming horde. "For all the amazing junk you people can do, has it never occurred to a single sorcerer that it might be useful to be able to grow wings?"

"I've done some work on it," Dante said. "But the ducks keep dying before I can get them all the way sewed on."

Blays and Volo paddled with everything they had, drawing them into the darkness of the forest. Much of the forest enclosing the settlement was too dense to pass through, but the citizens had carved pathways through it, including the one the five of them were now using to escape. Dante extended his mind into the trees and the nether within them, harvesting great tangles of branches to close off the passage. The lead canoes crashed into the unexpected growth, the Blighted hissing in fury and whacking at the branches with ineffectual paddles.

Blays glanced over his shoulder. "Can't be that easy, can—?"

Light seared through the fresh growth, incinerating it along with at least one unlucky Blighted who had flung herself into the branches to rip at them with her hands. As she burned, she tipped back her head and smiled at the sky. Her smoking husk plopped into the water with a sizzle.

"Stop your craft and bend your knee." The White Lich's voice rang through the woods. "Mercy can be yours. But it requires the humility to accept it."

The Blighteds' canoes shot through the opening in the foliage, cinders clinging to their clothes and hair. Volo and Blays were paddling with everything they were worth, but the furious strength of the undead would slowly overtake them.

Gladdic twisted in his seat, ether circling his fingers and wrists in shining bands. "What you call mercy is the abnegation of the self. You would snuff out every sense of choice, and once our thoughts can be of nothing but you, you would tell us that is freedom at last."

"I know you." An edge of amusement entered the lich's voice. "You are the one who hastened my liberation. Ah, the anguish on your face when your ambush failed. I have seen such looks many times before. Did you think that destroying me would make them forget the evils of your soul?"

Gladdic made a choking sound. Rod-straight bands of ether rushed to his hands. He sent the light blazing behind them, shredding into the closest three canoes. The Blighted shuddered with the impact. Severed limbs spun into the water. As soon as they splashed down, the surface roiled with ziki oko feasting on the gifts of flesh.

The second line of enemy canoes swept past the de-crewed vessels. Gladdic drew another stream of glittering lines and slung them at the Blighted. As the light closed on its targets, a tide of shadows poured from behind the undead, enfolding the ether and smothering it into nothing.

"You consider what you have to be great power, don't you?" The lich's words sheared through the patter of the rain. "You have worked a lifetime for it. Now, for your stubbornness—your refusal to accept the truth before you—you have tossed it aside like a pot of waste."

The canoes pursuing them broke to either side, leaving a clear avenue through the water. The air there darkened to twilight.

Gladdic thrust out his hand, his forearm as sinewy as if it had been skinned. "Galand!"

Stiff cataracts of light poured from Gladdic's hands. And then

Dante felt it: the monstrous wave of nether thundering toward them. He called a great flock if it to himself, sending the energy careening in the wake of Gladdic's ether. The light hit the torrent of enemy shadows first, the two forces exploding into a mass of madly-spinning sparks. The lich's nether carried onward, forcing past Gladdic's efforts like a man wading through deep snow.

Dante hit it with everything he could. Limbs of nether tussled against each other like battling dogs. The air blackened until the trees within it were bare silhouettes. Still the lich's attack ground forward, pushing Dante's defenses back foot by foot. It was the strongest attack he'd ever encountered. Trying to hold it back felt like trying to pull up a mountain by its roots. Sweat popped out from his brow. He wanted to yell out, but he was bearing down too hard to speak; the slightest slip of concentration, and the nether would rush forward, annihilating them.

His hands shook. The lich's shadows pushed a foot closer, then lurched forward by ten. Dante felt himself about to give way.

Gladdic extended his fingers, spraying beams of light into the pressing wall of darkness. These carved away at the shadows, biting deep, whole portions falling away and dissipating. The nether slowed. Dante pushed back with some final reserve, causing the shadows to buckle along the seams Gladdic had sliced into them.

Everything came to a halt. Both sides strained against each other, neither advancing nor retreating. Gladdic adjusted a single beam by a matter of inches. It cut into the underside of the shadows. Without warning, the lich's entire attack collapsed, fluttering away like black ash.

Dante fell back, chest heaving. His jabat was drenched with sweat.

Blays glanced back, still paddling for all he was worth. "Was that as close as it felt?"

"Not sure," Dante said. "Did it feel like we were about to get ripped into a pile of bloody guts?"

"That wouldn't be entirely bad. At least I'd finally get to shake hands with my liver for all its fine service."

Dante groped clumsily at the nether, gathering more to defend against the next assault. Behind them, the Blighted paddled harder yet through the last specks of decaying shadows.

Gladdic gripped the gunwale, sweat tracking through the wrinkles of his forehead. "He fears overextending himself while he remains weak. Either the Blighted will overwhelm us, or we will deplete ourselves slaughtering them."

"Nice plan," Dante said. "Would be a shame if someone decided to thwart it."

He felt down for the soil beneath them. For the most part, the swamp's waters varied between ten and twenty feet in depth, but some portions of the bed were no more than two or three feet beneath the surface. He located one such spot just ahead of them. As they passed over it, he pulled the dirt upward, mounding it until it was inches from breaking into the open. The Blighted plowed onward, gaining steadily. When the enemy canoes were ten feet from the shallows, Dante yanked the ground upward into a series of jagged rills and spikes, hardening it into stone.

The canoes crashed into it with the hollow splinter of broken hulls. Pale bodies flew out with the impact, still gripping their paddles. The second wave of ships crunched into the first, snarling themselves against the barrier of rocks.

Naran made an obscene gesture at the pileup. Blays and Volo opened up space, heading for a small tunnel through the trees. Behind them, ether glimmered across the raised stones, which sank beneath the water, returning to their original state of silt. A handful of boats stopped to pick up the Blighted from the wrecked canoes. The others didn't break speed.

But Dante's maneuver had put them several hundred feet ahead of their foes. They sped through the gap in the trees, entering a maze-like profusion of trees and minor islands. As Volo steered them down one of the many pathways, guided by some Tanarian trail marker Dante couldn't make out—or, perhaps, guided only by her completely reasonable terror of all the things chasing them—Dante harvested the trees across the waterway behind them.

"You should save your strength," Gladdic said. "A few branches won't so much as slow him down."

"Unless it makes the Blighted think there's no path there at all."

He had lost one of his dragonfly spies at some point—most likely, his focus had lapsed while they'd been fending off the White Lich's onslaught—but he sent one of the two survivors to keep watch over the hidden pathway. The Blighted entered the maze-like area and slowed, gnashing their teeth in confusion.

The lich stopped, surveying the trees dispassionately. He tilted back his head, then waved his hand. Ether danced along the branches. When it reached the section Dante had altered, it lit up like a lantern. The lich's mouth twitched. He flicked his hand, returning the trees to their unaltered state. The Blighted raced into the tunnel.

"I have successfully bought us several whole seconds," Dante announced. "We might want to consider going faster."

"Then *you* might want to consider paddling," Blays said.

"With what? My hands? And after the ziki oko eat them, should I use my elbows?"

"Or your face. No one will miss that."

Dante spared a dollop of nether to soothe their strained muscles. Even so, the Blighted gained ground, with the White Lich right behind them to undo Dante's attempts to block or snarl the trail.

"We got a plan here?" Volo's voice was as tight as a harp string. "Or are we just hoping the dead people will get tired soon?"

"I thought we'd discourage them by paddling until we're too lean to have any flavor," Blays said. "Or we could give them Gladdic. He's so sour they'll probably let the rest of us go."

Dante's mind chased its own tail. They couldn't outrun their foes. Couldn't hide themselves or their trail. So what was left? Face the White Lich and his armies and hope Gladdic had been wrong about everything?

As the enemy canoes closed distance, divisions spread to the left and right, preparing to hem them in. Standing in his command vessel, the White Lich lifted his hands. A storm of geometric lightning crackled toward their canoe. Gladdic met it with a cloud of nether that boiled away in the face of the driving light.

Dante kept one eye on the sorcerous battle and the other on the way ahead, searching for some way out. Volo had angled to port to avoid a string of islands ahead. As they got closer, the many islands turned out to be a single long mass. Outside of the Wound, it was one of the largest pieces of land Dante had seen in the swamp.

"I grow weak." Gladdic sounded more disappointed in himself than angry or afraid. "Another minute, and he will have sapped me dry."

The oversized island grew closer, forcing Volo to veer further to port, and closer to the left flank of the enemy formation. The Blighted bared their teeth hungrily.

Dante grinned back at them. "Turn back to starboard. Take us to the island."

Volo shot him a glance. "To make a stand? That's the best we can do?"

"Sometimes," Naran said, "that's all you *can* do."

She and Blays corrected course toward the island. Gladdic

beat down another multi-pronged thrust of lightning. Dante reached for the nether, gathering it from all the death the swamps had hosted throughout the ages.

"The walls are sheer," Volo said, squinting at the sides of the island, which were at least eight feet high and completely vertical. "I'm not seeing anywhere to make landfall."

Dante reached forward. "Aim for the middle."

She redirected course again, steering them closer toward the center of the island. A hatchet splashed into the water behind them, followed by a second. The next one struck the side of the hull with a dull clonk. As the Blighted drew within range, some dropped their paddles and took up weapons. Saliva spilled from their mouths.

Lightning flashed behind them. Gladdic grunted, fighting it off with a shuddering hammer of nether. The island loomed ahead. Volo dragged her paddle in the water, back-beating to stop them from crashing into the rock.

"Don't slow down!" Dante yelled. "Straight ahead!"

Volo darted him a scared glance, then paddled on, shoulders straining. Dante reached into the stone, liquefying it and pulling it away to open a passage straight through the low cliff. Water spilled inside and they followed it. The air smelled cool and like freshly-broken rock.

The light dimmed around them as Dante bored onward. Behind them, an enemy canoe raced toward the opening. Dante yanked the entrance shut, locking them in utter darkness. The other boat crunched against the stone seal.

The splash of their paddles echoed through the narrow space. Gladdic sent a ball of light to hover beyond the prow, illuminating the tunnel as it cleaved open just feet in front of them. At the same time, Dante closed the way behind them, pushing the water forward along with their canoe.

"How far is it to the other side?" Blays said.

Dante felt ahead. "Don't know."

"Is there a chance you could run out of juice before we get to it?"

"Anything's possible."

"Unfortunate," Blays said. "Don't worry, though. If we get trapped in here, I'll bash you against the front wall until either it cracks open, or you do."

The canoe sped on through a space that, while it advanced steadily, never grew any larger. Instead, as they continued, Dante shrank the gap to more tightly fit them and conserve his own energy. Everyone fell silent, as if speaking up would some-how acknowledge the impossibility of what they were doing and cause the universe to immediately correct itself.

After a few hundred feet of travel, Dante felt his strength fad-ing. Should he conserve energy and stop sealing the way behind them? But that would thin out the water until the canoe ground to a halt. It was light enough that they could carry it forward, but that would slow them down drastically. Maybe enough to al-low the lich's soldiers to circle around the island and ambush them as they —

Light exploded in front of them. Dante threw his hands over his face. Someone cried out — possibly Volo, but it was hard to be sure — and they shot into a dreary, rainy day. After the blackness of the tunnel beneath the island, it seemed as bright as a coastal morning.

They took two seconds to ensure they were alone, then struck out with all speed, vanishing into the depths of the swamp.

Trees and miniature islands unrolled around them. Water, too. Lots of water. Volo insisted she knew where they were, but under questioning, she revealed that meant "a part of the swamp that didn't really have anything in it and hence wasn't worth knowing much about." In other words, she might know where they were in relation to the other bits of Tanar Atain, but she didn't actually know her way around that particular slice of it.

Still, their goal at the moment wasn't to reach a specific location so much as to get to anywhere that they might finally not be in danger of being slaughtered. In good news, there hadn't been any sign of Blighted or the lich since they'd carved their way through the island. Dante had sent a dragonfly to keep watch on the lich, but he hadn't even spotted their foe yet when he'd felt a presence grasping through the shadows. It had taken hold of the insect and darted back along the line of nether connecting it to Dante. He'd cut the nethereal cord as fast as he could. He hoped it had been fast enough.

He and Naran spelled the others at the paddles. Dante started counting inside his head. Blays fell asleep forty-two seconds later. After another hour of travel in a random direction, they put in at a crescent-shaped island that smelled faintly of sulfur. As the others dragged the canoe ashore to hide it in the weeds, Dante slew a handful of flying bugs to form a perimeter around the island.

At the camp, the Andrac kneeled a few feet from Gladdic, hanging its head. Dante didn't know if they could feel pain, but it seemed exhausted at the least, listless and half-broken.

Dante moved to stand across from it. "I need to see its claws."

Gladdic gestured to the demon. It lifted its head, staring at Dante as if it somehow knew about the others of its kind that he'd destroyed, and held out its long talons. Dante moved his mind along their curves. The nether that formed the demon was dense and unmistakable as anything but itself. It took him virtually no time at all to conclude his search for the lich's blood.

"It's gone." His voice was flat. "The blood must have washed off when the Andrac was swimming away from the lich."

"Every drop?" Gladdic bent forward, lips moving soundlessly as he examined the claws for himself. His face soured. "You are right. I see nothing."

"Uh uh," Blays said. "That can't be possible."

"There is nothing to be found. Look for yourself if you fail to believe me."

"Oh, I believe you. But I won't *let* it be true. Because it means we're completely screwed."

Dante dropped to sit on a fallen log. "We could try again. Send dragonflies in with the Andrac. When the Andrac wounds the lich, the dragonflies can dip themselves in his blood and bring it back to me."

Gladdic pinched his mouth together in a frown. "While the Andrac is left behind? That is a callous use of one's people."

"Yes, it would be. Except that we'll cunningly replace 'people' with 'soulless demons that no one would ever miss.'"

"Are you so certain of that? The Andrac are made from traces of humans. The traces come from very deep within us. Perhaps they are made from a dark part of our own souls. A part we deny possessing."

Dante blinked. The demon drew back its jaws in a smile. Gladdic cocked his head at it, then snorted and smacked his leg.

He turned to Dante. "Hold out your hand."

"My hand?"

"The appendage you relieved me of. Hold it out to the demon."

Making sure the nether was close, Dante started to extend his right hand, then thought better and put out his left instead. The Star-Eater stared into it like he was searching for fish within a shaded pool, then lowered its head and opened its fanged mouth. Its throat convulsed. It deposited a silvery puddle into Dante's palm—the blood Dante had seen it lick from its claws early in the fight.

The blood lay in his hand with the weight of quicksilver. "The demon did this on purpose?"

"If they bear a portion of our soul, is it surprising to think they might also bear a portion of our intelligence?"

Perturbed, Dante moved into the blood. It was so shot through with ether that for a moment he could see no hint of nether at all. Yet there it was, threaded through the light like the tiny veins within an eyeball. He reached for it.

The pressure in his head boomed like thunder. He swooned and blacked out. He found himself lying halfway on his side. The others had just started to move toward him; he'd only been out for an instant.

"Well." He wiped a sudden sheen of sweat from his forehead. "If we want to go say hello to the Eiden Rane, that won't be a problem."

Gladdic drew back his shoulders. "Do you have a link to the prime body?"

"Right now, what I have is a headache. And an old man nagging me to be perfect at something I've never even tried before." Dante returned to the log he'd been sitting on before. "The lich's signal is overwhelming. This could take a while to sort through."

He leaned his elbows on his knees and closed his eyes. If the nether's connection to the lich was like the crash of a waterfall, he had the impression the link to the original body would be the patter of a single raindrop. He cast about for a second thread. A minute later, having found nothing—why couldn't it ever be easy?—he shifted his attention to the main signal of the lich, hoping that in understanding it, he might better search for its counterpart.

"What if this 'prime body' is nothing more than a myth?" Naran kept his voice low, but not so low that it didn't penetrate the back of Dante's mind. "What if there's nothing else to be found?"

"You worry worse than Dante." Blays threw something small into a puddle of rain water. "Wail and gnash once we know it's time to wail and gnash. Until then, let's find a better use for our time. Like staring silently into the distance."

"When you travel from port to port, there are countless rumors of treasure and wealth to be found if you're bold enough to chase them. Poor captains leap at them, assuming they're all real. Good captains ignore them, assuming they're all false. Great captains venture after them knowing they're probably chasing a phantom—but make plans to feed and pay their crew even if they fail."

"Our current situation is so desperate that our big plan is to run off and stab somebody in their second body, which is something that I've never heard of anyone ever having. If you have a backup plan for that, I'm dying to hear it."

Naran muttered something Dante couldn't pick up. Dante continued to examine the contours of the main link. In form, it looked roughly the same as they always did, except massive and on the brink of painful to interact with. But that could only go so far to explain why the second link didn't seem to be there. Was that because it wasn't?

Or was it hidden?

Keeping his eyes closed, he stood and turned in a slow circle. The pressure rotated around the inside of his head. He held his breath, attempting to shut out all outside stimulation, but still felt nothing but the main pulse.

He opened his eyes and said several rude words. "I can't feel it."

Naran folded his arms, glaring at Gladdic from the corners of his eyes. "Then this was all a waste of time?"

"It was a great use of our time," Blays said. "Now that we tried our best to kill the lich, we're off the hook, aren't we? So it's everyone else's fault if he goes on and destroys the world."

Gladdic considered the ground, drops of rain rolling from his close-cropped hair. "How does this skill typically function?"

"Like I told you," Dante said. "The nether in a drop of blood is connected to the nether in the rest of the body. Get the blood, delve into the nether, and the link opens to you."

"Yet the second link isn't there? Or is it that the connection to the Eiden Rane is too powerful to see it?"

Dante shook his head. "Could be either one. Trying to feel if there's another link is like trying to feel a feather's touch while you're being punched."

"Should I start punching you?" Blays said. "To help you practice, of course."

Dante tilted back his head. The sky was overcast, just as it had been for days. It was starting to feel like the sun would never return to the land again. He turned once more to the pressure in his mind, seeking its edges. How did you pick out a single raindrop from the middle of a raging storm? Or pluck a leaf from within an all-consuming flood?

He lowered his chin with a snap. In both cases, you couldn't find what you were looking for from *outside* the storm. He gazed into the maelstrom of the link to the lich, then dived into the nether. It closed over his mind with cruel weight. Shadows howled about him, buffeting his ears; though the sensations were entirely in his mind, tears sprung from his eyes. He struggled to stay afloat, fighting to kick his way toward some sort of surface—then relented, letting his mind's body be carried along by the stream until the shadows and his consciousness were traveling at the same pace.

Though the current raged, he floated within it. Peering ahead, the channel of shadows led to a great hazy mass. He turned back to the stream itself. Every tendril of nether seemed to be flowing toward the well of the lich. On a hunch, Dante swam toward the center of the current. Amid a swirling mix of shadows, he came to a stop, once more matching the flow around him.

There, a single strand of darkness flowed away from him—or

rather, he was flowing away from it. He reached for it, closing on it with a final lunge. The stream was so thin and weak that his touch threatened to tear it apart. He held tight, binding it together, feeding it with nether. It blackened to opacity. Watching it for any sign of cracks, he drew it away from the river until he and the strand floated alone amid nothing.

With a disorienting lurch, he returned to the physical world, holding one arm out for balance. He felt for the strand. As soon as he touched it, the faintest pressure toyed within his head. He turned in a circle until the sensation centered in his forehead. He was facing due north. Almost directly away from the lich.

"I found the second signal," he said. "The prime body is real."

4

Gladdic's mouth fell open. "His original body exists? And you can find it?"

"This was *your* idea," Blays said. "Are you that shocked to finally be right about something?"

"Don't you understand? If it is real, then it can also be destroyed."

Naran followed Dante's gaze into the trees. "How far away is it?"

Dante tilted his head, trying to gauge the pressure's properties. "Hard to say. It's extremely subtle. I don't think I'll be able to judge until we're underway and I can feel how much closer we're getting."

Blays swore. "Why do all of your solutions involve work?"

Dante got up to help relaunch the canoe. Gladdic moved to the Andrac, which had crouched among the shrubs at the perimeter of their camp. Its shoulders were hunched high and it was still leaking shreds of shadow from the wound the lich had opened in its chest, which remained unhealed.

Gladdic communed with it. It unfolded stiffly to its feet and followed him into the trees. When Gladdic returned, he was alone.

They got into the canoe and shoved off, paddling along at a

sustainable pace. For the first few miles, Dante didn't say a word, keeping all of his attention on making sure his link to their target didn't slip away. Once he was beyond certain the connection wasn't going to vanish, he sat back in the stern, blinking at the occluded afternoon sunlight.

"We're not getting much closer," he said. "It's got to be at least forty miles away. Maybe twice that. And almost straight north. Volo, do you know what's up there?"

"Swamp," she said.

"Interesting. Any particular kind of swamp? Or just the kind with a lot of water in it?"

"It's hara dim. Abandoned land."

"What happened to the people who abandoned it?"

"They got smart." She jabbed absentmindedly at a large purple fish that had taken a close interest in their boat and was following alongside them. "I've never been there. I guess we get to learn about it together."

"Whatever is to be found there, it will be employed in service of protecting the prime body," Gladdic said. "Our task will not be easy."

Blays paused mid-paddle. "Are you suggesting the invulnerable centuries-old wizard might try to protect his only weakness? Truly, your insight is too valuable to go without."

Naran uttered a murmur of dissent. "Even if we have located the prime body, we can't be certain that killing it will also kill the lich. If it were so vulnerable, why would he leave his weakness where he can't protect it?"

Gladdic raised a white eyebrow. "The fact we are the first to ever find it should more than answer the question. He fought to keep its very existence a secret. You cannot kill what you do not know."

Dante was tempted to push them to complete the journey in one long go, cycling between paddlers and salving their muscles with nether, then decided it probably wasn't the most brilliant idea to arrive at the White Lich's secret lair completely exhausted and low on nether. They continued for a few hours after dark, Gladdic lighting the way with a ball of ether, then made camp on an island. There had been no sign of Blighted along the way, nor of pursuit, but Dante kept his dragonflies on patrol throughout the night.

They started out again at first light. The swamp had a heavy, unhurried air to it, and now that they were miles away from any settlement, animals glided in and above the water with little concern for the humans. Once, hearing the chattering of a pack of branch-swinging, flesh-eating boko mai, they diverted for half a mile before correcting course to the north.

The trees grew denser and taller, thick scarves of cobwebs hanging between them. As the delicate pressure mounted in his head, ruins sprouted from the larger islands. Others lurked below the surface, suggestions of a lost past. Rather than heaped rubble, some looked largely intact, as if they'd been built beneath the water — or like they'd been built at a time the water had been lower.

By the next morning, the pressure in Dante's head was strong enough to be irritating. Three miles later, it was pulsing steadily in his brain, peaking to the point of pain. His heart thrummed even harder.

He called them to a stop and motioned to a wide island just visible through the spiderwebbed trees. "We're right on top of it. Has to be over there somewhere. Ready to go put an end to an abomination?"

Blays loosened his Odo Sein swords. "Are you ever afraid our enemies are saying the same thing to themselves when they're creeping up on *us*?"

Dante sent two dragonflies winging ahead into the ruins scattered across the island. After a minute of searching, he frowned.

"I don't see anything. He'll have it hidden. Possibly disguised. Be ready to kill anyone we meet."

He brought the nether to him. Behind him, he felt Gladdic call to the ether. Volo paddled forward toward the island. The pressure behind Dante's brow grew by the second until it hurt with each heartbeat. With the island still a hundred yards away, the pain peaked, knife-like, and then began to abate.

But the relief was far from welcome.

"Stop." He grabbed the gunwale. "Back up. Slowly."

Volo gave him a confused look, then backbeat her paddle. The pain of the pressure ramped up again.

Dante held up his hand for her to stop. He leaned over the side of the canoe, but the water was far too murky to see more than a few feet down. "The prime body isn't on the island. It's beneath us."

Blays stared at him, then gave the water a deeply skeptical look. "I find that hard to believe. Unless the Eiden Rane started life as a very gifted trout."

"Why not? Where better to hide something you don't want people to know exists than in a place where it can't be seen?"

He closed his eyes and sent his mind down through the water, descending twenty feet before he reached the thick silt of the swamp bed. He regained his bearings and probed further. After a few more feet, he bonked into something solid. Something that didn't want to let his focus inside it. Scowling vaguely, he moved along the dirt piled on top of it instead.

"There's a structure buried under the mud," he said. "But it's made of something weird. I can't manipulate it."

"Then how do we get down to it?"

"I don't know yet. I can't even find an entrance."

"No worries, we'll just learn to breathe water. And grow hammer-hands to bash our way in with."

Naran cleared his throat. "This so-called prime body is alive, yes? And hence in need of the necessities of life?"

"I will confess my experience with two-bodied people is pretty limited," Dante said. "But I'd assume you're correct."

"Then there must be some entrance to convey these necessities to the body. It may even have caretakers of some kind. They would require an access point."

"This is not necessarily true," Gladdic said. "In my younger days in the priesthood, we were faced with a challenge. We needed to conduct certain scholarship on the matter of Taim potentially having bequeathed to us an incomplete calendar. And yet if it were to be made public knowledge that we were questioning the god's measures, the peasants would have called for our heads. Requiring vows of secrecy from the participating monks did not seem sufficient for such a grave matter, yet the king himself insisted the research must be done.

"I was the one who came up with the solution. We sank a deep pit in the king's woods, lowered the monks into it, and sealed them inside. A small hatch allowed the provision of food and water, but it was not large enough for a person to pass through. Once the monks' work was complete, resulting in a small amendment to the calendar, we sent down their final supply: a bottle of poisoned wine."

Blays gawked. "What an inspiring story of problem-solving!"

"The monks knew their sacrifice was for the well-being of the kingdom and the virtue of Taim himself. Without it, the church might have fissured, resulting in the loss of countless lives. They volunteered gladly." Gladdic swatted at a mosquito. "While there was no way inside their lodgings, we would have been able to sustain their lives indefinitely. The Eiden Rane may employ a similar system to protect his prime body."

"What does any of this matter? We're here to kill the prime body, right? So rather than wasting time looking for a way inside the lich's secret lair, why don't we smash the roof in and let the gigantic pool of water do the work for us?"

"Tempting," Dante said. "But he's got to have a way out in case there's a flood. We could lose the target."

"And then you use your magical powers to find him again."

"Assuming we can get to him before the lich rushes in to stop whoever's messing with his one vulnerability. We'll find a way inside—and we'll end this here and now."

Reasoning that the entrance would have to be above water, he ordered Volo to take them to the ruin-choked island. As the others wandered about looking for hidden doors, Dante sank his consciousness into the soil, searching for tunnels or stairs. The ruins were lodged in the dirt like raisins in a lump of uncooked dough. Any one of them could have a secret staircase into the space beneath the water, which seemed to be hundreds of feet wide and descended to unknowable depths. With an inner grumble, he poked his mind down into the quiet stone of the first ruined building.

He'd only been at his task for five minutes when Volo's voice rang out from the neighboring island. "Hey guys! Over here!"

Dante ran around the corner of a tumbled-down building, drawing the nether to him, but although Volo was jumping up and down and waving her arms above her head, she didn't appear to be in the process of being menaced or mangled by anything.

Dante cupped his hands to his mouth. "Yeah, we'll be right over. As soon as you bring us the canoe."

Volo straightened in embarrassment, then laughed and ran to the bank of the island where she'd left the boat. The others gathered next to Dante as she pulled up to shore. For some reason, she was dripping wet.

They piled inside the vessel and crossed to the smaller island. This had zero structures on it whatsoever, meaning they'd ignored it. Volo tramped a third of the way up the shallow slope and stopped in front of a tall and unpleasant-looking tree with a snake-like mess of roots and spiny branches that looked like they were reaching forth to strangle you.

"Aha," Blays said. "You've found us a *tree!*"

Volo wagged her head. "Isn't just a tree. It's a jana kang. Stores water in that pot belly-looking part of itself. Well, I swam inside it—and on the other side, there's a tube down into the darkness."

Dante took a step closer to it, reaching into the nether in its trunk like he'd do if he were about to harvest it larger. Just as Volo had claimed, past the vast barrel where it kept its water, a woody tunnel ran deep into the earth. Much deeper than any root had any business going. The interior seemed to be dry and was wide enough for a grown man to crawl through on his hands and knees.

He rubbed the back of his neck. "How in the world did you find this?"

Volo shrugged. "I looked around until I saw something that shouldn't be here."

"You find it unusual to find trees in a forest?"

"You can't see it because you don't even know what you're looking at. And you won't know there *is* something to look at unless I tell you." Concern bent her face. "What if owning knowledge is the most responsibility a person can have? Does having it oblige you to figure out where you need to share it?"

"Ease your burden by sharing it with me now. How did you know?"

"Jana kangs suck up brackish water with those roots there. By the time they store it in their belly, it's been made fresh. You travel around the swamps as much as I do, you have to know where to get good water. But this is the thing about the jana kang: they *only* grow where it's brackish."

"And we're two hundred miles from the nearest ocean."

She made a little "there you go" gesture. "Even if you knew it was strange for one to be here, the belly's filled with water. You'd never see the entrance unless you were already looking for it."

Dante motioned to Blays. "Well?"

"If you're suggesting I go first," Blays said, "then I suggest that you go defile yourself."

"But you're great at climbing inside trees."

"And I'm even better at telling *you* to do it."

Volo rolled her eyes. "What's the matter with you? I've already been inside it. It's dark, that's all."

She threw herself at the tree and scampered up its trunk toward the woody shelf overhanging its so-called belly. Dante watched her youthful lack of care with an annoyance largely aimed at himself. In prior times, he'd done any number of things far more foolish and dangerous than climbing inside a strange tree, yet rather than emboldening him, the experience of age had made him hesitant.

Volo slipped beneath the shelf and into the belly of the tree. Dante set his jaw and started up after her. The gnarled bark made for easy climbing. He reached the wide hole at the top of the belly and swung a leg inside, ducking his head. The interior held a pool of dark water six feet wide, four across, and unknowably deep. It was sloshing about slightly, but there was no sign of Volo.

He lowered himself into it. The water was warmer than he'd expected and smelled clean in a way the swamp absolutely didn't. He groped about with his toes but couldn't feel the bottom. He conjured up a dot of ether. The white light stretched across the belly. Six feet underwater, a large hole stood open in the back of the chamber. Dante took three deep breaths and dropped below the surface, kicking toward the hole. He fit through without issue. After a few feet, the passage bent upward.

He surfaced in a hollow space the size of a small wagon. Volo treaded water across from him, her black hair slanted over her stark white face like a wind-ripped veil. His breath and the splash of water echoed tightly, but the close space was interrupted by another tunnel into the trunk. This one was above the waterline. Dry.

Before he could think to turn around and go back for the others, Blays surfaced beside him, blowing water from his nose. He was followed by Naran, and then a couple seconds later by Gladdic, who extended his wrinkled neck to keep his mouth above water.

Blays eyed the old man. "You look like a drowned terrier."

"Some day, so will you," Gladdic said.

Dante grabbed the lip of the tunnel and pulled himself up. "No more insulting each other until we're sure we're not about to be crushed to death by a sentient tree."

The tunnel was only four feet high, obliging him to crouch his way forward. Within a few feet, it descended in a spiral staircase. The steps' edges were smooth, as if they'd been grown rather than carved. The floor and walls sweated condensation. Between the slipperiness of the steps and the lowness of the ceiling, he was so concerned with not bashing his head or tumbling downward that he had no mental space left to be worried about whatever they were walking into.

The air cooled. A whiff of decay joined the smell of must. The tunnel leveled out, expanding to six feet high, then eight. They were no longer walking on wood: rather, it was the bone-like grimstone.

Dante tried and failed to reach inside it. "I can't manipulate this stone."

Blays glanced at the floor. "Have you tried telling it that it's ugly first?"

"Is that a coincidence? Or did the lich build this place to protect it from people like me?"

The floating blot of ether Dante was using to light the way spilled over a tall stone door. Blays started to draw one of his swords, but as the blade lit up with purple sparks, drawing on the nether of his trace, he thought better and resheathed it.

Dante made eye contact with the others, then pulled the nether about him like a cloak and reached for the door's ring-shaped handle. He expected it to be locked, or even rusted shut, but it swung open handily, an unseen counterweight pulling it along its hinges.

The room beyond was too vast for the light of the ether to fill. The floor was patterned grimstone. The air smelled distantly of death. As Dante stepped forward, white lights glowed from the high walls.

He froze. "Gladdic, did you do that?"

"I was about to inquire the same of you."

After several seconds of silent waiting, Dante muttered to himself and moved to his right, following the sweep of the wall. Round white pillars connected the floor to the ceiling. These were inscribed with foreign writing in a language Dante had never seen before. He passed by three of them before it occurred to him to stop.

"These columns," he said. "There's writing on them."

"*All* columns have junk carved on them," Blays said. "You think a king's going to pay for some big fancy temple and just leave all his columns blank?"

"I thought Tanarians didn't use writing."

Volo reached for the symbols, which looked grimy but not particularly weathered. "We don't. The Drakebane's priests used to tell us that anything worth carrying forward should be made simple enough to remember."

Gladdic bent forward like a blade of grass grown too long to support its own weight. "It isn't Tanarian. It's Yosein."

"Yosein?" Dante wrinkled his brow. "The people who used to live in the Hell-Painted Hills before the lich drove them out?"

"Indeed. I would suggest they were the original architects of this place."

"What does the writing say?"

"I do not know. Regrettably, I lacked the foresight to see that I would someday find myself in an underwater palace covered in Yosein script."

"I might be able to read it." Blays leaned close, running his fingers over the letters. "I think it says, 'This has nothing to do with why we're here.'"

"I'm not so sure about that," Dante said. "We keep seeing connections between the Eiden Rane and the Yosein. If anyone would know about him, it's them."

"Yes, and if we kill him according to plan, none of it will matter."

Dante was half tempted to make a rubbing of the inscriptions with the bit of charcoal he kept for such purposes, but even if they weren't in the middle of something extremely dangerous, there were dozens of pillars in the room. He'd only be able to record a tiny fraction of the text from a single pillar. Even if he found a way to translate it, the information would be so incomplete it would almost certainly be useless.

He moved away from the pillar, drawing his knife and poking himself in the arm. Nether lay heavy in the damp air, strangely skittish. Fifty feet from the passage through the tree, they came to a corner of the room. Dante followed the new wall, walking between it and the pillars. Another pair of torchstones glared to life ahead of and above them.

Leaves rasped over the floor, but there was no breeze.

Dante stopped in his tracks and stared hard into the darkness to their left.

Naran murmured, "Did you hear — ?"

Pairs of light winked from the gloom, faint as stars. Gladdic lifted his hand. Ether blared across the chamber, lighting up a mob of lean-limbed ghouls. The Blighted bared their yellowed teeth and charged. They made no effort to coordinate, but so equal was their fury that they advanced with the discipline of a king's guard.

Blays drew his swords, the purple-black charge of nether racing from the hilts to the tips. Dante and Naran did the same. Volo got out her long knife with its heavy guard. Gladdic stood his ground, fist clenching portions of both nether and ether.

Dante flicked his hand, sending black scythes whirling into every other Blighted on the front line. They fell like fumbled crockery, rage burning with the last light of their eyes. Blays and Naran carved into the thinned ranks. The nether-enhanced swords cut through bone like it was flesh and flesh like it was cheesecloth. Blood sprayed the floor in red curls.

The Blighted climbed over their own dead, throwing themselves at Naran and Blays. Ether streaked from Gladdic's hand, straighter than any arrow, taking the enemy in their foreheads and chests. They thumped to the ground, their withered hands groping for the swordsmen's ankles even as they died.

Blays stepped pretty through the corpses, lunging forward whenever a Blighted stumbled or tripped, running them through and then yanking his blade to the side, releasing their blackened guts to thud wetly to the ground. Dante slung a second round of nether, cutting down ten of them in an instant. Ether seared through the gloom. Purple swords swung in arcs, trailing their dark light behind them.

As always, the Blighted fought to the last. At the end, limbs and gore lay tossed across the stone, white islands in a swamp of blood—a grotesque copy of the Wound of the World itself.

Blays wiped his swords on a dead man's clothing. The fabric was too tattered to tell exactly what it had been. "How long do you suppose these bastards have been down here? Getting chopped to bits was probably the most excitement they've had in a century."

Volo kicked a pair of legs, then looked disgusted with herself. "If this is the best the lich can do, maybe he isn't so scary after all."

"Their wrath and speed is more than enough to overwhelm normal men," Gladdic said. "But they are more than soldiers. They are also eyes. The Eiden Rane now knows we're here—and if he knows, it is possible that the prime body knows as well."

Dante swiveled his head in a slow semicircle. "It isn't going anywhere yet. Maybe it can't even move on its own."

Blays sheathed his weapons. "We're on a mission to kill a bed-ridden old man? If you see something running away from us at full speed, don't worry. That's just my honor."

Gladdic stepped over a torso. "Honor is nothing but a way for the powerful to excuse their own power. We will find the prime body, and we will destroy it. Or the White Lich will find us."

He strode onward, passing over the bodies rather than de-touring around them. Dante kept a lump of shadows in his fist. They came to the far wall and turned left. Halfway across the room, they came at last to a door. Blays drew his weapons and nodded to Dante, who pulled on the ring handle. It was heavier than the first door had been, but opened without trouble.

The room beyond was a downward stairwell. Blays led the way, Dante one step behind him. After a single flight, the stairs ended at another door. This opened to a tight corridor. Two inches of water lay on the floor. The air was now as cool and neutral as a cavern. Blays stirred the water with the toe of his sandal, provoking a stagnant smell, but no movement from any-thing within it.

He put away one sword and stepped forward, remaining blade held low before him. Gladdic lit the way with a ball of ether whose light was soft yet penetrating. The corridor was just wide enough for two people to stand shoulder to shoulder, but not wide enough to fight side by side, and they advanced single-file, Blays in front.

Stone ground behind them. Dante whirled. Gladdic called up a second spot of ether just in time to catch the door slamming shut behind them.

Blays swept back his hair. "Probably just the wind, right? A gust from the massive storm we've got going on down here?"

Rather than waste time arguing whether they should go forward or back, Dante continued down the hall, tromping through the water toward the door Gladdic's light had shown at the far end. The water felt warmer on his sandaled feet. He stopped. A current ran over the top of his foot.

"The water," he said. "It's getting deeper."

He jogged forward, water spraying from his heels to splatter the tight walls. Dante came to the door at the end of the passage, grabbed its steel ring handle, and pulled. The door didn't budge in the slightest. He tugged again, getting nothing.

Hot prickles ran up his back and arms. "It won't open!"

"Have you tried not being an idiot?" Blays yelled. "Use the nether!"

The water continued to flood in, now reaching their shins, foamy and lukewarm. Dante shaped the nether into a dense spike and rammed it into the middle of the door. Chips of grimstone flew everywhere, a large crack spreading from the impact. Dante hit it again, opening a hole to the other side.

Warm swamp water jetted from the hole and sprayed him in the face.

"It's a trick!" He backed away, nearly falling. "It's not a door, it's a wall!"

As he stumbled back toward the other end of the hallway, Gladdic waded forward, his face hardened with resolve. He lifted his hand. Light speared from his palm to the hole in the wall.

Dante's heart jumped. "What are you — ?"

The ether coalesced into the hole and settled into the cracks. It went solid white, then faded away, revealing a smooth and un-marred wall.

Gladdic smiled in brief satisfaction. "Your nether is apt at de-stroying. It might even be used to create that which is new. But the highest virtue lies in preserving that which already exists."

Dante rolled his eyes. "*True* virtue lies in finding where the gods damn water's coming in from before we drown."

"Shit!" Blays yanked his right foot out of the water. A hand-sized silver fish dangled from the blade of his foot, blood drip-ping from its jaws. "Now that's just rude!"

Dante felt as though he and the world had slipped out of joint from each other. He knew the feeling well: they had entered a situation where if you slowed down to think, you would get swept out to sea. The only thing left was to act and hope your in-stincts were well-honed.

"Light!" He pointed at the water. "As much as you can!"

Gladdic spread his fingers wide. Dots of light spread through the water, flashing from the scales of the wriggling ziki oko. Darkness darted from Dante's hands. A fish blew apart in a red and silver haze. He struck at a second and then a third, clouding the water with their blood and filmy guts.

Blays grabbed Volo and hauled her from the water, boosting her up on his shoulder. He bugged his eyes at Dante. "Here's a suggestion: get us out of here!"

Dante nodded, but had no intention of doing any such thing. He had the feeling, and it was a strong one, that if they aban-doned the corridor to let it flood, the water would stick around for a good long while before it drained. Long enough for the White Lich to arrive. And if they lost the prime body now, he knew they'd never see it again.

He exploded four more fish. Naran yelped and jerked up his left leg, taking aim at the ziki oko clinging to his ankle and skewering it with his Odo Sein blade, nearly severing his own foot in the process. Dante blasted two more as they streaked toward the commotion Naran had kicked up.

The light was still spread across the water, shining crazily with the tossing of the surface. Another fish zipped toward Blays, apparently from nowhere. Dante reduced it to a cloud of silvery chunks and slogged toward it. Another fish raced in toward the expanding cloud. Dante dispatched it and followed its track back toward the wall.

Gladdic grunted and stepped up beside him. Yet another fish swam in, seemingly straight from out of the rock. Dante blew it apart. Gladdic frowned and thrust forth his palm. A flurry of ether tumbled toward the base of the wall. The air crackled as the water there turned the milky white of quartz. Frost shot up the wall, glittering in the pure light of the ether. A wave of cold blew past Dante's face.

No more fish came. The surface was still tossing and turning, but it already seemed calmer. Dante waded forward and nudged the ice with his foot. "How long is that going to hold?"

"Longer than it should," Gladdic said. "Yet likely not as long as we'd like."

Blays swung Volo from his shoulders and placed her into the water. She tipped back her head at him. "You held me from the water. But what would you have done if the fish had come for you?"

"Scream, I expect." Blays made a quick inspection of his legs. "If I didn't know better, I'd almost think someone doesn't want us to be here."

"A common reaction to your presence." Dante waved his hand, sealing the small bites Blays and Naran had taken to their feet. "Does anyone see anything resembling a door?"

They poked and peered at the walls. Other than the false door, there was no other sign of an exit from the corridor. Dante couldn't manipulate the grimstone itself, but he could follow its edges with his mind — something he should have done when the flooding began, but which he hadn't thought of in the heat of the moment. As it turned out, the chamber they were inside jutted out into open water, a dead end.

But there was another level below them.

A search of the floor turned up a trap door. Blays and Naran hauled it open, revealing a staircase. Though some of the water had drained from the false corridor, several inches remained, and it poured down the steps, leaving an unpleasant trail of scales and fish eyes.

Dante took the lead to the landing below. Past a foyer, another pillared chamber yawned into darkness. He'd been tamping down the pressure in his head so he could pay better attention to his surroundings, but he allowed himself to feel its full strength. So close to the target, it was hard to be sure, but the feeling indicated the prime body was somewhere ahead of them yet, and possibly deeper still.

He entered the chamber. Torchstones lit up from the walls to right and left, spilling over the faces of another score of Blighted. Seeing the living humans, they stampeded forward. Perhaps Dante was imagining it, but for once the frustration in their expressions looked more resigned than furious, as if they understood they had no chance but still couldn't stop their compulsion to attack any more than a rock, when dropped, could stop itself from falling.

Dante and Gladdic cut them down before they had the chance to close on the others. Those that didn't die right away glared up at the darkened ceiling, curling and uncurling their fists.

Along with the pillars, the chamber held a number of long, sturdy tables covered in grime and fine white mold. Slabs of solid grimstone served as benches for the tables. The latter bore books—some of them left open, the pages ruined by mold, which Dante found highly irritating—along with glass flasks, neat arrangements of bones, and copper cubes carved with symbols half-obliterated by a green patina.

Dante motioned to Gladdic. "Does any of this have any significance to you?"

The old man made a brief inspection of the table's contents, then pushed back. "Research. Perhaps alchemical, perhaps sorcerous. Sophisticated, if I had to guess. Quite possibly involving knowledge we no longer possess." His cheek twitched. He picked up one of the cubes, turning it in his hand. It was clear that its corners had once been sharp and crisp, and that the symbols etched into it had been precise and artistic, but everything had been blurred and disfigured.

Gladdic dropped the cube on the table. "In Mallon, we are taught to praise Taim as the highest of the gods. As the one who brings order to our lives with the gift of time. But time is a curse, isn't it? It doesn't bring order. It brings *chaos*. Breakage and decay. To the bodies of ourselves and everyone who will ever be."

"Odd," Blays said. "You look like an eighty-year-old man. Yet you *sound* like a fifteen-year-old boy whose girl just told you she can't see you anymore."

Dante picked up one of the cubes. Its weight felt right. He bounced it in his palm, then tucked it into his pocket. He moved on past another set of tables, giving them a once-over for anything interesting, more torchlights winking on as he advanced deeper into the chamber. The rasp of his sandals echoed from the blank walls.

Another set of torchstones came to life, casting their light on a great throne of grimstone and iron, which had rusted over the years, the ruddy fluid staining the chair's sides like old blood. Dante stopped short, breath catching in his throat. A man sat in the chair.

He was motionless. Desiccated. Dante reached into the nether and felt that it was quiet.

"He appears dead," Dante said. "Then again, so does everything the lich is involved with."

A silver crown rested on the man's head, blackened with age. His robes looked like they'd once been exceedingly fine. Tarnished silver bracelets and rings adorned his hands, but atop his shriveled skin, they resembled a wealthy child dressed up in his parents' jewelry.

Naran appeared to be about to take a step forward, then thought better of it. "Do you see his jaw? The planes of his cheeks?"

"Looks an awful lot like the Eiden Rane, doesn't it?"

"Is this it? The prime body?"

"No." Dante moved closer, keeping the nether locked in his left hand. "The blood's telling me the real one's lower down. But I'm sure the White Lich wants anyone who finds this to believe it's the prime body."

Blays drew his sword. "Step aside."

"I just told you this isn't it."

"And I am replying to say there's no reason to take that chance." He twirled his sword. "Besides, chopping things is fun."

Dante glanced reflexively at Gladdic for guidance, then frowned and stepped aside. "Chop away."

Blays flicked his wrist, sending his nether-coated blade through the body's brittle neck. The head took a moment to topple over, as if it had to wake up first. It hit the floor with a dull clonk. The dead man stirred. Blays grunted and lifted his weapon, but the body was just leaning to the right after having been relieved of the weight of its head.

Dante tapped his temple. "Pressure's still there. Congratulations, you have successfully defiled a corpse."

"Well if he's down here, he probably did *something* bad."

"We'll tell everyone he drew his sword on you first. Come on, help me find the next door."

He walked behind the throne. There, a mural lay across the floor. Beneath the grime, the tiles illustrated a scene of a great battle, legions of men in lacquer armor arrayed against an icy white titan while the world around them burned.

The walls were all blank stone. Dante closed his eyes and felt down into the nether. As he'd thought, it seemed as though there was another level below them. Unable to feel anything about the grimstone other than that it was there, he instructed the others to spread out to search the floor manually for another trapdoor. But where the corridor had been tight, limiting the grounds of their search, this room was a massive open space. Searching all of it carefully enough to reveal a concealed door could be the work of hours.

Yet as with any overwhelming task, the only solution was to ignore the intimidating scale of it and start chipping away at what was in front of you. Dante made his way across the floor, bent like an old water-carrier, poking at cracks in the floor with his knife.

"Galand." Gladdic's voice echoed across the room. Standing beneath one of the wall-mounted torchstones, he beckoned with a bony finger. "Join me."

Doing nothing to disguise his irritation, Dante crossed the room to join the priest.

Gladdic gestured upwards. "Do you see this torchstone?"

"You mean the source of light making it possible to see any-thing at all?"

"Indulge the possibility I am not a complete fool, and imagine that I am asking you to examine it."

Dante sent his mind into the torchstone. Though they were notoriously difficult to craft—in fact, as far as he knew, the ability had been lost altogether, although possibly it was merely that everyone had run out of the proper resources — the design itself was quite simple. The ether in the gems was converted to light, which was in turn enhanced in brightness by the nature of the stone itself, allowing for a small portion of ether to illuminate a space for a disproportionately long time. Dante was no expert in the stones, nor the ether, but everything in the item appeared perfectly standard.

"I'm looking," Dante said. "It looks like a torchstone."

"It does. Now indulge me a second time, and examine this stone." Gladdic walked away from the corner toward the center of the long wall. He stopped beneath the next torchstone.

Dante moved into the ether — at least, as best as he could — then gave a shake of his head. "I don't see anything strange."

"Then you are poorly trained. Look again. Knowing that the device is attempting to deceive you."

"How can you be so old and still be so bad at making your point?"

Dante sent his focus back into the glowing stone. On the surface, everything appeared the same as the last torchstone. Pointedly aware that he was missing something that was apparently obvious, he pressed closer yet. On instinct, he sent a wisp of nether into the stone. The light flickered — and so did the wall.

Dante clapped his hands. "It's not just lighting the room. It's casting something onto the wall."

"Shall we find out what?" Gladdic squared himself to the wall and lifted his hand. Ether winked between his fingers and the torchstone. The light wavered, then flashed and went out.

Their section of the room dimmed considerably. But the remaining stones provided enough light to show the door set in the wall.

"A sophisticated act of trickery," Gladdic said. "The illusion is only deployed when someone enters the room, triggering the torchstones to activate. Additionally, this facility has employed the torchstones since we first entered it, and never as anything but a source of light. Only now, when we have long since grown used to their presence, and would not suspect them of any oddness, are they used to hide the truth from us."

Dante motioned the others over to him. "Yeah, well if I'd been around for a thousand years, I bet I'd be able to come up with a pretty clever lair, too."

Once the other three were assembled at the door, Dante pulled it open. Gladdic's ether lit up a cramped descending staircase. The smell that wafted from the depths was of something very old. Something that never saw the sunlight.

Dante headed down, stepping softly. Someone—Volo, he thought—was walking down the steps with their sandals slapping. Just as he grew annoyed enough to curse the offender out, he reached the bottom of the staircase. Holding the nether at the ready, he entered an expansive room. Torchstones sprung to life along the walls, raining light through a chamber that at first glance seemed identical to the one above it.

Dante touched his forehead, which felt ready to give birth. "It's just ahead."

Beside him, he felt Gladdic reach for the nether. Blays, too. Volo drew a pair of throwing knives with leaf-shaped blades. As before, a line of pillars ran parallel to the two longer walls. Dante moved to the left side of the room and advanced along the columns, knowing the cover they provided was more psychological than real.

By the fourth pillar they passed, he noticed one difference in this room: rather than the columns being etched with Yosein script, they were carved with images of demons boiling up from the ground and ripping people apart with long claws. The next pillar showed a field of bodies on bare, ravaged ground. At the edge of the carving, nothing but demons remained alive.

Near the far end of the room squatted an iron and grimstone throne identical to the one they'd seen in the previous chamber. As before, a gnarled and shrunken body sat upon the throne, hands resting on the seat's broad arms. The corpse was bearded, swaddled in a moldering robe.

Dante came to a stop. The pressure in his head had grown so painful he had no choice but to clamp a mental lid on it. "That has to be it. The prime body."

Blays moved beside him. "More like the prime mummified corpse. So what's our approach? Shred it into person-jerky?"

"This and everything hence is beyond any man's knowledge," Gladdic said. "It may be as simple as destroying the body. But it might require destroying the body's trace as well."

"Sounds like it's time to start experimenting." Blays drew one of his swords with a crackle of nether. "Tell me when to stop hacking."

He took a step forward. On the throne, the corpse lifted its head and opened its eyes.

Dante choked. Blays spat out a word that sounded like multiple curses ground up into a sausage-like slurry of nonsense.

The dead man's eyes were a washed-out blue. He regarded each of them slowly, his expression foggy, as if he was examining a scroll written in a language he didn't understand.

Blays lifted his empty hand. "Er, hello?"

"You are the first ones to ever find me." The decrepit man spoke passable Mallish, accented the same as the Eiden Rane, with his S-sounds honed toward the sharper edges of a Z. His first words were halting, but grew more fluid as he went along. "How have you done this?"

"It wasn't easy," Dante said. "We—"

"Tell him nothing!" Gladdic pointed his finger at Dante's head. "You know nothing of what sits before you. His master is more treasonous than a winter storm on the high sea. And he will serve that master without any hint of human compassion."

"I thought everything that came hence was beyond all knowledge."

"Think, fool. Should we tell him, and we somehow fail, his master will ensure that the same trick may never again be used against him."

The prime body braced his arms on the throne, as if trying to lift himself, then groaned in pain and slumped back, head resting against the chair. "Finding this place was no accident. No commoners could have reached this chamber. You are sorcerers."

"That is too obvious for comment." Holding the nether and ether together in his hand, Gladdic paced sidelong in front of the prime body, keeping his distance. "Do you understand what you are?"

The man smiled as thinly as it was possible to smile. "I am nothing. A regretful leftover that must yet be preserved. And so I am a prisoner."

"Is there anyone else here?"

"This place is not a house for the living."

"You have no caretakers? No protectors?"

"This temple was built to be all the protection that I would require. As for needs, I have none—none, at least, that will be tended to."

Dante kept both eyes on the man in the throne. Though he was a long way from healthy, he already looked less frail. "Didn't you just tell me that he couldn't be trusted?"

"And he cannot," Gladdic said. "Yet it may be possible to judge the quality of his lies."

The prime body gazed at them flatly. "Why have you come here?"

"You will answer my questions first. What continues to keep you alive?"

"The will of my master."

"Can this will — this power — be generated by those who are not under his sway?"

"If a thing can be done once, it can be done again."

Gladdic chewed on this a moment. "How did the Eiden Rane become the Eiden Rane?"

The man laughed, a disturbing rustle. "How is all power gathered? By taking it from others, and placing it within yourself."

"And how is this done?"

He closed his eyes. "I no longer remember."

Gladdic strode forward, light and darkness glaring from his hand. "You lie. Refuse me the truth and I will torture you to madness."

"I will answer no more questions, for I no longer have one of you. You have come here to destroy me."

"That's right," Dante said. "But we will make it fast."

"Would it surprise you to learn that I welcome an end?"

Blays cocked his head. "You *want* to die? Haven't you had an awful long time to take care of that for yourself?"

"Do you think my master would go to the trouble of locking me away from all harm without also ensuring that I be made impotent to harm myself? When I am trapped in this tomb, century on century without sunlight, without the songs of the birds and the girls, without the taste of meat or even the sweet taste of clean water? Who, in such situation, would not go insane, driven to claim their own life and at last bring about an end? When I have not felt a real life for so long, what would it lose me to end it?"

"Surely there are ways to pass the time down here. You could have started up a mold collection."

The prime body swung his head from side to side, an act that seemed likely to snap his fragile neck. "I have *been* for long enough. For nothing has meaning that has no end: and that which goes on forever can never be loved, for it becomes too familiar, as common as the earth or the air, and just as unremark-able. While all around it fresh seeds sprout and grow tall, bloom in all their color, and then die—only to be replaced by the flow-ers of their own seeds. Tell me this: would you trade my life for your own?"

The question was fully rhetorical, the prime body plowing on with more in the same vein, waxing on about how he no longer had true memories of life outside the tomb, but rather memories *of* memories, which he was no longer certain were accurate. He seemed capable of talking for eternity. Almost as if he wasn't quite ready to die after all. Had he gone senile? Or was his chat-ter a form of self-defense: a ruse to prattle on at them until they died of old age and left him alone?

Dante's eyes widened. Sick with the certainty of their mistake, he lifted the tamp he'd placed on the blood bond connected him to the prime body. It exploded forward, dazzling him. He waited for his senses to return.

And found that, while the sense of pressure remained over-whelming, it had diminished, and was getting further away with each moment.

He swept the nether into both hands. "This is not the prime body."

Gladdic gave him a scornful eye. "But your signal brought us to it."

"And while that thing sits in its throne yapping at us, the sig-nal's running away."

Gladdic's face stiffened. He drew his power to his hand. "King of deceit! I will put your lies to their death at last!"

With startling agility, the man in the throne popped to his feet. He clasped each hand to the opposite forearm, nails near his elbows, and tore downward toward his wrists, opening shallow channels in his skin. He was so withered and pale that he looked as though his veins couldn't be running with more than an ink bottle's worth of fluid, but blood dripped readily down his arms.

The man smiled, eyes narrowing to malevolent slits. "I am much older than you know: and I have waited a long time to kill again."

Dante and Gladdic lashed out with a pulse of shadows. The ancient sorcerer flicked his left hand, whip-like, spraying drops of blood toward his foes. Nether streaked toward them from all sides of the chamber, multiplying beyond the force exerted by the sorcerer. The summoned shadows swarmed against Dante's attack, dispersing it like sand in turbid water. Gladdic's was dashed apart an instant later.

One of Volo's knives flicked through the air, catching the light of a torchstone. The blade disappeared into the folds of the sorcerer's cloak, seemingly without effect. Blays dropped into the nether and sprinted through the shadows. Without so much as glancing his way, the ancient one twirled his left index finger. He ejected Blays from the netherworld with such force that he hit the ground and skidded backwards.

The sorcerer—who was, it was now clear, a sort of under-lich left behind as the final defense of the prime body—snapped his left hand forward, flipping more blood toward Blays. Nether gushed to the droplets, as hungry as ziki oko, forming a barrage of darts.

Blays kicked hard, scooting away along the floor. Dante tossed a chaotic handful of shadows toward the darts, but he could already see that he was too far away to intercept the strike. His heart clenched tight. As the barrage swept closer, an eye-blink away, Blays vanished into the shadows.

The attacking nether buzzed in confusion, spinning randomly through the space Blays had exited. As the sorcerer cocked his hand, ready to force Blays back into the physical world once again, Dante's strike rammed into the circling swarm, erasing it.

Blays reappeared to Dante's left. "Have I ever told you I hate wizards?"

"Technically, you *are* one."

"If sneaking about counts as sorcery, then why do cats still need you to open the door for them?"

Before the throne, the under-lich flicked his arm, robes flapping, turning aside Gladdic's rain of ether with another shower of blood-augmented shadows. Both sides paused, assessing.

"This fighting is foolish," the ancient one said. "You show strength. My master would welcome you to his service. Just as he did me."

Blays wheeled his sword through the air. "Yeah, that deal seems to have worked out so well for you, Mr. Hasn't Seen Sunshine in Five Hundred Years."

The man fixed Blays with an interrogating eye. "Your talent isn't known to us. It would make a welcome addition to our ranks. Regarding myself, it's true that I have spent ages in what some would call imprisonment. But my lord returns, and my wait is at its end: he will claim the world, and I will be granted my share."

Gladdic drew the nether to his remaining hand, beginning to shape it, but Dante held up a hand. He knew that they couldn't afford to delay—that every second they spent dealing with this under-lich was another second for the prime body to make its escape—but he knew also that a great mystery stood before him. And that the owner of that mystery liked to talk.

"Did you join him willingly?" Dante said. "Or did he enslave you?"

The ancient one smiled in crusty amusement. "What does it matter? I serve happily. And so will you."

"If he's so powerful, why does he need people like us to help him?"

"Can one man be in two places at once? To complete many tasks, one needs many hands. The lord understands that it takes more than one candle to light the darkness."

"Has this deal made you immortal?"

"Not even the master knows for certain, for there have been none like him before." His eyes twinkled. "But I look forward to finding out."

Before Dante could say more, Gladdic curled his lip and lashed at the servant with a patchwork blend of ether and nether. Posing with the arrogance of a fencer, the under-lich spun from his right foot to his left, pelting the assault with his own blood and the nether that it drew.

As the two energies pounded each other into sparks, some of Gladdic's nether appeared to defect, or perhaps simply to turn neutral, too engaged by the presence of fresh blood to continue its original task. Though the struggle played out too quickly to be sure of its exact nature, one thing was clear: the under-lich was using less power to defend himself than it seemed like he ought to need. Even if Dante and Gladdic were able to wear the enemy down, his ability to defend himself would buy the prime body precious minutes to make his escape.

Gladdic seemed to draw the same conclusion, stomping forward and hammering at the under-lich with a storm of prismatic light that overwhelmed the torchstones like the sun blotting out the stars. Dante flanked Gladdic's assault, smashing at the undead with a mallet of nether.

Volo tossed another throwing knife. It took the enemy in the shoulder, but he paid it no mind, as if he felt no pain at all. As the under-lich spun and whipped his limbs, beating back each attack with a sprinkle of blood, Blays slipped into the nether, attempting to circle around to the sorcerer's back. From the corner of Dante's eye, he caught Naran trying to edge forward, only to be driven back by a stray loop of nether; those shadows were under Dante's control, but in the chaos of the fight, Naran would have no way to tell.

The under-lich thumped Blays from out of the netherworld. Blays rolled backwards and blinked back from sight before the enemy's followup lance of nether could strike him.

The scratch Dante had opened on his arm at the start of the fighting had started to coagulate, leaving the nether sluggish. Almost grumpy. He used a razor of nether to lengthen the wound. A warm bead of blood slid down his arm. The shadows spun with enthusiasm. And Dante smiled.

As Gladdic tried and failed to brute-force his way through the ancient one's guard, Dante peppered the robed man with tight shots of nether. The sorcerer spun like a dust devil, his spilled blood driving the nether before him like a herd of black beasts, smiling his arrogant smile, as if mocking Dante's own.

Dante felt the ether about him: crackling between Gladdic and the lich; glowing softly from the torchstones; present in the design of all things. In perfect stillness, he emptied his mind, like two cupped hands holding nothing. And asked the ether in the lich's arms to heal the wounds there.

The sorcerer continued to whip his arms about like a practitioner of a strange martial art, but the nether that had orbited him drifted away from his now-bloodless limbs.

Dante summoned as much nether as he could hold together. "Now!"

He unleashed the shadows in a single long flood. Gladdic jabbed forth his palm, matching the nether with a column of light. The under-lich scrambled backward, his once-smug eyes going wide with alarm. He raked fresh cuts across his arm. He'd only started to bring up the nether when the wave of energies broke over his body.

He disappeared in a haze. Nether teemed around him like dark wasps. Ether streaked forward like lost bits of shooting stars. When the air cleared enough to see again, the under-lich had fallen to his knees. One of his arms had been ripped free and was lying against the throne behind him. Half his face had been shredded to the bone; something that might have been the remnants of an eye lay upon his exposed cheek.

The other eye swiveled toward Dante, brimming with hatred. "You will mourn what you have just done when you sit at his feet. When—"

His half-flensed jaw swung free from its hinge, hanging from the side of his mouth. A look of dismay entered his eye, and then it rolled upward, seeing nothing. The under-lich lost what little color he had left, whitening like snow. He lifted his hand to the ceiling. His fingers curled to his palm, snapping off one by one and falling to the ground with the sound of crumpled parchment chucked aside.

With a burst of blue light, he collapsed into dust. The grimstone beneath him was stained with pure ether.

Dante edged closer to the stain. "Is he dead?"

"He better be." Blays nudged the pile of dust with his sandal. "Otherwise, the only one who can slay him now is a charwoman. Don't we have a prime body to hunt down?"

Dante made a once-over of the others, but no one had taken more than a few scratches during the fight. Not surprising. The under-lich had been too caught up in fending off Dante and Gladdic to launch many counterattacks of his own.

This done, Dante reopened the link to the prime body in his mind. The pressure pointed directly to the wall behind the throne. After brief inspection, they found another door concealed by the illusion cast by the torchstone above it. Dante grabbed the ring handle and pulled the door open.

A wall of lukewarm water poured over him, sweeping him from his feet and slamming him against the back of the throne. Volo sailed past him, scratching about for a handhold. Gladdic scrambled to the side, avoiding the flood's full strength.

He approached the doorway from the side, water pouring

over his bare shins as he craned for a look inside. "Half the wall is open. The only way out is back the way we came!"

Dante wanted to argue, but the roar of the water coursing through the wall was convincing evidence for Gladdic's point. He turned and ran toward the staircase, snagging Volo by the arm and helping her to her feet.

Dante touched the center of his forehead. "It's getting further away. They must have gotten it into a boat."

Blays grunted. "Let's hope it wasn't ours."

Dante took the steps three at a time, reaching the hall where they'd first discovered the illusion-hidden door and sprinting across it, his sandals smacking wetly. The next staircase brought them up the trapdoor and into the corridor where they'd nearly drowned. Water leaked through cracks in Gladdic's ice, threatening to blow the plug loose at any moment. Dante ran to the entrance, ready to shatter the door if he had to, but the door opened without complaint.

They dashed across the first chamber they'd entered, the ground scattered with the corpses of the Blighted, and made their way to the tunnel up through the tree. Dante took a deep breath, dived into the belly, and swam out through its opening, emerging into a warm afternoon day. All in all, they'd spent a full two hours locating the tomb and making their way to its end, and hardly two minutes getting back out of it.

Despite Blays' worries, the canoe was still there. Most of it, at least. What was left floated in splinters, bobbing in the swamp's subtle currents, as the link to the prime body grew fainter by the moment.

5

Every organ in Dante's torso seemed to sink three inches, as if someone had pulled a plug from within his body and everything inside him was draining away. The chunks of the canoe floated serenely, warmed by the sun, which had finally fought its way past the clouds.

"No!" Volo charged into the muck at the shore, plucking a broken board from the water and holding it across her palms like a dead infant. "This was my way-boat. I was supposed to die with it!"

Dante was too brain-numbed to wonder what in the world she was talking about. As he stared stupidly at the wreckage, Gladdic stumbled toward the bank of the island, dripping water after their swim through the pot-bellied jana kang tree. He lifted his intact arm and showered the pieces of wood with ether. They stirred, beginning to drift back together. A ghostly image of the canoe wavered above the water. Splinters of wood quivered.

A bead of sweat dripped down Gladdic's temple. The image of the canoe thickened until the water beneath it was as dim as a distant hill in a morning haze. Just as it looked ready to knit back together into an unbroken whole, the process stopped. After a final shudder, the pieces of wood fell back, going still. The ideal of the canoe faded away into nothing.

Gladdic lowered his hand and his face. "I lack the power. What's done can't be undone."

"Well, it's not like we're totally screwed or anything, is it?" Dante said. "Which one of you volunteers to be the new boat?"

"A complaint only reveals that the speaker cannot solve the problem before them."

"Oh, fuck off!"

"This land has more vessels than any seven kingdoms put together," Naran said. "Perhaps there is an abandoned boat someone on this island, or one of its neighbors."

He jogged down the shore, sandals squelching. Volo had crouched down and was still cradling the piece of canoe she'd fished from the swamp.

"There won't be another boat here," Dante said. "Or else whoever's helping the prime body would have destroyed it, too."

Blays wandered forward, arms crossed. "Build a raft?"

"Unless we also build it a set of wings, we'll never catch up to them."

"We'll just raise a sail and power it with the wind of your bitching."

Dante snorted. "Right. You start gathering wood for the raft while I grow a field of hemp to beat into the sail."

Blays tipped back his head. "Or we could skip all that and you could grow us a canoe."

"From my canoe-seeds! I knew I was forgetting something!"

"Find yourself a plant and harvest it into a boat, you stupid ass. I know it'll be hard to find a tree in the middle of this gigantic forest, but I have faith in you."

"That's...a pretty good idea." Dante turned back to the island's interior. "Help me find a tree, then. Something young, but that's already got some growth to it."

Blays headed into the trees. As Dante went in a different direction, Gladdic moved beside him. "You are able to do that?

Grow a boat from a tree?"

"Theoretically. It's a skill I picked up in the Plagued Islands. It's amazing what people will share with you when you're not busy trying to conquer and enslave them."

"It was not my intent to enslave the Plagued Islands."

"Much more noble of you to prop up the bloodthirsty Tauren and have *them* enslave the place."

Gladdic clicked his mouth shut, gazing into the distance. "All my life, I thought myself a beacon of moral clarity in an ocean of diseased minds. Visions of power turn us away from the gods. We are all worms in the same rotting log."

"Even if your hypothesis is true, some of us worms are less gross than others."

Dante quickened his pace, intending to avoid a philosophical debate when he had boats to grow. Blays hollered out from his right. Dante jogged over and found him standing in front of a ten-foot tree with leaves shaped like the feet of fat-toed geckos.

"I'm no expert," Blays said. "But judging from the leaves, trunk, branches, and fruit, I'd say this is a tree."

It looked more than suitable: large enough to be established, but small enough to have a lot of growth ahead of it. Dante jabbed his arm with his knife, closed his eyes, and moved into the nether inside the tree, examining its structures. He was, at that point, a fairly decent Harvester. He'd practiced the art on and off for over a year. He'd practically restocked the Collen Basin's granaries single-handedly.

That, however, was relatively simple. It was one thing to make a plant grow as it wanted to. It was another thing altogether to make it grow as *you* wanted it to.

After half a minute of poking around in the nether without finding anything obvious to help him, he concluded that sometimes, the best way to learn was by diving in without caring if you failed. He focused on a low branch, gathering the nether near its base. A twig sprouted. Dante drew it downward until he had a vine-like extension long enough that its tip was resting on the ground.

He stopped for a moment to walk around his creation. "Someone get Volo over here, will you? As long as I'm doing this, I might as well do it right."

Blays waved his hands over his head and yelled for Volo, which was not what Dante meant for him to do at all. She trotted over dutifully. She was no longer carrying the bit of her ruined boat, presumably having buried it, pushed it off into the swamp, lit it on fire and rubbed the ashes into her hair, or whatever it was that Tanarians did to properly dispose of the remains of their cherished boats.

"I'm about to grow us a new canoe," Dante said. "You're the first person I've ever seen cry about losing one, so I'm guessing you have strong opinions about what makes a good one."

Some of the sorrow left her young face. "Canoes are what lets us trade. And visit each other. And get away from each other. They're what lets us explore new places and what lets us escape when trouble comes to our village. When something is so important to everything we do, isn't the fool the person who doesn't care if he has a good boat or a bad one?"

"Yes. Agreed. Debate over. Just tell me how to make the damn thing. We'll start with the bow and work our way to the stern."

"That's your first mistake, dirt-walker. In a good canoe, there *is* no bow or stern. They should be identical. That way, when you're in tight quarters, you don't have to flip the boat around — just turn yourself around, and start paddling the other way."

After some questioning about angles, width, and depth, Dante kneeled next to the tip of the vine and reached into the nether. Green matter flowed from the end of the vine, expanding rapidly into the nose — or, he supposed, the stern — of the canoe. As Volo watched, her eyes were as intensely focused as a surgeon operating on the king, but the gleeful smile on her face was that of a madwoman.

She offered a few pieces of criticism about the sharpness of the prow. As Dante fixed this and moved on to expanding the body of the boat, the finished end hardened from a green, leafy texture into hardwood that was as dark as unadulterated coffee.

The wood seemed to want to grow, and by leading the way with the nether, the tree extended itself happily, as if he were painting a boat in the middle of the air. When it was a third of the way finished, its growing weight caused it to tilt to the side. Volo dived forward and caught it before it could snap free of its fragile vine.

With disaster averted, Dante finished the middle of the boat and moved on to sculpting the other end. The wood creaked pleasantly as it came together in a sharp point. With the hull finished, he extended seats across its interior.

Volo's grin was wide enough to sail the canoe through. "It's gorgeous!"

"Not quite done."

Dante branched a smaller vine from the one that he'd used to grow the boat. Once the new vine was long enough, he sprouted a bud from it, extending this into a short crossbar handle, then a long smooth pole. At the far end, he flared the greenery into a shape resembling a flattened bottle of wine. After ensuring it met Volo's approval, he hardened it into wood, then duplicated it twice more.

He cast the vines away from the completed pieces and stepped back from his work. "What do you think?"

Volo dropped beside the boat, giving one end an exploratory lift. "It's so light. And as smooth as glass. Completely seamless. Bet it cuts through the water like an Odo Sein sword. I'd kill for one of these!"

"Unless it's the White Lich, no murder necessary. The boat's all yours."

She swung up her head, searching his face for signs he was tricking her. "I can't take this. It's a masterpiece."

"Well, I can't carry it home with me. So you might as well take it."

Volo popped to her feet and hugged him tight. "Thank you. When I pass this down to my children, I'll make them thank you too."

He reached for the gunwale. "Don't start thanking me yet. An hour from now, and the prime body's guards could be bashing it into toothpicks."

They picked it up and portaged it to the shore. It slid into the water like a knife being sheathed. The pressure of the link to the prime body had lessened significantly, but it remained steady enough to follow without difficulty. Dante oriented them southward and they struck out with all speed.

Blays drove his paddle into the water. "Any idea who the prime body's got traveling with him?"

"Well," Dante said. "As far as I know, today was Bob's shift. But he might have had to take time off to tend to his mother. She's got that swelling in her feet, you know. In that case—"

"Forgive me for wanting to know who or what we're about to do battle with."

Volo twisted around, not missing a single stroke of her paddle. "When it could be anything, isn't it better to prepare for nothing? What if you prepare to fight a fish, only to be rendered helpless against a bird?"

"Then I'll aim higher."

"She's right," Dante said. "If it's Blighted, they won't be any trouble. If it's another sorcerer, then I expect it'll be weaker than the one they left behind to try to destroy us. Then again, I'm starting to think we've only seen a fraction of what the White Lich can muster."

"At least tell me we're gaining on them?"

Dante delved into the bond of blood. "They've got several miles on us. We're not obviously gaining, but I don't think we're falling any further behind. It'll be a while before I can tell if the gap is growing or shrinking."

The canoe whisked along so swiftly the water hissed against its hull, a steady accompaniment to the rhythmic churn of the paddles. Dante closed his eyes and immersed himself in the link to the prime body. Were they gaining? Or was that just a trick of —?

Something tickled the far end of the link. If Dante hadn't been concentrating on the connection, he might not have felt it at all. The presence took up the end of the thread and began to advance along it with almost perfect stealth, its movement as subtle as the strokes of a norren line painting.

Dante popped open his eyes. He knocked down an iridescent blue wasp that had been droning along beside the boat, reanimated it, and sent it buzzing south above the canopy with all the speed its wings could provide. Stone ruins peeped from the tree-coated islands. As the wasp flew closer to the prime body, the presence crept onward along Dante's bond to it.

It was halfway to him when the wasp spotted the boats rushing on through the forest.

"The White Lich." Dante's throat was so tight he could barely speak. "He's less than ten miles ahead. And he'll reach the prime body long before we do."

Gladdic startled as if he'd been stung, making the canoe roll back and forth. "How can this be so? It's been a mere three hours since the Blighted in the tomb first saw us."

"He must have already been on his way there. To cover his only weakness."

"Which will pass into his hands in a matter of minutes. We have failed. He will never let the prime body from his sight again."

Dante expected someone to pipe up with an argument—perhaps even for one to stir in himself—but everyone was quiet. Naran lifted his paddle from the water and laid it across his lap. Blays followed suit. After a few more strokes, Volo did the same. The canoe drifted forward on its own momentum before coming to a stop in the middle of the sun-dappled water.

"So that's it?" Volo said. "We're just giving up?"

Dante ran his hand down his face. "We can't go after the prime body. The lich will smash us like we're a spider crawling toward the crib."

"Then what do we do?"

"There is nothing more to be done." Gladdic's voice was the monotone of the utterly defeated. "This was our one chance to stop the disease before it can become a plague. With every day that passes, the Eiden Rane will convert more and more Tanarians into Blighted. Each one swells not only his army, but also his personal strength. And we are already too weak to defeat the enemy head-on. What shall we do against this? Attempt to rally allies to our cause? Most would scoff at the threat; others might believe, but will be too afraid to fight; those willing to heed our call will discover that, in the time it required for us to go to them for aid and then to return with them here, the enemy has become invincible."

Gladdic tipped back his head to the sky. "The only power that can save us now is the gods. And they will do nothing, for most do not care—and the rest *like* to see us suffer."

The finality of his words knocked them into a second silence. Bugs hummed along between the plants, a few stray bees visiting the fire-colored flowers that were beginning to bloom from the vines that looped between the trees.

"The lich is tracing the connection between me and the prime body," Dante said. "Once he reaches the end, he'll know exactly where we are."

"He'll come straight for us." Gladdic's voice lacked a single drop of doubt. "The idea that we almost killed him will make him furious. You must sever the link."

"I know. But there's one thing I need to do first."

While they'd been talking, the spying wasp had been following the lich's armada from on high. Now, Dante sent it north, back in the direction of the prime body. Aided in his hunt by the link in his head, he located the lone boat within five minutes.

With the White Lich closing in on his mind—an outcome which, if it came to pass, Dante feared might grant the enemy much more than the ability to feel where he was—Dante ordered the wasp to plunge down through the canopy. The boat was a double-hulled canoe crewed by a team of Blighted boatsmen, overseen by a motionless figure whose face was the same color as his bleached white robes.

A platform stretched between the two hulls, mounted by a small cabin. Dante sent the wasp straight toward it. It had no windows or portholes, but something between a door and a hatch was set into its rear. The frame was warped just enough for the wasp to wriggle through.

The interior was dark, lit only by thin slices of light seeping through the edges of the door. In the center of the cramped space, a skeletally thin man lay curled fetally. He was nude, the prongs of his vertebrae stretching his skin, his knees and elbows as knobby as a malformed branch.

Dante relocated the wasp to the ceiling for a better look. And almost retched. The body's eyes and mouth were sewn into tight black lines. He was hairless and his skin was a patchwork of seams, as if chunks of it had been replaced repeatedly across the centuries. His fingers were as long and thin as twigs and he was missing most of his nails. He was twitching his fingers, drawing them over the cabin floor. He seemed to be tracing letters or symbols of some kind, but if so, it was from a language Dante had never seen.

The tickling in his mind became a trembling, then a violent shaking as the White Lich surged toward him across the blood--bond. Dante cut the bond to the prime body—and their hopes with it.

Lacking any real plan, they headed east, veering south once Dante was sure they were well away from the White Lich's forces. Nobody said much except for mundane matters like asking for a water skin or a break from paddling. As dusk neared, Volo put them in on an island half covered in frogs whose skins were cornflower blue.

The swamp typically stayed warm enough at night that there was no call for a fire, which was good, because Dante felt far too demoralized to try to drag together some dry wood. The five of them sat in a loose circle, gazing at the grass.

Blays frowned, leaned close to a green stalk, and held his hand to it. He lifted it, holding an insect that looked exactly like a stick with legs.

"The White Lich only cares about enslaving humans, right?" As the stick-bug reached the end of his hand, Blays flipped his palm over, letting the creature crawl to the other side. "Clearly the solution is to disguise ourselves as humble animals of some kind. Cats ought to work. He doesn't strike me as the sort of fellow to care for cats."

"Sheep are better," Dante said. "They're about the right size, and we could all hang around in the same flock. With plenty of normal sheep, of course. We wouldn't want to look like idiots." He reached for a handful of sour purple berries Volo had found upon their landing. "Gladdic, do you have any other ideas for how to come at him? Any other rumors? Old stories? Things the Drakebane was too scared to try?"

The priest appeared to be trying to stare through the horizon and into the other side of the world. Just as Dante was about to repeat himself, Gladdic said, "It is a miracle that we were even able to locate the prime body. If there were any other effective solutions, someone would have executed them long ago."

"Can we seal him back up? Let him be dealt with by whoever's around the next time he busts out?"

"Even if I knew the process, which I do not, we would have to bring him back to the Wound. He will know better than to fall for any tricks to get him there."

"Then what can we do?"

"Make your peace, if you can," Gladdic said. "And then do what we are all here to do: die."

Blays transferred the stick-bug to his other hand. "We could leave here and never talk about this again. That way no one has to worry about their coming doom until right before they're Blighted."

"A breathtakingly humane proposal," Dante said. "Remind me to nominate you for sainthood the next time we're in Narashtovik."

No one had any other ideas. Dante hadn't really expected any. Walking to the other side of the island, he wondered if they shouldn't all just kill themselves. It would have the added benefit of stopping him from having to loon Nak and explain everything that had happened, which he wanted to do about as much as he wanted to fall asleep with his feet dangling in the water.

However, if there was one thing age and responsibility had taught him, it was that the overall pain of procrastination was higher than that of getting the chore done right away. With the daylight getting short, and fish rippling the water everywhere to bite at low-flying bugs, Dante opened his loon connection to Nak.

"Yes?" Nak's voice was as upbeat as ever. "Lord Dante?"

"Hello, Nak."

"I was beginning to fear something had gone wrong! What happened, then?"

"That depends," Dante said. "Remind me what was I about to do last time we talked?"

"Well, you were about to sail in with that rebel outfit—the Righteous Monsoon, isn't it?—and finally put an end to Gladdic."

"Yes, that's what I was afraid of."

"Something *has* gone wrong. Don't tell me he escaped yet again!"

"No, he's in our custody. Listen, Nak, do you remember when I asked you for anything in the archives about Tanar Atain, and you told me that fairy story about the vampire of the deep swamps?"

"I won't apologize for that. My intention was to provide you with everything I could find and to let *you* decide what, if anything, was useful."

"It turned out to be wrong. But not in the way we expected. The vampire is real—and he's far, far worse than the stories told."

Dante had a little less than an hour before the loon shut down, and so he explained in only moderate detail about their attack on the Wound of the World: and how they had indeed found Gladdic, but hadn't realized that Gladdic was actually in the process of attempting to destroy a long-buried evil that the Monsoon was attempting to use to destroy the Drakebane Dynasty. And how, after learning what the White Lich was, they'd deemed it necessary to keep Gladdic around, both for his knowledge of the lich and of Tanar Atain. Dante then summarized their recent efforts—and failures—to stop the Eiden Rane.

"No one's ever been able to destroy him," Dante concluded. "But if we don't find a way, I believe it's possible that he's going to conquer everyone."

"By turning everyone into these Blighted?"

"Or things like them."

"But won't he eventually run out of power to raise more? Every nethermancer has limits to how many undead he can command. Even Jack Hand himself had a limit to how many rats he could get to march to his tune."

"This is different. The larger the White Lich builds his force, the stronger he seems to get. That implies there's a point of no return. Once he crosses it, *nothing* will be able to defeat him."

"Come now, that violates everything we know about sorcery."

"Over the years, it has become readily apparent to me that most of what we know about sorcery is that everything we thought we knew about it was wrong."

Footsteps sounded through the loon; Nak was pacing. "If I was the one telling you this, you'd tell me that I was an ignorant fool. So rather than it being the case that this White Lich is such an exceptional figure that he doesn't have to obey the known rules—and who is, in fact, capable of the exact opposite of what all experience has shown us to be true—isn't it more likely that you're wrong, and that he will shortly reach the end of his ability to command more Blighted?"

"Nobody here seems to think so!"

"The Tanarians know everything, do they? Haven't you always been the sort to scoff at local beliefs, then attempt to expose them as ridiculous superstition while you uncover the real truth of the matter?"

"You could be right," Dante said, calming himself. "We're in a strange land that's virtually unknown outside of its own borders, and the only person we know here is somebody I've spent the last year alternately trying to kill and avoid being killed by. Meanwhile, the enemy we're contending with is like nothing I've ever seen before. Given all of the above, it's not easy to know what's true. We could be overestimating the White Lich."

"Ah, it's been so long since I heard the sweet tune of sense! I thought I'd never —"

"However, the point remains that we are at least partly responsible for his release. And even if he's not capable of consuming the entire world, I've already watched him consume a Tanarian village. He'll cause far more death than that before he's done. We have to find a way to eliminate him, but we don't have the strength to do it ourselves."

"It might have slipped your mind, busy as you are, but you do rule an entire citadel full of some of the most highly-trained priests and monks on the continent. I could dispatch some of them to you."

"We'll do that, but it'll take months for them to arrive. Who knows how powerful the White Lich will be by then. And we need to plan for the possibility, however remote you might think it is, that he *is* as dangerous as the Tanarians say. Preparing a defense against that is going to require more than a few months."

"Hmm. Have you considered diplomacy?"

"Well, we and the White Lich have already tried to kill each other three times now, and he keeps trying to enslave me. But I'm sure we'll be able to hash out our differences over a nice pot of tea."

"Not with *him*, you fool. Er, foolishly great leader. I was referring to our allies. And potential allies."

"Like who? Gallador?"

"They have a few sorcerers around, don't they? And they're exceedingly loyal. Especially since you completed that tunnel for them into the Western Kingdoms."

Dante scratched the side of his jaw. "They'll help us, but they can't afford to send much. Not with the Gaskans itching to return them to the empire's grip."

"The Collen Basin? They are much closer, and it seems as

though they should owe us as much as Gallador."

"Unfortunately, they're too morally stunted to realize their obligations to us. Besides, as far as I know, they only have a single sorcerer in the whole place. Mallon stole away anyone else who showed the talent."

"The norren, then? They're loyal. Sort of."

"No nethermancers there, either. And I doubt their woodsmanship would be much use in these swamps. Still, a few of them might be useful to have around. Warn the rest that it might be a good idea to cut back on their feuding for a little while."

"There's always Pocket Cove," Nak said. "Although after they got us into Weslee, they probably think that *you* owe *them*."

"This might sound insane, but our best bet for an ally might be Mallon."

"Mallon?! You've been halfway at war with them ever since the Plagued Islands!"

"And their leadership has just been forcibly replaced by scheming foreigners. We could offer to help them restore order in exchange for their help putting down the White Lich."

Nak grew thoughtful. "How exactly are you going to broker this alliance? It will take at least a month to get our envoys down there."

"Raxa and Sorrowen are still in Bressel. They can start right away."

"You want to unite two ancient enemies in battle. And you plan to do this using an acolyte and a thief as diplomats?"

"Raxa's not a thief. She's an assassin. Given what Mallon's up against, they might take her more seriously than some oil-haired dandy."

"Wouldn't that be something. Mallon and Narashtovik working together as friends! Do you think such an alliance could last?"

"We're too different for that. But better to have peace until the time when we remember to start hating each other again. I want you and the Council to come up with ideas to make this happen."

"We shall convene at once."

"Beyond organizing whatever aid we can muster, right now what we need most is information. Records of the White Lich or anything like him. Hopefully, we'll turn up something we can use to kill him."

A quill scratched in the background. "Shall I dispatch a ship to the Houkkalli Islands?"

"Bearing gifts. I'm not sure their monks have the highest opinion of Narashtovik. Send your fastest rider to Pocket Cove, too. They were establishing themselves around the same time as the Eiden Rane. They might know something about him."

"I could send a rider to Pocket Cove. But it seems to me that it might be faster to simply ask Minn."

"She's still there?"

"She was operating on the foolish assumption that you two would be back when you said you'd be."

Nak left to go fetch her, shutting down the loon connection so as not to drain the nether. Five minutes later, the loon pulsed in Dante's ear.

"Dante?" Minn sounded slightly distant; the loon was bound to Nak and she was likely standing next to him.

"Have you ever heard of someone called the Eiden Rane?" Dante said. "The White Lich?"

"The what? Do you realize you have the strangest conversations?"

"He's a…person. Of sorts. A sorcerer who has supposedly been alive since about the same time your people founded Pocket Cove. I wondered if you knew anything about him."

"No. But there's a lot at Pocket Cove that the elders keep to themselves. Is this serious?"

"Extremely. Can I convince you to go ask them for me?"

"Yes, although I feel like I ought to extract a concession from you in exchange."

"Name it."

"Grant us a title of some kind," Minn said. "It doesn't have to be proper nobility. I just want to be able to browbeat people when they get snotty with me."

"Very well." Dante swatted at a fly that wouldn't leave him alone; they were running out of Volo's anti-bug paste and had started to ration. "I hereby declare you and Blays to be the Fishmaster and Fishmistress of Canal Street."

"Isn't this the strangest thing. It seems I just forgot where Pocket Cove is."

"Okay, hang on. Make that the Honored Tri-Barons of the Sealed Citadel."

"That's a lordly-sounding mouthful. I'll leave tomorrow morning. Oh, and one more request."

"Yes, Minn?"

"Don't let Blays get hurt."

"I never do."

"He gets wounded all the time!"

"And always comes home without so much as a scratch."

"I wouldn't mind a scar or two," Minn laughed. "I'll be at the Cove within a week." Her footsteps retreated from the room.

Nak said, "While I was off finding her, I was thinking about how odd it would be that the founding of Pocket Cove was taking place at the same time this lich of yours was first attempting to seize Tanar Atain. And how, right before that, you had the Rashen and Elsen locked in a deathly struggle for Narashtovik that resulted in the finding of Cellen, the raising of the Woduns, and all of that business. What was in the air back then that so much was happening in such a short period?"

"Greatness doesn't emerge from a vacuum. It inspires itself in others." Dante smacked the back of his leg, which had been brushed by what he hoped was a sprig of grass. "Or maybe it's about being challenged. The nethermancers of Narashtovik have learned more in the last dozen years of strife than in the two centuries before that. Now think about all the troubles they were going through a thousand years ago."

"That would explain why they seem to have known so much more than we do. Yet how was all of that lost?"

"I suppose they finally ran into a challenge they couldn't overcome."

They both fell quiet. Before they could stare too deeply into the abyss, Nak brightened. "I'd better get to it, then. As they say, the only cure for hard times is hard work."

"Get a team to check the archives, too. And summon the Council. Tell them everything I've told you. And that I need all the ideas I can get."

He closed the connection. Twilight had fallen, casting the swamp into surreal shades of purple and steel. The voices of the others drifted from the camp. Dante had no new answers, but speaking with Nak had cleared his mind. If nothing else, the outside world would soon be aware of the darkness spreading across Tanar Atain. And the great gears of Narashtovik were rolling into action: priests gathering to share counsel; monks paging through the stacks in search of lost secrets; riders spilling forth from the gates to seek the wisdom of other lands.

It was almost enough to make him forget that all this activity was happening over twelve hundred miles away.

Before he could lose his motivation, Dante pulsed Sorrowen's loon. He wasn't certain the boy would answer—before, the acolyte had kept the loon hidden away, only wearing it for pre-arranged talks—but Sorrowen answered immediately.

"Lord Galand?" The boy's voice pitched up. "We haven't heard from you in days. We thought you were dead!"

"No," Dante said, and was right about to begin to explain when he realized he had no energy to go through it all again. Fortunately, Sorrowen was of grossly inferior stature, and Dante owed him no explanation whatsoever. "We've run into difficulties. They're ongoing. But I have news for you. That new fleet Mallon built? It wasn't to invade the Collen Basin. They're using it to transfer Tanarians into Bressel."

"Ah. Right. Why?"

"It's related to the difficulties here. The extremely condensed version is that it turns out Gladdic, as evil as he is, was here to destroy something even more evil. Being ignorant of this, when we tried to enact justice for his crimes, we ended up stopping him from destroying the thing that's much worse than he is. And now things are so terrible that the emperor decided to move everyone he likes to Mallon instead."

"That explains the riots. And the priests turning on each other. And all the warring. The city's in complete anarchy!"

"But it hasn't fallen to the insurrection yet?"

"No, but I would say it's about to."

"How can you be sure?"

"Uh," Sorrowen said. "Well, for one thing, the king's dead."

"King Charles?!"

"Wasn't that the name of the king of Mallon?"

"Yes? You grew up in Bressel!"

"Yeah, then it was definitely King Charles. That was a few days ago. The Pikes of the Faith—that's what the rebels call themselves—have taken more and more of the city ever since."

"They're going to take control of the entire thing once the emperor brings back his first fleet-load of Tanarians. If you and Raxa haven't already figured this out, you guys don't have to worry about Mallon invading the Collen Basin anymore. They've got way too much on their hands for that. But I've got a new job for you. After the Drakebane takes command of Bressel, there's going to be a resistance movement. I need you and Raxa to join it."

"Er." The loon picked up the sound of Sorrowen scuffing his shoe in the dirt. "But didn't you just say the resistance is about to lose?"

"Yes, so if I'd asked you to fight in it, or take charge of it, you might have something to worry about. Which makes it a good thing that I'm merely telling you to join its fringes and see if you can identify its leaders."

"What if Raxa says no?"

Dante swore, abruptly certain that she would. It was most inconvenient to need things from people who weren't required to follow your orders. "Tell her there's no time to negotiate now, but that she'll be paid fairly."

Sorrowen sighed. "She's going to yell at me. But I'll do my best."

"See that you do." As Dante reached to tap the loon, he stopped his hand. "One last thing. If at any time you haven't heard from me in a week or more, pack up your things and return to Narashtovik. And tell Raxa she has no further obligations to the Citadel."

"You think you might..?"

"Do you understand me?"

"Yes, lord."

"Good. Keep yourself safe."

Dante closed down the loon. Stars reflected from the dark water. After staring at them for a minute, Dante turned and rejoined the others. Everyone but Gladdic was asleep, or at least attempting to be. They'd lost nearly all of their gear when the canoe was destroyed, however, leaving them without blankets or coverings of any kind other than the clothes on their backs. They didn't have much food, either. Would have to do something about that. Such details seemed very tedious, but Dante supposed that tending to them would give them something to do until they came to terms with the idea that they'd blown their only shot.

While the others slept, Gladdic sat apart from them, back turned as he scratched something out onto a palimpsest. Now that they weren't actively pursuing the White Lich, the old man's presence felt different. It would be exceedingly easy to draw a sword and put it through his back.

Gladdic looked up from his work, glancing over his shoulder. Dante turned away and started tamping down the grass to make his bed. He supposed they should set watch.

Then again, if the Eiden Rane came for them that night, what would it matter?

There was something disproportionately uncomfortable about sleeping without any form of blanket, and Dante found himself waking time after time, tickled by the grass or the tiny legs of what he fervently hoped weren't spiders. He got up for good at the first graying of the east, happy to be out of the grass even though he was still completely exhausted.

When Blays got up a while later, he took one look at Dante and laughed. "You look like you've been Blighted."

"Good. I won't feel guilty when I eat your limbs for sustenance."

"How much *do* you have left to eat?"

"Just what I had in my pack."

"Split it with me? I don't have anything."

"That's because you ate all yours last night."

"Look, I'm the one doing *you* a favor. Either you can share part of it with me, or I'll steal all of it for myself."

Dante reached for his bag. "You think so?"

"Yes, I—" Blays vanished into the shadows, rematerialized at Dante's back. "Do."

Concluding that the only way to end this torment was to comply, Dante split the rest of his nuts and dried fish. It wasn't enough for either of them, and they made a quick pass of the island, turning up a few more of the purple berries they'd eaten the day before. Dante was almost sure they were the same kind, anyway, but being generally not a fan of the type of diarrhea that often accompanied the consumption of the wrong type of berries, he double-checked with Volo, who confirmed they were edible.

She eyed her share. "Isn't much to fill you up, though."

"Well no," Blays said. "But if we plant them in the ground, and water them and care for them for several years, then it won't matter how few of them we had to begin with, as we'll all have starved to death."

Dante motioned into the trees. "We need to find a village. Or a city, if there are any of those nearby."

"What about the whole 'invincible lich and his undead army' thing?"

"We'll go back to ruminating on our utter failure after we've secured the basic necessities of life."

Volo pinched her upper lip. "Halo Vaye isn't far. But it's back toward the Eiden Rane."

"Get us there. I'll make sure that we're not seen."

He knocked down a pair of dragonflies, which he'd found to be the fastest and stoutest of the available insects, and sent them whirring ahead. The five of them piled into the canoe, discovering that the one upside to having no supplies was that that meant you had nothing you needed to pack.

The day was the warmest yet and the paddlers were all soon sweating. Blays and Volo chatted some, but Naran hardly said a word, and Gladdic spent the time looking like he was trying to remember how to perform advanced mathematics. It was mid-morning and everyone's stomach was growling by the time the dragonflies broke into the village clearing.

"The village is there," Dante reported. "The people who live there are not."

Blays winced. "Blighted?"

"I'm not seeing any remains. Or bloodstains. If the lich Blighted this place, his first order to his new servants was to scrub it spotless."

The canoe entered the wide clearing that held the village. No smoke rose from the communal ovens and grills. No people tended the stands of banana trees or the tuber paddies.

Blays stopped paddling. "How many more villages are we going to see like this?"

"It wears at the soul," Naran said.

Volo ducked her head, surveying the silent fields and empty house-boats. "If you see enough of it, that wears your soul down to nothing, right? And you can't go on any more. Does that mean there's a limit to how much good any of us can do before we give up?"

Gladdic shifted on his bench. "Is that what happened to the gods?"

"Ah!" Blays pointed at one of the stands of trees at the edge of the village. "Bananas!"

A large bunch hung from the crown of one of the trees. Most of the fruits were still green, but a few near the end were yellow, and those at the very end had fallen to the ground, the peels browned and splitting. The uncollected fruit drove home the desolation even more than the abandoned homes.

Volo altered course toward the small square island, bringing them onto the soft dirt of its fringe. Blays hopped out, drew his sword and hacked through the trunk; rather than being hard wood, this was made of a dense and fibrous pulp closer in consistency to a giant stalk of celery, and yielded easily to steel, the tree splashing down in the water.

With a flick of his wrist, Blays severed the banana bunch from its thick green stalk. He wiped down his sword and hefted the bunch, trying to avoid the absurdly sticky white sap that gushed from where it had been cut.

As if by mutual decision, they each ate two of the fruit to quell the rumbling in their stomachs, dropping the peels into the water. They stashed the green ones in the back of the canoe. Volo directed them to the gates in the nets surrounding the village proper.

"They're wide open!" Her jaw dropped in horror and affront. "That's a beating for sure!"

A shadow passed over Dante. "They didn't bother to close it because they knew they weren't coming back."

They docked on the long pier bisecting the net-enclosed water. Dante entered the nearest of the raft-mounted shacks. Only a bit of dirt lay on the floor, suggesting that, as with the bananas, the villagers had left within the last few days.

Feeling mildly guilty, Dante made his way through the household's possessions, collecting spoons carved from bone—in the swamps, even tin was too precious to waste on cutlery—and some bottled foodstuffs. In contrast to the spoons, glassware was so common in Tanar Atain that even village peasant-farmers kept their pickles and preserves in colored glass containers that would have sold for good money in any northern market.

To conserve what little space they had, the beds were framed with a lightweight plant similar to wicker or bamboo and slung against the walls, where they could be secured upright when not in use. The raft's beds had been left down, the blankets rumpled. Dante lifted one and sniffed it. It smelled like another person, but not especially unpleasant. Even so, the idea of using a stranger's bedding, and likely a dead stranger at that, struck him as more objectionable than sleeping in the grass. After considering it for a moment, he called forth a wave of nether to beat at the blanket. When he lifted it, no vermin fell from it, yet he felt mollified nonetheless.

They picked through a few more houses, replenishing their lost equipment, then gathered in the shade of a vine-covered trellis that ran down a third of the dock. While the others had been salvaging, Volo had used a fishing line and net to bring in a few fish. They lit one of the communal grills to heat the fish, leaving the skin on, then sat down for a proper meal, laying the meat on banana leaves and accompanying it with various pickled vegetables Dante had never seen before.

"Well," Blays said as the meal wound down. He leaned back and planted his palms on the dock. "We've robbed our way back to competence. Do we have a new plan? Or is it time to try out the life of the vagabond?"

Dante used a fish bone to pick a shred of onion from his teeth. "I spoke with Nak. He's making arrangements to send us a team of nethermancers. But it'll take two months before they're here."

"Too long." Gladdic nodded to the empty village. "By then, the Eiden Rane will have an army."

"You guys know his weakness," Volo said. "Why don't you go and kill the prime body?"

"Because he'd slaughter us." Dante flicked the fish bone into the water. "There's no way to get close to him without him knowing about it."

Blays pressed his fist to his mouth and belched under his breath. "What if we got everyone to evacuate the country? Without fresh blood, the lich won't be able to make more Blighted. Or swell his own power any further."

"How does that beat him? Do you suppose he'll die of loneliness?"

"I *suppose* that it will cause him to stagnate, buying us time for our friends to arrive. At which point the smiting happens."

"Where do we evacuate tens of thousands of people to? A big

mass on the coast where the lich can kill them all at once?"

"That's one option, but how about anywhere that isn't here?"

"They won't have any homes. No food, either."

"If they stay here, they're going to *become* food."

"By the time we sail around to even half the villages, he'll have taken the other half. Besides, most people won't go, because some of them will be idiots about it, and some of those who wouldn't typically be idiots about it are even bigger idiots who support the Righteous Monsoon, which thinks the Eiden Rane is going to lead them to freedom. It won't work."

Blays scowled. "It'll save a whole bunch of people. I'd call that 'working.'"

"It would only save them temporarily while taking up all our time that we could be using to save them permanently." Dante tapped his fingers on his knee. "Maybe the best thing to do is hang back, watch him closely, and see if he makes any mistakes that we can pounce on. Gladdic, what do you think he'll do from here?"

The old priest gazed blankly into the rows of empty boats. "He has lived and planned for too long to make basic mistakes. He will continue to pass from settlement to settlement, absorbing them to himself. Once he and his legions are of sufficient size, he will bring them to bear against a city. There, his power will be doubled in one blow."

"That wasn't at all what I wanted to hear."

Blays got to his feet and paced across the dock. "Figure out which city he'll hit and fortify the hell out of it. Set up traps to separate him from the prime body. Urban warfare is always a nightmare, it'll be a wonder if it doesn't open up a shot at his weakness."

"Not bad," Dante said. "But it's very contingent. And if we prepare well enough to actually take him down, it's likely he'll hit somewhere else instead." He blinked in thought and turned to Gladdic. "You and the Drakebane had a plan to kill him in a straight-up fight. Why wouldn't the same thing work now?"

Gladdic gestured in simple dismissal. "The Eiden Rane was at his weakest then. Even if we had the same force right now, it wouldn't be enough."

"It wouldn't be the same force. It would include me and Blays. And we wouldn't be attacking the White Lich—we'd be ignoring him while we put an end to the prime body."

Gladdic raised his white eyebrows, but his interest died the next moment. "Our attack relied on the Knights of the Odo Sein suppressing the lich's sorcery. Without them, we stand no chance in direct battle."

"Let me guess. There aren't any of them left?"

"Most died fighting the lich or the rebels. Those that survived left with the Drakebane. They would never desert him."

"Ah. Shit, then."

"Indeed. This is the first time I have felt hope since the prime body fled from us."

"We should take this idea to the Drakebane," Naran said. "If it's that sound, it should convince him to return with his knights."

"Impossible. The Odo Sein are key to his ability to hold onto Bressel. He would not risk losing them." Gladdic smiled darkly. "Besides which, the Drakebane fears the Eiden Rane worse than death itself. He agreed to the assault at the Wound of the World because he believed it was his last chance to save his nation. It is clear that he believes this land has passed beyond saving."

Dante folded his arms. "We have nothing to lose by trying. I have agents in Bressel. I'll have them speak to the Drakebane."

"And when they fail? What then do we do?"

"I don't know. See about Blays' plan to fortify a city. Or maybe we can see if Volo can infiltrate the Monsoon, if she's willing. We may be able to feed them fake information to try to lure the lich into a trap."

Gladdic said nothing. Somehow, this was worse than any spoken criticism.

Dante stood. "We'll make for the nearest city. We need to start recruiting the Tanarians to our cause."

"Hang on," Blays said. "Gladdic, you said that every Odo Sein is dead or gone. Where did they come from in the first place?"

Gladdic lifted his bony shoulders. "Their powers are a great secret. Anyone who shared such information, especially with worthless hari foreigners, would be skinned from the waist down, tied to the back of a canoe so that the legs and genitals dangled in the water, and then sailed about until the swamp took its course."

"They seriously do that? Or is that what *you* would do?"

"It is a punishment reserved only for crimes that could undo the empire itself."

"Whatever happened to good old-fashioned beheadings? In any event, the Odo Sein don't fall out of the womb dressed in dragon scale and waving their magic swords about, do they? Don't they need training of some kind?"

"They have an academy." Gladdic rocked back his head. "You wonder if there might be any trainees there."

"The Drakebane lit out of here like he was being chased by a thousand-year-old madman, right? What are the chances he swung by the academy to pick up all the knightlings on his way out?"

"There may be some with the skill to help us. But it can't be done. I don't know where the academy is."

Blays motioned to Volo. "You seem to know the location of every drop of water in this swamp. You know where this academy might be?"

"I didn't even know there *was* an academy," Volo said. "The stories I heard were that the knights were immortal servants.

Like zombies, but people."

"I don't suppose it's a great use of our time to comb the swamp for something that we have no idea what it looks like. For the record, though, I think this was a pretty great idea."

Gladdic lowered his chin. He had that faraway look on his face again. "I don't know where the academy is. But I know someone who does."

Dante spread his palms in a shrug. "So what? I thought they wouldn't tell a foreigner anything about that. On pain of having their balls eaten by ziki oko."

"Those were the old rules. With the coming of the Eiden Rane, my source may be made to see reason."

After a quick and fruitless sweep for survivors in the village of Halo Vaye, they struck out for Dara Bode. According to Gladdic, his source, an official named Fade Alu, lived there. Or had, at least, prior to recent events like the Righteous Monsoon's rebellion that had seized the capital. And the release of the White Lich. And the fleeing of the Drakebane to Bressel, along with his soldiers, cabinet, and thousands of others.

A lot had changed, in other words, and as they carried on southward, moving back toward Tanar Atain's particular version of civilization, Dante worried that they'd wind up wasting their time searching for a man who was no longer there.

Then again, it was the best plan they had. And at least it would be much easier to get in and out of the cities than back when Dante had been trying to hide his skills from Volo.

During the day, they passed two other settlements. Both times, they diverted to approach the people there and warn them what was happening further north. The villagers looked back and saw three wretched foreigners in the company of a Tanarian girl who barely looked old enough to own her own boat. Yet their scorn fell apart like damp bread when Volo challenged them to send a scout to Halo Vaye and see for themselves.

As they paddled away from the second village, Blays turned about to watch them send a boatsman out past the nets. "Ah good, they're actually sending someone. Finding all their friends dead will teach them to insult *our* credibility."

"Well it will," Dante said. "Along with the side benefit of possibly saving their lives."

"This feels like madness. The Drakebane's gone and the Monsoon *wants* to feed these people to the lich. There's no one to protect them. They'll be slaughtered."

"And? We're doing the only thing we can to stop it."

Blays shook his head. "I know. But I wish we could do more."

As the day wound down, Dante's dragonfly spotted a double-hulled war canoe patrolling their way. Until quite recently, the swamp's routes had been held down by the Drakebane's soldiers, but this ship flew the colors of the Monsoon. Volo turned hard to port, detouring for half a mile before continuing to the south. With dusk coming on, they paddled a few hundred yards away from the watery thoroughfare to put in at another island for the night.

They ate and made camp. It was starting to sprinkle, so they strung up an oiled canvas tarp they'd taken from Halo Vaye. Once this was up, rather than moving under it, Gladdic continued to sit in the rain, letting the droplets flatten his white hair to his head. For some reason, his refusal to get up and move to the shelter not ten feet away annoyed Dante worse than a horsefly.

When he couldn't take it anymore, Dante got up and stood over the old man. "I don't know if you've noticed, but we've just now invented a way to keep the rain off our heads. I think we'll call it a 'rain-beater.'"

Gladdic didn't bother to look his way. "Have you come to the realization yet?"

"That it's annoying to be asked vague questions?"

"The Eiden Rane points to a single conclusion: that in the end, we cannot win."

"Sure we can. I'd bet you three tons of silver that you used to think you could never be beaten, either."

Even this didn't provoke so much as a glare. "Even if we are able to slay the lich, and disperse all remnants of what might be called his soul, eventually, a power like him will arise again. And again. Some day, that power will *not* be defeated. And all of the world will fall."

"You have no way to know that. As far as we know, he's the only one who's ever figured this out. Which is supported by the fact that nobody's been able to replicate his work in the last thousand years."

"People always seek power. Over each other, and over death. Do not tell me that you have not pursued immortality yourself."

Dante crossed his arms. "And I've failed quite spectacularly to find it. I certainly have no idea how to turn everyone on earth into my undead slaves."

"You don't want to believe this because it hurts to do so. Then turn away from the pain, if it is too much for you."

"Even if you're right, and it's inevitable that one day, a great sorcerer is going to destroy everything, what does it matter? Each one of us knows we're going to die someday, but that doesn't mean life isn't worth living. Perhaps someday the world *will* end. Until that day comes, people will keep loving, and fighting, and being afraid, and finding the courage to go on. We can't save the world forever. But we can save it for now."

At last, Gladdic glanced at him, briefly and sidelong. "Is it true that you have seen the afterlife?"

"Where'd you hear that?"

"From one of the many people I sent to spy on you."

Dante pressed his knuckles to his mouth. He still wasn't sure how to treat the matter of revealing his knowledge to the priest. Assuming they did go on to eliminate the White Lich, they still had to deal with Gladdic, didn't they? However much good the priest did here, it wouldn't undo the murder of Captain Twill, to say nothing of the thousands of lives lost in the Plagued Islands and at Collen. There would be a reckoning. When it came, Dante didn't want Gladdic to know all of his tricks.

At the same time, there was zero guarantee that they would win. The best way to increase their chances was to pool knowledge and work together without reservations. Countless lives depended on it. The calculus was ugly, but it was clear.

"Yes," Dante said. "I've been there. So has Blays."

"Is it like they say it is? Like *we* say it is?"

He laughed out loud. "Not in the slightest."

"I thought not. Will you tell me the truth of what awaits us?"

"It isn't a singular place. In fact, it's three. The first is known as the Pastlands. Usually, it takes the form of a good memory, or something you've always wished for. When you're there, you don't know you're dead, or that anything's wrong. You just repeat the same things over and over—and to you, there's nothing wrong with that, because it's what you've always wanted. Except that the Pastlands is a trap. It doesn't want you to leave."

Gladdic furrowed his brow. "Why?"

"Hell if I know. Maybe the landlords get to charge our souls rent. Or maybe the gods meant this as a reward. Live out your dream in perfect peace over and over until the day you finally get disillusioned of it. Whatever the case, once you find your way out of the Pastlands, you reach the Mists. It's both everyday and idyllic. Your normal life, but without violence or death. If I had to guess, it's a way to live out anything you missed before you died, leaving you without regrets. And to make peace with the fact that it's over."

"That does not sound unpleasant."

"It isn't. But after a while, everyone moves on. Into the World-sea. I never saw it. Only the dead can go there. My understanding is that when you cross over, you become a part of everyone that ever was, and drift as one forever."

The old man considered this, then gave Dante a piercing look. "Then there is a way we can escape his power. We can die. And enter a world that will be forever beyond him."

"While you are technically correct, I feel as though that would defeat the purpose here."

"Perhaps." Gladdic lifted his left hand to the side of his head and closed his eyes. Ether sparked from his fingers toward his temple.

Dante shouted out and grabbed for a chunk of nether. He clubbed it into the light, dispersing them both. "What the hell are you doing?"

"What does it look like? I am thwarting the lich."

More light beamed from Gladdic's hand. Better prepared, Dante thrust at it with a dagger of shadows.

He grabbed for Gladdic's hand. "Stop that! You can't just fry your own head off!"

The others had rushed from beneath the tarp to watch from ten feet away. Gladdic flapped his hand at Dante. "You are welcome to join me. It will solve everything. Or you can waste your days hovering over me like an overbearing mother, until the lich has won his prize, and you have done nothing to stop him."

Dante ground his teeth together, keeping the nether tight and pacing in front of Gladdic. "If there was no White Lich to worry about, and you found a way to live for as long as you liked, how long would you stick around?"

"What manner of question is that?"

"You can find out by answering it."

Gladdic snorted. "No less than centuries. Perhaps as much as forever. There is always more to see, and if you traveled across the world, by the time you returned home, you would find that it was now a new place, and so was everywhere else that you had once visited."

"Right. Which is decidedly untrue of the Mists. First of all, from what I can tell, you are confined to a relatively small por‐ tion of them — either the land you died, or where you consider home, I'm not sure. I didn't really die, so I might not have been subject to the same rules. All I know is that you don't get to trav‐ el wherever you please. If you died now, you might find your‐ self stuck in the Mistly equivalent of Bressel, unable to leave the city. Or you could be trapped right here in the afterlife's version of this fetid swamp.

"Second, as it turns out, most people don't stay in the Mists for more than a couple hundred years, and a lot leave within a single lifetime, or even a handful of years. There isn't the sense of danger that we have here, the urgency. Here, you *have* to get things right. There, it doesn't matter. There's no striving to better yourself. No history to participate in. The Mists are boring, you fool. That's why everyone moves on, usually sooner rather than later. To pass into the Worldsea. And then whatever *you* are ceases to exist."

Gladdic stared at Dante for a moment, then lowered his hand from his head to his lap. "That is why they lie to us about the af‐ terlife. Because if we knew the truth, we would not be afraid to do wrong. Not when there are no punishments or repercussions. We would be free to do anything."

Sensing the drama was over, the others quit watching and moved back under the tarp. Dante soon joined them. Gladdic sat alone in the rain for a while yet, then crawled beneath the shel‐ ter.

In the morning, they struck out as soon as it was light enough to see whether there were any swamp dragons in their path. Volo told them it would take two days to reach Dara Bode.

Crossing under the boughs, with the morning sun poking through in yellow fingers, Dante wondered what the Eiden Rane was up to, then realized he didn't have to wonder. The lich would be ensuring no harm could come to the prime body. And once that was done, he would be traveling from village to village, absorbing the people there into himself.

Blays stifled a yawn. "Say Volo. Considering that you are the only right and honorable Tanarian among us, and that the rest of us are a bunch of filthy hari, you think we'll have any problems getting into the city?"

She shook her head, her dark ponytail sweeping her shoulders. "Nah. By law, any settlement has to let the people who do my work inside. Even the capital."

"That was the law under the Drakebane. But that revolution you were a part of is calling the shots now."

"I don't think even the Monsoon would be *that* heretical."

Dante was less convinced, but supposed they'd be in better position to find out once they were upon the city. And they were still dressed in Monsoon jabats, which might make things a little easier.

He spent most of the morning in thought. As noon neared, he turned to Gladdic. "That thing the lesser lich was doing. Throwing his blood at us. Have you ever seen something like that before?"

Gladdic gave a quick jerk of his chin. "You neither?"

"Never even heard of such a thing. Did it seem to you that he was...amplifying his powers?"

"More that he may have been expending somewhat less energy than typically necessary to achieve such results."

"Which might be a way of saying the same thing. He was just flicking his blood around. Any ideas as to why that would work?"

The priest narrowed his eyes, deepening his crow's feet.

"Blood attracts nether. You yourself employ it to magnify the shadows' strength. Yet you do so in a passive way. Perhaps a more active use results in more active nether."

"Plausible."

"What are *your* thoughts?"

This time, Dante only hesitated a moment before deciding to reveal them. "Along similar lines. But I don't think it's as simple as just flinging your blood around. If it was, somebody else would have figured it out a hell of a long time ago."

"Whereas what the lesser lich did had the whiff of a lost art. Or one he developed over centuries of isolation."

"Exactly. We already know certain skills have been lost to time. It isn't hard to believe there's been others." Dante drummed his fingers against the gunwale. "Who was that guy, anyway? A sorcerer, right?"

"The only other possibility would seem to be an unusually talented dancer."

"So when the White Lich turns you, he doesn't have to turn you into a Blighted? You can keep your powers? Your personality?"

Gladdic shrugged. "If he was able to turn himself into the Eiden Rane, why would he be incapable of replicating the effect in others, if only to a lesser degree?"

"How much independence do they have?"

"I have gathered a selection of stories on this matter. They agree that while the lich's lieutenants are able to think and act of their own will, ultimately, they are each bound to the Eiden Rane's commands to such extent that thoughts of treason would be inconceivable to them."

"This sounds like bad news. If we send sorcerers against him, can he turn them against us?"

"If they choose to join him, absolutely. But if they are unwilling, I am not sure." Gladdic toyed with a loose thread on his jabat. "Would you like to know why I collected these stories of the lesser liches?"

"I don't know, so you stood less chance of getting murdered by them?"

"I was considering whether it would be better to join him, or to be destroyed."

"And you chose to be destroyed?"

"Indeed. I thought it would please Taim." Gladdic's shoulders jerked. He broke into laughter, its peals drowning out the buzz of the insects.

Deciding that the canoe was perhaps not the appropriate venue for sloppy bloodshed, Dante waited to begin his experiments until they made landfall for the night. As usual, they camped near the center of the island to hide themselves from passing boats, so Dante padded toward the north shore. There, he produced his knife and cut the tips of his ring fingers enough to bleed steadily. Cutting his fingertips took a much more concerted mustering of willpower than the back of his arm, but he promised himself that he would heal the damage soon enough.

He was too self-conscious to do any twirling about—Blays would never let him live it down—so he contented himself with flicking his wrists like whips, snapping beads of blood from his fingers. The nether darted after it, as quick and hungry as ziki oko, but not in any way that looked noticeably different from when it came to a cut on his arm.

Still, was it more effective? How could he even measure such a thing? He crouched over the ground, drew a small portion of nether to his palm, and frowned. He got up, meaning to go back to camp and fetch a spoon, then spied a nutshell on the ground. One half had cracked and the meat inside had been eaten by fungus. He scooped out the remains and removed the cracked side, leaving him with an intact half.

He summoned the nether again, filling the nutshell to the

brim. Once he was satisfied the surface was level, he brushed aside the leaves from a patch of bare ground and sent the shadows into the earth, softening the soil and drawing it aside until the nether ran out. The resulting depression was roughly a cubic foot in size.

Dante filled the nutshell again, ensuring it was to the same level as before, then snapped his right hand at the ground. At the same time, he commanded the nether toward the falling specks of blood. The shadows swirled violently as they plunged into the ground. Again, he used every drop to soften and remove the dirt.

The second hole looked no bigger nor smaller than the first. He measured them using his hands and found they were the same size, or at least close enough that he couldn't tell the difference. Cursing under his breath, he repeated the experiment just to make sure nothing funny had happened, but the results were the same.

It was possible, however, that the blood-flicking—he made a mental note to come up with a more impressive name in the event he discovered how to harness its power—simply didn't apply to earth-moving. The lesser lich had used it on offense and defense. He searched about for and found a smaller nutshell and filled it with nether. Shaping this into a small bolt, he rammed it into the trunk of a large tree. He refilled the shell, flipped blood at the tree, and struck it again. Leaning close, he couldn't see any difference between the two holes he'd knocked in it.

With the sunlight getting scarce, he backed away from experiments in favor of simply whipping a bit of blood around, sending the nether to it, and observing the results. By nightfall, this had gotten him exactly nowhere. He healed his fingers and trudged back to camp.

The next day kept him busy watching the path ahead with a trio of nimble dragonflies, warning Volo whenever they were neared by a Monsoon patrol boat. Now that they'd seized the capital, the rebels seemed to have taken on a new set of colors: a white flag set with two circles, one light blue, the other dark. Their soldiers were dressed in similar colors. The uniforms Dante and the others wore had become outdated.

As they neared Dara Bode, the patrols grew more frequent, detouring them on five different occasions. By sunset, they were still miles from the capital, but Volo paddled on.

Blays laid his paddle across the gunwales and motioned to the west. "I know it's easy to miss now that the sun's going down, but did you notice that the sun's going down?"

Volo didn't break pace. "What, are your arms getting tired? We can be there in two hours."

"Silly me. I forgot that city guards love letting foreigners inside the walls after dark."

"It's better this way. We Maggots come at all hours of the day to collect our bodies."

"What about us four hari?" Dante said.

"You're...advisors. Brought here to speak to the Monsoon." She brightened. "About the Drakebane's plans in Mallon, which is where you are from."

"That's more plausible than half the stories we've used to get into places that didn't want us there. Still, now that the capital's under rebel control, we should treat it like hostile territory. Let's do our best to not cause any battles."

They carried on, the woods darkening around them. As they neared the city, the foliage grew denser on both sides until there was only a single wide lane of open water providing access to the capital. To Dante's complete lack of surprise, it was blockaded near its end by a small flotilla of Monsoon sailors flying their white and blue.

Working on the assumption that every entrance to the city would be similarly patrolled, they approached the soldiers and were ordered to present themselves before a double-hulled war canoe. The soldiers asked Volo several questions, made a few disparaging remarks about the poor quality of her foreign cargo, and waved her on to the capital.

The forest opened before them, exposing an enormous clearing. The capital was laid out like any other village, but the scale was immense, with the outer ring consisting of four hundred feet of open water (though some of this was taken up by fish pens) before the agricultural islands and paddies marking the outside of the city proper. Past that, oil lanterns flickered from swathes of raft-houses and in the windows of the stone manors that populated the many islands in the center.

Volo steered them around to the passage through the netting that surrounded the capital, calling out a greeting to the guardsman watching their approach from one of the docks supporting the gate.

The man stood, tottering to the edge of the dock and lifting his lantern to spill light over the black canoe. "Volo? Is that you?"

She shielded her eyes from the sudden glare of the lantern. "Hobron? They got you on the *gates*?"

"You didn't think Commander Barain was going to leave the Drakebane's soldiers in charge of the gates, did you?"

"Yeah, but I expected him to put someone *good* on the job."

He flashed a toothy grin and beckoned them onward. "Tie up and hop out, will you?"

Volo obliged. She hopped from the canoe and entwined the fingers of her right hand with his, a gesture that appeared intimate to Dante's standards, but which seemed to bear no more weight than a handshake. Dante climbed onto the dock, trying to look inoffensive as Hobron gave them a once-over.

"Nice to go a few days without rain," Volo said when the sentry was finished making sure they weren't obvious threats. "Then again, if you consider the fact that—"

Hobron bulged his eyes and lunged forward, clapping his hand to her mouth. He glanced down the dock to where two other guards chatted and laughed with each other.

He released her and stepped back. "Sorry about—"

"What the hell was that?" Volo stamped after him. "I'll shove you off this dock!"

Hobron dropped his voice so it could barely be heard above the wash of water against the dock. "How have you not heard? The Monsoon has banned dana kide. Just like they promised."

"I thought that was just...something they were saying. How can they ban dana kide?"

"We already *know* the truth. What's the point in arguing different? It's just meant to confuse us. To muddle our minds and make us forget what's right. You know this."

"I know," Volo said softly. "That's what they told us."

"And they're right. So what's there to worry about?"

"What do they do to you if they catch you doing it?"

"They glass you."

"Shit and scales. They're serious."

'There's nothing more serious than protecting the truth from those who would slander it." Hobron smiled, then grew sober. "You sailed north with them, didn't you? Into the Go Kaza?"

She nodded.

Hobron lowered his voice again. "Is it true what they say? That we've freed the Eiden Rane?"

"Yes."

He whooped and clapped his thigh. "Then Tanar Atain is ours!"

"Yeah." Volo did her best to smile. "And they'll never take it back from us." She jerked her thumb toward the city. "Hate to rush things, but they're waiting on me."

"What's your business here, anyway? In case my captain asks."

"Hauling bodies. As for the hari, they're here to advise the Monsoon."

Hobron gave the four outlanders a skeptical eye. "Advise us in what? How to smell bad? How to kneel to little statues of false gods?"

This time, Volo's laughter was genuine. "Our leaders know what they're doing, don't they? Who are we to question if they want to hear hari gibberish?"

"I don't get it. But I guess I don't have to." The guard rocked on his sandaled heels. "Well. Try to see me again when you're leaving?"

Volo stepped into the canoe. "I'll do that."

"Clear waters, Volo."

She waved. "Clear waters."

The others reembarked. The metal gates, painted blue against corrosion, creaked apart. Volo guided them through the entry and into the farmlands, which were dark and smelled of damp leaves. The clouds were thin and were rippled like a spoon dragged through whipped cream, allowing the full moon to shine through. A tear slid down Volo's cheek.

"Er," Blays said. "Is something the matter?"

She dipped her paddle in the water three times before answering. "I can't believe they did it."

"Banned dana kide? Your peculiar way of saying hello?"

"I bet it looks pretty funny to you, doesn't it? A couple of Tanarians meet each other, and maybe they haven't seen each other in years, but the first thing they do is argue about whether the rain is good or bad. Or whether beauty is proof of virtue."

"'Hello' *is* a lot shorter."

"Dana kide isn't about rain, or beauty, or any of that crap. It's about always hunting for the most elusive prey in the swamp: the truth. Our devotion to the hunt is what made us who we are. Then the Monsoon came along, and told us *they* had the truth, and anyone who argued otherwise was trying to pollute our minds and keep the peasants locked in the Drakebane's chains. Their supporters believed it — and so did I."

"There's no shame in being wrong," Dante said. "Only in re-fusing to admit it."

"And in spouting wise-old-grampa wisdom like you just came up with it." Blays swept his paddle along. "What'd he say about the punishment for dana kide? That they'd glass you?"

Volo nodded. "At high noon, they chain you to the middle of a dock. And they bring out a glass lens. And use the sun's rays to burn your crime into your skin."

"Congratulations," Naran said. "Your people have discovered a way to make hanging seem like a kindness."

The watery farms looked undisturbed by the recent unrest, but as they passed into the sprawling neighborhoods of rafts, Volo had to dodge around numerous planks sticking from and floating in the water. Four-man Monsoon canoes cruised down the canals. The raft-filled slums had always been boisterous, laughing places, but that night, the loudest voices Dante heard were people coughing.

Gladdic provided Volo with the address of their destination. This was a manor in the well-heeled island districts. His contact was an elderly man named Fade Alu. According to Gladdic, Alu's official position within the Drakebane's cabinet had been that of a roving tax collector assigned to many of the outlying villages. But for reasons that were obscure to Dante, Gladdic sus-pected Alu's job was actually a cover for his true task: traveling about and identifying potential talent to join the Knights of Odo Sein.

Alu's home was one of a score built onto a shallowly sloping island. Volo guided the canoe up to one of the island's docks and tied it to a cleat. Gladdic stepped off and waited for the others.

Dante crossed over the platform. "Are we all going with you?"

"He will not wish to reveal his secret," Gladdic said. "He might kill to protect it. By arriving en masse, we may intimidate him away from such ideas."

He made way to the thoroughfare that bisected the island, running from its low point to its highest. Cobbled paths wound away from the street to the gates of the high walls that enclosed each property. Alu's manse was located at the far end of the island, which at an elevation of some hundred feet rendered it one of the highest points in the capital. From its vantage, the only thing blocking sight of the entire city was the heart of Dara Bode: the fortress of the Bastion of Last Acts.

Gladdic followed the path to the gate in Alu's brick wall. The grilles were wrought iron, sealed by a chain whose links were as thick around as a man's wrist.

Blays cocked his head at the distant house. "Shall we yell?"

Gladdic slashed his hand downward. A blade of white light flicked across the air. The chains fell away with a weighty clank. He pushed the gate aside and entered the garden, which remained well-kept despite whatever troubles had riven Dara Bode over the last few weeks. Gladdic took another path to the stoop and its oversized front door. The knocker boomed through the house.

The door opened with a mutter of hinges, revealing a middle-aged servant in an orange jabat. He flicked his gaze across the five of them with increasing disgust. "Do you even know the hour?"

"Later than you imagine. I am Gladdic of Bressel, and I will see Fade Alu."

"Then you will depart, and only return once the sun has given you permission." The servant moved to close the door. Gladdic extended his index finger. The door quit moving. The man blinked at it and put his weight behind it, but it wouldn't budge. He fell back a step. "Who are you?"

"A former servant of the Drakebane. Your emperor has fled. But I remain here to save your country."

The doorman's eyelid twitched. "You will wait here."

He made to close the door, which held firm until Gladdic gave a small nod. The servant slammed the door. His footsteps retreated into the interior.

Dante gave the priest a look. "You catch more flies with honey than vinegar."

"Yes," Blays said, "but you catch the most flies with shit."

Gladdic didn't respond. A minute passed, then another. Volo wandered to the edge of the stoop to gaze down on the quiet city. Naran had a distant look on his face, as if remembering old times. A lantern lit up one of the third-floor windows, then receded from the room.

At last, the door swung open again, the servant stepping adroitly to the side. "Enter, guests."

Dante moved in behind Gladdic, bringing a trickle of nether to his hand. The servant spun on his heel and led them through a brick corridor and into a sitting room, or more aptly a kneeling room, considering that its furniture consisted of a few knee-high tables and vast numbers of rugs and cushions.

A man rose from the main table. He was about sixty and his slicked-back hair had gone almost entirely silver, with a few streaks of deep black hanging around what remained of his temples.

He took in Volo and the foreigners before settling his pale eyes on Gladdic. "Gladdic. You're aware our new rulers have outlawed dana kide?"

Gladdic inclined his head. "I have just learned as much."

"Then you'll understand that I'm being purely *rhetorical* when I greet you by asking whether it's in the best interests of a people to strangle their ability to speak themselves toward truth."

"I could not say."

"Good, because I didn't ask. Just as I didn't ask whether the best way to win the hearts of a conquered people is to stamp out their holiest traditions."

"If such a question were to be asked, I would tell its asker that the best way to ensure that a conquered people will never rebel against you is to reshape them to be the exact same as *your* people."

"As a former taxman, you'd think I'd have more appetite for grinding people under my heel. But I don't even have the stomach to think such things." Fade smiled with half his mouth. "It's good to see you. I'd have guessed you'd be dead or long gone."

The priest moved a half step in front of the others. "An unexpected calling has kept me here. I do not expect to see my homeland again."

Fade made a subtle gesture to the others. "And because you can't go back to Mallon, you've brought friends from Mallon to visit you instead?"

"We would not call each other friends. But we have all found ourselves being swept along by the same strange tide."

"Let me guess. The one flowing from the north?"

"Indeed. First, though, what of matters here? Have you and your family been safe since the revolution?"

"Got them all packed up and shipped off to Bressel. House has felt damn near empty."

"Then why do you remain?"

Fade pulled his lopsided grin again. "You're not the only one with a calling. I aim to wrap things up and skip town soon as I can. The way things are going with the Monsoon, I'd leave even if there were no northern threat."

Gladdic nodded thoughtfully. "Yet there is. You are wise to go."

The other man lowered his eyes to the stump of Gladdic's right arm. "Looks like you got firsthand experience there." He

THE LIGHT OF LIFE

winced. "Pardon the pun."

"It's no matter. As I said, I have already accepted I will not survive the coming storm. Losing an arm better prepares me to face death, when it comes, without flinching."

"You're even more fatalistic than the last time I saw you."

"Gazing into hell will do that to a man." Gladdic tilted his head to the side. "Do you know why I am here?"

"To make sure I don't get any sleep?"

"The Eiden Rane has returned. I have seen him. We have *fought* him. And we think we know a way to destroy him."

"Oh, batshit. The Drakebane did everything he could about that. If there'd been another option, he'd be out there on the front lines right now, not digging himself a new nest in Bressel."

"You don't have to believe. But the Drakebane has abandoned you, and *I* am still here."

Fade scowled and motioned to his servant, making a drinking motion. The servant vanished from the room.

"Can we get to the thrice-cursed point already?" Fade said. "Why *are* you here?"

"To save Tanar Atain. Our plan requires the Odo Sein. Do you know where they used to be trained?"

"Why in the nine waters would I know that?"

"There were rumors that you worked for them."

"You can tell a lot about a man by which rumors he's eager to swallow." The servant swept into the room, presenting Fade with a green glass. Fade tipped it back, emptying it, and set it back on the tray. "The location of the training grounds was one of the biggest secrets in the Empire. If I had so much as stumbled on it, my bones would be hanging in a cage in the deepest swamp."

"Then you don't know where it is."

"Hell no. I wouldn't *want* to know."

Gladdic turned his profile to Fade, taking two steps toward

the wall. "Do any Odo Sein remain in the capital?"

"You know they'd never leave the Drakebane behind. Any that survived the fighting sailed away with him to Bressel."

"That was the conclusion I reached as well. In that case, I need you to stop lying to me."

"Excuse me?"

"You know precisely what I am saying."

Fade motioned to his servant again. "Trying to keep track of all your Mallish gods must have driven you crazy. I don't know anything about the Odo Sein."

"Do you understand that this is the last hope for your country?"

"There *is* no hope, you loony bastard. I can't help you. I suggest you find someone who can."

Gladdic turned to face him. The priest's eyes were as sunken as wells. "We didn't get a chance to engage in dana kide. I will rectify that. Are we agreed that liars are bad people?"

"What kind of a question is that?"

"Do not attempt to dodge me. Dana kide is the search for truth, which is holy. If truth is holy, then lies are unholy. And liars are their vessel."

The servant came back with a refilled glass. Fade didn't reach for it. "If a man lies to save his life, does that brand him a liar?"

"It does when a man's lies will cost the lives of everyone in his country. Now stop dodging and answer my question. Are lies unholy?"

"Depends entirely on the why, doesn't it?"

"If a man lies to save himself from death, that is merely the act of using one unholy act to protect oneself from another. The lie, itself, remains unholy. How, then, might we rid ourselves of lying? If we killed every liar, do you think the next generation would be raised without knowledge of falsehoods?"

"I think if we killed everyone who ever told a lie, we'd have done the Eiden Rane's job for him."

"Indeed. For lies are a disease that seems to run as deep as our own blood. Do you know the only way to be cured of them? To lose everything. Every single part of you and what you love. When everything is taken from you, and you have nothing left to lose nor to fear, at last, you can see the truth."

Gladdic swept his left hand through the air. Ether glittered across the room. Scores of footsteps lit up across the floor, a shimmering pattern of chaos. Most of them were adult-sized, but two pairs were much smaller. They led out the rear of the sitting room, accompanied by a set of larger prints. Gladdic followed the trail out the door and into a hallway.

Fade made a choking noise and lurched after him. "The hell you think you're doing?"

Blays trotted after them both. "Does anyone know what's going on?"

A thought stirred in Dante's mind, but he left it unspoken. Gladdic tracked the footsteps past the kitchen and down another corridor, with Fade hectoring him in increasingly strident tones. The small footsteps led to a dingy door that might have been a pantry. They stopped there. The larger set that had traveled with them reversed and headed back down the corridor toward the sitting room.

Gladdic set an ear to the door, then pulled back his head and lifted a quizzical eyebrow. "What do you keep in here, Fade?"

"Food! Roots and such!" Spittle flew from Fade's mouth. "Get out of my house!"

Gladdic reached for the door handle. Fade stormed forward. He was a heavyset man with some muscle to him and if he struck Gladdic it was likely the old man would fall. Gladdic glanced at Fade's feet. A white glow outlined the man's sandals. His lower body locked up, his upper body swaying forward; he windmilled his arms for balance, but his feet and legs were so firmly rooted in place he couldn't have fallen over if he'd been struck in the back with a mallet.

Gladdic smiled at him so briefly Dante wasn't sure that it had been there at all. The priest swung open the door. The room beyond exhaled the smell of dirt and tubers and spiced sausages. Windowless, it was as dark as a cavern. Gladdic lifted a finger and flooded the room with gentle light.

Two young children huddled on the floor, arms wrapped around their knees. Between their identical haircuts—long on top, short on the sides—and the softened features of childhood, Dante couldn't tell whether they were boys or girls. In tandem, they stared at Gladdic, then at Fade, who remained half-frozen behind the priest.

"Grandchildren?" Gladdic said. "Stand, please."

Fade wheeled his arms, but Gladdic was out of reach. "Don't you *dare*. You foreign shit, I'll bait my hooks with your balls. I'll —"

The priest jerked a thumb at Fade. The man's jaw clamped shut. He stood as static as a statue.

"Come out, children," Gladdic said. "Into the light."

The one on the left stood, motioning for the other one to do the same. Hesitantly, they walked out from the pantry, stopping outside the door.

Gladdic didn't move. "Are you afraid?"

The one who'd stood first, the shorter of the two, nodded. "Yes, sir."

"You should be. For your grandfather would rather sacrifice you, and everyone else in this land, than to break his word to the coward who's abandoned him."

"Grandpa? Did we do something bad?"

"No, child," Gladdic said. "You are innocent. But innocence is the weakest shield of them all. It splinters the first time it meets a blade."

Gladdic made a chopping gesture. Fade's head jerked forward as it was released from its bonds. "Stop, you son of a bitch! *Stop!*"

Ether sparked on Gladdic's fingertips. "I haven't yet begun."

"Right." Blays moved forward, reaching for the hilt of his sword. "If this is going where I think—"

Gladdic gestured again. Whiteness traced Blays' figure. He stopped in his tracks, immobilized except for the raging of his eyes. Gladdic ignored him, staring right back at Fade, whose neck worked and strained.

A halo of ether formed around Gladdic's index finger. He hovered it over the top of the braver child's head.

"Get away from her!" Fade shook his head side to side like a dog that's taken a snoutful of pepper. "You're a monster!"

Gladdic snorted in contempt. "Your words have no power, fool. If the Eiden Rane is not stopped, these children are already dead."

He shaped the halo into a long needle, lowering it to the girl's face. She backed away, her back thumping into the wall. "Grandpa!"

Dante's heart beat like the wings of a manic bird. Gladdic moved across from the girl, trapping her against the wall, and maneuvered the glowing needle to her ear. Dante called forth to the nether.

The girl screamed.

So did Fade. "The Hell-Painted Hills!"

Gladdic halted the needle. "What of them?"

"The training grounds are tucked away in the Hell-Painted Hills. You want to find whatever's left of the Odo Sein, that's where you need to go."

EDWARD W. ROBERTSON

6

Gladdic touched his chin. "The Hell-Painted Hills."

Fade nodded, sweat dribbling down his brow, chest heaving. "That's why no one's ever found the place. Only the Odo Sein's power is enough to keep a body from getting poisoned by the old magics."

"The Hills run for hundreds of miles between the coast and the mountains. Where within them is the academy?"

Fade rattled off a slew of precise directions to the Hills. "That will take you to a spot known as Frog's Reach. It's right there on the fringe. The Silent Spires — that's the academy — is miles past the border. There's no road, no proper path neither, but the way is marked in gold. Follow the gold, you'll get you to the Spires." He curled his lip. "Except you'll drop dead before you get a mile in. And in the Hills, there isn't even any dirt to bury your foreign corpse."

Gladdic turned his head to Volo. "Are his directions plausible?"

She swallowed. "I know where Frog's Reach is, yeah. But nobody travels through the Hills. It's death."

"Thank you, Fade. At last, you have found a way to speak the truth."

Gladdic closed his eyes. The needle blinked away. Fade and

Blays stumbled forward, released from their invisible bonds. The girl ran past Gladdic and into her grandfather's arms.

Fade gazed over her shoulder with sheer loathing. "Now get your half-rotted carcass off my land. I don't care what kind of sorcerous devilry you got in your veins—I ever see you again, I *will* plant my knife in your heart."

"I would not blame you." Gladdic bowed. "Thank you for your cooperation, Fade Alu."

They made way for the front door, the sobs fading behind them. Outside, the night air was sluggish and humid. Dante had been getting used to it, but at that moment, it felt suffocating.

"What," Blays said, batting aside a low-hanging bit of shrub, "in the orgy of the gods was *that*?"

Gladdic looked as untroubled as a man waiting on a shaded bench on a spring day. "The guiding of a man toward the light."

"By paralyzing him while you threatened his granddaughter with a knife made of ether? Would you have hurt her?"

"I don't know."

Blays skipped ahead and planted himself in the middle of the path, blocking it. "That's not good enough! I didn't spare your life to watch you hurt *children*!"

"And I didn't go on living in order to watch you fail because you lack the courage to win."

"You asshole, do you even—"

Dante stepped between them, barring his arms to the side. "You idiots! Have you forgotten that we're in the middle of enemy territory? How about we wait to accuse each other of war crimes and cowardice until we're somewhere the authorities won't burn us with glass or feed our lower halves to the fish?"

Teeth gritted, Blays nodded once. Gladdic made an "as you wish" gesture. Dante wasn't entirely sure they had proper inns in Tanar Atain—conceivably, if you went to visit another city, you could simply pole your raft-house to it and live in that—but upon asking Volo, she confirmed that, though rare, such establishments did exist.

They got in the canoe and Volo guided them through the endless canals. As soon as they exited the island district, she came to a stop in front of a three-story building skirted by wide porches. Laughter rolled out of the open windows. Rather than being built on land, the structure was held up by thick stilts, as though it had once been a dock until its owners thought of a more profitable use for it.

Otherwise, it was more or less like any inn you'd see in Narashtovik or Mallon, with the exception of the "stables," which took the form of a miniature marina enclosed with fences above the water and nets below it. It was overseen by a guard whose egg-shaped body was a local rarity, given that most everyone spent a good portion of their day poling or paddling boats around, hacking at plants with machetes, or shaping beams into new rafts and docks. Volo didn't leave her new canoe behind until she had thoroughly impressed into the guard that if her boat got stolen, she would in turn steal no less than one of his testicles.

They secured a room (third floor, which Volo said would get a better breeze) and headed up to it. Dante bolted the door behind them. Blays and Gladdic separated like combatants in an arena. Volo sat on a mat in a corner, looking downcast. Naran moved to a wall, hands clasped behind his back.

Blays stood across from Gladdic, held apart by a shin-high table. He hadn't taken off his sword belts yet. "You were going to do it, weren't you? You were going to kill that little girl."

"Killing her would have been inefficient." It had been a long day of travel and most men Gladdic's age would be hunting for a chair, but he stayed on his feet. "Her grandfather broke before she'd felt the slightest sting of pain."

"But if he hadn't buckled, you would have hurt her until he

did."

"Bask in your self-righteousness. I above anyone know how good it feels. How intoxicating it is to condemn your enemies as evil and yourself as the wielder of virtue's sword!"

"Quit with the speeches," Dante said. "You sound like a mad priest."

Gladdic smirked at that, then sobered. "Look to our results. No one was hurt. And we gained the location of the last remaining Odo Sein."

Blays flung out his hands. "No one was hurt *this* time! But if we hike out to these Silent Spires, and they tell us to go fuck ourselves running, what's your plan then? Start torturing the youngest person in sight?"

"If such an act was required to stop the Eiden Rane, you would spare one child and sacrifice the world instead?"

"Some things aren't worth compromising on, you son of a bitch. Like, I don't know, *baby-killing*!"

Gladdic lowered his face and pinched the bridge of his nose. "Conventional morality works against conventional threats. But the threat posed by the lich is beyond all scale. If we don't accept the nature of what we face, and adapt to its horrors, we will lose."

Blays' face had gone scarlet. "This was a bad idea."

"I'll fight the lich with everything I have," Dante put in. "But I won't become a monster. We can't give up our souls to this."

Gladdic rubbed his jaw. "That would make our task much harder."

"Then we'll work harder."

"As if we weren't already? Restricting our methods will only increase the risk of our defeat."

"Then we'll risk it! Gods damn, man, I've done more than my share of killing. And I'd do most of it again. Despite that, I still think I'm a decent person — or that I'm at least capable of being saved. But if I start torturing children, then I don't get to believe that anymore."

The old man considered him for some time. "So be it. But know that if I must sacrifice my soul to end this, I will do so in a heartbeat."

"Not much there to sacrifice," Blays muttered.

Dante shot him a pointed look. "The darkest solutions are often the fastest. The easiest. The surest. But sometimes, there are other methods. We have made a long and ridiculous career out of finding those alternatives. Let's try to do the same here. Agreed?"

"Agreed," Gladdic said.

Blays folded his arms. "We'll do more than try."

Dante sighed heavily. "Then it's settled. With such an enlightened agreement in place, I'm going to descend to the common room and acquire a bottle of local liquor. On second thought, I'll get two."

"No." Naran pushed off from the wall, wandering toward the middle of the room. "I can do this no longer."

"But I just told you we're done arguing. Don't tell me you're against drinking time."

"I mean that I can't participate in this alliance. Not with him."

"Ah." Dante hesitated, unsure how to approach the awkwardness of the situation, then remembered he didn't give a damn about Gladdic's feelings. "I'm not particularly thrilled about palling around with my worst living enemy, either. But the cause we're working toward is much greater than our differences. Right now, the five of us are the only thing standing between—"

Naran held up a hand for peace. "There's no need to argue. I am already convinced that what you are doing is right. But I cannot continue to fight alongside a man who would threaten a child. The same man who murdered my captain."

EDWARD W. ROBERTSON

Everyone looked Gladdic's way, but the priest seemed perfectly uninterested in defending himself. Because he knew he
was guilty? Or because he knew that they would never understand the reasons for his innocence?

"Naran," Blays said. "You can't just flounce off. Not after everything we've been through."

Naran smiled a little. "It has been an experience like none other. But it's also because of everything that we've been through
that I must go."

"But we need your help here."

"Do you? Volo knows these waterways like I know the middle seas. As for the three of you, you can do things that would
make most gods jealous. Myself, however? I am just a man with
a sword. I can't stand against what you fight now. But I can be of
more use elsewhere."

"What's the plan?" Dante said.

"I'm not yet sure. I may attempt to find the spice route for
Lady Vita in order to win Alebolgian allies. They'll be closest to
this menace if the White Lich breaks free of the swamps. I'm sure
our war coffers wouldn't mind the assistance, either."

"I hope this will be over long before it comes to that. But if it
does stretch out, we're going to need every ally we can get, and
every person we've got working to the best of their talents. Are
you sure this is what you want?"

"I have spent too long away from my ship." Pride warmed
Naran's eyes. "It's time I served my crew again." He unbuckled
the belt bearing his Odo Sein blade and held it out to Dante.
"You may find someone who will put this to better use than I
can."

"I can think of no better use for it than for you to use it defending yourself." Dante ran his hand over his mouth. "Which
you might need to do sooner than you'd like. We can't send Volo
to bring you to Aris Osis. We need her to help us find the Odo

Sein."

"I understand. I know how to navigate the waters. I will find my own way."

Volo scoffed. "You buffoon. If you aren't eaten alive by a swamp dragon, the Monsoon patrols will lock you in a tower until you're as old and gray as *he* is." She jerked her chin at Gladdic, then smiled. "So it's a good thing for you that you know me. I got friends here. Others like me. One of them will take you to Aris Osis."

"You would do that for me?"

"You're the one rushing around the swamps to do battle with the craziest things I'll ever see in my life, all for the purpose of defending Tanar Atain, a place you've never even seen before. And you're asking *me* if I'll help *you*?"

Naran laughed. "Tanarian logic is a formidable enterprise. How long will it take you to make your arrangements?"

"Better make it tonight. I expect our friends here want to get moving at sunup."

He made for the door. "Then let's be on our way."

Blays reached for his arm. "Hang on, Captain. How about a drink before you run off on us?"

Naran clasped his forearm. "No, my friend. There is nothing for us to drink to. Not yet."

He released his grip, nodded to Dante, and stepped outside, Volo right behind him. The door closed. Sandaled footsteps rasped down the hallway.

"Well," Blays said. "I'd hate to waste a good pub just because one of us is too busy 'getting things done.' Shall we?"

Dante nodded, stood there a moment, then walked out with Blays. They headed downstairs. The common room wasn't overly crowded, the local liquor was of decent quality (if inexplicably fishy tasting), but they didn't seem to have much to talk about, and they were drawing stares from the Tanarians. After a single if strong drink, they returned to their room. With nothing else to do, they went to sleep.

Volo had been out for half the night, but as the sun broke through the eastern haze, she rolled from her cot with an eagerness that made Dante acutely jealous that he was no longer young. After a quick meal downstairs, they headed for the "stables," retrieved Volo's canoe, and departed the capital.

According to Fade Alu, the Silent Spires of the Odo Sein were located roughly eighty miles from the coast in the middle of the Hell-Painted Hills, which separated the southeast border of Alebolgia from the northwest of Tanar Atain. According to Volo, everyone said the Hills were still as hostile to life as when the Yosein had first poisoned them against the White Lich.

"I once knew a boy named Goss who said he'd spent a day in them," she said. "But he used to bite off his own toenails. And tell us that if you went deep enough into the Go Kaza, the fish had wings and flew through the sky while the birds had fins and swam in the water."

Dante shifted on his seat. "Do you know of anyone who's stepped foot in them? You don't drop dead the instant you touch them, do you?"

"I didn't. Not when me and some other Maggots decided we had to explore them. But we were only in the Hills for a few minutes before we all started to feel like it was a really bad idea."

"Because you were scared? Or because the land was imposing that feeling on you?"

"I think that it was a lot of both."

"What exactly did it feel like? Did you get an impression of what would have happened to you if you'd stayed?"

Volo screwed up her mouth, eyeing the patchy clouds beyond the canopy. "It felt like I was becoming someone else. And that if we'd stuck around much longer, whatever I am would have been lost."

"Well," Dante said. "I hope very much that you're wrong."

Gladdic smoothed the front of his jabat. "What if it is only possible to travel into the Hills while in the presence of a Knight's sorcery-deadening field?"

"Then we're completely screwed, aren't we? What kind of question is that?"

"The kind we must never be afraid to ask ourselves if we are to succeed."

Volo estimated the journey to the Hills would take four days. Within the first hour of leaving Dara Bode, they were stopped twice by Monsoon patrols, but apparently Volo's status as a corpse-carrier was still valued under the new leadership, as they were let on their way without issue. After the second stop, she took more obscure passages wherever she could.

She'd assured Dante that she'd left Naran in good hands, but he feared what would happen if Naran's escort were stopped by the Monsoon. Given local hostility to foreigners, Dante wondered if it had been a mistake to let Naran go. Or if they should have accompanied him to the port of Aris Osis themselves.

A nice thought. But it would have cost them a week or more of travel. Gladdic was, to a certain extent, correct. They were a long way beyond niceness. Dante thought it could be a long time before they had that luxury again.

Late in the day, they passed by the town of Yeli Pade, which was nowhere near the size of the two cities they'd been to, but a dozen times larger than the outer villages. It had fallen to—or pledged allegiance to—the Monsoon. The white banner flew from its small stone fort. On it, the two blue orbs, which Dante suspected were to represent the eyes of the lich, watched over the town.

After they made camp, he spent an hour working on the blood-flicking, but nothing he tried provided any results whatsoever. He was starting to think it never would: things were always passing from the world, devoured by the blind jaws of time. When they were gone, there was no getting them back.

That night he dreamed of sailing out to sea and coming to an immense edge that stretched from one horizon to the other, the ocean spilling over it in a colossal waterfall to nothing, dragging all the water and all the land behind it into the abyss.

The next noon, as they approached the town of Uru Hine, the clamor of battle swelled in the distance. They diverted, approaching stealthily, and watched as the Righteous Monsoon overwhelmed the town, which had apparently remained loyal to the Drakebane. The rebel soldiers seemed to be taking special care to take as many of the residents alive as possible. Not out of respect for their countrymen. It was to provide the White Lich with as many bodies as possible.

There was no talk of intervening.

Beyond Uru Hine, a swath of settlements had been gutted. There were no obvious signs of violence, and as far as Dante knew, the lich remained in the deep swamps of the north, laying the foundations of his power. It was possible the Drakebane had evacuated the people to be transported to Bressel.

Yet for some reason Dante suspected the Monsoon had gotten there first, and that there was, at that very moment, a flotilla of prisoners on its way to the Eiden Rane's hands.

He heard from Nak while they were two days out from the Hell-Painted Hills. The conversation didn't take long. The monks had scoured the archives. And the boat had returned from the holy men of Houkkalli Island.

Both of them had reported the same thing: they knew nothing of the White Lich, nor anything that resembled him.

"Great," Dante said once Nak was through. "Well, I suppose it's a good thing we kept Gladdic around."

The old man turned around in the canoe and lifted an eyebrow.

"I'll continue the search," Nak said. "Who knows what might turn up? And I assure you that I have nothing better to do."

Dante thanked him and shut down the connection. Later that same day, his loon twinged again. He answered hopeful that Nak had turned up an overlooked tome, but was greeted by Sorrowen's hesitant voice.

"There's been a lot of fighting," the boy said. "Like, a *lot* of it. For a while, nobody was sure which way it was going to go. Today, though, the rebels turned the tide. They drove the king's loyalists right out of the capital."

"Couldn't happen to nicer people," Dante said. "But we might need to get them back in power if that's what it takes to ally with them against the lich. The Bresselian resistance movement has likely already started. I need you and Raxa to join it and work your way toward the top. Show them the powers you can wield for them, if that's what it takes."

"Um," Sorrowen said. "That sounds dangerous. For us."

"Trust me, I'd be ecstatic to switch places with you. Work slow and steady to gain their trust, Sorrowen. When they see what you can do for them, they'll be clamoring to bring you into the fold."

After a bit more talk, Dante concluded the conversation. He spent the rest of the day thinking through the shape of an alliance between Narashtovik and Mallon. Cally would be turning in his grave at the mere notion of such an outrage, but things had changed for the stranger. Dante believed the old systems were about to be ripped out by the roots.

As they neared the Hell-Painted Hills, the air cooled by several degrees. Frequent winds shivered the branches of the trees, which stood taller and taller, vines dangling from their boughs like colonies of sick snakes. The pockets of land grew few and far between, but blades of rock lurked just below the surface, obliging Volo to slow down and feel the way forward with a pole.

There were no more villages, no more wandering fishermen, no more signs of human life at all. Enclosed beneath the lumbering trees, the swamp grew darker. The canopy shook with the wind, but below it, the air lay still.

After some miles, the way ahead brightened as swiftly as if the sun were passing from behind a cloud. The colors of flame and soot appeared behind the trees. And then the trees were gone, and the sky opened above them, and the swamp came, at last, to an end.

Blays rested his paddle on the gunwale. "We're supposed to walk into *that*? Are you sure there isn't a safer route? Like off the edge of a cliff?"

The landscape was a slope of rock as jagged as the just-cooled stone on the north coasts of the main Plagued Island. Most of the rock was shiny black, but it was streaked with the colors of flame, the more distant of which seemed to dance in the sunlight. After weeks in the flatness of the swamps, the heights seemed monstrous, like a vast black wave about to pound down on the shore. Not a single tree, shrub, or blade of grass grew from the land.

Except on the very border. There, the division between the Hills and the not-Hills was as stark as if it had been cut by a knife. Everything to the northwest was barren, but on the few blobs of earth that extended from the southeast of the line, yellow spring flowers bobbed their heads in the wind.

"We're here," Volo said, then blushed. "In case you hadn't noticed."

Blays reached his paddle across the border, nose tilted back like he was expecting the instrument to burst into flames. "Is it remotely safe to go in here? This place looks like an army of demons has spent the last thousand years barfing in it."

Dante shielded his eyes against the sun. "Does anyone see any golden streaks? Volo, is this Frog's Reach?"

"Sure is," she said. "And so are the twenty miles to either side of us. The frogs like it here because the fish don't."

"Frog's Reach is that big?"

"I don't think people are that concerned about giving a name to every little piece of the land they never go into."

"It would have been nice if Fade had mentioned that. Then again, I suppose he was a little preoccupied with stopping his granddaughter from getting slaughtered like a pig." Dante squeezed his temples with one hand. "We've got two jobs here. First, we find the trail. And second, we figure out if it's safe to follow it."

"The answer to the second question may be before us." Gladdic extended his knob-knuckled finger. "Consider the insects."

Dante peered into the sunlight, uncertain what he was looking for. Gnats and flies weaved through the air on their drunken little missions. "What am I looking at? A bunch of pests?"

"A bunch of pests who cross the boundary without falling on their backs and crossing their legs above their bellies."

"So it isn't so treacherous after all!" Blays said. "It must be sheer coincidence that the Hills don't have a single bird, mouse, tree, or blade of grass on them."

"If it's that poisonous, you might finally be able to get the mold out of your smallclothes." Dante called to the nether. "I'll see if I can find us the path. Then we can argue about who has to go first."

He knocked down two dragonflies from the countless number of them that were cruising around, then reanimated them, sending one along the border to the southwest and one to the northeast. Unsure how bright or conspicuous the gold markings might be, he leveled the insects out at just sixty feet up, moderating their speed.

Ether and nether stirred behind him. After a moment of panic, he realized Gladdic was poking at the boundary of the Hell-Painted Hills, seeking answers.

Within ten minutes, gold glinted in the vision of the northbound dragonfly. Dante descended, confirming that the color was a part of the rocks rather than a lost piece of royal jewelry, then swung the insect about to fly directly away from the boundary and into the wasteland, gaining altitude as it went. Two hundred feet further into the Hills, a second blotch of gold shined from below.

"Got the trail," Dante said. "It's only a few miles north."

As they paddled toward it, he recalled the second dragonfly, sending the one that had found the gold marking inland as fast as it could. By the time they'd gotten the canoe up to the first marking, the inland-bound scout had crossed a good ten miles of the Hell-Painted Hills. In all that time, it hadn't seen a single sign of life. Not even bones.

A lobe of grassy land extended from the barren border. They brought the canoe up to it and climbed out.

"I'm still on the trail." Dante motioned into the hills. "But I have no idea how long it'll be before I find the Spires."

"Assuming Fade was telling the truth about them being here," Blays said.

"He was," Gladdic said. "I have no doubts."

"Why would you? After all, why would a man lie to save his family?"

"Would you like to make a wager on the matter?"

Blays grinned. "Since when were Bressel's high priests allowed to gamble?"

"Bressel is no longer Mallish, is it? Nor part of the Mallish faith. Hence I have no church left to answer to."

"If it's good enough for you, who am I to argue? The only problem is I've spent all my money in this damn place." Blays rubbed his chin, then brightened. "Aha! Penny-pinching Dante

over there always has extras hidden away. Probably tucked behind his balls. I'll bet you ten of his silver that the Spires aren't
here."

"You won't," Dante said.

"As an agent of the Citadel, I haven't been paid in months.
Fork it over and I won't charge you interest on what I'm already
owed."

Dante was too distracted by his dragonflies to do more than
don an unpleasant look.

"Very well." Gladdic produced a pouch from beneath his jabat
and gave it a jangle. "Ten silver. If Fade Alu was lying, it is
yours. But if the Spires are there, then yours is mine."

Blays stretched. "I assume you won't be insulted when I ask to
see the color of your money first?"

"According to you, 'cheater' would be the least of my crimes."
Gladdic made a thoughtful noise. "Which would, in fairness,
only make your suspicion all the more reasonable."

He opened the pouch. Having only one hand, he was obliged
to pour the coins into Blays' palm.

Blays inspected them, then dropped them back into the bag.
"Well, I know whose corpse *I'm* looting first."

As the two dragonflies zipped their way deeper into the
phantasmagoric hills, Gladdic hunted through the grass until he
found a shield-shaped green beetle. He placed it inside an empty, narrow-mouthed ink bottle, then walked to the knife-sharp
edge separating the live land from the dead stone. He set the
bottle on a naked black rock and stepped back.

Mile after mile of black slag-land passed beneath the dragonflies. The trail of gold blots carried onward, spaced irregularly,
sometimes as much as an eighth of a mile apart from each other.
Sometimes, however, two to five of the marks were clustered
within a few feet of each other.

Just as Dante was starting to worry about how much further

his scouts could fly before the connection dropped, a spot of green drew his eye. Unlike the sharp, jagged angles of the hills, this was fuzzy.

He took the dragonfly higher. The greenery poured down the side of a slope and into a valley, forming a circle of trees and grass hundreds of yards across. Within it, a ring of towers jutted from the hillsides like the spokes of a cage with its roof torn off.

"Bad news, Blays," Dante said. "You owe Gladdic ten silver."

"I don't see how that's bad news for *me*," Blays said. "Go on and pay the man. And if you have any decency, wash the coins first."

"The other bad news is the Spires are at least twenty miles in. Maybe thirty. Even if we—" The dragonfly's sight blacked out. Dante felt for his connection, but it had been snipped like a loose thread as it had been right about to pass over the edge of the trees. "Lost my scout. Probably closer to thirty miles, then."

"Of some of the worst terrain I've ever seen. We'll be lucky to make it in two days."

"Two days in a land that supposedly kills everyone who hangs around in it for more than a few minutes. Volo, how long were you and your friends in the Hills before you turned back?"

She scrunched her mouth to the side. "More than an hour, less than two."

"Excellent," Blays said. "Then all we have to do is cross thirty miles of horrific terrain in under two hours to get to the Spires, which may or may not be just as toxic themselves."

"I think it's okay," Dante said. "They have plants there. Trees. Whatever's keeping life out of this place doesn't impact the Spires."

"Mind set at ease, then. Race you there!"

"Maybe it's just superstition that's keeping people out. That and rough terrain."

"People explore everything. They'll travel for hundreds of

miles across the ocean, which is essentially a bottomless pit of salty poison. If the Hills were safe to travel through, *someone* would have found out by now."

Gladdic moved to the boundary, crouched, and picked up the ink bottle. He returned and held it before them.

"Behold." The green beetle strolled around the bottom of the bottle, antennae twitching. "It lives."

Blays placed his hands on his thighs and bent in for a closer look. "So you're saying all we have to do to survive the Hills is turn ourselves into beetles?"

"Young Volo has already ventured into the wastelands for a modest period of time without suffering harm. If we begin to feel ill, we will do as her friends did, and turn back."

"Is this the brightest way to go about this? What if we sail to Bressel, kidnap one of the Drakebane's pet Odo Sein, then bring him back here? You guys can tie him to a pole and wave him at the lich while I move in for the stabbing."

Gladdic tucked down the corners of his mouth. He turned his back to them and waded through the grass toward the boundary. As he neared the line of blasted rock, he wavered, then set his shoulders and stepped across.

He tilted back his head and breathed through his nostrils. "Wait here, then. I will return with an acolyte of the Odo Sein, or not at all."

He walked onward into the fiery kaleidoscope of stone. The wind ruffled his hair. He didn't look back.

"Gods damn it," Blays said. "Are we about to let a crazy old man shame us into committing suicide?"

Dante shrugged. "Look at the bright side. If we drop dead, you can spend the next nine hundred years in the Mists calling him a moron."

He braced himself and stepped onto the black pan of rock. There was no thunderclap from above, no wilting in his chest.

Blays did some swearing and joined him. Yet as they made to follow after Gladdic, Volo remained standing in the grass, her eyes wide as she stared down at the lifeless ground before her.

"What's the matter?" Blays called. "So what if this place was hostile enough to drive out the White Lich? It's *probably* safe for squishy little humans."

Volo didn't look up. "When I joined the Maggots, we were told we had free current to go anywhere in Tanar Atain except two places: the Go Kaza, and right here."

"You can stay on that side, if you like," Dante said. "You've taken us far enough."

She stamped from one foot to the other, then slapped herself in the face. "I can't walk away. If the Monsoon hadn't gotten me to trick you into helping them, then maybe none of this would have happened."

Baring her teeth, she stepped over the line separating life from nothing. She froze for a moment, as if coming face to face with a bear, then hurried after them. "Come on. If we move fast enough, maybe I'll forget this place wants us dead."

Gladdic hadn't slowed down for them, but despite his spryness, the others caught up with little effort, making good time over the gently sloping land as they moved from the first gold marking to the second. A quarter of a mile in, the ground shot upward in a series of blade-like ridges and deep valleys.

Blays came to a halt. "Anywhere else, and I'd say we should take the ridges. Valleys would be choked with more shrubbery than a brothel's merkin locker. But somehow, I don't think undergrowth will be a problem here."

"There's not even any rubble in them," Dante said. "It's just solid rock. Like it was draped on top of whatever was here before."

"Or the surface was melted. Like a good cheese."

"Cheese?" Volo said.

Blays gaped in horror. "You don't know what cheese is? That's the real reason the Drakebane seized Bressel, isn't it? Not to escape the White Lich. But to get his hands on Bressel's famous Temple Yellow."

Dante scowled. "Will you stop making me think about cheese?"

The valleys would be protected from the wind, but their rear walls looked too steep to climb. They hiked up a ridge instead. The sunlight was only mildly warm on its own, but the black rock baked like a fire was crackling beneath it; completely exposed, with their limbs bare, the four of them were soon sweating like a stone brought up from the springhouse.

"I don't know what's worse," Blays said. "The sun, or the footing. It's a damn good thing we have these rugged sandals to protect our feet from the jagged, jagged rocks."

Dante already had an oozing scrape on one of his toes. "Let me know if you hurt yourself badly enough to need the nether. The code word will be 'Oh hell, I just sheared off three of my toes.'"

With the worsening ground, they had to place each step carefully, cutting their pace by a third. As Dante's jabat dampened with sweat, he summoned a shadowsphere above their heads, flattening it and stretching it out until it was the consistency of a thick mist. With the sun blocked, the wind dried their sweat, suddenly cold.

The slope leveled out. They stopped for a look around. Behind them, the swamp was a mat of treetops, water sparkling from beneath the growth. Ahead, the land rolled on and on, each hill a little higher than the one before it.

Volo buckled her knees, reaching for the ground with one hand, as if she might collapse. "What's wrong with this place? Why is the ground all bendy? Is that from the magic?"

"Disturbing news," Blays said. "Everywhere is like this. It's your swamp that's the weird place."

"How can that be? If it's all a bunch of bare rocks, how can your boats get anywhere?"

"Because we put wheels on them. And build little streams for them. Except instead of water, we use bare dirt, or paving stones. We call it 'roads.'"

Volo regarded him suspiciously, then bit her lip. "If the rest of the world is made of land, and hills, why is ours so different?"

"You should be happy about that," Dante said. "Coming from a unique place has made your people unique, too."

He didn't tell her that it might not always have been that way: that the lifting of the Woduns, and the great changes that had seemed to have flooded across the land in the years before and after the last coming of Cellen, might have forged Tanar Atain from something mundane into its current shape. So that if not for his forebears, the land might never have been locked away from the rest of the world, to become the breeding ground for the White Lich.

They moved down the ridge and ascended the next. After so long in and around the water, Dante found himself with an odd case of sea legs. On the positive side, though the rills in the ground were as sharp as knives, there was no dirt or grit to slip on.

A few grueling hours and miles onward, no one had reported feeling any signs of illness. *Was* it superstition that kept everyone out of the Hills? Maybe there had been an enchantment protecting the land, but it had faded away long ago, while the memory of it lived on. Whatever the case, other than a general sense of exposure, and the low-grade anxiety of being in a place that would offer a person no hope of survival if they were to get lost in it, everything seemed normal enough. Gladdic had brought the beetle in the ink pot along with him, and it showed no signs of trouble.

Sunset poured across the land, the oranges and reds matching the smears of color on the rock. None of them had seen an uninterrupted sunset since the last time they'd been in Aris Osis, and they watched it until it was almost all the way down before descending into a valley where they'd be out of the wind.

"We're somewhere over a third of the way there," Dante declared once they got a tarp up and had progressed to arranging their blankets in a futile attempt to spare them from the hardness of the ground. "We'll want to be out before dawn if we want to avoid spending a second night here."

"Because of the invisible wolves?" Blays said.

"You've not seen them, too?"

"Stalking after us, unseen. Howling to each other, unheard. When they bite us, it might not look like they're doing any harm, but that's only because you can't see the blood."

Dante wrapped his blanket over his shoulders. The wind had driven the humidity down and the late spring evening was much colder than in the swamps. "It's about more than the Hills themselves. We're going through our water faster than I thought we would. We'll have to ration it until we get to the Spires."

Volo got a funny look on her face. "Ration *water*? You guys make it sound like you've had to do this before."

"Nobody tell her about deserts until the morning," Blays said. "Not unless you want to carry a wet blanket the rest of the way to the Spires."

They arranged a watch schedule—more than watching for intruders or animals, it was to observe each other for signs of illness—and did their best to sleep on the mercilessly uncomfortable ground. Dante got up for good a few minutes before first light. His thighs and feet were achingly sore.

He was usually the first to get up, but Blays was already sitting up and blinking his eyes, and Gladdic had had last watch. He sat at the edge of the tarp, illuminated by the tiniest trace of ether.

Dante shuffled over to him. "How's the beetle?"

Gladdic lifted the ink bottle to the light. The green beetle twitched an antenna but was otherwise still. "Sluggish."

"From the aura of the Hills?"

"Perhaps. But I pray that if I were confined to a bottle without sustenance for a day that I would be doing half as well."

"How are your legs? Strong enough to travel?"

Gladdic smiled thinly. "I have eased my soreness enough to continue. But your concern is appreciated."

Dante rousted Volo. They ate and packed up. Gladdic lit the way onward with the ether until the sun broke clear of the eastern ridges. The Hills were as rugged as ever, yet they made steady progress. Dante kept the fog of nether over their heads to protect them from the sun, but the day warmed quickly, and sweat trickled down his sides. Limiting himself to scant sips of water, he found his hands were shaking.

Late that morning, they stopped in the shade of a cliff to rest. Dante had been keeping his remaining dragonfly relatively close to ensure that they weren't wandering off course nor that there were any unexpected threats lurking ahead of them. Meaning to see how far they had to go, he sent it whirring along until it spotted the pocket of greenery that made up the Silent Spires.

To the best of his judgment, they were ten to twelve miles out. Doable by nightfall, if they pressed hard. He sent the dragonfly closer, searching for the best approach by foot, as well as any defenses they might have. As soon as it flew above the outermost trees, it blacked out.

Dante swore. "Just lost my other scout."

"To what?" Blays said. "The invisible air-wolves?"

"It wasn't far enough away for the link to degrade. It dropped dead at the same spot as the first one. Something stopped it."

"And this upsets you? Sounds to me like it's proof they've got active Odo Sein there."

A half mile later, as they trudged up an incline as steep as a set of stairs, Volo's right sandal snapped, spilling her to the ground. As Dante swept away her cuts with the nether, Gladdic waved his hand, restoring the sandal with a glare of ether. Yet the strap wasn't pristine, merely reverted to a state of being heavily worn but not quite broken. It looked as if it would give out after another couple of miles. Even if Gladdic used the ether to fix it again, the state it was returned to would be more worn than it was now, meaning it would break again even sooner, with the cycle repeating until the ether could do nothing at all.

Dante bent his mind to the problem, yet it vexed him more with each minute that passed. Broken things could be fixed by hand, but only if you had the materials to replace or reinforce what had worn down. There were no plants here to work with; should they shred one of their blankets to wrap around her foot? Carrying her was out of the question. It would make whoever was carrying her ten times more likely to unbalance and fall off the ridge, and anyway, even Blays wouldn't be able to bear her on his back for more than ten or fifteen minutes at a time.

An hour later, Volo's sandal snapped again, sending her reeling to the edge of the ridge. Blays caught her, falling down in the effort. She landed on top of him.

Gladdic peered at the broken strap in angry confusion. "Why would it do that? Doesn't it know that we need it to function properly?"

He snapped his hand back and forth as if he were dueling with a miniature sword. The ether glared at a skewed angle, knitting the strap back together. Gladdic spat on it and walked onward, wobbling a little.

Volo roughly wound the straps around her feet and calf. "This sandal is stupid. *Feet* are stupid. They should be hard enough that you don't even need shoes."

She ran after Gladdic at a speed that seemed much too fast. Dante walked after them, frowning deeply. Could he make her feet harder? Grow a lot of skin on the bottom or something? But he couldn't do that, could he? Unless...*what if* he drew the rock up around her foot, encasing it in a thin stone booty? He could remove it once they reached the Spires! It would—

Stars flashed over his vision. He crumpled to the ground; he'd kicked a clump of rock. His toes were mashed and bloody and one of the nails was split. It should have turned his stomach, but he wanted to laugh. He muttered to himself. The nether came slowly, as if confused, then settled onto his wounds, erasing them.

Blays snorted at him. "Forget that rocks are stronger than feet, idiot?"

Dante got to his feet. "Let's find out if your face is harder than my fists."

"I could fight using only my face and you'd still lose."

Dante stomped to within two feet of Blays. "Then let's find out! You want the first swing?"

Blays drew back his fist, mouth twisted into a leer. As his elbow reached its apex, he paused, eyes darting to Volo and Gladdic, who watched eagerly.

"Dante," Blays said. "There's something wrong."

"That you're not bleeding from both nostrils? I'm about to correct that."

"Dante! *Look* at us!"

Dante's nails were digging into his palms so tightly he'd drawn crescents of blood. With difficulty, he relaxed and took a long breath. Across from him, Blays was wild-eyed, and despite the healthy tan they bore from months on months of travel, he was as pale as a Tanarian.

Gladdic was, too. Volo's face was as white as plaster, while her eyes were webbed with red cracks.

Dante could barely get the words out. "We look like Blighted."

The anger receded from Gladdic's eyes like a spell. He fumbled for his pocket, extracting the ink bottle. At its bottom, the green beetle lay on its back, legs folded over its thorax.

"The Hills," Gladdic said. "They have come for us at last."

Blays groped his own face, as if afraid it was in the act of changing form. "We have to go back!"

Dante wagged his head, dizzying himself. "Can't do that. We have to get to the Spires."

"I won't become one of them!"

"It's nearly twenty miles back to the swamp. We'll never make it there in time. The Spires are much closer — and there are people living there. It must be safe."

"For the Odo Sein, maybe. What if it isn't any safer for us?"

"Then we die! Or we join the lich's service like the other Blighted! Do you want to stand here arguing about it? Or do you want to run for your gods damned life?"

Blays snarled, then fought down his anger like he was swallowing his own vomit. He wiped his forearm across his brow and laughed. "We run, then. And hope the Odo Sein have a beer waiting for us on the other side."

Dante moved to the front of the column and broke into a jog. He drew a knife and cut his arm. Wherever the ridge was too spiky with rocks to run over it, he reached into the stone and smoothed it before them. Behind him, he felt Gladdic drawing on the ether. Light glowed on Dante's skin.

He didn't look back. "What are you doing?"

"Attempting to preserve us," Gladdic said.

"Is that going to work?"

"I operate on the assumption that it will be better than nothing."

Whether due to Gladdic's efforts or the panic racing through his veins, Dante's head cleared, if only for the moment. He ran as fast as he dared, gaze flicking between the path immediately be-fore him and the next glint of gold marking the way forward. He no longer had a dragonfly to plot their course from above. If they lost the trail now, they were as good as dead.

Sometimes they fell. When the cuts and scrapes were bad enough to slow them down, Dante healed them. When all they were was a little blood, he let them bleed. A thudding redness encroached on the edges of his vision. Every time he stumbled, or couldn't see the next golden marker, rage choked his lungs like he'd inhaled a draft of water.

Volo's sandal broke a third time. Gladdic mended it with the ether, but they'd been running less than ten minutes more when it came apart yet again. The next time, it hardly lasted five before it sent Volo crashing to her knees. She screamed and hurled the broken sandal off the ridge as hard as she could.

Gladdic spat a curse. "What will you do now, you fool?"

"Run until my foot bleeds," Volo said. "And keeping running until it stops."

She hopped in place, then broke into a dash Dante could hardly keep up with. It wasn't long before her foot left was leav-ing shiny dark blots on the stone. Nether darted from Gladdic's hand, healing her, if only for another minute.

Dante couldn't say how long they ran for: even if he hadn't been distracted following the markers and smoothing the path, the red fog was suffocating his brain as badly as the haze of the Pastlands. At some point, Volo lost her other sandal, too. Dante's right foot felt warm. It was covered in blood. Rather than pain, all he felt was anger. He needed to find someone, and he needed to hurt them.

Bare skin smacked against the rock. Dante glanced back and saw that Gladdic had fallen. Blays and Volo ran on. Dante glared after them, teeth clenched so tightly they squeaked.

"Get up!" he yelled over Gladdic's body. "Get *up*, you worthless shit!"

Drowning in fury, Dante drew back and kicked Gladdic in the ribs. The old man didn't stir. Dante kicked him again, hard enough to rock him on his side. His legs jutted from his jabat, as thin as the back legs of a dog and as wrinkled as a shirt tossed in the corner for days. Pathetic.

Dante drew back his foot again. Something bobbed to the surface of his mind. Clarity. He calmed himself, the wrath raging around him like a windstorm while he was tucked away inside his house. The ether came. He let it flow down his body.

Everything got...better. Dante crouched and shook Gladdic's shoulder. Nothing. The priest's skin, the easily-tanned complexion of a Mallisher, was now so white Dante could nearly see through it.

He picked Gladdic up—the old man was as light as he looked—and stumbled onward. Blays and Volo were starting up the next hill. Dante slogged along, only smoothing the path where it was most treacherous. When he reached the top, he had to kneel and catch his breath, sending the nether into his muscles to wipe away their complaints.

He didn't catch up to Blays and Volo for another mile. They were slumped next to an upthrust fist of rock painted with red swirls. They were as pale as fish bellies and their eyes were closed. As Dante approached, Blays' bloodshot eyes fluttered open.

"Oh." Blays' voice came out in a croak. "Was going to ask if you'd carry Volo for a bit. But it looks like your hands are full."

Dante sank down beside him, propping Gladdic against the rock. "When was the last time you saw a mark?"

"Time ago. Some of it."

"Do you remember which way we were going?"

Blays swung his head about, mouth hanging open, brows lowered. "Up? Weren't we going up?"

Dante grunted. "North. Which way is north?"

"The sun is...there." Blays pointed to it—it was currently hanging to their left, painful and yellow—then traced his arm across the sky. "That means it came up over there. And *there* is up."

"North."

"Yes. North." Blays tried to push himself up, but his legs gave out. "My lower arms aren't working."

Dante thought for a moment, then glowered at the dark stuff until the shadows rolled across their limbs. The fog pulled back a little. Able to think again, he stilled his mind and touched them both with ether, which seemed to help. He meant to turn it on Gladdic and Volo, but his supply was exhausted.

"Not sure we'll get much further," he said. "That was all I had."

Blays cracked his neck, looking a little better. "Don't worry, Volo and Gladdic are already asleep. If we all die, we can tell them it was *their* fault and they'll never be the wiser."

They hoisted their charges and shuffled onward. Their progress was creeping. They'd barely made it over the next hill before the red fog stole in from the sides of their minds. Dante pushed on, barely able to see the way ahead, lost in the huff of his breathing and the thump of his wrathful heart. When his legs threatened to quit working, he called to the nether again. He wanted nothing more than to become part of the swirling darkness, to lose himself in its coldness, its hunger for blood.

Blays lifted a shaky arm. Beneath his pale skin, his veins stood out like worms. "Look."

Beyond the next line of hills, a single tree rose into the empty sky.

Later, Dante couldn't remember crossing the final leg of their pilgrimage. All he could remember was the rage that seemed to define his every desire. And then, like being splashed with a bucket of water from a mountain-fed stream, it fell away: he had stepped out of the Hills and into the trees.

He set Gladdic down and sat, leaning his back against a trunk. Blays found a spot across from him. The color was already returning to Blays' skin.

Blays rubbed his hands into his eyes. "Care to tell me what just happened to us? Other than something horrible?"

"This land kills all life," Dante said. "That's the only way the Yosein could turn back the White Lich and his armies."

"But the Yosein are long dead. How can their enchantment have lasted this long?"

"Maybe that's a reflection of just how much they hated him."

"In other words, you have no idea."

"Correct."

One of Dante's dragonflies lay dead on the dirt twenty feet away. He reached for the nether, but it wouldn't come. Not because his strength was exhausted, though he knew he was close. But because the power of the Odo Sein refused to let him. Examining the others, everyone had a few cuts and scrapes on their elbows and legs, and Volo's feet oozed blood from the soles, but he didn't see anything critical.

Gladdic's eyes fell open. He considered the trees around him and the towering pillars of stone at the bottom of the valley. "I exist."

"And I mean to have strong words with the gods about that some day," Blays said. "In the meantime, we've got a job ahead of us. One that you insisted we do, I'll note."

"What is our plan to make contact? To walk into their most secret temple, and pray they allow us to live?"

"I was thinking I'd wait for them to send us a carriage." Dante pulled himself to his feet. "But now that you mention it, your way sounds faster."

It was another minute before Volo came back to her senses. In that time, Dante didn't see anyone moving in the windows of the towers or in the green fields around them. There was a dirt path just to their right and Dante followed it downhill. After the neutral emptiness of the Hell-Painted Hills, the smell of leaves and pollen stopped up his nose like a bung.

The path leveled out, delivering them from the forest. Pressure lifted from Dante's shoulders: he could reach the nether again. He was tempted to use it to heal their abrasions, but not knowing what awaited them at the academy, he saved his strength.

In an echo of the settlements in the swamps, the grounds of the Silent Spires were composed of concentric circles. In the outermost ring, fruit trees grew unfettered, festooned with blossoms of every color. Next came a ring of tidy crops starting to sprout from the jet black soil. After that came a ring of statuary, well-tended squares of decorative greenery, and a form of pavement achieved by smoothing out the natural rock of the Hills into a high gloss, then etching patterns and glyphs into the stone.

And within it all rose the circle of towers. Seven in number, they soared two hundred feet high, capped by black domes marbled with the colors of fire. Their faces were peppered with arched windows, some of which opened to balconies.

All of the rings were empty. There were no workers in the fields, no worshippers at the small shrine that stood in the center of the plaza between the towers. Wind buffeted the sprouts in the fields and tousled the flowers in the gardens.

Dante swallowed. "Tell me the Drakebane didn't bring everyone from the Spires with him, too."

He'd been angling for reassurance from Gladdic, but the priest said nothing.

Dante touched the hilt of his sword, pulling the shadows close like a thick blanket on a winter night. He passed into the shadow of a tower, then back into the late afternoon sunlight as he entered the paved grounds in the middle of the towers.

He stopped there and turned in a slow circle. "Hello? I'm a friend of Tanar Atain. We come seeking the order of the Knights of the Odo Sein."

A leaf fluttered across the courtyard. The windows stayed silent.

Blays waved his hands above his head. "Hey, people who dedicated your existence to not getting destroyed! Guess what? You're about to be destroyed!"

Silhouettes moved within the windows. The tips of arrows winked in the waning sun. Dante shaped the nether into killing darts, but a great blankness slammed down upon him, locking both ether and nether in place.

EDWARD W. ROBERTSON

7

Dante scrabbled for the nether with all that he had, but there was no defying the power of the Odo Sein. That was the very thing that had brought them to the Spires. Though he, Blays, and Volo were armed, there was no hope of fighting back. They were exhausted. Which ruled out running away, too.

"Ah!" Blays quit waving his hands and held them above his head. "That destroying I was talking about? Not by us. By the Eiden Rane!"

Archers advanced onto balconies, sighting down the white shafts of their arrows. As many as a score per tower. More than a hundred in all.

"He tells no lies," Gladdic boomed. "The Eiden Rane has been released from the iron prison of the Riya Lase. He slaughters your people as we speak. We have fought him, but we cannot stop him. Not without your help."

With the archers in position, quiet overtook the grounds once more. White cloths embroidered with orange patterns hung from either end of the temple in the center of the plaza, flapping away at themselves in a wind that felt as if it might never stop blowing.

A door creaked open in the base of a tower across from them. Six men or women dressed in hooded white robes swept from the entry in perfect silence. They kneeled down in two rows of three, arrows trained on the intruders.

A seventh figure walked into the light. She wore a robe, or something like it, but unlike the warriors, her arms were bare and her face was uncovered. She was tall and neither young nor old. Something in her bearing was so commanding that Dante hardly noticed as another six archers trotted from the doorway to join the others.

She walked toward them, the wind pinning her robe to her legs and torso, rippling the orange stitching. Half of the warriors advanced with her while the others held their bows trained on the four outsiders. After thirty feet, the first grouped dropped into a crouch, arrows nocked, and the others popped up and dashed forward to flank the priestess.

She came to a stop across from the four of them. Her light skin and dark hair marked her as Tanarian, but she was taller than most — taller than Dante, in fact, and nearly even with Blays and Gladdic. Despite being a priestess, and one in the middle of a rocky desert at that, the muscles of her arms and shoulders were fit for hard labor.

Her stature would have drawn looks, but her face would have stopped feet. She was at least five years past the stage of life when nearly all young people were pretty, but that extra time had carved the excess softness from her cheeks and chin, granting her the beauty of a noble warrior.

Her eyes locked on Gladdic. "Gladdic of Bressel. I know you."

"I do not think so," he said. "I would have remembered if we had met."

"The Drakebane spoke of you. He wasn't sure he could trust you."

"Yet which of us is still here in service to your land?"

She snorted in a way that Dante found annoyingly charming. "You, a foreigner, stay in our land to fight a battle that isn't yours, while the Drakebane, our emperor, abandons our land be-cause he thinks that battle can't be won. One of you is a very big fool."

"I'd put good money on both," Blays said. "Don't worry, my friend Dante will cover me."

"You shouldn't have been able to get here. Not without adding four more gold markers to the trail. You two are war-locks." She nodded at Dante and Gladdic, then eyed Blays. "And there's something wrong about you, too, isn't there?"

"Crippled brain," Dante said. "I'm afraid he was born with it."

She nodded again, sympathetically. She frowned at Volo. "You're a roamer. Of the Veins? A merchant? No, there's some-thing unsettling about you. Like opening your door to find a sin-gle banana has been placed on your stoop. You're with the Mag-gots."

Volo bobbed her head. "Yes. Ma'am."

"Did you bring these dirty hari here?"

"No, ma'am. Is it ma'am?"

"It isn't," the woman said. "Is the purpose of titles to show honor to those that bear them? Or to degrade yourself before your betters, and train you to do their bidding?"

Volo straightened her back, looking deadly serious and a little alarmed to find herself in dana kide with someone of the wom-an's stature. "Do we know who first invented titles?"

"No more than we know who invented the first floor beneath our feet, or the first way to tell a man that his mother's a whore-dog."

"If the first title was invented by the one who bore it, then I'd say it was meant to degrade everybody else. But if it was made up by one of the everybody else, just another commoner, then I say it was meant to honor a good person."

"And since I already admitted we can't know who invented ti-tles, we can't know their intent. Classic dodge." She gave Volo a brief and not overly warm smile. "My title is Bel. I have a name, too, but it's mine, and I don't share it like drunks passing around their bottle. You can have it when you tell me your own names, and why I shouldn't kill you for trespassing in a place where no hari has ever set foot."

"I'm Dante Galand," Dante said, deciding that lying might only get him in trouble down the line—and that he might need to impress her. "High Priest of Narashtovik."

If this meant anything to her, she didn't know it.

"Blays Buckler." Blays extended a hand, which the Bel ignored. "No title attached. Not because I don't deserve one, of course. But because a fancy title would only make it harder for me to do what I do."

The woman tilted her head. "Which is?"

"Save Narashtovik from disaster whenever its High Priest meddles in something he had no business with."

"That's what brings you here? Meddling?"

"If this is what meddling looks like," Gladdic said, "then we should all wish for our lives to have more priests and mothers -in-law. As stated, the Eiden Rane has returned. We seek to stop him."

"And I seek to find a way to stop aging that doesn't involve dying. I think I'll have more luck at my job than you will."

"I am inclined to agree. Yet we have faced him and survived."

The Bel laughed, her pulled-back hair swaying as she wagged her head. "Do you even care if I believe you? While you're at it, why not tell me you're my long-lost father, thus I'm obliged to help you however I can?"

"We got here to the Spires, didn't we?" Blays lifted his right elbow behind his head, stretching it with his other hand. "You know the weirdest part of it all? Between the way his eyes shift between blues, and those granitey features of his, the lich is a pretty handsome fellow. I don't normally say that about a glowing giant who's trying to cut me in half with a glaive as big as a church steeple, but it happens to be true."

She smirked, then swung her dark brows together like a closing gate. "But you saw him. You looked into his eyes, and then—the clash of weapons—an escape. How?"

"We had the help of a few of your knights. Unfortunately, they didn't make it out."

"They fought with great valor," Gladdic said. "They met their fate precisely as they were trained to."

"If you were able to stand against him, why are you *here*?" She strode forward, startling her guards as she shoved at Gladdic. "You have to go back! You have to go back and you have to rip his heart in half with your sorcery!"

With the guards on edge, Dante reached for the nether, but it was still being clasped in place by the knights concealed in the towers. "Why didn't we think of that *before* we poisoned ourselves marching through the Hell-Painted Hills? We can't stand against him, Bel. Not on our own. That's why we're here. Send your knights with us, and we'll destroy the White Lich."

"You said that you've already fought him alongside the Odo Sein. And that he killed my knights and forced you to run away. Why would I send more good men to their deaths?"

Gladdic straightened his jabat. "Have you heard of the theory of the prime body?"

She doused him with a look of sheer disdain. "If you think we're that negligent in our duties, why come here at all?"

"I don't follow your reasoning, my lady."

"That's because you haven't bothered to think it through. We're the ones who uncovered the idea of the prime body in the first place. Even if we hadn't, a moment of thought would have led you to the conclusion that, in the course of our sworn duty of destroying the Eiden Rane, we *might* have heard of a method that would allow us to do exactly that."

"Your people have sought out the body, then."

"We've been seeking after it for centuries, Gladdic of Bressel. Before you waste my time, I'd suggest *you* go and find it, and only then return to the Spires. I'll be long dead by then, but I'm sure my granddaughter will be very accommodating to you."

"But my lady, we have already found it."

Her jaw dropped open. "That's not possible. We've been searching —"

"For centuries. I heard you. But as you know, we are sorcerers. Warlocks, if you like. And though the group of us are not friends, there is one value we hold in common: we do not like to fail."

"If you've found it, then you don't need to battle the lich himself. You only need to suppress his sorcery long enough to strike at the prime body. For that, you don't need to travel all the way to the Spires. You could just use the Drakebane's personal guards." She tapped her front teeth. "Except you came here. Which isn't at all easy to do. The Drakebane's Odo Sein are all dead."

"Many, yes. The others fled with him to take Bressel."

"That actually worked?"

"Better than even he dreamed. And so we are left to come to you for aid."

"My name is Ara," the woman said sadly. "And there are no more knights left to help you."

Dante crossed his arms. "The next time you want someone to believe the Odo Sein are gone, you might want to warn your Odo Sein not to use the powers of the Odo Sein."

"I said there are no more knights here. Did I say that there was no one left with our talent?"

"Then give us a squire. Or a Pageboy of Odo Sein. I don't care *what* you call them, all I need is for you to send some of them with us."

"There are many reasons for a person to reason poorly." She began to pace across the paving stones, the white fabric of her dress flowing about her strong legs. "We know most of them as the Hana Ro. In your language—although these days it's as much our language as well—this translates to something like 'the Branch of Lacks.'"

Ara's gaze grew distant, as if she were searching for signs of infiltrators in the fire-colored hills. "Yes. *Something* like that, although not precisely that." Her eyes snapped to Dante. "Do you speak more than one language?"

"Two well," he said. "A lot of others not so well."

"Then you know that exchanging words between them isn't like exchanging coins between different countries, where you can weigh the metal in them against each other, and know that you're getting a fair deal so that nobody needs to be stabbed. With language, there are a lot of words that don't translate at all. You might dismiss this as the barbarism of a foreign culture that doesn't even have the concept of such-and-such, but that is arrogant thinking, which is lazy thinking, which is the slow death.

"*I* think that if you can't translate one of your terms directly to another language, such that it means exactly the same thing in theirs that it does in yours, that doesn't mean there's a flaw solely in the other language. For if your language lacks the specificity to be translated, then it is inaccurate as well, and strays from the truth in ways you can't even see."

"That...makes sense." Dante looked up at the balconies of the tower across from him. The archers were still crouched there, watching them with nocked arrows. "You were talking about the Hana Ro?"

"I was and am, so be quiet and let me. When you're reasoning, the Branch of Lacks is like a tree that bears the fruit of all the things that you don't have at your disposal. We in the Spires could spend all night arguing which fruits are borne most heavily, but I don't care about that right now, and will list them in no particular order. One common lack is the lack of information to reach a sound conclusion. If you think fire is cold, then you'll never understand why it keeps burning you.

"Another lack—and some of my peers will argue that every other lack is merely a sub-form of this one—is the lack of brains to guide yourself down the correct path. Just as a sick man is too weak to paddle across a body of water, your mind is too weak to paddle you toward the truth.

"A third lack, which might be a refined version of the second, is the lack of training to be able to reason well in the first place. Say you come to a fight with a spear of burnished steel. Your foe's only got a sharpened pole. But if he's spent years in training while you just picked yours up for the first time, you're dead on your feet.

"And lastly, at least for our purposes, there is the fourth lack: the lack of good intent, where you willfully deceive yourself with false logic in order to reach conclusions that reinforce your old beliefs, or that justify your poor actions.

"Now then. In not understanding why I can't send Odo Sein away with you, which fruit from the Branch of Lacks are you full of?"

"I'll save you some time," Blays said. "It's absolutely the brains one."

"I'm guessing it's lack of information," Dante said. In any other circumstance, he would have been highly annoyed that they were drifting so far off track, but listening to Ara philosophize was like watching a trained athlete run through an unfamiliar course without missing a step. "Given that I didn't even know this place existed until a few days ago. And that you deliberately hide yourselves out in a wasteland that sucks the soul out of anyone who walks into it."

Ara smiled, flashing her teeth. "You're already making your

way toward the answer. Yes: we founded the Odo Sein in the Hell-Painted Hills because their poison protects us from the Eiden Rane, to say nothing of pests like you. Are you aware that a knight, on finishing their training with us, never returns to the Silent Spires? Why?"

"Because the Drakebane needs them to fight off the endless monsters and rebels your land's always spawning?"

"If a fruit is grown from toxic soil, would you eat the fruit?"

"Of course not. It will be full of the same poisons it grew from."

"Even if the tree was grown in a clean land and then transplanted to the foul one?"

"It would still start absorbing the poisons as soon as it was taken here."

"Yes, it would. And so do we. This land was made to be so corrupt that *nothing* can grow here. We've carved out a small piece of it that we can survive in, but we can't keep all of the poisons out of it. Over time, they build up in you. We have ways to protect ourselves from them. But that changes our bodies forever. In ways that make the *normal* land toxic to us."

"The knights don't return because they can't," Dante said. "They'd get stuck here. Just like you are."

"It was lack of information after all." Ara smiled, the beauty of her face shot through with sadness. "Sure, there are some people here who possess the powers you need. But none of them can leave the Spires. They'd drop dead long before they met the Eiden Rane."

"I see." Dante nodded twice, finding that he'd been unceremoniously dumped into that numb and quiet space where all hope has been kicked from beneath you, and your mind decides that the only thing left is to lie down and wait for it to end. "Well."

"How about apprentices?" Blays motioned vaguely to the towers. "In a place like this, you've always got loads of young kids to sweep the halls and muck the stables in exchange for the privilege of being taught to serve their lords for the rest of their lives."

"Oh, they're long gone," Ara said. "The Drakebane recalled everyone we had to try to put down the Monsoon. Right down to the children. They weren't close to being ready to fight, but when a man feels his future slipping away from him, he'll mortgage it for pennies on the round. I expect the last of our apprentices were fed to the ziki oko weeks ago."

"But if any survived —"

"Then they'd be with the Drakebane, hustled away to Bressel. They're trained to obey him like your arm is trained to obey your mind. They can't leave his side any more than your hand can pop itself from your wrist and crawl away on its fingers."

Blays opened his mouth to reply, then closed it, giving a quick shake of his head. He seemed to lapse into the same hopeless acquiescence Dante found himself mired in.

"You say that you would die if you left the Spires," Gladdic said. "How long would this take?"

Ara rolled her eyes up and to the right. "For those of us that were born here, a matter of hours. For those who were brought here later in life, they might last a day or two."

"Which implies that those with the stoutest constitutions might endure longer than that. Long enough to depart the Hills. You must commit your people to us."

"I must order my people to commit suicide? You northerners worship so many gods that your brains don't know which direction they're pulling in, priest."

Gladdic leaned closer. Dante could feel him fumbling around in both the shadows and the light, but the soldiers of the Spires continued to keep both forces frozen in place as tightly as the glaciers of the Woduns.

"Do you suppose that you will survive here, the last island of free humanity, after the Eiden Rane has swallowed the rest of the world?" Fine bits of spittle flew from Gladdic's lips. "Once he controls the continents and the seas, he will rip these hills out by the roots. The only sanctuary for you will be that of death."

Ara held her ground. "Desperation is driving you to hysterics, you wrinkled sack. Don't feel bad. It's a common failing when you lack a real argument."

Gladdic's face flushed red. He made a great yank at the ether, grabbing at enough to level the plaza, only for the unseen negators to clamp down on it with everything they had.

"I make no hysterics." Gladdic closed his eyes, breathing through his nose until his hands stopped shaking. "Better than anyone, the Odo Sein must understand that if we fail, everything is gone, replaced by two ends: death, or the slavery of the Blighted."

"If I must understand it, why are you talking to me like I don't?"

"Because you, and everyone else I speak to, are incapable of understanding that your life was rendered worthless the instant the Eiden Rane crawled back out from the earth. Send your people and at least know that you tried!"

"It would only be a waste."

"Then send your lessers! What does it matter, you arrogant bitch? They are *meant* to fall in service of the Spires!"

Ara's right hand twitched. Her guards tensed. The cords stood out from her neck, but her voice was calm. "It's not logical to waste resources on a strategy we know will fail. Better to wait and see if the lich makes a mistake. Like trying to enter the Hills before he's strong enough."

"You know that he won't," Gladdic said. "He has fought your people before. He's had a millennium to plan his ascension. He will never strike before he is ready. The only choice is to take the fight to him before he's prepared."

"There's wisdom in that. But we can't help you do it. So if you're serious about stopping him—about taking the fight to him—I suggest you stop wasting everyone's time and be on your way."

Gladdic curled his hand as if to make another grab at the ether, then slouched his spine, dropping his gaze to the plaza tiles. "It is no wonder the world lies ever in darkness. Bring the answers before your leaders and wisemen, and they will prove themselves as cowardly as everyone else."

Dante turned to take in the slope they'd come in on. "Crossing the Hills almost killed us. If we leave now, will we be okay?"

"Once you enter our land, it'll cleanse the Hills' corruption from you within a few hours," Ara said. "But once you start off again, don't stop until you hit the swamp." She glanced up at the balconies; some of the archers had returned. "You should go. You can wait in the outer trees until you feel well enough."

Dante racked his mind for answers, but they'd exhausted every argument they'd come to make. Under the watchful eye of the archers, he walked away from the plaza and into the gardens that ringed the towers. He felt much better than when they'd arrived at the Silent Spires, but he could feel the exhaustion lurking in his legs. Even after some rest, it was going to be a long walk back to the swamps.

Blays kicked a rock, sending it skittering over the dirt. "Well, that was a lot of a bust. What are we going to do now?"

"I think," Dante said, "that we are going to do an unpleasant amount of walking."

"Why don't we ever travel to anywhere that you can reach by sitting?"

"Maybe Naran had the right idea. We should buy the fastest ship we can find and spend the rest of our existence sailing around somewhere warm."

"If we stick to the seas, the lich might not even be able to get at us. The Blighted would make awful sailors. They already act like they're drunk, just wait until they get put on a ship and get some rum in them."

Dante brushed past a shrub of blue flowers. "Taking to sea isn't a completely insane idea. Once we're out of the Hills, I'll loon Nak and tell him to start arranging for an escape fleet."

"You mean like what the Drakebane did, except with no destination at the end of the journey? If that's what we're down to, I'll start preparing a eulogy for the state of our ideas."

"We should go to Bressel," Volo said. "If we can find the Odo Sein and talk to them, maybe one of them would come back with us."

Dante grunted. "Everyone we've talked to seems to think that's about as likely as talking the White Lich into sitting on his own glaive."

"Then we'll kidnap one of the knights and *make* him fight the lich."

"Kidnapping someone who can strip our powers from us like dirty sheets might be our worst idea yet. Even so, just to cover our asses, I'll ask my agent in Bressel to see if she can run down an Odo Sein. Right now, though, everything we've seen indicates that traveling to Bressel would be a waste of weeks we can't afford to lose."

"That's pessimistic," Blays said. "I'm sure the White Lich will put his plans on hold if we write him nicely enough."

Volo wiped a bead of sweat from her temple. "What if we searched for one of the apprentice knights who fled with the Drakebane? Maybe they weren't able to train long enough to be totally loyal to him."

"If they were trained for—" Blays got a startled look on his face. He spun on his heel and dashed back toward the plaza. There, Ara had been speaking with her bodyguards and was just now mounting the steps of the tower.

Hey!" Blays waved his arms over his head. "Bel Ara, wait!"

Archers flooded back onto the balconies of the towers, aiming their arrows at Blays. He skidded to a stop, holding his hands high above his head.

"I admit running straight at your leader while yelling my head off wasn't the most diplomatic approach," he called out. "But can you wait to fill me full of arrows until after I've filled you in on how I'm going to save the world?"

Dante was already running after him, trying to take a posture that indicated he thought his friend was very stupid and that he was only trying to stop that friend from making things worse.

As Dante hit the plaza, Ara descended two steps to stand above Blays. "If you've come back to beg me, you'll have more luck begging a tree to grow you a wife."

"Oh, I already have one of those." He smiled tightly at the archers and slowly lowered his hands. "But if I can talk this tree into growing me a person who'll hear me out, then I'd be interested."

She squinted at him with one eye. "You're aglow with cleverness. That seems like a stupid reaction, considering I've already told you at length why we can't send anyone to help you. You want to argue more? Waste as much breath as you want. Words can change minds, but they can't change facts."

"You might say that, good Bel. But my companions and I are cursed with the foolhardiness of not knowing when a thing can't be done. With that in mind, I have a proposal for you."

"Make it fast or not at all."

"You can't send knights to help us because you don't have any. And the only other people here who have the power of the Odo Sein can't leave the Hills. Well, that's the end of it, isn't it? But then I got to thinking. *You* might not be able to leave here, but we can. And we can put a blade through the prime body's heart and bring down the lich—if you teach *us* to be Odo Sein."

Ara's black eyebrows twitched upward. A smile spread across her face like dye dropped in water. "I see why they don't give you a title, Mister Buckler. After all, what *would* they call you? The Minister of Alternative Solutions?"

"I prefer the Baron of Getting Shit Done." Blays turned to Dante, who had stopped a few feet behind him. "You think we could fit that on a signet ring?"

"If this works," Dante said, "we'll stitch it in gold thread on a thirty-foot banner. Well, Bel Ara? Can you train us?"

She descended another pair of steps. "Sure. In fact, the idea had already occurred to me."

"You're serious? You can train us to do what you do — the skill we need to counter the White Lich — and you didn't say anything about it? You were going to let us just walk away?"

"I have to come up with the ideas for you? You don't understand the Odo Sein at all, priest of the eleven-plus-one gods of the north. If you couldn't think this solution out for yourself, then you proved you're not ready to learn what we do."

"But I did think that thought," Blays said. "So that means you'll teach us?"

"Nope." Ara dropped down the final steps, putting her on the ground with them. "But I will bring your plea in front of the Argument of Seven Voices."

"Right. The good old Argument of Seven Voices. Will you think less of me if I ask you what the hell that is?"

"The rulers of the Silent Spires."

Dante licked his lips. "I'm sorry, I thought you were the ruler here."

"Then that was a faulty assumption on your part, wasn't it? Not a good thing, thinking the first person who wanders out of a fortress is in charge of the whole palace. I *do* have sovereignty over my own tower, and as the newest Voice of the Seven, I'm expected to handle irregularities like this. But in a case like yours, we decide as a group."

"As in you take a *vote*? You don't have a king? Or at least a chancellor of some kind?"

Ara snorted. "Trust a High Priest to argue that every governing institution's got to be ruled by a High Priest. Why would you believe one person can be right about every single thing at every single time? If you want to get to the truth, you don't assign it to a single man who's above us all. You put a bunch of good people in a room and you let them fight their way to the truth."

Gladdic moved next to Dante, looking more thoughtful than during his angry outburst earlier. "How will this hearing proceed?"

"I'm thinking we'll argue on three decisions. First of all, whether we're allowed to train those who approach the Odo Sein rather than vice versa. Second, we'll look at whether we're allowed to train hari to be knights. And last, I'm pretty sure the others are going to want to argue that foreigners who trespass in the Silent Spires should be put to death."

"Aha," Blays said. "On that count, might I suggest no?"

Dante shaded his eyes against the sun, examining the heights of the towers. "How will this process play out?"

"Like any process meant to get to the bottom of an issue," Ara said. "You'll tell the Seven who you are and what you're about. Then they'll question you until you're so sick of questions you'll spend the next five years ending every sentence with a period. Then we'll argue with each other until we've reached our decision."

A shadow fell over her face. "That's the process in theory. Like always, it's different in practice. As I hope you've figured out from the name, you'll be talking to seven people. But the truth is, three won't be listening. Not with an open mind. You'll have a pair of Boulders sitting in front of you."

"Boulders?" Dante said.

"Boulders are just like they sound: they're sitting in the exact same place they've always been in, and they won't budge from their spot even if you tied a team of swamp dragons to them. They're the preservers of our first ideals, and they'll never agree with what you're proposing. Their names are One and Five." Ara paced in front of them. "So if you want to win a judgment in your favor, you'll have to convince four of the remaining five lords of the towers to go your way. Sounds brutal, doesn't it?"

"Like trying to wrestle a bear. That you've just cuckolded."

"The good news is that of those five people—the five you have any hope of persuading—one of them is a River. Someone who's been pushing for change for a long time. His name's Seven and he'll support you in everything. That means you only need three of the other four. A little better for you. Unless you lose anyway, because your hopes will have been raised higher by it."

"That's a needlessly cruel way to put it. But I'm confused. You say there's two Boulders, one River, and four undecided. That's already seven people. Aren't you one of the Voices, too?"

Ara flashed her teeth again. "I am. And I haven't decided how I'll vote yet."

"Comforting. What are the state of your laws on the three matters we'll be discussing?"

"Our laws? What is a law?"

"The things people give to other people so that those people will be less inclined to be horrendous butchers toward each other."

"A law is a rule that was decided to be correct by a certain group of people at a certain point in time. Are those people here now? Is that time here now? I don't see those people. I don't see that time. I see *my* people, gathered at the current time, to determine what we believe."

"A truly enlightened state of affairs," Dante said. "How long do we have to prepare our arguments?"

Ara waved up at the seven towers. "Until I get the other six down here to hear you make them. Don't worry, it'll take a minute. Some of them are very old."

Before Dante could say another word, she strode toward the shrine in the inner ring of the plaza. There, she lifted a small mallet from the post it had been hanging from and used it to strike a bowl-shaped piece of brass that rang like the offspring of a bell and a gong.

Shouts carried down from the balconies. Most of the archers withdrew, replaced by people with the general bearing of trusted household staff. They leaned over the railings to look down on Ara. She swung back the mallet and struck the instrument again. At this, the staff dashed back inside. Ara replaced the mallet on the post and walked across the open-walled shrine to one of the seven seats that were arranged like a pincer beneath the structure's pitched roof.

"Well, this is unfolding rapidly," Blays said. "Suppose we should figure out what we're going to say?"

"You're not going to say much." Dante turned a stern look on Gladdic. "And *you* aren't going to say anything. Not unless you can refrain from calling the person you're speaking to a 'bitch,' or threatening to cut off their digits with a dull stone, or any of the other pleasantries you spit out the instant things aren't going your way."

Gladdic's mouth twitched. "Threats are often more convincing than rhetoric or facts. I will do what is necessary to secure our goals."

"You will do what is necessary to not make me punch your jaw out the top of your head. This could be our last shot, Gladdic."

"Then see that you do not fail, and require me to correct our course for us."

Dante curled his hand into something not far from a fist. "I have run my country for years. I've forged treaties. Alliances. I know when to extend an open hand and when to draw the dagger. You, on the other hand, solve your problems by murdering anyone you don't like. Before we begin, swear you'll follow my lead."

The old man smirked. "You suppose your efforts to control those around you are more moral because there are times when you *don't* employ violence? Yet how many have died in your wars?"

"*My* wars were fought to *free* people, not to enslave them to —"

A door boomed open from another tower. A tall man in a white, airy robe similar to Ara's plodded down the steps, surrounded by a small coterie of attendants. Like Ara, he was tall, with muscles more suited to swinging an axe than to poring over scholarship, but he was well into his middle age and bore a baker's layer of fat. He eyed the foreigners with naked suspicion, head swiveling to keep watch on them as he approached the shrine.

As he settled into his chair at one end of the pincer, another tower opened, disgorging a man with the lean build of a racing hound. He was about forty and he was nearly bald, sporting a tuft of black hair at the front of his forehead and not much else at the top. He glanced at the three foreigners with curiosity, then smiled quickly but warmly.

The next Voice to arrive was a woman whose wide shoulders and thick body were stout enough to house a small family. She gave them a look that was nearly as cold as the icy blue gaze of the lich, mounting the steps with the implacability of a draft animal.

"I don't like these people," Volo whispered once the woman was seated. "They look like they say mean things to babies knowing that the babies won't understand them."

The remainder of the council arrived shortly, consisting of four men and three women in all. Two of them were old enough to require assistance up to their seats. Two staff members appeared next to the outsiders, and through a process that was almost entirely nonverbal, indicated that they should step before the Seven Voices. As the servants guided them to their place between the two points of the pincer of chairs, they kept a twitchy distance, as if afraid the foreigners' leprotic arms were about to drop from their bodies.

"Voices of the Silent Spires," Ara said. "We have an unusual matter before us. One that I suspect we're going to have to spend an immense amount of words to untangle. First things first, let's make some introductions. We're going to know each other very well before this is over."

She introduced the outsiders, including Volo, then moved on to the Voices. Dante made special note of the Boulders, One and Five—the axe-swinger and the shelter-sized woman, respectively —and the River, Seven, the balding man who'd been the only one to smile at them.

"I'll summarize the situation to the best of my understanding," Ara continued. "With the aid of the rebels of the Righteous Monsoon, the Eiden Rane has reemerged from the deep swamps. The Drakebane tried to stop him. The Drakebane failed at this, and put into play the Exodus, abandoning Tanar Atain to the lich and his servants. We know this. There aren't any surprises there.

"What is a surprise is that these four people—including no less than three hari sorcerers—have kept fighting back. They faced the Eiden Rane at the Wound of the World. They didn't win a complete victory, but they did survive the battle against him, which would be counted as a win by most people who know what they're talking about. After this, they proceeded to do something impossible. Something we've failed to do for centuries. They found the prime body."

The other six Voices shifted in their chairs, scoffing and muttering to each other. Ara shrugged, waiting for them to simmer down. "If you can't believe it, that's probably because your ego doesn't want to accept that a team of degenerate foreigners have done what we couldn't. It doesn't help our pride that these hari were trying to save Tanar Atain while our own emperor was ducking out of here like the sun was about to drop on his head. It makes you wonder why we ever agreed to such a plan."

"We didn't agree," said One, pressing his fingertips together and leaning forward. "We were told. And we obeyed, as is our duty. Now quit sermonizing and get back to the point."

"The point? The point is that these hari, in all defiance of self-preservation, want to take a third shot at the lich. But they need Odo Sein to strip him of his powers while they strike at the prime body. When they learned that none of us can leave and help them, they came up with an alternative plan: that we should train *them* as knights, so they can confront the Eiden Rane themselves."

If her earlier words had caused a stir, these ones unleashed a storm. Again, Ara waited for it to grow quiet enough to be heard. "Do you want to sit here all day puffing on about how outraged you are, and how important it is for all good people to be exactly the same amount of outraged or be branded a traitor? Or do you want to talk through whether we *should* be outraged?"

"You're putting the stern before the bow," One said. "The first thing to decide isn't whether to train them to be Odo Sein. It's to decide if we should feed their guts to our gardens!"

"Do you think I'm so dumb that I've forgotten that I live in this place that I've never left? If you want to ask them why we shouldn't kill them, they're standing right in front of you. Interrogating them is your *job*."

One shifted his bulk to better glare at Dante. "What's there to ask? Outsiders who trespass in the Silent Spires are to be executed. Are you an outsider?"

"Is this question rhetorical?" Dante said.

"It's a good way to find out if you're lying or delusional."

"Yes, I'm an outsider."

"And were you invited here?"

"I think that, given the circumstances of —"

One flapped his hand like a yapping mouth. "Is that hari babble for 'yes'? Or do you think that trying to wriggle away like a greased eel makes you *more* trustworthy?"

"No," Dante said. "We came here on our own. Because —"

"There you have it. They're outsiders. They came without permission. Hence they've forfeited their heads. Now where is my sword?"

Dante looked to Ara for support, but she'd taken a seat and was watching them with bland interest. To his right, a guard drew his sword, looking uncertain, but his confidence was bolstered when four other guards unsheathed their blades too.

Seven, the balding man, cleared his throat. "We've always held that, yes, trespassers are to be executed. It's just good policy. Can't have the wrong people sniffing around our secrets. But it occurs to me to ask: have we ever *had* a trespasser?"

One's face grew stony. Five pressed her lips together until they disappeared.

Ara said, "They've tried, haven't they? The gold marks where they fell are scattered over the Hills like spilled grains of rice. But has anyone ever made it here? No. Not a single one."

"Then it would follow," Seven said, gesticulating tightly, fingers splayed as if he were working a skein of threads, "that we've never had to — rather, had the chance to — test our tradition. To bring it from the clean room of the mind to the grimy grounds of the real."

One snorted. "That's the most obnoxious thing I've ever

heard!"

"If it offends you, feel free to rephrase it in a way that's less upsetting to your tender ears."

"There's nothing to be tested," Five rumbled. She had a streak of gray running back from her right temple. "The Knights of the Odo Sein are the land's only defense against the Eiden Rane. The Silent Spires is the institution tasked with the grave responsibility of replacing those knights. Anyone who compromises our security, and our ability to save our citizens from annihilation, must be destroyed."

"That would be challenging to argue with indeed," Seven said. "But now that the Drakebane's gone, are we still the same institution? Now that we're not training more knights, what *are* we? If our responsibilities have ended, what's left for these outsiders to threaten?"

Five thrust out her jaw. "We don't know that we won't be needed again."

"This is all irrelevant, isn't it?" Dante gestured southeast, back toward the unseen swamps. "We're not here to compromise your security. We're here to fight the same thing you are. What do you have to lose by teaching us the power of the Odo Sein?"

"It's very simple," One said. "Our principles."

Blays rubbed his jaw. "I don't think he knows that word, good sir. You might want to try something along the lines of 'the ruthless pursuit of your goals.'"

Dante shot him a look. "Exactly what principle is at stake here?"

"The tradition of the Spires. Our loyalty to the emperor. Our pledge to our people to never let foreign powers influence our protection of Tanar Atain. Take your pick."

"Is any of those principles more important than not being consumed by the lich?"

Six, who looked to be the oldest man among the Voices,

cleared his throat. "I'm sorry, but have we decided *not* to kill them? Or did I nod off during that part?"

One crossed his arms over his broad chest. "If that's a call to vote, then mine is for death."

Blays rolled his eyes. "Great thinking. Let's get those heads rolling. I'm sure that the next outsiders who march into the Spires will be another group of friendly and extremely effective allies, and not the White Lich looking to feed you to his troop of enraged zombies."

"My vote is for life," Seven put in.

One scowled. "The tradition is as clear as the air in front of your face. Foreign intruders get introduced to Tanarian steel. How in the bottomless waters can you deny that?"

"Since arriving, they haven't caused any trouble. They spoke with Three peacefully enough, and whatever they had to say impressed her enough to induce her to summon an Argument. It seems to me that the obvious interpretation of the tradition is that we're to kill foreigners who come here to *harm* us. What sense would it make to execute those who come to *help*? If a foreigner came to us to guarantee that he could kill the Eiden Rane, and all he needed was a single speck of dust from the Spires, would we still execute him, because tradition can't be violated no matter what?"

Ara glanced across the pincer of chairs. "Who wants to let them live?"

Seven raised his hand. So did Two, then Six, then Ara herself, followed by Four.

"I count five." Ara stared at One. "Unless you've got four extra arms hidden in your pockets, you lose."

One shook his head in disgust. "Get this over with before my lunch escapes my throat."

"So that you all understand." Six jabbed his bony finger at the foreigners. "Anyone else had come and wandered in here from the Hills, and I'd be cheering as the servants swabbed the blood from this shrine. But these aren't normal times. That's why I'll listen to what comes next."

"This is exactly what I was talking about before your vote," Dante said. "This is an extreme time. The White Lich has escaped his confinement. There's no one else left to stand against him. During times of peace, there's nothing more important than principles. But in times of extremes, when whole futures hang in the balance, the normal rules break down. It's what you do when your principles fail that defines who you are—and whether you survive or fall."

Five chuckled. "Do better, Sir Galand."

"Excuse me?"

"You think you're speaking reason. But you're speaking about emotions. Why we should let our fear of what's out there change what we do in here."

"Aren't you afraid?"

"Don't see how that matters."

"Answer the question and I'll tell you."

"Sure I am," she said. "Anyone who isn't afraid of the Eiden Rane is so stupid they wouldn't even notice when the Blight stole the rest of their minds away."

"You've always been able to stick to your principles because the Spires have always been protected from the outside world. But your insulation's about to be ripped away from you. You're afraid because for once, you *can* be hurt."

Five sank back in her chair, glaring hard. But he thought he saw doubt in her eyes.

One cursed. "We're way off course here. We've always chosen our recruits. What we *should* be talking about is how it's wrong to train any random person who comes to us."

Seven cocked his head. "I don't understand why that would be so."

"We can't trust them. They might have hidden motives. They might be infiltrating us to do us harm. There are reasons we seek out our own talent."

"And do you think we find all of the talent that's available?"

"More than enough!"

"I'll make this quick," Ara said. "You might not know our history, One, but I know it and I know it well. Ever hear of Fadan the Cleaver? He came uninvited to the Spires to become a knight. And it was a good thing he did, because if not for him, we would have lost the Second Battle of Dara Bode. Then there's Rika Marn. She turned out to be something-and-a-half. Less than a century after that, and we took in the Dalaw Brothers. I can keep going if you want. Or you can accept that if you have the talent, and swear to serve the Drakebane, the Spires have allowed any number of those who came to us to serve the emperor."

One tossed a glance at the foreigners. "None of those people you rattled off were hari."

"Are we talking about hari yet, One?"

He didn't look at her. "No."

"Then I call for another vote."

This time, it was four to three, with Four defecting to the other side. Dante didn't know what to make of the loss of one of their Voices, particularly when Ara's history of them doing exactly what they were voting on seemed so ironclad. He was suddenly aware of the gaping rift between the actuality of the Voices' personal opinions and his assumption that he'd be able to stroll in and talk them right to his side.

But these weren't half-drunk peasants in Narashtovik who would scramble to do anything he asked. They were an institution every bit as venerable as Narashtovik. One that was vital to the ongoing existence of Tanar Atain. They would have a deep culture of their own — and a will to match.

"Glad to see not everyone has lost their minds," One nodded at Four. "Now then, Three, you got any history lessons about all the outlanders we've taken in over the years? Because I just did a quick count and came out with...let me see here..." He lowered his head, counting off on his fingers. "Oh right. Zero."

"You're right," Ara said. "No hari has ever been trained in the Odo Sein. As far as I know, they've never even been allowed to set foot in the Spires. I'm as interested as you are to hear the foreigners explain to us why we should break that streak."

"It's just as I've said." Dante kept close watch on the faces of the undecideds: Two, Ara, Four, and Six. "We're the only ones who can stop your enemy from conquering you—and the rest of us in turn. Why *wouldn't* you train us?"

One got a good laugh from this. "You're warlocks, right? Great big powerful ones. Except when you oppose the Odo Sein, of course, when we render you just another man with a sword. Back in your frigid homelands, if your enemies came to you, would you teach them the ways of your dark magic?"

"That depends. Is my homeland being ripped apart by an invincible lich who I'm powerless to stop?"

"If we're so powerless, why are you begging us for aid?"

"Now who's getting off track? Yes, I would train my enemies if that's what it took to hold off the enemy that would destroy us both. What other choice would I have?"

"An easy answer to give. Now let's think this through. You and your enemy have always run at a stalemate. Maybe you're the big guy one year, and the next year his kingdom's looking a little stronger, but neither one of you has been able to conquer the other. You're evenly matched. Now they come to you and you teach them all of your strengths. Together, you march against the new foe. And you beat him! Wow! Great job."

One leaned back in his chair, looking down his long nose. "Then you go home. Soon enough, the old conflicts flare back up.

Only this time, you're not evenly matched anymore. You've taught your enemy everything you know. And they use it to put you to the sword."

"That's paranoia. We're not your enemies. Until a few months ago, I didn't even know you people existed."

The bulky man exchanged a smug look with Five. She smacked a meaty hand on the arm of her chair. "You ask us for the one skill that is uniquely Tanarian. The one weapon we know how to forge that no one else does. You say that you're not our enemy? Perhaps not. Perhaps not for now." She pointed to Gladdic. "But his people surely hate us, and if they ever cast off the Drakebane, they will come for their revenge. Or the Alebolgians will buy the secret from the Mallish, and send their greedy ships to plunder our wealth from Aris Osis, reducing us to poverty. Your claims that *you* are not the enemy are disingenuous. When you pour a bottle of spirits into the swamp, there's no putting it back in the bottle. If we allow our secrets to leave Tanar Atain, one day, they *will* be used against us."

"You might be right," Dante said, keeping his words slow to mask his annoyance. "But I still say it doesn't matter. Not when the alternative is your total destruction at the hands of the lich."

"The wisdom of the Odo Sein lies at the core of who we are as Tanarians." This was spoken by Two, a man in his fifties with the lean-limbed build of one of the runners the Galladese used to swiftly deliver messages across the rugged terrain of the rift valleys. "If we pass it along to foreigners, and it's no longer our own, then haven't we lost who we are?"

"How so? You'd still be right here."

"You fail to look deeply enough. If the process of saving ourselves requires us to destroy who we are, then what have we saved?"

"Aside from the world?"

"Joke all you want," One said. "You're not the one being asked to surrender all of Narashtovik's treasures to outsiders."

"I just don't see how sharing a piece of Tanar Atain can destroy Tanar Atain. If anything, it will spread your influence and your prestige." Dante rested his arm on the pommel of his sword, then blinked. He reached for the handle, the gently tapered horn of a swamp dragon, and drew the blade. Purple nether forked along the black metal.

One shot to his feet and thrust his finger at Dante. "That's one of our swords!"

"Right and wrong." Dante held up the weapon for them to see. "It's modeled after your weapons. But I crafted it myself. Your design has saved me several times already, allowing me to find my way to the Spires, where we *will* find a way to kill your mad wizard. Meanwhile, though I've borrowed from their traditions, the Odo Sein still exist, completely untroubled by my 'theft.' And the same will be true if you teach us to be one of them."

He held the sword up another few moments. Each Voice stared at the swirling nether, which continued to flow even as every other shadow lay trapped by their power. Dante let the moment linger, then sheathed the blade with a forceful click. He allowed himself a small smile.

One chortled. Ara sighed. Seven cleared his throat, then looked down, a touch of red coming to his cheeks.

"Rhetoric," Ara said. "You're trying to stir our guts. But has it occurred to you that sword you carry is the physical embodiment of what we profess to fear?"

Dante shook his head. Sensing his bewilderment, Blays stepped up beside him, giving the audience a small bow. "Forgive me for making a suggestion that's almost stupidly simple. But what if we just promise not to tell anyone else what you teach us?"

Five laughed some more, her belly shaking. "And no man has

ever lied? No *foreigner* has ever broken a promise to people he has no loyalty to? No, hari, we can't accept your word as if it's made from pure gold."

"The main problem here is that we're not Tanarians, right? Then how about if we solve that whole mess by *becoming* Tanarians?"

This caused the Voices to exchange glances. Frowning at his lap, Seven said, "That would be an elegant solution, yes."

"But?"

"But," One said, "you *aren't* Tanarians. Look at yourselves. Your features are as fat as a blowfish."

"The fish aren't going to like it when that gets back to them. Surely you don't think the way a person looks determines what land they belong to. If we'd been born in Dara Bode, and raised as right and proper Tanarians, would you still think we were nasty hari?"

"A convincing counter," Five said. "But irrelevant, as you weren't born in our land, nor raised as one of us."

One's face bent with contempt. "It's not *that* convincing. If you jump in the water and swim for an hour, does that make you a fish?"

"Mostly, it makes me hungry and sleepy," Blays said. "I daresay that fishiness isn't defined by the specific piece of water the fish lives in. You can take a fish from one pond and put it into another and it'll do just fine in its new home."

Six eyed them, the wrinkles deepening around his eyes. "You'd become Tanarian, would you? What can you tell me about the Body?"

"The body? It's fleshy? Some bones inside to keep it from flopping around? An excellent way to travel from one place to another without the need for expensive horses or canoes?"

"I refer to the Body of Tanar Atain."

"Yes, me too. As I was saying, something about how you're all a part of it. And you have...duties. To the rest of it. All pulling together, you might say. Just as a body's lungs, heart, spleen, and so forth set aside their differences and work together to keep the physical body, ah...alive, and happy, and so forth, so must the people of Tanar Atain work together to form what you might call a Body of the country."

Seven was looking embarrassed again. Six applied one of the most patient expressions Dante had ever seen. "You aren't Tanarians. You could live among us for another dozen years and you might not yet be one of us. Do you suppose the Eiden Rane will give us that long to find out?"

"Maybe if we got him something to distract him. Like a large quantity of pinwheels."

"This is all hypothetical, isn't it?" Ara motioned to Dante. "Would you actually pledge to serve Tanar Atain when it means you'd have to sever all your ties to your homeland? You'd renounce your titles and pledge to serve as knights in the Drakebane's service?"

Dante shifted on his feet. "I have a responsibility to my people. I can't abandon them."

"Then you can't become Odo Sein."

"We could make it—"

She made a cutting motion through the air. "This will never work. You can't be a master of one land and a servant to another."

Blays shrugged at Dante. "Well damn, that trick worked with the Broken Herons."

"I have a solution." This came from Gladdic, who drew a thin, hooked knife and set it against his throat. "Once our work is finished, I will destroy myself, and my knowledge of the Odo Sein will perish with me."

"Finally, we're getting somewhere." One grinned at Dante and Blays. "And the two of you? Would you make such a pledge?"

"Absolutely," Blays said. "To be honest, I've been looking for an excuse to off myself ever since I found out my favorite baker closed shop."

Dante gazed across the seven waiting faces. "Do you realize how easy it would be to lie to you? We could complete our training, slay the Eiden Rane, then return to our homeland, and you wouldn't be able to do anything to stop it. You're trapped here. So yes, I too promise to commit suicide once our mission is complete."

Ara pressed her knuckle to her upper lip. "For some reason, I feel as if I can't trust you on this one."

One tilted his head toward her. "I'm not hearing bold ideals. I'm not hearing a compelling counter-morality for us to explore. All I'm hearing is ways for them to weasel past our beliefs. Are we ready to vote?"

Several of the others nodded. From the bored and exasperated looks on their faces, Dante could tell which way the vote would swing.

"Stop," he said, and found he had nothing else.

One regarded him with heavy-lidded eyes. "Why?"

"Because you're about to vote no."

"That's the first time you've been right during this entire Argument. Voices, let's get this done with. Everyone who is convinced that the Silent Spires should train hari in the way of the Odo Sein?"

No hands went up. After two seconds, Seven lifted his arm, though he didn't look happy about it. No one joined him.

Gladdic laughed, a sour and caustic thing. "Look at these wise elders who condemn themselves to death."

One smirked. "The time for talking is over, priest. We've made our decision."

"It must have been easier to reach that decision knowing that soon, no one will be alive to write the history of your cowardice."

"Enough. Guards, he might look old, but that'll only make him easier to drag away."

Soldiers moved in from the sides. Blays' hands drifted toward the scabbards on his hips.

Dante laughed. "You won't train us because you fear it would lead to the loss of Tanar Atain. But what does it matter when you've already let that happen? Your culture's in its death throes. Train us in the Odo Sein, and I'll save it from vanishing forever."

The soldiers paused, waiting for orders. One swore. "I told you, no more talk. The Voices have spoken."

Ara stood, drifting a step toward Dante. Her eyes seemed to grow sharper while the rest of her face blurred. "We should listen. I see inspiration in him, One. Don't you?"

The large man glared at her in disgust, then considered Dante. His anger relaxed. For the first time, doubt crept across his face. "Damn it. Shit and scales, I see it. Speak, priest. And be fast with it."

"The idea is very simple," Dante said. "The execution will be complicated. You need to put your language into writing. You need to put your ideas and your history into books. And I will help you."

Six started to speak, then coughed, his elderly eyes watering. A servant leaned in to help him only to be smacked away by the old man.

After a gulp of air, Six found his voice. "You know nothing of Tanar Atain. You think we've never heard of writing before? Of *books*? We have our reasons for doing things as we do."

"I understand perfectly well. What is it you once said about this, Volo? That Tanarians want their truths written in water, which naturally changes its form to suit its surroundings, rather than chiseled in stone, which can never be altered?"

"Close enough," Volo mumbled, wide-eyed and clearly reluctant to be dragged into the talk.

"Congratulations," Six said. "You listened to one thing that one of us had to say. We have no need for your writing. It's stifling. We've passed our knowledge along just fine without it."

Dante took a step to his right, looking past the towers in the direction of the distant swamps. "That worked before, when everyone thought the same way that you do about the value of being able to exchange ideas with anyone willing to listen. But once a group breaks away from that, and clamps down on what can be said, they'll destroy anything they don't like. You're seeing it now with the Righteous Monsoon. They believe they have all the answers, that there's no need to pursue other ideas — that any others are a *threat* to them. As a result, they've already banned dana kide. Put an end to your daily quest for new truths. Soon, they'll be imprisoning or killing the heretics who deny their faith, if they haven't started already. Even if we kill the lich, the Monsoon will kill everything you consider Tanarian, until your former culture is as barren as these hills."

All seven Voices watched him thoughtfully. He raced onward, letting the idea Gladdic had provoked in him unfold. "The only way to protect your heritage is to write it down. So that if you're killed, your ideas and knowledge won't die with you. So that other Tanarians don't have to come to you to find your wisdom, but can share your books as easily as they'd share a meal. Books can be burned, or wear out with time, but in most ways, they're stronger than us. They never get too tired to go on. They don't need to eat. They can be hidden away for years without harm. This is how you last in the face of strife."

Dante returned to the center of the shrine's floor and faced Ara. "As I said, the idea's a simple one, but getting it done will be as complex as any sorcery. Here's my offer. If you train us in the Odo Sein, then I will bring Narashtovik's scholars to you. They'll train your own scholars and archivists. They'll show you how to craft an alphabet. To record yourselves on parchment. To fill libraries with the story of Tanar Atain. That way, you can persist through the Monsoon without losing your past to the flames. So that even when the day comes that Tanar Atain eases into the past, its history will remain alive forever."

Five stirred, jowls creased with a frown. "Are you finished?"

Dante folded his hands at his waist. "I think we're all hoping the answer to that is a massive yes."

"Then I call for a final vote on the matter of whether to teach the hari the skills of the Odo Sein. All those in favor?"

Still meeting Dante's eyes, Five raised her right hand. Dante swung back his head in surprise. Seven was next to follow, and then the others, until only One remained with his hand down.

"Six to one," Five declared. "The Argument is concluded. The Voices have spoken. Ara, you are hereby authorized to train the four before us in the ways of the Odo Sein."

EDWARD W. ROBERTSON

8

"Are you ready?" Ara waited until each of them had nodded their affirmation. "Then you may begin your practice."

"Right." Blays shifted his knees on the mats Ara had laid out at the edge of the forest, the bleakness of the Hills spread before them. He looked down, adjusted his jabat, then took a sharp breath through his nose. "Pardon my comically deep foreigner's ignorance, but did I miss the part where we were taught what to do?"

"No, I shouldn't think so."

"That's odd. Because I'm pretty sure you just told us to get to it. But what *is* it?"

"It is the Odo Sein," Ara said.

"I've managed to pick up on that much. But aren't you going to, er, teach us?"

"How should I do that?"

Blays looked at Dante. "A little help?"

"Oh no." On the mat beside him, Dante shook his head vigorously. "I think you've got the matter well in hand."

"I'll admit I'm not much of a teacher myself. Unless you'd like to learn how to chug a mug of beer without spilling down your shirt. But it seems to me that you might try teaching us the same way you taught your other students."

EDWARD W. ROBERTSON

Ara touched her finger to her lips. "Interesting. Are you my other students?"

"If so, I must have delivered a few too many chugging lessons, because I don't remember any of it."

"If you aren't those other students, then how can I teach you the same way I taught them?"

"With terrific skill and aplomb?"

"It's critical to the understanding of the Odo Sein that the student learns its processes on their own."

"Why is that?" Dante said.

She fixed her eyes on his. "Think. Why *might* that be?"

"You're a radically isolated group of practitioners of an obscure form of sorcery. The most likely answer is because you're loony mystics who've spent too much time cut off from human contact, and have either gone insane, or adopted unique practices that are indistinguishable from insanity. But I'm guessing that's not what you're going for?"

"Why are you framing that as a joke when it's a perfectly reasonable conclusion?"

"Am I *right*?"

"You'd better hope not, hadn't you?"

Dante leaned on one palm. "If learning the processes on your own is vital to the process itself, that suggests the Odo Sein is based on private revelation."

"Or the very process you're engaged in right now," Gladdic said.

"Reasoning? Deduction? Getting mired down in silly arguments? This is sorcery, not philosophy."

"Both the nether and ether follow predictable rules. One might even say that they are logical."

"Oh yes, they're practically arithmetic. You remember that time I added two to three and it killed twenty Monsoon soldiers?"

"You're not very smart," Ara said to Blays.

He laughed. "We've only met today, and yet it's already like you've known me forever."

"A minute ago, you told me you don't know anything about the Odo Sein. But you're wrong about that. And not only a little bit wrong, but so wrong that I have a hard time believing you're not deliberately lying."

"I think I preferred it when you were calling me stupid."

"How do we figure things out?"

"Huh?"

"Yes, by grunting dully until someone takes pity on us and does it for us. That's one method. But let's pretend you're a person who respects themselves."

Blays tilted back his head, contemplating the late afternoon sky. "By beating it out of people for being too cryptic?"

"We reason," Dante said.

"How do we begin to reason?" Ara said

"Several ways. Extrapolating from personal experience. Abstracting out our thoughts. Observing repeated patterns of behavior or natural forces."

She stared at him levelly. "Let's start with personal experience. Do you suppose you can think of an experience you've had with the powers of the Odo Sein?"

"Several." He felt the blood rushing to his face. "Like the one we just had twenty minutes ago."

"Do you need me to keep holding your hand? Or are you ready to take a step on your own?"

"We don't know *how* you do what you do. But we've seen its results. Normally, the nether's like water. It flows easily, because that's its nature. But when the Odo Sein is applied to it, it becomes icy. Like it's frozen in place. And you can't move it."

"Are you sure that's true?"

"Yes. I suppose. For me. Gladdic, how did you experience it?"

"Similarly," the old priest said. "With the ether as well. Typically, one is able to bring it forth the same way that one might open the shutter in a dark farmhouse, allowing the light to spill forth upon the interior. Beneath the oppression of the Odo Sein, I can still see the light outside, but it no longer shines through the open window, and the house remains dark."

Blays shifted his weight on his knees. "Normally if I try really really hard, I can make a little piece of nether do something that may or may not resemble what I want it to do. But when your knights are around, I don't even get the chance to fail, because the nether just sits there. It reminds me of the early parts of my training, when I'd learned to see the nether, but still hadn't figured out how to touch it."

"That points us to the general mechanism," Dante said. "We all agree the shadows and the light are still there. The Odo Sein isn't taking them away. It makes them inert." He lifted his eyebrows at Ara. "Are we supposed to be able to reason this out further?"

"If I tell you no, is that because it's true? Or because your belief will make it true?" Ara smoothed her robes over her thighs. "When it comes to learning, most people cripple themselves by running to their teachers for help the instant things get hard. Yet if you train yourself right, you can reason your way forward far more often than you'd think, using far less hard knowledge and evidence than you'd believe possible. Getting good at that process is vital. If you try to rely on me for all your answers, you're never going to reach them."

Dante, Gladdic, and Blays fell into a longer conversation about how they'd encountered the Knights of Odo Sein during earlier conflicts, specifically when they'd freed Naran from the Blue Tower, and then the confused battle at the Wound. As they spoke, Volo wriggled around on her mat like a dog seeking to bed down in the grass. Dante didn't feel as though they were making much headway, but they'd at least confirmed that the experience had always been the same: one of being unable to reach the locked-down shadows.

Ara hadn't been paying much attention to them until the conversation petered out to half-hearted rehashes of things they'd already rehashed twice before. Annoyed disappointment grew on her face with each moment.

When she couldn't stand it any longer, she stood, knocking the grass from her robe. "You're slowing down like you've been hulled. Try this. Look out there, into the desert. You see it?"

Blays shielded his eyes with the blade of his hand, peering into the streaked black hills that started just feet away from where they were kneeling. "You mean the freaky-looking stuff surrounding the Spires for thirty miles on all sides? I'm having to squint pretty hard here, but I think I've got it."

"Today, it's nothing but naked rock. But that wasn't always so. A long time ago, the desert was a forest."

"Where the Yosein lived," Dante said. "Before the White Lich came. Their only way to stop him from destroying them was to destroy their homeland instead."

"A simple version of the facts, but I suppose that's the best I can hope from you. It's true, though, that people lived here. Animals, wild and domestic. Trees. The whole land thrived with life of all kinds. I want you to look out there and I want you to imagine what it was like."

"Then what?"

"Quit worrying about the then before you've even started the now. You've been whining that I wasn't giving you any instructions, and now that I'm trying to give you a lesson, you can't even do what you're told?"

"I'm sorry, Bel Ara."

"You can apologize to me by doing your damn job. Gods, teachers always make the worst students."

251

Dante inhaled and exhaled, clearing his mind in the same way he emptied it for the arrival of the ether. He stared out into the field of jagged rock. It looked unreal, like a glimpse from a hellscape inversion of the Mists. A layman might think it was impossible that such a place could once have been a bountiful forest. But Dante had seen other places time had changed just as much. Plains into mountains, forests into deserts. The only reason the earth looked eternal was because a person's span upon it was so brief.

His first thought of how this place had once looked was the pine forests surrounding Narashtovik, with their towering rough trunks and the carpets of slippery needles on the forest floor. But this was obviously wrong: it had to have been closer to the great leafy forests of Mallon, although probably different from those as well, as it often snowed in Mallon, and he wasn't sure that it ever did in Tanar Atain.

The jungles of the Plagued Islands, then? With their flowering vines, thickets of bamboo, and lush trees? He thought that might be closer, at least. Then again, the Yosein and their forests had ceased to exist something like a thousand years ago. Had the trees and flowers back then even looked like the ones that existed today? From what he'd pieced together, the people from that time period were nothing like the ones that were here now. Did everything change over time? Or were birches always birches and bears were always bears, and specific groups of people were the only ones that didn't last?

The sun tilted westward. As it went, the wind picked up, driving at them in uncertain bursts. As Dante contemplated what type of forest might have covered the area, he kept a general awareness of the nether to see if this little exercise was affecting it, but it looked perfectly normal. It wasn't long before his mind started to wander, first to what the purpose of this exercise might be, and then to ways to stop the White Lich.

He looked up and saw that Ara was gone. The winds were now gusting as if enraged, blowing in every speck of dust from the rocky wasteland, stinging their faces and eyes. A servant arrived, his face masked with an almost translucent piece of fabric stretched over a small wicker frame. He indicated they should follow him back to the Tower of Three, which Ara commanded, or stewarded, or however it was that the Voices considered themselves to govern.

The tower door was solid iron covered in symbols that resembled the runes of the Riya Lase. Dante had the immediate suspicion that there was a layer of iron within the walls as well, built to keep out or (more likely) at least slow down the lich.

The foyer's ceilings were fifteen feet high, the semicircular space filled with the mats, low tables, and glasswork typical of most of the nicer residences and establishments elsewhere in the country. Ara had been speaking with another servant.

Seeing them, she motioned the servant to depart. "Did any revelations come to you from out of the desert?"

"That depends," Blays said. "Does two tons of dust count as a revelation?"

Gladdic's lower eyelids were sagging with exhaustion. "How long might it take us before we are able to command the power of the Odo Sein?"

"You're asking me to guess when you, a person I'd never met before today, is going to be able to learn a skill you might not ever learn?"

"If you are able, yes."

"I'm not. It takes as long as it takes."

"But will it be soon enough to stand against the Eiden Rane before it's too late?"

"How should I know?" She jerked her thumb at the staircase. "If these are the best questions you've got, we're done here. Go get some dinner. Some sleep. Whatever it takes to make you

EDWARD W. ROBERTSON

worth teaching."

After that rather demoralizing speech, they were led upstairs to simple stone chambers furnished with rugs and tapestries, where they were fed bread—having not eaten any since entering Aris Osis, Dante hadn't realized how much he'd missed it—stewed beans in a thick, salty sauce, and fruit tarts that tasted both sweet and sour.

The staff removed their dishes as soon as they were finished. One remained to show them about their rooms, finishing at the doorway, where he indicated a chain hanging from a hole in the wall.

"The room should not be left. If assistance is required, pull this chain."

Blays gave an experimental tug of the small brass links. "What's it do?"

"A bell is rung. A servant is summoned."

"A fellow is thanked for the explanation."

The servant gave him a blank look and left. Their beds were the typical wicker frames that could be secured against the wall by day. Dante rolled onto his thin mattress and was immediately so weary that he wasn't sure he could get up again.

Blays blew out the candle—which was neither tallow or beeswax, and smelled like a variety of stout, shiny plant they'd seen here and there in the swamps—and shuffled across the dark room to his bed.

"We're sure this isn't a prank of some kind?" Blays climbed onto his mattress. "The other Odo Sein had to go through this as well?"

"Why don't we ask them and find out?" Dante said. "Oh wait, there aren't any left, which is exactly why we have to go through this in the first place."

Dante typically woke up a few times during the night, but on that occasion, he didn't stir until a servant swung open the door

254

just before the sun broke from the horizon. Dante had slept for a good ten hours, but felt almost drunkenly groggy, and his legs and back were so sore from the long march the day before that he was obliged to soothe his aches with nether on his way to the privy.

Breakfast was flatbread stuffed with potatoes and beans. There were few spices to speak of, just a bit of salt and herbs. It was immensely different from the heavily spiced fish, root mash, bananas, and rice they ate in the swamps. Did the people of the Spires cling so fiercely to the idea of Tanarian culture because they understood that they weren't truly a part of it?

After eating, Ara arrived to lead them back to the boundary between the forest of the Spires and the bleakness of the Hell-Painted Hills, where she instructed them to think about the lost forest once more. Within an hour, everyone but Gladdic was fidgeting. A little after that, Blays began to snore.

Ara cursed and rolled her eyes. She gave Blays a shove. "Wake up, you idiot. If you want to sleep the day away, you can do that back in the swamps."

Blays rubbed his eyes. "I wasn't doing a very good job imagining the old place by myself. I thought dreaming about it might help."

"Are you being serious?"

"That depends. Will believing in what I said get me out of trouble?"

She got up and walked back to the seven towers.

"Well done," Dante said. "Next time, try killing yourself. You can tell her that you thought you could imagine the forest better from within the Mists."

Blays got up, planting his palms on the small of his back and stretching backwards. "If I have to spend one more minute imagining a bunch of stupid trees that died a thousand years ago, I *will* kill myself. What are we even doing? How is this going to teach us to nullify sorcery?"

"I don't know. But given that Ara is one of the only seven people authorized to teach the Odo Sein, I'm going to go out on a limb and assume she knows what she's doing."

"I'd rather endure the training at Pocket Cove again."

"Didn't they try to drown you? Make you die of exposure?"

"Exactly."

Ara didn't come back until after they'd been brought their lunch, another meal of stuffed flatbread. She directed them to continue envisioning the forest. They obeyed dutifully.

"I imagine you're growing so bored you're thinking about killing yourself," she said after another hour. "First of all, that would be stupid. The smart play would be to kill *me*. Second, since repeated failure is toxic to the will to go on, and you don't seem to be able to do anything but fail, let's try a new course. Take up your foul magics."

Dante reached out to the nether. Blays made a clumsy swipe at it while Gladdic summoned a perfect pattern of light. Without so much as a twitch, Ara locked the two talents in place. Dante gave a peremptory tug at the shadows.

Ara lifted her hand, palm up. "See that?"

"The part where you made three extremely dangerous people look like sad children?" Dante said. "Yes, I might have noticed."

"But did you *watch* it?"

"I didn't know that it was coming."

"Do you take that same mindset to a sword fight? Or when you're dueling one of the other warlocks?"

"Of course not. That's a fight for my life."

Ara laughed mockingly. "You're working to combat the Eiden Rane, and you don't think it's a fight for your survival? Your life is on the line every second of your training. And so is mine. And so is the life of everyone in this country. When you're with me, you watch and you listen. Always. Do you understand?"

Dante nodded, keeping any bristle out of his voice. "What was I supposed to see?"

"Watch again. And tell me."

She ordered them to draw on their abilities again. Just as before, she slammed down on them, sealing the ether and the nether as firmly as the world's own skin.

Dante glanced at Gladdic and Blays. They shrugged and shook their heads. Ara repeated the process a third time, then a fourth and a fifth.

She scratched her armpit. "See anything yet?"

"You're locking it down," Dante said. "If there's more to be seen, I'm missing it."

"Then maybe you should look harder. Or would you rather go back to imagining the forest?"

"Please no." Blays covered his heart with one hand, extending the other for mercy. "At least have us imagine a hot springs. Somewhere people might like to bathe. I guarantee you I'll be able to describe it to you in perfect detail."

Ara snorted, but seemed at least half amused. "We'll try a few more. But like I said, too much failure in too little time turns bold men into timid children."

Yet Dante got nothing out of the next few attempts, either. Ara had them contemplate the Hills some more while she thought — or pretended that she was thinking while she was actually punishing them for their stupidity — then snapped her fingers.

"I'm stopping you from accessing your unholy magics," she said. "But there are ways for you to slip past me. You're going to try."

Dante bit his lip.

If Blays had similar thoughts of discretion, he promptly ignored them. "I suppose it's too much to ask *how* we might do that?"

Ara didn't bother to respond. She motioned for them to summon their powers. They complied and she once more froze the light and shadows in place. Dante bull-rushed toward the nether, meaning to batter right through whatever she was doing, but it was like running full tilt into a wall. Sensing that was a dead end, he retreated, whispering to the nether with all the subtlety he could summon.

He thought he sensed a quiver. But as soon as he turned toward it, it went as still as the rest of it. No amount of wheedling could get it to twitch again. Ara gave no sign she'd seen anything move at all.

Blays begged off five minutes later, his powers exhausted. Gladdic and Dante persisted for a good while longer, getting to a whole lot of nowhere. With the day running short, Ara stopped their practice, told them to imagine the forest, and walked away.

When dusk fell, the servant arrived to bring them to dinner. Blays clapped his hands. "At last, something I'm good at."

Dante barely tasted his food, lost in contemplation of what Ara had attempted to show them so far. Was the business about imagining the lost forest merely a thought exercise to push them into the correct mindset to be able to see whatever it was that Ara was attempting to show them? Or was it an important exercise in its own right?

Furthermore, if she was serious that there was still a way to reach the nether when the Odo Sein was opposing you, then wasn't it possible that, even if they learned the skill themselves, the White Lich would still be able to muster his sorcery against them?

He didn't say anything of this latter doubt. Yet he would have bet everything he owned that Gladdic had already arrived at the same question.

The third day followed the same schedule as the second. Dante shouldered on the best he could. Volo couldn't access either the nether or ether and spent nearly the entire day gazing out into the fiery wastes. Blays managed the occasional joke or jocular complaint. While Gladdic smirked more and more as the day wore on, Dante thought it had little to do with Blays' efforts, and more to do with the old man's growing conviction that they were doomed to fail, squandering their final days on nonsensical lessons while the White Lich continued his inexorable advance from the depths of the swamps.

It was both cruel and merciful that every day had to end eventually. That day was no exception. As they parted ways, Ara didn't even bother to insult them. She just shook her head and headed to her tower.

If anyone said a word at dinner, Dante didn't hear it. They retired to their quarters.

Blays tossed a mat against the wall and sat on it with a heavy thump. "Here's an unpleasant question. How long do we stick around here getting nowhere until we cut our losses and move on?"

Dante unfolded his bed from its ties. "To what? Admitting we were wrong and asking the lich for jobs in his new empire?"

"I *told* you it was going to be unpleasant."

"I wonder if we aren't meant to learn a thing," Gladdic said. "Perhaps the Odo Sein are toying with us. Teaching us nonsense until we grow so frustrated we leave of our own accord."

Dante flicked a beetle from his sheet. "Why would they do that?"

"To prevent us from reaching the inconvenient conclusion that we can never learn their skill in time, and that the only way to confront our foe is to bend the Odo Sein to our will by force, and make them come with us after all."

"I think you're mistaking this for the sort of thing that *you* would do."

But now that Gladdic had planted the thought in him, Dante

couldn't evict it from his mind. It was a long time after the candles were out before he fell asleep.

Their fourth day at the Silent Spires opened to an unbroken sheet of wind-hustled clouds. It was drizzling and the grass was wet, but Ara took them out to the boundary anyway.

"The forest is still out there," she declared. "Find it, and you'll be on your way."

Dante sighed in a way that could have been mistaken for meditative breathing and closed his eyes. He smelled the rain on the leaves. Somehow it hadn't occurred to him before, but there were still some trees in the Hell-Painted Hills, weren't there? Right there in the Silent Spires. He opened his eyes and swiveled his head to gaze at them. Once he'd committed them to memory, he closed his eyes again and used them as his model for how he imagined the old forest must have looked.

Whenever his attention wandered, he nudged it back to the exercise. Half an hour into it, as he was imagining himself walking through the barren hills with the woods sprouting up around him as he went, he opened his eyes. They didn't *have* to learn the Odo Sein themselves, did they? Not if they could find a way for the Voices to be able to leave the sanctuary of the Spires without dropping dead.

Ara walked up behind him. "What is it? What do you see?"

Dante snapped his eyes shut. "Tall trees. Like these ones here."

"That's it?"

"There are animals, too. Squirrels. Things of that nature."

"Right," she said. "Keep looking."

He did, but was beyond relieved when she finally called a halt to their activity, if you could call it that.

Blays stood, walking in small circles. "I don't think I could spend more time thinking about forests if I *was* one."

Gladdic stretched out his spindly legs, rubbing his right hip with his left hand. "Bel Ara, I can no longer hold my tongue. I see no sign that we're making progress toward our goal. Am I wrong?"

"Probably not," she said.

"Then why not offer us specific guidance? Why not teach us what we're looking for and how we might find it?"

"Did you not listen the first time I told you? Is that why you're having such trouble with this? If we wanted to smother you, we'd use our hands, not our dogma. Find your own way or give up trying."

Dante got to his feet. "It's hard to find your way when you don't even know what your destination is. At least give us some direction."

Ara's face radiated scorn. "What do you think these exercises are? A joke? A merciful way to let you spend your last days dreaming about peaceful woods before the Eiden Rane comes to stomp the life from your body? I'm giving you what you need to learn. If you're not getting it, blame yourself."

"Why let us wander in circles when you know a threat like that is on its way?"

"You want me to act as an institution? To hand down my precious knowledge from on high? To hell with that. Institutions only stray further and further from the truth they once held, lost in the swamps of their own dogma, drawn astray by charlatans and profiteers. The only way to remain pure is to get every new student to reconfirm the truth for themselves."

"That's not always true. I run one of the largest institutions in the north. It's been around for centuries, and we're still dedicated to the pursuit of what's true."

"Are you, priest of the eleven-and-one gods?"

Dante folded his arms. "Why do you keep calling me that?"

"Because I think it's hilarious that you northerners need an entire army of gods just to explain to you that some things are right and others are wrong. Tell me, defender of dogma, have you never found anything in your endless scriptures that rang false? That didn't mesh with what your own eyes were showing you?"

"Sometimes, yes. But—"

"Shut your mouth. You know I'm right but will defend your institution to the death because that's what they do to you. They enslave you. Blind you. Twist you from supporting truth to supporting *them*. We make you find knowledge for yourself. Does that make it tougher for you? Too fucking bad. Because in doing so, you're constantly bringing us new wisdom, and exposing the falsehoods within our beliefs."

"Don't move too quickly now." Blays held out a warding hand to Dante. "I'm afraid she's just disemboweled you."

Ara switched to the second exercise, flipping on and off the influence of the Odo Sein while the others watched. When she decided she'd punished them with this for long enough, she moved on to clamping down on their powers while they attempted to sneak, wriggle, or wrest themselves free.

Volo swung her mat to face the fiery hills. Dante felt bad for her: she couldn't participate in anything involving sorcery, meaning she likely wasn't going to have much at all to do once they got into the swing of things. She couldn't make it back through the Hills without them, either. Even if she tried, she had nowhere to go; she'd broken away from the rebellion she'd been a part of, a move that must have cost her most of her friends. As far as he knew, she had no family—although he felt mildly guilty for not being sure.

A pebble struck him in the face. He flinched, much too late. Ara bounced another pebble in her right hand. He gave a nod of apology. She told them to reach for their sorcery and he did so.

A servant was making his way from the towers to bring them their midday meal. Before he got to them, Volo shot to her feet.

She scrabbled away from the border so hard that she fell on her rear in the grass. Face contorted with panic, she continued to kick herself away from the Hills.

Ara swept herself to her feet, seeming to close on the girl in a single stride. "What did you see?"

Volo tipped her face toward Ara, staring up at her with spooked eyes. "It. I saw it."

"Speak like we're not privy to every one of your thoughts."

"The forest. The people. They were right there. They were there and it was like I wasn't me anymore and—"

Ara slapped her across the face. "Do you think it's useful to babble like you've been kicked in the head? Slow down, and calm down, and think through what you just saw. Quickly now, before you lose it."

Anger flashed across Volo's face, but it was gone as fast as it had appeared. Absently, she rubbed her cheek, gazing into the wasteland. "I was sitting here. And I was thinking about how it must have looked back then. And how it would look if it came back. And then it was like..."

She rolled her hand through the air. "I saw these flashes out on the rocks. Bits of gold. And then everything lurched and I was still looking out at the hills except they were covered in trees. People were there, too, singing to each other as they took water from a stream. Only I didn't recognize any of the words. The people didn't look right, either. They looked hari."

"What else did you imagine?"

"That's just it, Bel Ara. I don't think I was imagining anything. It was like I was *there*!"

"Then what?"

"One of the men at the stream looked at me. He looked so surprised, I know that he could see me. That's when the vision popped. Just like a soap bubble. And I was sitting on my mat again. It was like falling asleep in one place and waking up in another. That's why I yelled out."

"You sound sheepish. Don't be. It's always startling to be given a Glimpse."

Dante rubbed the back of his neck. "A glimpse of what?"

"That depends," Ara said. "In this case, I'd say it was the past."

"The past? As in the actual past?"

"Ask better questions or don't ask them at all."

"How could she have seen the past? It's gone. It's *past*. That's what it does."

Wind gusted from the hills. Ara stepped beneath the cover of a tree, casting her face into shadow. "You're a warlock. By waving your hand, you kill people from across a field. With a nod of your head, you heal lethal wounds. You crossed the Hell-Painted Hills, which no one who wasn't Odo Sein has ever done, and even the Eiden Rane can't yet do. And you find this so unbelievable?"

"Yes?"

"Then you're welcome to keep going along as you have been. Or you could find out what the girl did that you couldn't."

"Let us accept that this is real," Gladdic said. "What, then, is a Glimpse?"

Ara smiled. "Why, it's a function of the Odo Sein, old man."

"You say she saw into the past. How? Was she granted a vision? Does memory exist independent of the body, and she caught a passing scrap of it? And what does this have to do with the ability to neutralize sorcery?"

"Good questions. Going forward, you'll want to try to answer them."

Blays motioned to Volo. "This was the first time you've seen anything like this, right? You've been at this for days. Were you doing anything different this time?"

Volo tucked her chin, thinking. "Before, I was just thinking about trees and things. As if I was sitting there watching the leaves blow in the wind. But this morning, I started thinking about how I've never been in a forest like this, have I? I'm a swamp rat. That's all I've seen. So *first*, I had to think about what it would look like for everything that dies to fall on the ground and just stay there and not get swept away like it does in the swamp. And that got me thinking, things can just run around on the forest floor, can't they? They aren't confined to some little island or routes through the tree branches.

"Then I started to wonder what it must be like to not be a swamp rat, but to be a ground rat. So that's what I imagined myself as: just a little rat, running through the grass, trying to find seeds, hiding when I saw an owl or a taka ito. And how the ground must be dense with fallen leaves, and what that must smell like, and what lives in the leaves. And then I got sad, because it had all died when the lich came. All those trees. All those birds. Even the rats.

"But I don't like being sad. So I started imagining something else: how some day, the poison will be gone from this place. The dirt will build up in the valleys. Seeds will blow in from the fringes and take root in the new soil. Flowers will grow and bees and flies will come to them, and then lizards will come to eat the bugs, and birds will come to eat the bugs and the lizards, and all of this stuff will be crapping and dying and making more dirt.

"Until one day, there's enough dirt for a tree to grow. And become tall, and drop its seeds, and form a grove, who drop *their* seeds, and become a forest.

"And then I, the little rat, come back to the woods that I thought were gone forever."

Volo fell silent, blushing like she'd accidentally flipped the hem of her jabat over her head.

"That's when this Glimpse came?" Blays gestured in a circle. "While you were out ratting it up?"

"I felt weird a few times before that, but I didn't know what it was. It was like it wanted to show up but it wasn't quite ready yet."

Dante raised an eyebrow at Ara. "She's taken a step forward, hasn't she? Maybe a big one. Yet why do I have the impression that you're not going to tell us anything about what this means?"

Ara shrugged. "Because you're finally starting to learn."

"All right, but what in the world does seeing a moment from the past have to do with locking the nether in place?"

"Nothing. There's no direct connection. At least not one that we've ever thought of. I'll tell you that much to spare you from getting lost in an eel warren pursuing answers that aren't there. Now get back to work."

She resumed holding the shadows down while the three of them attempted to break free, but Dante could barely focus. As impossible as it would have been for him to believe a few minutes earlier, he was ragingly impatient to kneel down on his mat and think very hard about old forests.

For reasons that were probably sadistic, Ara kept them at their current practice for another half an hour before sending them back to their mats. At last, Dante closed his eyes. What had Volo been doing that he hadn't? Was it the specificity of her vision? That she'd placed herself as an active participant in the scene rather than a passive observer? Or was it the highly dynamic passing of time she'd employed?

The simplest test would be to try to mimic exactly what she'd done and see if he got the same results. Dante pictured himself as a humble rat, not much different than the countless rodents he'd slain to use as scouts. He went about his ratly duties, foraging for fruits and seeds, hiding from things with bigger teeth and claws, building a cozy nest.

Initially he got so lost in the vision that he forgot what he was doing it for. With this realization, he got excited—it seemed like the sort of thing that would trigger a revelation—but nothing seemed out of the ordinary. He certainly hadn't been struck with a Glimpse.

He moved on to visualizing the destruction of the forest, the current state of the Hills, and the gradual return of plants and life to the wasteland. Nothing came of his efforts except annoyance at Volo for being the first to achieve a breakthrough while the three trained nether-wielders were still sitting around like morons.

They finished the day without any further excitement. At dinner, Dante drilled Volo over everything that had led up to her Glimpse, but her story was the same as before.

He woke in the morning with the sense that he'd been dreaming. An idea shook loose from the tattered and fading hints of the dream: trying to duplicate Volo's work was foolish. Time and time again, Ara had stressed the vitalness of self-discovery. Blazing your own trail.

That morning, as they kneeled on their mats to face the emptiness of the Hell-Painted Hills, Dante let his mind rest empty. Once he felt ready, he called up the same basic forest he'd been imagining for the last several days, a blend of the growth you could see down in the swamps mixed in with the more temperate forests of Mallon.

Previously, he'd drifted through these woods like a speck of matter, with no defined features of his own; he hadn't understood that, as Volo had done, it was fine to take a more active role in the forest. This time, he imagined himself there. He found a game trail and followed it to a shallow stream with a pebbly bottom. He was poking around the banks for fish and aquatic insects when he heard a woman scream.

He blinked, receding from the vision. No one else had noticed, meaning the scream had to have been in his imagination, there in the lost forest. He'd never thought about people being there before, but of course they'd existed, the Yosein and whatever other groups whose names had been lost to time. Before he could start thinking too hard, he imagined himself racing toward the scream. Fighting past branches and thorns, he reached for the nether.

He scrambled up a short incline. Ahead, men with spears and axes held a ragged line against a rush of grub-white attackers. The Blighted outnumbered the humans five times over. Behind the line of spearmen, women and children huddled together, the women bearing sticks or bone knives.

The Blighted crashed into the line of humans, impaling themselves on the bronze spears. Despite their wounds, the undead continued to push onwards, raking at the men and bowing the middle of the line to the point of collapse.

Dante spread his hands wide, sending a storm of nether over the heads of the humans and crashing into the Blighted. They fell with looks of angry betrayal. The survivors charged into the gap opened by the deaths, only to be hammered down by a second wave of shadows.

The humans now stood alone. Several stared at Dante in shock. A beam of sunlight broke through the branches, golden and dazzling, half blinding him. The people fell to their knees in worship.

He felt as though he was tipping forward. Into something unknown and not entirely safe. He pulled back, yanked out of the vision, which had felt half dreamlike, unfolding on its own, and half artificial, a story he'd been telling himself. He felt as though he'd been very close to something—maybe not a Glimpse, but *something* – but as much as he tried to slip back into that liminal space, he could no more do that than he could wake from a dream, get up for a glass of water, then lie back down and resume the dream where he'd left off.

He closed his eyes and started a new vision. The forest was there, and so was he, and—

"That's more than enough." Ara slapped her hand against her thigh. "It's a good thing you can't see how stupid you look while you're dreaming away, or else I'd have to take away your swords to stop you from blinding yourselves."

Blays got to his feet, bending down to stretch his hamstrings. "If I carved on myself every time I was made to look foolish, you'd currently be talking to a three-foot stack of roast beef."

"Do you people really eat those things?"

"What? Stacks?"

"Cows. Lumbering piles of festering meat."

"You think eating cows is gross? Then I won't even tell you about pigs."

Ara switched them over to the practice Dante had come to think of as the Freeze. Before, he hadn't been certain whether imagining the forest (a process he'd mentally labeled, with great creativity, as "Forest") was no more than a mind preparation technique.

Yet after Volo's Glimpse, he was now certain that it was actually a skill-honing exercise. Further yet, that it was clearly related, if indirectly, to what Ara was trying to teach them with the other techniques. What, then, were the central lessons of Forest? To be detailed and reasoned? And to pair this with the perhaps contradictory ability to be unbound, to let your thoughts run free and take you where they may?

This seemed to have almost no relevance to Freeze, which involved watching passively as Ara took the nether and the ether and locked it in place. Either it was a comically poor exercise, or he was a comically poor student, because he still couldn't see *how* Ara was stopping the magics, only that she *was*.

So far, he'd worked out what he thought were three reasonably good theories about the underlying premise. The most obvious was that Ara was freezing the light and shadows in place such that they couldn't be moved no matter how hard you tried.

Alternately, that she was somehow tricking the two powers into thinking they weren't being summoned at all, deafening them to the sorcerers' calls. And lastly, that the Odo Sein had discovered a way to satisfy the nether and ether such that they didn't *need* to answer the call.

Across from him, Ara locked the powers in place. The nether was still stirring, but it was heavily subdued. If it were a creature, he'd have thought it was falling asleep. She left it in this state for a minute, then withdrew. The nether awoke, stirring like grass in the wind.

Drawing on the lesson of the Forest, Dante untethered his thoughts, letting them float wherever they wanted to go. Ara let another minute pass, then froze the shadows again. It made no sense: if she was manipulating the nether, or setting the two forces in opposition to each other such that neither would budge, he should be able to see the work she was doing with the shadows to produce this result.

She unlocked them once more, letting them pulsate and sway. Acting on impulse, Dante threw himself into the nether, drinking it down, breathing it in, just as he'd let himself get lost in the half-dream of the Forest.

Ara came for the nether again. Dante popped from the shadows like a seed shooting from a squeezed lemon. A layer of buttery light flashed between himself and the nether.

Seated on his mat, he looked up. Ara was gazing at him. Not with her usual impatience and irritation, but thoughtfully.

Each time she released her hold on the nether, Dante immersed himself in it anew. He didn't act further. Not yet. Before he'd learned anything further, Ara called a halt to Freeze and turned them to the third practice of trying to wield the light and shadows despite her efforts, which Dante had named the Struggle.

Earlier, he'd focused his efforts on holding tight to the nether as she pulled it from them. This time, he plunged into it. During the Freeze, he'd learned to feel her presence as she approached. As Ara arrived, claiming the nether, Dante braced himself, tangling the shadows within himself with those around him. Rather than being squeezed out with a sudden pop, he was slowly pulled from it, like a man drawing a sledge full of firewood up a snowy slope.

The next time, he not only entwined himself in the nether, but he sent it whirling about himself like hailstones caught in a storm. A handful of motes of light chased after the madly weaving shadows. The whits of nether dropped like dead bees to the ground, stricken from his control, but the effort took Ara twice as long as it ever had before.

She dropped her hold over the dark and the light. Normally, Dante had taken this time to reflect on what he'd just tried and why it might have failed, but he found himself in a space where his ideas were assembling themselves without conscious work on his part.

As Ara loomed forward to quash the nether, Dante drew on his own trace, extending it into many tendrils which he enmeshed with the nether around him. He sprayed this mixed nether out into a whirlwind of shadows. Ara's power fell on them like the boom of a closing door, yet the nether, tied to Dante's trace, which even the Odo Sein couldn't lock down, stood full against her assault, its motes dropping by twos and threes rather than in whole flocks.

Across from him, Ara narrowed her eyes. Her skill swelled larger yet, battering against the maelstrom of nether. Pinpricks of light flickered from within the stormcloud. Rather than the stark silver-white of starlight, their color was the warm yellow glow of a fire.

Dante's command of the surviving fragments quivered, then shook, then at last fell apart. The nether tumbled to the ground and lay there as if resting. Ara pulled back her power. Dante's heart was beating like it might never slow down, but his mind was clear.

He bit his lip until he tasted blood. Shadows rose around him like strangers gathering just beyond the light of a campfire. He took up his trace again; part of it had been temporarily spent, but enough remained. He threaded it into the exterior nether once more. As Ara mustered the Odo Sein, Dante reached into the nether within her body. He expected to see it arranging itself against him, but it seemed utterly uninterested in events around it.

He whipped some of his shadows into an erratic frenzy while splitting others into small pieces and burrowing them into the earth like black worms. Ara rumbled toward them. Next to him, Blays' nether crumbled like he wasn't even trying. Gladdic's wavered but was already starting to collapse on the edges. Dante's black worms held fast to their tunnels while his storming blots swerved and dodged. Beneath Ara's assault, the first of them dropped to the ground, dispersing into the soil.

A thought sprung fully-formed to Dante's mind. He delved back into the nether in Ara's blood, withdrawing some and leaving the rest, spinning a connection between himself and her that might be comparable to a very crude loon or an excessively weak version of the link he formed between himself and a reanimated rat. Completely uncertain what it would do, or even whether it would do anything at all, he opened the connection.

The air around him blazed with tiny golden fires, so many and so bright that Dante threw his hands up over his head, rocking back.

The blots of fire whirled around him like little gobs of liquid sunlight. A few dozen harried Gladdic, with a handful of stragglers remaining around Blays, but the majority were looping around him, a swarm of miniature golden bees.

He dropped the connection between himself and Ara. The gold motes blinked away, all except for the occasional minute wink that might have been no more than a passing reflection of sunlight. More and more of Dante's shadows withered and dissolved under Ara's onslaught.

He tried to draw the nether out from her again, but the weight of the Odo Sein was far too heavy for him to push back. He watched as his shadows were dispersed. And he smiled.

When all was still, Ara turned to him, dark eyebrows lifted at the outer corners. "What exactly are you trying to do?"

"I didn't try. I did." Dante found that he was shaking. He took a long breath, but it did nothing to help. There was nothing to do but plow on. "You aren't turning the nether against us to wield the Odo Sein. You aren't using the ether, either."

Speaking the words made him feel as though the world had fallen away from beneath his feet. "You're using a third power. Something none of us has ever seen before."

EDWARD W. ROBERTSON

9

They all stared at each other. Ara lifted the weight of the Odo Sein from their shoulders. Dante plucked a thread of nether from her and bound it to himself. A few of the golden flecks spangled the air, but nearly all of them had already vanished.

Gladdic beetled his brows. "What do you mean that she wields a third power?"

Dante motioned to the air, although he doubted that any of them could see the specks there. "I mean that there's the nether. There's the ether. And there's whatever the hell the Odo Sein use."

"That is impossible. That's—"

"Heresy?"

"People in *your* country would be hanged unto death for heresy like this. Yet heresy was not the word on my mind."

"Then what?"

"I'm not certain, as I was having a difficult time locating one that matched the depth of my contempt for your intelligence."

Ara laughed, brushing a strand of hair from her eyes. "By rights, I should let you two argue amongst yourselves to reach a conclusion on your own. But given the exceptional times we live in, I'm going to relax our rules. Dante is right. The Odo Sein doesn't come from ether or nether. It is a third power."

Gladdic scowled at her. "That cannot be possible. You must be wielding the abilities of the sorcerers the Odo Sein professes to hate, while disguising them under a different name in order to make it palatable to yourselves."

"You've gone senile, old man. If the truth scares you, you're free to leave."

"I have studied the ways of sorcery for longer than most people live. I have traveled as widely as a sea captain and read more volumes than a monastery. And I have never heard of any suggestion of a 'third power.'"

"We like words here, as you can tell. We spend them like they're worthless. But sometimes, words aren't enough."

Ara gazed into nothing. A point of light winked in the air, no more significant than a speck of dust caught in a beam of light. Then again, there were no beams of sunlight there in the shade of the trees. She lifted her finger, tracing a cryptic symbol before her.

The air lit up with a stream of golden light. It flowed more smoothly and cohesively than nether, but didn't shape itself into crisp lines and geometric patterns like ether was prone to do. No one could look away from it, the warm light shining from their faces.

Gladdic batted at the air. "That proves nothing. I can make the ether any color I please."

Ara rolled her eyes. "Then quit looking at its *color* and look at what it *is*."

The old man took a hesitant step toward the river of gold, craning his head forward. He whispered under his breath, then fell silent. He stepped back, eyes darting back and forth.

"You know how to use both the nether and the ether," Dante said. "So go ahead. Try to wield *that*."

"I already tried." Gladdic's words caught in his throat. "I could not."

Ara gave a small shrug, dismissing the golden band. "Too bad. Would have made my job a hell of a lot easier." She tossed her head at Dante. "Well done, incidentally. You're a quick learner."

"You think that was fast? We've been at this for days."

"Most trainees take months. I had one dullard who took a year and a half to see it."

"Someone sat here imagining forests for eighteen months?" Blays said. "When they killed themselves, did you bury the body? Or were you so ashamed of what you'd done that you threw it down a ravine?"

"Is it that hard to believe it would take so much effort?" Ara said. "Most normal people aren't filthy cheating warlocks."

Blays started to chuckle, then broke into full-on laughter, pressing his hands to his face. "The two of you run entire religions dedicated to proving which power is superior, nether or ether. And neither of you had so much as a clue that there was a *third* power. Doesn't that make the last thousand years a little embarrassing!"

"We are no different from any other priest," Gladdic said. "We are all liars, for none will admit to ourselves that we don't possess the full wisdom of the gods, or else we would have no authority to demand tribute from the peasants."

Dante peered into the air, searching for hints of the golden light. "What do you call this third substance?"

"That's pretty obvious," Blays said. "It's gold, right? So we should call it gether."

"We should absolutely not do that."

"You're right. Nethold is much better."

"We already have a word for it." Ara seated herself on her mat, smoothing her robes over her legs. "But that word's for us. You hari trash should come up with your own."

"I'm still voting for gether," Blays said.

"Hang on." Dante eyed Ara. "The Voices were so concerned about the loss of Tanarian culture that you almost voted to kill us rather than see it diluted. We should use your word for it."

She sucked her lower lip between her teeth. "Odo Sein. The Golden Stream."

"Funny." Blays stroked his chin. "I once knew a fellow named that very thing. But his title referred to his liking to get prostitutes to stand over him and—"

Dante punched him in the arm. "The Golden Stream it is."

"That's its formal name," Ara said. "Among ourselves, we usually just refer to it as the stream."

"All right, the stream. And what exactly can it be used for?"

"Much less than ether or nether. But it has its uses. You'll learn them in time. Or not, because you are stupid."

"Do you insult people so often that you don't even know you're doing it? If so, I'd love to bring you to the Gaskan court some time."

"And maybe I would go, if I could. Or if I knew or cared what Gask was." Ara grew serious. "You shouldn't be worried about what you can do with the stream. You're a long way from being able to wield it. You should be concerned with helping your friends to see it. You'll all progress much faster if you can argue about it together rather than relying on your insight alone."

"A few days ago, I would have complained that as the teacher, *you* should be the one to take the lead on that, but I know you'll just tell me to think it through. All right, then. At first, I tried to copy what Volo imagined. This got me precisely nowhere. But when I got lost in a world that was just as deep as hers, but was uniquely my own, *that's* when I first saw the gold in the air, although I didn't know it at the time. Then when Ara was wielding the Odo Sein, I kept seeing little flashes of it. But I wasn't sure what I was seeing until I used the nether to see what *she* was seeing."

Gladdic tipped back his head. "How did you accomplish that?"

"By drawing on the shadows within her and connecting myself to them."

The priest grunted. "Ingenious."

"From what I saw, the stream comes from inspiration. Maybe it *is* inspiration. Am I right?"

Ara crossed her arms. "How would I know?"

"Because you're the only one of us that knew about it until ten minutes ago! Because you *do* know!"

"I know what I think is true," she said calmly. "But I might be wrong. If it *is* inspiration, the following of your own path to sudden knowledge, then won't following your own path to understanding it only make you a stronger wielder of it?"

"That's an annoyingly tight logical loop." Dante seated himself across from her. The grass smelled good, especially after so long spent in the half-stagnant waters of the swamps. "Assuming the stream is real, and not a misunderstanding—or a bizarre stunt on your part—why doesn't anyone else know about it? If it comes from inspiration or thinking or what have you, why aren't other people seeing it all the time?"

"Who says they aren't? Who says *you* haven't seen it before? How has it appeared to you so far?"

"The first was in my vision. It was like a sunbeam, only more buttery and glittery than normal. After that, it showed up as flecks of golden light."

"Which might have been sunlight. Or the little spots you see in your eyes all the time. What does the nether look like? Shadows?"

"More or less."

"And if nobody knew what the nether was, and someone caught a glimpse of it, just a little shadow, would they instantly jump to the conclusion that it was magic?"

"Probably not."

"Not *probably* not. Absolutely not. Because you'd be crazy to think that. The same reason applies to the stream." Ara motioned to the grove and the bleakness beyond. "Besides, this place makes it easier to perceive. There's more than one reason we founded the Spires here."

Dante leaned forward, frowning. "This might sound like a silly question, but if knowledge of the stream is so obscure, how do you people even know about it?"

"Because we invented it."

"You can't *invent* sorcery! That's like claiming you invented air."

"Well, we did. Where do you think your own powers arose from?"

"The gods."

"So it was invented — by your gods. Who, by the way, are not the same gods they have on the other side of the world, but who also certainly know about your ether and nether despite their lack of faith in the one true way." Her point was outrageous, but Ara looked pretty satisfied with it. "You get these beliefs from your holy books, don't you? Books so big and thick they could choke a swamp dragon. And what are they filled with? Old, dead ideas. That's why we're not so fond of books."

"But you agreed that you wanted — "

"Oh, shut up. Our hand has been forced into needing to use them for now, but if we battle off the White Lich and outlast the Monsoon, maybe we'll destroy them all again. My point is that books stop you from thinking the deeper questions. You should be asking yourself this: how long has this world been here? How long have we been in it?"

"Over a thousand years, at the very least," Dante said. "I've read histories that run back nearly two thousand years. *The Cycle of Arawn* is vague on the matter, but two thousand years or so fits with its teachings as well."

"Well, that feels like a very long time, doesn't it. Two thousand years. But what if it's much longer? What if we've lost the eight thousand—or eight hundred thousand—years of history that came before the tiny sliver we can still remember? In so much time, how many other figures as powerful as the White Lich might have arisen, to eventually be cast down in wars so great their memory echoes down in time even as the details are lost? Would they all have been evil? How many of them were neutral or even benevolent figures, and rather than ravaging humanity as the lich would, they helped it grow, until their eventual ascension into other realms? What if the echoes of these titans rang down through history until they become the names of your gods?"

Dante was stunned. Gladdic looked like he didn't know whether to laugh or strike her.

Blays whistled. "Now *that's* heresy!"

"With that much time to work with," Ara said, "it's not hard to imagine that there was once a mortal individual who was the first to discover the nether. Just like we did with the stream."

Dante swore. "At least I finally have proof that the gods are merciful, since they're allowing you to go on speaking rather than converting you into a pile of ash in a smoking crater. This line of talk obviously isn't going to go anywhere pleasant, so answer me this: if you invented the Golden Stream, how'd you do it? What's the story of the Odo Sein?"

Ara shook her head. "Can't say."

"Oh, come on. You're not about to tell me to just think it through. That might work on a logical problem, but it's not possible to reason your way through history."

"I'll take a whack at it," Blays said. "Once upon a time, the Odo Sein got exceedingly pissed off at a group of not-Odo Sein, and so great was their anger that they were inspired to invent a totally new way of beating the shit out of their foes. Am I close?"

Ara's cheek twitched, but there was no holding back her smile. "And Dante thought there was no way to think your way to history. I can't tell you how the stream was invented because that would taint your minds with our understanding of what it is. You need to explore it on your own. If and when you reach the point where you can wield it, I'll tell you what we think we know." She shot upright. "So why don't you get back to work?"

"Right." Dante turned to the others. "Well, I've told you what I did to see the stream. So just do that."

Blays scrunched up his eyes. "Get good ideas, then look out for flashy little gold bits?"

"That's what worked for me."

"That's what you *say* worked for you," Ara said.

"Careful there. You wouldn't want to infect us with the actual facts." Dante found a more comfortable position on his mat. "This time, when you imagine the forest, get lost in it. Let your ideas flow as they will and carry you along with them."

"Question," Blays said. "Do we have to think about a bunch of trees? Or can we think about whatever we please?"

Ara shrugged one shoulder. "Do you think you need my permission?"

"Even if I did, I suppose that's never stopped me before."

They bent to their tasks. Dante built his inner world of the lost forest layer by layer: trees, grass, birds, and so forth. With each piece he added, he spied subtle sparkles of gold. If he hadn't known what they were, he likely would have mistaken them for tricks of his mind. He couldn't be sure, but he didn't think he'd ever seen them at other points in his life when he'd been daydreaming or brainstorming.

Not five minutes into it, Volo jumped to her feet. "I see them! They were glimmering in the raindrops!"

Dante laughed. "You were imagining weather?"

"We've got weather in the present, don't we? Why wouldn't they have it in the past?"

The idea was so obvious it hadn't even occurred to him—or, alternately, he still hadn't been thinking flexibly enough, defaulting to visions of pleasant sunshine. When he closed his eyes again, he imagined himself struggling through a snowstorm, fighting for every mile he could get before sundown. Within the barrage of snowflakes, one in a thousand glittered gold.

The day's end was nearly at hand when Gladdic inhaled a loud breath through his nostrils and opened his eyes. "I have seen the stream."

Dante clenched his fist in triumph. "How? What technique did you use?"

"I wasn't imagining the forest of days gone past. Rather, I envisioned Tanar Atain as it stands now. Its boisterous cities and its hard-working villages. Then I envisioned the White Lich falling upon them and ravaging them. The way the Blighted would fall upon the citizens like a pack of rabid wolves; how they would bite for the vulnerable softness of a woman's throat, and peel away the still-throbbing muscle from a man's calf.

"The villages were small enough to be slaughtered wholesale. After, the blood hung in the still waters like the stink of death. In the cities, some were able to flee into the wild swamp, to fall victim to the ziki oko or venomous snakes. Others wasted from disease or starved down to their bones.

"I watched as one man paddled his family away from the Blighted as they gave chase. Hour after hour, he paddled with all his strength. Yet the Blighted were tireless. As their boats closed on the man's canoe, he pushed himself to his absolute limit. His arms spasmed; he lost hold of his paddle, dropping it into the water. His canoe drifted to a stop. The Blighted flung themselves inside. And the man, who was too weak to even lift his own arms, barely had the strength to close his eyes as they ripped apart his wife and children.

"At last, I saw a mother attempting to flee the Blighted, tugging her three young children along behind her. As the savagery unfolded on all sides, and the monsters closed in with their mad eyes blazing, she lost all reason to her terror. She raced away from her children, leaving them behind to be devoured. When they screamed in pain and terror, she hoped their cries would drive her mad—yet she was still sane when the Blighted leaped from the water and began to eat her alive. And in her clarity of mind, she spent her last moments understanding that when her children had died, the last thing they saw was their mother's back as she ran away from them."

"I'm sorry," Blays said. "Does anyone have a spare noose? I seem to have displaced mine."

"Mock me as you wish." Gladdic stared out into the jagged landscape of punished stone. "When I saw the horror contort the mother's face, as potent as burning acid, that's when I saw the gold shining from the depths of her eyes."

Dante was too excited to have another of them able to see the stream to care about the gruesome process Gladdic had taken to get there. He felt as though it was only a matter of time until Blays would call out that he too had witnessed the new power, but when the sun sank into the dust-filled sky, reddening it like spilled blood, Blays still hadn't found his way to the stream.

That evening's dinner tasted especially good: cauliflower in nut oil, along with black bean mash and slices of tart green apples which the servant said were from the year's first crop.

"This is about as good as you can make a plate of stuff that's too dumb to run away from you." Blays spoke through a mouthful of food, jabbing a fork at the air for emphasis. "But don't you guys ever eat meat?"

The servant smiled wryly. "Something in the Hills makes the animals' flesh taste unwholesome. It's not such a bad thing, though. We don't have space for livestock. We must use all the plants that we grow to feed ourselves."

He retreated to the kitchens.

Dante nodded to Blays. "Be sure to eat your fill. You've got a long day of holding us back tomorrow."

Blays laughed and lifted a heaping spoonful of herbed beans. "Really, only one of us needs to learn the Odo Sein, right? If the three of you have that covered, it's probably best for me to get out of your way. Preferably in a hammock somewhere."

"What have you tried imagining?"

"Right now, I'm imagining that you're not being a conde-scending jackoff. But it's not a very realistic vision."

"Well, keep trying. Ara seems intent on making us muddle through this on our own. The more of us we have working on it, the faster we'll go."

The next morning was a warm one, with unusually low winds. Ara met them at the boundary and sent them straight into the Forest exercise. It took him several minutes of focused effort, but Dante could now see the stream almost every time he tried. Forty minutes in, he stood from his mat and motioned Ara a short ways into the trees.

She looked inclined to ignore him, then sighed and joined him. "Did I say you could take a break?"

"It's all right, I imagined asking you. You said yes."

"What do you want? To remind me that you haven't bathed in days?"

Dante fought down the flush in his cheeks; they were stand-ing close together, and she smelled like honey. "While everyone has the nether within them, very few of them will ever be able to do anything with it, no matter how long they spend in training. Is the same true of the stream?"

"You're worried that your friend might be an idiot."

"I reached my conclusions on that front almost fifteen years ago. I'm just worried he might also be an idiot with the Odo Sein."

"All of you have the potential to reach the stream."

"The potential to do so within a month? Or only after a lifetime of study?"

Ara shrugged. She'd worn a lighter robe to deal with the day's heat and her shoulders were bare. "I can't know the answer to that. Like so much else, you'll have to figure it out for yourselves."

"That's not good enough this time. The White Lich doesn't give a big white shit about our inner quest for personal understanding of the Golden Stream. We spooked him enough to make him conservative in his advances, but sooner or later, he's going to realize we're not running around the swamps anymore. He'll start claiming people again. Bigger and bigger settlements. Within a matter of weeks, he'll become too powerful for us to resist."

"You want to learn our secrets in *weeks*? If you're crossing a desert many days from water, and your friend breaks his leg, what do you do to make it onward?"

"Carry him."

Ara raised an eyebrow. "Or?"

Dante thought for a moment. "You leave him behind."

Dante returned to his mat. This time, rather than envisioning the woods, he thought. Blays had as much theory about the stream as the rest of them, but he still wasn't breaking through to where he could see it. Tapping himself into Ara had let Dante see through her sight and witness the stream. What if he could tap himself into Blays and figure out why Blays *wasn't* seeing it?

He waited for Ara to call out for them to take a break, then stood next to Blays. "Still being terrible?"

Blays lobbed a pebble across the border into the naked Hills. "If I'd seen the stream, do you think I'd *not* have demanded Ara bring me nine bottles of celebratory wine?"

"Let me try something."

Dante moved his mind into the shadows within Blays' blood, withdrawing some and binding them to those within himself. On a lark, he tried to access Blays' sight and hearing the same way he might in an undead rat, but it was like bouncing against a blank wall. This made a certain amount of sense: when he re-animated a rat, a dragonfly, or even a person, he had total command over it. By contrast, his connection to Blays was extremely tenuous. It was the difference between clasping hands with Blays and actually *being* Blays. In fact—

"Er." Blays pointed into the air around Dante. There, two small bits of gold spun about each other in expanding orbits. "You're talking about those little guys? The ones that look like extremely expensive gnats?"

"You see them?"

"Unless I'm hallucinating after I drank so much of that cele-bratory wine that I forgot I'd had any. How am I doing this?"

"I was trying to see through your sight, but I think I made you see through mine."

"So you did all the tough work, then magically passed your hard-earned knowledge over to me? Can we make this standard practice?"

Dante met eyes with Ara. "We've figured out that the Golden Stream exists. We've all learned how to see it. Now how do we learn how to wield it?"

EDWARD W. ROBERTSON

10

Dante didn't really expect for her to tell them that. This turned out to be a wise mindset, because he turned out to be exactly right.

"You need me to tell you how to be sorcerers?" Ara said. "Three of you *are* sorcerers."

"More like two and a half," Blays said. "Or two and a quarter. Actually, what's the smallest fraction more than two?"

Dante tapped his chin. "Why don't you ask your penis?"

Gladdic stuttered with unintended laughter.

Blays shook his head at them both. "Since our mentor insists on being as helpful as a hemorrhoid, why don't we just try to grab the stream?" He closed his eyes and clenched his face. They were nearing midday and it was hot enough for a bead of sweat to appear on his temple. He opened his eyes, breathing hard. "Nothing. And if I bear down any harder, I'll need to change my jabat."

Dante examined the two bits of gold that had appeared next to him. They were already shrinking, dimming. He extended his mind toward them. He could see them, but it was as if there was nothing there for his mind to sense. An idea presented itself to him. Before he could think about all the ways it wouldn't work, he summoned the nether and wrapped it around the two dots of stream. The sparks seemed to brighten for a moment, but remained invisible to his inner eye.

He shook his head. "It's like trying to move a limb I don't have."

"Now I understand," Blays said. "Not having one would explain why you think they can talk."

Gladdic seated himself cross-legged and scowled up at the two flecks of gold. Volo walked in a circle around Dante, mouth twisted to the side. A part of him expected her to unlock the secret right away, as she'd done with the Glimpse, yet the sparks didn't show any sign of being affected. The four of them spent the next minute in near silence. Without warning, the two pieces of stream winked away, nowhere to be found.

"Did someone do that?" Dante said.

Gladdic lifted an eyebrow. "If we had, would that not be proof of the talent to move them, and hence a favorable outcome?"

"We can stare at the stream all day without getting anywhere. How do we actually wield it?"

"What if we're getting ahead of ourselves?" Blays rubbed the back of his arm. "When I was at Pocket Cove, they broke our training with the nether into several sections. First, they taught us to see the nether. Second, to touch it. And lastly, to grasp it. Right now, we're trying to skip straight to the grand finale. But maybe we should try to learn how to touch the stream first."

"That's inefficient," Dante said. "When I learned the nether, I went straight to using it. I didn't even have to see it first."

"You seem to be forgetting that you had the original *Cycle* lending you a hand. And that you turned out to be one of the greatest nethermancers of our generation. These people don't even have a broadsheet calling the emperor a wanker, let alone a holy book that teaches you how to wield the stream's power without you knowing that you're being taught. I'd say that baby steps are all we've got."

"Agreed," Gladdic said. "Many of the acolytes within the Mallish church show little potential, but even modest talent in the ether is too valuable to be thrown away. Those who are strong may leap to the top of their studies in a handful of bounds. For those who are weaker, more steps are needed to convey them to the heights."

As they spoke, two dabs of stream returned from nowhere, circulating in the air between them.

Dante let out a huff of air. "Fine. We'll try to learn to touch it. How'd they teach you to do that at Pocket Cove?"

"Er." Blays tipped back his head. "I don't wholly remember. I think it involved a lot of naked swimming. And searching for exotic sea snails."

"We'll just find where the Odo Sein keep their ocean, then. How can you not remember learning to shadowalk?"

"Because unlike the rest of you who get into these things, I'm not an obsessive mooncalf about it. I'd tell you to loon Nak to ask Minn what she taught me, except she's over in Pocket Cove right now, isn't she? I think the process involved breathing."

"Breathing? Like with your lungs? That sounds like an arcane process to be sure."

Blays paced about the grass. "Hang on, part of the reason I'm having a tough time remembering is because I ripped through it like used cheesecloth." He snapped his fingers. "That was it! I employed my Waves o' Muscle technique, and once my head was all calmed down, I swooped in on the nether from the side. Caught it completely off guard."

"Waves o' Muscle? I veto this discussion."

"The name more or less describes exactly what it is. The technique's a way to train yourself to be able to murder your foes at maximum efficiency, but it's also a good way to get your brain to shut up and let you think. What you do is isolate a group of muscles—the ones around your ears and eyes, say—then tense them hard when breathing out. Then as you inhale, you relax them. On the next breath, you move down to the next set of muscles, the ones in your jaw and neck, and repeat the process all until you get down to your feet."

Dante found that he was already flexing the muscles on his face and ears. He made himself stop. "What does any of this have to do with learning sorcery?"

"Beats the hell out of me. And Minn. All I know is that I did it, then came at the nether like a big sexy hawk, and it worked."

Dante glanced at Ara, expecting to see her rolling her eyes or drooling with scornful laughter, but she was presently looking uncharacteristically nonjudgmental, which only happened on the rare occasions they weren't saying something she found unbelievably stupid.

"This seems dumb," Dante said. "But it also seems like it'll only take a few minutes to test out. You might as well go first."

Blays rolled his shoulders. "The women present might want to avert their eyes to avoid a sudden loss of consciousness."

Volo giggled. Ara's expression reverted to its natural state of "witnessing unbelievable stupidity."

Blays inhaled deeply through his nose, then cocked his head. "I've spotted a flaw in this plan. I can't seem to see any of the stream."

"That's because you're bad at..." Dante trailed off, turning in a confused circle. "Hold on, where *did* it go?"

Volo and Gladdic looked about, but they too couldn't see a single golden speck.

"This makes no sense," Dante said. "We're all able to see it. We've taught ourselves that much. So why can't we see any of it right now?"

Volo quirked her mouth. "Maybe it's gone?"

"Gone where? The nether's all around us. So is the ether. Once you know how to see them, they're always there. So where is the stream?"

"Perhaps our skills remain weak," Gladdic said. "Hence it is only when we actively focus that we can see it."

"And all four of us are exactly as bad at seeing it? So it disappears from all four of us at the exact same time?"

"When phrased as such, it does not seem likely."

Dante rubbed the corners of his eyes. "Then is it disappearing somewhere? Hiding?"

Blays stretched his arms over his head. "I know one way to get it to show its face: show it a pretty mind-forest." While he was still mid-sentence, a little golden firefly appeared behind his head, circled to his side, and drifted in irregular loops. "Now that's strange, isn't it? I hadn't even thought of a single tree yet."

"You didn't need to. Because you were just inspired."

Gladdic's mouth fell open. He tilted back his head at the blue of the sky like he was being granted a vision from the gods. "You're suggesting that unlike ether and nether, the stream isn't permanent. Rather, it is *created*."

"That's not what I'm suggesting at all," Dante said. "That's impossible."

"Why so? Because the elements that we are familiar with do not act in the same fashion? You yourself stated that the key to seeing the stream was to think deeply and in detail about the forest. What is this but a focused way to find inspiration?"

"All right, that's plausible. And if the stream is constantly fading away, that's another reason that nobody else even knows it exists. Most of the time, it isn't there."

"Look!" Volo pointed above their heads. There, a dozen slivers of gold had sprung into existence, tossing gently in slow circles. "You guys just made those. While you were talking."

"While we were debating." Feeling light-headed, Dante gawked at Ara. "That's why you invented dana kide, isn't it? To turn your entire society into an ongoing source of the stream for you to use!"

"Close enough," she said. "Close enough to be given the truth. In practice, the Golden Stream fades away much too fast for us to get any use out of what the people spark up while they're arguing away with each other. But what this custom *does* accomplish is to train every single citizen to be a potential Knight of Odo Sein. As with your warlock degeneracy, most of them show little talent for it. Through dana kide, those who are good at it become very easy to spot."

Blays scratched the back of his head. "That's a bit manipulative, tricking your whole society into arguing all day long just to make your job a little easier."

"The concept of dana kide is wrong, then? When they reason their way to a better premise, and share that new idea with those around them, they aren't making themselves and their people wiser and stronger?"

"*That* part sounds noble enough. It's the part where you're totally deceiving them that feels deceptive."

Ara laughed in derision. "So what if we lie to them? We improve their lives with dana kide, while also using it to prevent them from being turned into the Blighted — or from being eaten alive by them. How horrible! How *shameful!* Your brilliant foreign logic has lifted the blinders from my eyes. We'll go serve our citizens up to the Eiden Rane at once."

Blays held up his hands. "All right! Goodness, for someone who thinks arguing is so great, you sure hate to be disagreed with."

"Your arguments stink like fish carcasses. You're not angry at me when you make a bad one, you're embarrassed at yourself for having made them." She swept a strand of hair from her brow. "If you're done condemning the Odo Sein for preserving our people against a threat that would have destroyed any of *your* worthless countries centuries ago, I'd like to congratulate you. It only took you a week to discover what it took us fifty years to work out."

"That's how long it took to found the Odo Sein?" Dante said. "Does that mean we're ready to learn your story?"

"Just how much do you think you've actually accomplished here? So you've worked out a few facts we've known about for hundreds of years? Get back to work."

The flickers of stream they'd generated earlier were nearly all gone. Blays started in on his flexing and relaxation routine — Dante refused to even think of it by name — but before he could finish, and "swoop in on" the golden dots, the last of them vanished.

"Unless we get extremely lucky, we're going to need a steady source of the stream," Dante said. "Volo, you're the best at generating it consistently. Mind dreaming up a few forests for us?"

"Yeah," she said. "But I'll do it anyway."

She smoothed out her mat, took a seat, and closed her eyes. Blays resumed his routine. Ara watched him for a moment, but grew bored of the sight almost immediately, which Dante found gratifying.

"It will be some minutes before the girl has assembled her inner world in enough detail to begin generating sparks," Gladdic said. "In the meantime, shall we take up the Garnassus of Ohelion?"

Dante looked at him as if Gladdic had suggested they disrobe for a wrestling match. The Garnassus was a historic debate between two Mallish scholars named Halwick the Stout and Bordrang the Black. Dating back four hundred years, and concerning the trials of a man named Tarlan who is repeatedly wronged and seeks a variety of revenges on his foes, it was primarily used to provide a framework within which neophyte scholars could debate the nature of moral action, particularly whether it was absolute, or influenced by the context around it.

"Ohh," Dante said. "You want to see if we can create some stream of our own? Do you want the position of Halwick? Or Bordrang?"

"Bordrang." Gladdic sounded like he was tasting the word and finding it to his liking. "I have always chosen Halwick. It is time to try a different course."

They set to arguing, with Dante going first. He'd usually found Halwick the Stout to be safe and predictable, but Gladdic made his counterpoints so fiendishly that Dante fought to keep himself on tenable ground. As Gladdic argued that Tarlan's vigilante killing of the man who'd stolen his flock was a fully appropriate response to an attack on Tarlan's ability to clothe and feed himself, a glimmer of gold appeared between them.

Blays' eyes darted to it. He exhaled in a rush. Scrunching up his brow, Blays inhaled and exhaled again. Dante and Gladdic resumed the debate.

A minute later, the glimmer dwindled away. Blays shook his head. "Nothing."

Dante broke off mid-argument with Gladdic. "You swooped?"

"I swooped. Then I swerved. And for good measure, I tried a flying backwards triple somersault. Still couldn't touch it."

Volo's exercise produced her first blot of stream. In almost no time at all, she was putting out a slow but steady flow of the substance. By contrast, Dante and Gladdic's production was sporadic and spotty.

Twenty minutes in, Blays straightened and stretched back his neck. "I don't feel like I'm getting anywhere. Anyone else want to take a shot?"

Dante took his place while Blays started up a raucous argument with Gladdic. Performing the Wave o' Muscles felt ridiculous, but it *was* oddly relaxing. Regardless, Dante was soon so wrapped up in trying to reach the Golden Stream that he forgot about how ridiculous he might look.

One attempt after the other came to failure. It wasn't even like he was bouncing off the motes, or sliding across them. It was more like they weren't there at all. He deployed every trick he'd learned in his life-long efforts to not be terrible with the ether, but none bore fruit.

When he grew frustrated, he switched out for Gladdic, who switched out in turn for Volo. They lunched, then spent the remainder of the afternoon beating their heads against the wall of the stream. At last, the setting sun informed them it was time to call it quits.

"It's no wonder the stream has such limited use," Dante said. "You can barely gin up enough of it to *see* it. And a speck of it barely lasts long enough for you to get mad at it before it fades away."

Blays clapped him on the shoulder. "You make it sound like we spent the day failing so badly our mothers don't know whether to disown us or blow our inheritance on hemlock. I say we made a lot of progress today. A few more steps forward like this and we'll be ready to go bash the lich's big white head in."

Dante wasn't too sure about the last part, but he was heartened by the rest. He'd let himself get dragged down by nothing. Just like always, the elation of success had been as short-lived as a mayfly: for today's success became tomorrow's normal. And when failure rose over your head like cold water, the memory of your last successful gasp of air was no comfort at all.

He was asleep, and enjoying it very much, when something twitched in his ear. This startled him so violently that he fell halfway from his wicker bed. The pulse came a second time. A loon.

He touched his ear. "Yes?"

"My lord?"

"Most likely. Who's this?"

"Why, it's Jona, sir."

Still drunk on sleep, it took Dante a moment to place the name: Naran's mate from the *Sword of the South*. The room in the tower was utterly dark except for a band of moonlight slicing through the gauzy curtains. The others were snoring, but if Dante kept up his conversation, they wouldn't be for long. Dante slipped out the door and into the stairwell that connected the two rooms comprising that floor of the tower.

"Jona," he said. "I understand that the Collen Basin is far away from here, but I'll assure you that it's the middle of the night in Tanar Atain as well."

"Oh, most sincere and severe apologies for waking you. But I bring news from Aris Osis."

"Aris Osis? How?"

"Well, being that that's where I am, sir."

"I thought you were in the Collen Basin, Jona."

"Yes, I was. Right up until I wasn't."

"Your presence there was a way to keep us in contact with the entire region. Who authorized your departure?"

"Why, Captain Naran did. Lord."

"How? He couldn't possibly have made it to Collen already."

"He's authorized me *now*, you see."

"Now that you're in Aris Osis? He authorized you retroactively?"

"Indeed. It's a mariner thing, you see. Wouldn't expect a man of your stature to be bothered with our customs, crude as they can be."

"Try me, Jona. Why did you feel you could leave Collen without my authorization?"

"Well, Captain Naran is my captain, my lord. And you're just some lord."

"I suppose there's no arguing with that." Dante frowned

down the dim stairwell. "You're right. You're not my subject, Jona, and I'm grateful for your help over these last few months even though you owed me nothing. Naran made it to Aris Osis all right, then? Why are you two still there? Looking for passage out?"

"That would be somewhat redundant, I'd think, since we have the *Sword of the South* right here. The crew snuck back into port some time ago to search for the captain."

"I was worried Naran might never see his ship again. Thanks for letting me know."

"You're welcome, lord. But I didn't wake you at hell's own hour of the night to let you know that everything is well and good. There's been an attack on Aris Osis."

"By the Monsoon?"

"They were a part of it, to be sure. Along with a horde of ghouls."

Dante had been pacing about the stairwell. Hearing this, he stopped short. "The Blighted? Was the White Lich with them?"

Jona repeated the question, voice faint; in the background, Naran's voice answered, too indistinct for Dante to make out. Jona said, "Captain doesn't think so, but there was certainly a lesser lich at hand. I don't know what such a thing as that might be, but I'm guessing the both of you do. It was an ugly night. Very ugly. Even after we'd turned the tide, and were driving the ghouls from the city, they were carrying captives off with them. Young and old alike. Don't think I'll forget their screams for some time."

"How were the defenders able to drive off the lesser lich? Were there sorcerers present?"

"Oh, it was quite a scene, my lord. The lich and his ghouls seized the outer districts with hardly a loss. The fighting in the city proper was as vicious as you'll ever see, yet one by one, the towers fell. The Tanarians retreated to make their last stand on

Turtleback Island. They knocked down the only bridge to it, but the ghouls waded through the water like they had no need for air at all. With the lich at their backs casting his sorcery about, they broke the front ranks of the defenders.

"But just as they were set to break through, and capture the whole port, two knights in scaled armor charged in with blazing purple swords! Gods, it was a sight. The lich's foul magics stopped dead. One of the knights was dragged down by the ghoulish hordes, but the second cut the lich clear in twain. After that, the ghouls fought like the demons they are. Looked ready to die to the last of 'em. But just like that, they turned and retreated from the city in a great mass, snatching up whoever they could grab along the way."

Dante's mouth had gone dry. "You said one of the Odo Sein — the knights — died in battle. What about the other?"

"Why, he's being showered with meat and ale as we speak, lord."

"I need you and Naran to find him. You can't let him leave the city. He may be our only hope of victory."

"The captain had similar thoughts. You see, sir, the Tanarians might have won this battle, but they suffered most horrible losses. And the Drakebane's already drawn off most of the city's best soldiers in his boats. Captain Naran thinks that if the devils muster a second attack, the entire city will fall. The slaughter that would come after would make what happened in the Collen Basin look like a slap-fight. Tens of thousands of people, sir. Captain Naran thinks you're the only one who can stop that from coming to pass."

"If the next attack is led by another lesser lich, he may be right. But if it's headed by the Eiden Rane, we'll all die. But we're in the middle of learning to use the Odo Sein ourselves. We can't afford to abandon our training right now."

"Yes, the captain thought you'd say something like that."

"Then I assume he also knows why we can't go."

Jona chuckled. "As a matter of fact, he's got a theory, the crafty devil. He figured you'd say that even if twenty thousand souls are lost in Aris Osis, breaking away from your training would guarantee the loss of infinitely more."

"That's exactly what we're looking at. No matter how gruesome things become in the short-term, we have to think about what will save us all in the long-term."

"Captain Naran understands that, surely he does. But he also asks if you might not find a way to continue your most important training *and* stop the city from falling to liches and ghouls."

Dante puffed his cheeks with a sigh. "To have any hope of that, you have to enlist the surviving Knight of Odo Sein to our side. Do you understand me?"

"Quite clearly, my lord."

"Good. Let me know if and when you've got him. I'll see what I can come up with on my end."

He closed the connection to the loon. The stars indicated he had three hours until dawn. Judging that the situation wasn't quite an emergency, Dante went back to bed, but he didn't get much sleep. He finally dropped off only to be shaken awake what felt like minutes later. His eyes were dry and scratchy, but he was lost in a pleasant stupor until he wandered out to the stairwell and remembered that everything had been upended.

The others were already at breakfast. He ran down to join them, casting a glance about for lurking servants before explaining everything that Jona had told him.

"Shit," Blays said after Dante finished. "Rains of it. Hoist the shields high and don't come out until the splatter stops. There's no way we can go to Aris Osis."

Dante gave him a puzzled look. "If we made it through the Hills once, there's nothing to stop us from doing it again. Aris Osis is only a few days from here."

"Yes, and if we make that journey, we might as well find a planet-sized knife to cut the world's throat with. I thought we were here to learn how to stop the White Lich ourselves."

"We are pathetic acolytes and the gods only know how long it'll take for one of us to gain real skill. Meanwhile, there's a fully-trained Odo Sein who might be willing to help us."

"One person. Who we've never met before. And who *might* be willing to help. And who *might* not get targeted by the White Lich's advance agents, or exposed in a gambit by a lesser lich, or any number of other plans the big fellow will devise in response to the Odo Sein thwarting his first attack on the city."

"Aren't you normally the one who wants to try to save every last man, woman, child, dog, rodent, and cockroach that comes into harm's way?"

"Sure," Blays said. "But I've also never run into an enemy who might qualify for godhood. Before, no matter what we were up against, I always thought we stood a chance."

"You don't now?"

"This is the first time I'm not sure that we do."

"I fear that we have no choice." Gladdic dabbed his mouth with a napkin. "By using his pet sorcerers as proxies, the Eiden Rane has found a way to move more aggressively than we anticipated. If he swallows Aris Osis, he'll have an army of no less than twenty thousand Blighted. With a force like that, he will absorb the rest of Tanar Atain as fast as he is able to move his troops."

Blays shrugged. "So we bide our time until we're ready, then ambush him."

"Impossible. He'll keep himself in the middle of an entire horde of Blighted. We will have no way to get close to him."

"Then I'll shadowalk through the horde. Or Dante will tunnel in beneath the lich. Or we'll deploy any of the thousands of other ways we've learned to kill people over the years."

"You forget that as his army grows, his personal strength swells as well. It is likely he will reach a point where he is immune to the effects of Odo Sein — or even to sorcery as a whole."

"It's 'likely,' is it? And what are you basing that on? A long personal friendship with the White Lich? Or was it just the first thing you found when you inserted your head up your ass to search for ideas?"

Gladdic's white eyebrows knitted together. "I am reporting to you the same information that I have heard from the Drakebane, his mystics, and his historians. I suppose your expertise is superior?"

"What have you actually done for us, though? Told us about the prime body, which plenty of other people seem to have known about?"

"I got you here! The place which you now believe is vital to our enterprise!"

"All *you* did was threaten an old man and his grandchildren. I'm reasonably sure I could have done that much. Assuming I could stop vomiting at the thought of it."

Dante noted, with mild irony, that their increasingly acrimonious discussion was causing a few stray bits of stream to drift above the low-slung breakfast table.

Gladdic pounded his open palm on the table, drawing a look from a servant mopping the other side of the chamber. "I have proven my loyalty to our cause time and time again. Now is not the time for division!"

"Maybe that's exactly what it's time for," Blays said. "If you think you can go to Aris Osis and put down the lich, nobody's stopping you. I think *my* efforts are best spent learning to become the only thing that can make him weak enough to stand up to."

Gladdic drew back from the table. "A perfectly reasonable suggestion. Who, then, will go, and who shall stay?"

Dante saw two paths opening before him—and he was afraid which one he would take. He planted his hands on the table. "Think this through, you fools. The choice doesn't have to be one or the other. It doesn't even have to be made right now. First of all, unless Naran can convince the knight to join us, the whole thing is moot, and we'll stay here. Second, the White Lich might not press the attack until he's had time to regroup in the swamps and add to his ranks. There's no need for us to go anywhere until we know there's going to be another assault on Aris Osis. Until both those conditions are met, we'll continue to train at the Spires."

Blays scratched his thumb against his upper lip. "And what do we do if they *are* met?"

"We get to Aris Osis as fast as possible. We stand against the White Lich or whoever he sends in his stead. If we die, we die. If we kill the Eiden Rane, we throw ourselves a party and we won't stop that party until the Tanarians get sick of us and throw us out. But if we only push him into retreat, then we'll come back to the Silent Spires and continue our work."

A couple of golden motes were tumbling near his head. Suddenly annoyed with them, he tried to swat them away, but he couldn't touch them with his hand any more than he could with his mind.

"Sounds smart to me," Volo said. "But you guys never care what I have to say."

Dante wanted to assure her that that wasn't true, except it was.

Blays watched Gladdic, waiting for the old man to make his move, then swore. "Yes. Righto. A plan that accounts for all of our concerns and contingencies. Only a complete jackass could say no."

Gladdic smirked. "Heavens forbid that after all I have seen and done that I be labeled a 'jackass.' I will agree as well—on the condition that Naran liaises with the Tanarians to ensure that enough scouts are deployed to detect a second strike well in advance."

"I'll tell Ara our plans." Dante stood. "If she gets mad about it, try to collect at least part of me to return to Narashtovik."

He stepped out of the dining hall and bumped right into Ara, who'd been steaming toward it to drag them off to the day's practice. He quickly explained what he'd heard was happening in Aris Osis, as well as their plans to deal with it.

Ara narrowed her eyes. "If we'd had any interlopers show up to bring you this news, I think I'd have heard them screaming under our knives by now. How did you get this information?"

"Through wicked sorcery."

"I guessed as much. Though you would have surmised that I *would* guess as much, and fed me a lie you knew I would happily swallow. Be aware that if you've smuggled another of your people into the Spires, we will kill you and feed you to our crops. Or maybe we'll eat you ourselves. It's been a very long time since we tasted meat."

Dante called on the nether and swept his right hand in a long oval pattern. Beside him, the shadows took on a human shape. He gestured broadly, more out of show than of need; the figure clarified into a tall woman, dark-haired, lean but strong, capable of swinging a sword or running for an hour straight. Gesturing and working more subtly, Dante added another layer of refinement to his work, honing the woman's eyes and nose and chin.

Ara's eyes had gone wide. With the illusion complete, a smile spread across her face. For once, it wasn't wry or mocking. It was the simple joy of being caught off guard by something delightful.

Hesitantly, she reached toward the vision. "That's how you see me?"

"It's not how I see you, it's how you *are*. If I can duplicate you like this, you can trust that I'm more than powerful enough to speak with people from a distance, and don't have any need to sneak people into your sanctuary."

Ara kept her eyes on the vision. "It's a good plan. If and when the time comes, we'll help you get back to the swamps."

"You don't mind interrupting our training?"

"*You're* the ones who forced your way into our home and demanded to learn all our secrets. But let me make this clear: even if you go to Aris Osis and slay the Eiden Rane himself, that doesn't absolve you of your promise to us. You will teach us to capture our history in books so that we can add an eighth spire to this place: the Library of Tanar Atain."

"Running out on our deal never crossed my mind. Even if we were victorious, do you really think I wouldn't come back to finish learning to use the stream?"

Ara smiled, half mockingly. "In that case, maybe I'd rather you die in Aris Osis."

She led them back to the half-wild forest that stood at the edge of the dead-blasted Hills. They picked up where they'd left off the day before, with three of them generating flecks of the stream while the fourth one tried to access it.

After a full round of failure, Dante folded his arms, tapping his elbow. "Bel Ara, will you touch the stream for us?"

"Surely. Don't discouraged by how easy I make it look."

She lowered her chin. The slowly swirling chips of gold assembled into a loose spiral. It looked something like a clock spring, but it looked less like something hammered into shape by a human hand and more like something made orderly by nature itself, like the smooth flat roundness of pebbles in a rushing stream. Ara let the power hang there a moment, then flicked her hand, shattering it back into discrete pieces.

"And a second time? Give me a moment first." Dante reached out for a strand of nether from within himself, grabbed another from Ara, and melded the two together.

She snapped her head about to stare at him. "What are you doing?"

"Watching the process for myself. Like you told us to do."

"I didn't tell you to use your black magic. That's cheating. You're supposed to observe and reason it out on your own."

"That's exactly what I'm about to do. To accomplish this, I'm using a perspective none of you have access to. You should appreciate that, as it can only add a new dimension to your knowledge of the Odo Sein."

Ara grimaced. "I don't know what I hate worse: when you are ignorant, or when you're able to twist your logic that far without it breaking. Go on, then. Subvert your learning with your shadows."

"It's always worked for me before." He checked the link between them to ensure it was secure, then nodded.

Ara reached out for the stream. Through the nether, Dante loomed forward as closely as he could. There was a brief moment of friction between Ara and the sparks. Something seemed to rotate, then to clunk into place; this achieved, the stream came to Ara's hand, waiting to be used.

"Would you do that again?" Dante said. "Slower this time?"

"While I'm at it, why don't I just tell you exactly what I'm doing?"

"It *would* make this go a lot faster. But I agree that it's more important to preserve your traditions than life as we know it."

She gave him a long look. The corner of her mouth twitched. She turned away and moved her mind toward the stream. This time, she slowed herself tenfold. Like the first time she made contact with the golden matter, there was a straining, a kind of friction.

To Dante's complete shock, Ara reached out to three different sections of the stream at the same time. After a moment of intellectual panic, he focused on one section, watching as she turned the fleck of gold this way and that. Her motions had a logical flow to them, like a mathematical formula or a piece of good music.

Before he could forget their sequence, he darted out to the stream himself. At first he couldn't so much as feel it, but as he began to repeat the sequence, it resisted, as if trying to pull back. He quickly repeated the process several times, etching it into his mind.

He asked Ara to show him again. She obliged. This time, he observed the second sequence, practicing both it and the first until he had them memorized. He had Ara move on to the final sequence. He repeated it eight times before he was positive he had it down. Taking a deep breath, he held the third sequence in place, then manipulated the stream with the first and second.

The stream held fast, refusing to be unlocked. Dante backed off, then tried again, progressing from the first sequence to the second to the third. The stream didn't seem to notice. He swore.

"I've been able to watch what you're doing," he told Ara, "but I must have got one of the sequences wrong."

She stared back at him. "Sequences?"

"The way you have to interact with the stream three times to get it to open up to you. I must have made an error somewhere. Can I see you do it again?"

If he didn't know better, he would have said she was hiding a smile. She accessed the stream anew, keeping her motions deliberate and slow. Watching the first sequence, Dante saw that he was right about one thing: the sequence *was* different from what he was doing.

But not in the sense that he'd made a small error that could be solved with a tweak or two. Rather, it was *completely* different. From start to finish. And it was different from his memorization of the second and third sequences, too.

With a sinking stomach, Dante asked Ara to access the stream yet again. The first sequence was radically different from both other times he'd watched her execute it.

He banged his fist against his thigh. "Son of a bitch! You have to change your approach to the stream every single time you want to use it?"

Ara relaxed her hold on the stream. "This comes as a surprise to you?"

"When you summon nether, it's like channeling a stream of water. Ether is more like emptying yourself and then allowing yourself to be filled with light. In both cases, the general process is the same every time."

"Well, apparently that's not true of the stream. Deal with it."

He weighed the option of launching into an angry tirade versus getting to work. The tirade would provide immediate short-term satisfaction, but it would only delay the greater and long-term satisfaction of actually knowing how to use the gods damned Golden Stream. Also, Ara would only mock him for it.

With the grim self-congratulation of doing the responsible thing, Dante moved toward a small gob of stream, turning it about at random. As he fumbled with the patterns of gold, Gladdic extended a nethereal link to Ara, observing the process for himself. Blays shadowalked to see if he could spot any clues from within the netherworld, but soon declared this an utter failure. Volo worked quietly on her own pursuits.

Dante accessed one of the sparks. As soon as he attempted to wield it, it pushed back—the tension he'd seen in Ara's efforts. After some fumbling around, he released the spark to see if he'd have an easier time with one of the others. It was just as impenetrable as the first. Several attempts later, he'd concluded every one of the golden sparks was unique, resisting his efforts with differing pressures and vectors. In each case, the pushback held a logical suggestion about how to negate that push and delve deeper into the spark's "lock."

The process of mapping this out felt like fitting pieces into a puzzle, or indeed like tripping the tumblers of a lock, yet it was far more abstract than that. Once he realized this, Dante was able to make rapid progress through the sequence of responses necessary to access the spark. Sometimes it slipped away from him, obliging him to start over, but as their mid-day break approached, he completed his first sequence.

Grinning, he gave himself a moment to admire his work. But only a moment. He moved on to the second sequence, advancing carefully from one tumbler—or note, he wasn't sure what best described it—to the next. He was still working on the third note of the sequence when the two he'd previously worked out changed shape, expelling him.

Rattling off a stream of salty oaths, he switched back to the first sequence. And found that the "lock," which he'd thought he was all done with, had also expelled his previous work. He'd have to work through a completely new sequence to begin to open the stream.

He pushed his palms against his face. "This is ridiculous. It's like trying to pick a lock, right? You have to trip the tumblers in the right order. Only the lock keeps changing shape while you're working on it. And after you've already opened it!"

"That's correct," Ara said.

"What are you so pleased about? This is a huge setback."

"But it's not impossible, is it? Or else we wouldn't be having this conversation, because I wouldn't be Odo Sein, since it wouldn't exist. And if there were no Odo Sein, then we wouldn't be able to talk in the first place, as the lich would have slaughtered our ancestors before they could have us."

"Look on the bright side," Blays put in. "At least this time she actually told you that you were right about something."

Not knowing whether to laugh or throw things around,

Dante resumed his practice. He'd gotten one sequence finished and was trying to zip through a second before the first one could change when his loon throbbed.

He hopped to his feet and walked away from the others, particularly Gladdic and Ara, then activated the loon. "Yes? Is that you, Jona?"

"Hope I haven't woken you again, sir."

"It's the middle of the afternoon."

"Oh yes, I've noticed. But I wouldn't know nothing about how a nethermancer structures his days. I'd imagine you'd have to stay up awful late to get to talk with the imps and demons."

"Imps and demons don't exist," Dante said. "And the ones that do are up and about during the daytime as well."

"I must say I find that most unsettling, sir."

"Then let's stop talking about it and start talking about why you looned me."

"Well, we've found the Knight of Odo Sein, lord. In fact, Captain Naran's speaking to him in the other room right now."

Dante clenched his fist in triumph. "And has he agreed to help us?"

"That's the exact matter I need to ask you about. The good knight is most interested in destroying the White Lich. I'd go so far as to say he's fanatical. Thing is, he doesn't believe in the slightest that the Odo Sein at the Silent Spires would ever agree to work with a bunch of dirty outlanders such as yourselves."

"We came to an agreement with them. I was in the middle of our training when you looned me."

"Oh, I'll just tell him that, then. He didn't believe me the other times I told him as much, but I'm sure this time will be different."

Dante scowled into the distance. "Tell him that Bel Ara is as beautiful as a sunrise, but her dedication to fighting the Eiden Rane has made her nearly as terrifying as he is."

Jona chuffed with laughter. "One moment, lord."

The loon went dead. Dante sat there, idling with the pathetic helplessness that was so specific to waiting for someone to re-open a loon connection.

It was only a minute before it pulsed again. "Well?"

"The good knight says that if you think Bel Ara is bad, you should try being trained by Five. He would be honored to give his life fighting the lich by your side."

Dante clenched his fist again, punching the air for good measure. "You have to keep him safe in the meantime. Don't even let him be seen in public."

"Suppose we'll cancel the knife-swallowing contest, then."

"One more thing, Jona. We're planning to stay here until we know that the White Lich plans to attack again. That means we have to know the instant he starts marching on Aris Osis. That means *you* need plenty of scouts. And some way for them to re-lay information back to you in as little time as possible. Signal fires or the like."

"Captain Naran had that same exact thought, sir. He's already got Tanarians ripping about in their canoes. If you hadn't no-ticed, they make top-notch watermen. Would love to get a few of them signed up to our crew."

"Even if we depose the main threat, the Tanarians will still have to deal with the Righteous Monsoon. I'm sure you could find a few sailors who'd be happy to get out of the country for a while." Dante gave a thumbs up to the others. "I need to return to my work. Let me know the instant you see signs of war from the lich. Even if it means interrupting me in the middle of the de-mon impregnation ritual."

"It will be done," Jona said. "I'm glad to know milord takes the matter so seriously."

Dante shut down the loon and returned to the others. "Our friends in Aris Osis have secured the help of the surviving

Knight of Odo Sein. Bel Ara, if the lich makes a move, we're going to need to be able to leave at a moment's notice."

"It's already taken care of. Do you think we're stupid?" She
looked him up and down. "Do you suppose the Eiden Rane will
make a second attack on the city?"

"I thought you guys were the experts on him. What with your
entire existence being devoted to stopping him."

"As far as I know, you four are the only people currently alive
who've squared off against him and survived. If I were an expert
on the Eiden Rane, and wanted to maintain that expertise as time
went on, I *might* want to go to sources such as yourself for more
current information."

"Despite having a conversation or two with him, I don't know
much about him. Most of our talk centered on things like how I
would join him or die. He was a bit one-note on that front. But
it's clear that he's smart and that, while he's far from reckless,
he's willing to make limited gambles. That's a dangerous opponent. Furthermore, he knows that *we're* a dangerous opponent. I
expect we've come closer to killing him than anyone has in a
long, long time."

"You sound proud of yourself."

"Shouldn't I be?"

"Did I say it was criticism?"

Dante gave her a skeptical look. "My point is that he can't be
confident that he can simply bide his time, slowly grow his power, and stick to the safety of the deep swamps until he's sure he's
invincible. Not as long as we're still out there. He moved on Aris
Osis because he thought it would make him strong enough to
slam the door on us. He knows the city can't withstand a second
assault. He'll be back to finish the job."

She nodded thoughtfully. "Then you're not likely to have
enough time to learn the Odo Sein."

"We'll see about that. If there's one thing I've learned about sorcery, it's that it doesn't work on the timeline you want it to—for good and for ill."

They broke for lunch. Dante hurried through it, returning to the Golden Stream as fast as he could, but his haste was in vain. Hard as he tried, he couldn't get through the second sequence before the first one changed shape on him, obsoleting his work. Often, he couldn't even complete the first one before it unraveled. The key to the stream seemed to be to pursue all three sequences at once, and to finish them in no more than a few moments, but doing that felt like trying to simultaneously pick three locks with two hands.

He went to bed that night afraid that Ara might be right after all.

He woke much too early, but knew within moments he wouldn't be able to fall back asleep. Instead, he put himself through the paces of the Forest, producing a speckling of stream, then reached out to it.

When he was halfway through his first sequence, Blays opened one eye, directing a filthy look at the faintly glowing pieces of gold. "That's disgusting. Can't you at least do that under the covers?"

Dante moved his mind into the nether in the thin rope running from the upper wall to the outer corner of Blays' bed frame. The rope severed with a crisp snip. The frame jerked downward, thumping Blays onto the floor.

"Damn Tanarian rope," Dante said. "It's the finest I've ever seen, and yet it will still fall apart on you at the worst possible time."

When Ara brought them to the field at the edge of the living land, the grass smelled of sunlight on dew. Dante's optimism for his progress was as bright as the skies, yet that day and the three that followed it passed with a dismal lack of concrete steps forward. Blays, at least, had finally gotten to the point where he was able to grapple with the stream, meaning that he was also able to join the others in the immensely frustrating business of participating in an activity very much like trying to build a sand castle as it was being washed away.

Even Ara, who was usually happy to laugh at and casually insult them for their stupidity, grew brooding and removed. Her lack of liveliness only made Dante feel less likely to succeed. He found himself working mechanically, trying the same methods over and over, making no real efforts to vary them. He told himself he was slowly growing his skills, but he didn't know if that was true.

Dante checked in with Jona every evening, but the sailor had nothing of particular interest. But on the fifth day after hearing that the Knight of Odo Sein had agreed to help them, Jona looned Dante during breakfast.

Dante stood from the low table and walked to the edge of the room. "Go ahead, Jona."

"We've just had a report from the swamps," the sailor said. "The White Lich is moving his forces to the east. The scouts believe he's on his way to a town by name of Ura Gall. That's several days away from us, but still a mite closer to Aris Osis."

"It goes without saying to keep your eyes peeled for any signs of a ruse. Is it possible to evacuate Ura Gall?"

"That won't be an easy thing to do, lord. If Aris Osis extends its lines to bring people down from Ura Hall, it will make them a very soft target. Too soft for the enemy to ignore, methinks."

"I didn't mean to send Aris Osis' troops to the town. I meant to get Ura Gall's people to flee to the north."

"But lord, that's the dead opposite direction from Aris Osis. That's a funny way to get them to safety."

"If the White Lich goes after them, it'd buy us another week to prepare. Small price to pay to save the rest of the country."

Jona made a thoughtful noise. "I suppose that's an easy decision to make when it's not your people on the chopping block."

"As a matter of fact, it is an easy decision, Jona. Furthermore, if Ura Gall heads north and the White Lich heads for Aris Osis instead, then we've exposed his ruse *and* removed the people of Ura Gall from harm's way. Something to think about as you're galloping around on your high horse."

"I was only thinking, sir. But that tends to be a mistake, don't it?"

"Have the scouts gotten an estimate on the number of Blighted?"

"Hard to say, given that they like to travel beneath the water, and also to rip apart anyone who gets close enough to count them. But they say it can't be anything less than five thousand. Mayhaps twice that."

Dante swore. "That was *not* the news I wanted."

"Should I go back and change it, lord?"

"It's all right. Raw numbers don't really matter. All that matters is the lich, and we still have a way to hit him."

He ended the conversation, then informed Ara and the others that they'd soon know whether there was an impending attack on Aris Osis. The idea that things were coming to a head helped Dante pursue the stream with renewed vigor, but by day's end, he still couldn't get two of the three sequences to stay open at the same time.

That night, long after they'd snuffed the candle and rolled into bed, the door to the room slipped open. Dante snapped open his eyes. A tall silhouette stood in the doorway.

"Get up," Ara said softly. "Don't make any noise. No lights, either."

Dante disengaged himself from the wicker frame, which was happy to dump you from it if you moved too fast. Blays and Gladdic were already stirring, but Volo was sleeping with typical teen vigorousness and had to be rousted with a good shake.

Ara wasn't carrying a lantern and the stairwell was so dim they had to feel their way down it until their eyes adjusted. Reaching the ground floor, she stopped to listen, then continued to the doorway.

Dante had spent very little time outside the towers after dark. A gentle wind blew in the heat of the captured sunlight that continued to be released from the mostly black Hills. The wind was blowing out of the northwest and Ara led them in the exact opposite direction, stopping at the last line of trees before the ground gave way to the warped nakedness of the Hills.

"I always think they look spooky at night," she said. "Like anything could come out of them."

Blays squinted into the darkness, the wind ruffling his blond hair. "*I* hadn't had that thought, but thank you for infecting me with it."

"Sit down. All of you. And get comfortable. We're going to be here for a while."

Dante lowered himself to the grass. It was dewy and cool. "What's this about? Now we need to practice in our sleep, too?"

"If you're going to get mad about this, you'll have to curse yourself, you dunce. I'm giving you exactly what you asked for: the first history of the Odo Sein." Ara plucked annoyedly at her robe. "We never reveal this until the night before a student is to be knighted and bestowed with their sword. But you're about to fight for us, and you might be about to die for us, and there's a small chance you might even win for us. So it stands to reason that you deserve to know who we are—and what you have become a part of."

She lifted her eyebrows. "Although it goes without saying that if you tell any of the other Bels that I told you this, it'll be a race to see whether they can kill you before I get to."

"Duly noted," Blays said.

"The story that most people know is that the Odo Sein were founded to put down the sorcerers and warlocks who were attempting to overthrow our rulers. But this is only partly true. It's like pointing to the base of a tree and saying that it grew from its roots. In a limited way, that's so—but you're forgetting all about the seed.

"Our seed dropped a few hundred years before the Eiden Rane. We're not sure exactly how long, because we didn't and still don't have physical records, and there's lots that's been lost in the chaos. What's important is that among the Yosein, there was a man named Shan Way. As a boy, he heard tales of the Arnad. Fierce nomads of what are now the Alebolgian prairies, the Arnad had disappeared a century before Shan's birth. Nobody knew why or where they'd gone. This, along with their prowess in battle, made Shan obsessed. He pestered all the adults he knew for stories of the Arnad, and when he played with his friends, he made them play as the barbarian nomads.

"Most childhood interests fall aside with age. Shan's didn't. As soon as he was old enough, he descended from the hills and into the prairies, visiting the villages the Arnad had burned, raped, and defiled over the years. There, he collected more stories of the Arnad. As many as he could. Where there were books or scrolls, he got those too, buying what he could and stealing the rest.

"His studies went on for years. He used to earn money by going to the squares and inns to tell the best stories he'd found. Soon, he was composing his own historical works on the Arnad. His interest in them *was* him. Yet despite everything he'd learned, he still hadn't figured out why the people of his obsession had disappeared.

"Finally, long after any sane man would have given up, he heard a story that the Arnad had disappeared into the Hitchcrag Mountains for reasons unknown. He set out on a pilgrimage into the mountains. Alone, because he was crazy. As he traveled, he imagined the path the Arnad had taken, all the reasons they might have left the plains, what he'd say to them if he found them. Within a few days, he'd gotten lost. As he tried to find a path back out, he stumbled into a shaded valley. Bones littered the ground. Half buried and covered in moss. Most of the clothes had rotted away, but Shan recognized their long knives at once. He had found the Arnad.

"Puzzled as to what had slaughtered such mighty warriors, he examined countless skeletons. Searched their effects for scrolls, especially those with orders from their chiefs, or communications from afar. Picked his way across the valley. Assembling the pieces like a mosaic, he put together a theory: the Arnad's shaman had had a vision that if they stayed on the prairie, their people would be wiped out. Not being fans of extinction, they headed into the Hitchcrags. Seeking sanctuary. Instead, they found death. Why? Shan ran through one possibility after another, envisioning how the Arnad must have been taken by surprise, pushed to one side of the valley, induced to make their last stand, and die.

"In the middle of his imagining this, something remarkable happened: Shan was given a Glimpse. He was *there* as the Arnad entered the valley. He watched as they were ambushed by a combined army of furious plains-dwellers. He saw the last of the Arnad fall. And he witnessed as a shaman in wolf furs hiked up a ridge to receive the rewards of his betrayal: three pouches of silver, and the hand of the firstborn daughter of the enemy king."

Seated in the grass, Ara tipped back her head and gazed up at the stars. "Shan was gobsmacked by what he'd seen. Understanding at once how and why he'd been granted the Glimpse, he remained in the valley, trying to attain another sip of the nectar of the past. Two weeks later, his wish was finally granted.

"But the Glimpse wasn't of the Arnad. Or of their foes. It was of a man and his pregnant wife crossing the valley in winter. They were dressed in buckskins, and though the stitching was skillful, the style looked older than anything Shan had seen. As the two of them climbed a ridge, the woman slipped in the snow. The man grabbed her hand and pulled her to safety, but lost his balance, tumbling down the slope to his death. Knowing there was nothing she could do, the woman trudged on. Shan didn't see whether she'd made it before the vision ended.

"Shan had finally found the Arnad. But he left the valley with a much deeper revelation: the past could be had again. Finding it became his new obsession. As he traveled and studied and practiced, he found that he didn't need to know everything about a people to catch a Glimpse of them. He only needed to think so fully about who they *might* have been that a gate would open to show them as they truly were.

"Shan saw the people who would become the Yosein as war pushed them from the Alebolgian coast and into the hills. He saw the Tracians, who built intricate earthen mounds only to pull them down a dozen years later, as if disgusted with their own work. He saw the Natyans, the forgemasters who brought us iron from the rusty hills.

"Each sight let Shan envision what led up to that sight. Letting him skip further and further back. He was now seeing people who had been completely forgotten. People he'd never heard of before. He saw people who rode horses without saddles. Then others who didn't know seem to know how to farm, following the herds and streams with the seasons. Then others who wore furs and chipped arrowheads from rocks. At one Glimpse, he saw a young boy summon a sphere of darkness. As he looked at it in wonder, the others of his tribe ran up behind him with rocks and beat him to death.

"Then something changed. Before, the cities had been gone,

but people were still plentiful. Now, there were almost none of them at all. The few Shan could find hid high in the mountains or in the deepest forests, living in the crudest savagery imaginable. He felt himself skipping more and more years with each Glimpse, but he had no idea how much time was passing. Only that at night, the stars were no longer where they should be, and that the beasts who roamed the prairies were bigger and more terrible than anything he'd ever seen.

"Then came a jump much longer than any before. One that made his head spin and his stomach drop. When the Glimpse resolved, what Shan saw nearly stopped his heart. Grand castles. Towering spires. Aqueducts that soaring down from the mountains. All of it was bigger and more beautiful than anything Shan had ever imagined. The people were tall and sleek and rode around on proud horses. The streets were so clean they dazzled. Markets sold food and goods that had to have come from every corner of the world.

"The Glimpse expanded further. Shan saw wizards wielding the light and shadow to raise immense monuments and dizzying towers to themselves. Others sat in finished spires reading their tomes. Each one had their own tower where they studied their art and performed subtle experiments while hundreds of guards and servants tended to the needs of the tower. They had made the realm. And they had made it great."

Ara paused to slip a waterskin from her robe and take a long drink. She cleared her throat and resumed. "The Glimpse moved away from the towers and into a darker mode. Shan watched as thousands of slaves worked the fields outside the city. Women whose minds had been hollowed out by sorcery swept and scrubbed the streets, collecting buckets of shit with grins on their faces. Men hacked blocks of stone from the hills, straining until they collapsed. For every person who lived well, four lived in agony. Kept in place by the unbreakable power of the warlocks and the twisted creatures they'd shaped to enforce their laws.

"Shan saw at last that the aching beauty of the realm was only made possible by an even greater horror.

"The sights afforded him by the vision began to speed up. Grim men and women worked in secret with a gold substance that glimmered on the air, hiding their activities from the wizards. In Shan's next sight, the people marched openly on the fields and quarries, freeing the slaves to join their ranks in rebellion. Time slid forward and the nether and ether were leaping through the streets of the cities, slaughtering the rebels by the tens of thousands. But those who bore the Golden Stream wrested the dark powers away from the warlocks. With the sorcerers reduced to mortal men, the rebels rushed in to string them from the rafters by their own guts.

"The sorcerers resorted to blasting whole neighborhoods into flattened rubble, clearing the way so that the wielders of the stream couldn't sneak up on their towers without being seen. Unchecked fires tore across the cities. Battles raged in the fields. Until everything that could be burned was burned. One after another, the sorcerer's towers were ripped down, the sorcerers bludgeoned into meat and fed to the dogs.

"The Glimpse slipped forward again. In one city, half the towers had fallen. Most of its districts lay in ruin. From the bases of the remaining towers, demons and monsters raced forth, carving through the mobs. Another slip and the demons were dead but human corpses layered the streets like autumn leaves. The skies were black with ash and the soot of the bodies.

"What was left of the rebels marched on the towers. Protected by the bearers of the stream, they pulled the warlocks down to earth. Only five towers stood between the people and their freedom. Then four. Then three. As the rebels moved to the third-to-last tower, its door swung open before they could attack it.

"A pack of abominations bounded out and scythed into the

mobs. Not human. Not demon. Not dead. But some measure of all three. And when they killed you—if they didn't eat you, or jam one claw up your ribs, another down your pelvis, and rip you in half—you became one of them. And when the entire mob lay dead or stood converted, and every soul in the city had been taken, the beasts returned to the towers and ate the very sorcerers who'd made them.

"The abominations spread faster than the news of them. Those places untouched by the war were gutted in a matter of days. Riders raced to rally people against the menace, but the resistance was overwhelmed before it could form. The survivors fled into the high mountains and deep wilderness. Only a few thousand scattered people withdrew far enough to hide. Everyone else was killed or absorbed.

"Until the abominations were all that remained on the earth.

"Even without humans to feed on, it took a long time for them to die. Hundreds of years, perhaps, although since they built nothing and grew nothing, the Glimpse gave Shan little indication of time. Eventually, the last of them passed. Even then, the people huddled in the peaks and jungles. Centuries later, when they finally emerged from their holes to see what had come of the world, the people were dressed in skins and carrying spears tipped with bone and rock.

"At last, Shan was released from what he would call the Long Glimpse. He was so horrified by what he'd seen that he didn't move for three days. When he stirred at last, a single thought rang in his mind. Sorcery had destroyed the world. A much better world than his own. And it was only a matter of time until it did so again. Worse yet—some day, it would destroy *everything*. All people. All beasts. All trees and fields and flowers.

"But he knew a way to fight it. The Golden Stream. Shan spent twenty years searching for it, guided only by what little he'd seen during the nightmare of his Long Glimpse. He was an old man before he finally found it and learned to harness it. Before he died, he taught it to three disciples. Three disciples who would watch sorcery spread across Tanar Atain—and who would found the order of the Odo Sein to combat it."

Ara bowed her head. She looked exhausted by the tale, as if the telling had taken a lifetime. The others exchanged a series of glances as complicated as semaphore.

"Okay, I'll say it," Blays said. "Isn't this utterly crazy?"

Ara looked up, a hard glint in her eye. "You're calling our history crazy?"

"First off, a man with no otherworldly training whatsoever was so obsessed with a gang of long-dead horsemen that he conjured up a heretofore-unknown form of sorcery. Except it wasn't *truly* unknown, because as it turns out, thousands of years before that, another group of anti-sorcerers deployed that same power against their slavemasters in a war that destroyed the world."

"Wrong. It wasn't thousands of years ago. It was tens of thousands."

"Well that makes it much more believable!"

"Shan was given Glimpses. Unlike people, Glimpses don't lie."

"Was Shan a person?"

"What else would he be? A jumble of cats walking around in a human skin?"

"If Shan was a person, and people lie, then maybe he lied about the Glimpses."

Ara gave him a disgusted look. "Do you people use this same scrutiny on your hopelessly complicated religions?"

"Of course not," Gladdic said. "For they are ours. And if you deny them, the powers that be send people like me to correct you."

Dante brushed what he hoped was a beetle from his foot. "You may think our beliefs are ridiculous, but I don't see how yours are ironclad. Shan could have made all of it up. Or more likely, he really did discover the Odo Sein, and his disciples invented a fabulous history for him in order to lend your order more credence."

Gladdic nodded once. "Even if Shan did see everything that he claimed, that is no proof of its historical veracity. One achieves Glimpses through profound expenditure of imagination. One might work oneself into such a fanciful mental state that one visits a delusion upon oneself in the form of a 'Glimpse.'"

"In other words, Shan might have imagined the whole thing while genuinely believing he was seeing our long-lost past."

Their discussion had generated a sprinkle of the stream. Ara waved at the flecks, looking simultaneously annoyed yet amused. "No one since Shan has been as talented as he was. We've never been able to go as far back as he did. But some of us have caught Glimpses of the more recent past. What we've seen matches up with his story."

Dante leaned forward in the grass. "What about the great cities he claimed to see? The castles and towers? Why aren't there any ruins around?"

"Most were annihilated in the cataclysm. The rest were eroded over the long passage of years—along with all memory of what had happened. Time annihilates us more totally than we know, priest of the eleven-and-one gods. It annihilates us more than we *want* to know."

The night was still warm, but a shudder passed over his body. The Hell-Painted Hills were a black sprawl of spiked and gnarled rock. The starkness of the land seemed to threaten that some day, everything would be just as empty as it was.

"I don't know whether what you've told us is true," Dante decided. "But I'm glad to have heard it."

"Absolutely," Blays said. "Nothing beats being yanked out of bed in the middle of the night and forced to consider the aching void of eternity and your pathetic insignificance within it. Why torture us—I mean, gift us—with this story, anyway? We still haven't heard a peep about the lich mounting another assault."

Ara pulled the collar of her robe tight across her neck. "I have a feeling that won't be true for much longer."

"Don't tell me you can Glimpse the future, too. If so, please don't tell me how I die. I'm really looking forward to being surprised by it."

"The Odo Sein can't see the future any better than anyone else can. But I am very cynical, which makes me more accurate than most of you."

"Bel Ara," Gladdic said. "I must ask—"

"No. No more questions. I've told you as much as you deserve. Get back to your beds. And don't talk about this again."

Dante fell back asleep more easily than he thought he would. When he dreamed, it was of walking through a grassy field where all people and animals had long since died, and the only voice left was that of the wind.

"Lord Galand." Jona's voice, typically musing and slow-paced, was taut and forced. "I have a new report for you, sir."

Dante was alone for once, out in the fields taking a walk to clear his head. "Go on, Jona."

"The people of Ura Gall were evacuated as ordered. They headed north. Fast as they could. For some miles, the lich and his army kept after them. But then the enemy broke south."

"To make for Aris Osis."

"I'm not paid to decide such things as that, lord."

"How long ago was this?"

"It was half a day before we heard from the scouts. I've kept as close to the front as I dared."

Dante did some quick mental math. "We have to leave now.

Otherwise, if he is headed for Aris Osis, we won't have time to get there before he sacks the city. Is there anything else?"

"Not yet, sir."

"Then I have to go prepare to leave. Tell me at once if circumstances change."

He dashed back toward the seven columns that made up the Silent Spires. As he entered the plaza between the buildings, he called out to a servant to help him find Bel Ara. Hearing Dante shout her name, she appeared on a balcony in her tower.

Dante cupped his hands to his mouth. "The lich is coming to Aris Osis. We have to get moving!"

For a moment, Ara looked bleak. Then she smiled, as mean as a falling rock. "Then I'd better help you stick a blade through the Eiden Rane's blue heart. Wait there."

She disappeared from the balcony. Dante instructed the servant to inform the others they needed to get ready to go at once. The servant jogged off at a speed that was fast enough to indicate respect but slow enough to indicate that Dante wasn't his master.

The door to the tower banged open, spraying servants into the plaza. They dashed off at full tilt—because Ara was right behind them, striding down the steps as her light robes fluttered behind her.

She stopped above Dante. "How soon do you mean to leave?"

"Immediately. We'll barely make it to Aris Osis ahead of the lich. We'll need every spare second to prepare the city."

"I thought you'd say that. I imagine your entire life consists of racing from one place to another at full tilt. Trying to save it all. That's why you're here, isn't it?"

"Not exactly."

"Oh? Then how *did* you come to be traveling about in a country where foreigners aren't allowed outside of the port, putting your life on the line to save us from a monster who's one of our own people?"

"A liar on an island pretended to be my dead dad."

Ara burst into unguarded laughter. "I'm deeply regretful that we didn't have time for you to tell me that story."

"It's a strange one. And probably longer than it's worth. But if we make it out of this alive, I'll be happy to tell you the tale."

"I might like that." She descended two more steps to stand beside him. "You actually think you can kill him, don't you?"

"So far, I haven't met anyone that I couldn't."

"I'll be honest with you, because it'll be funny. When you first came here, I thought you and your friends were a joke. That you'd exaggerated your encounters with the lich and would be pulverized by him if you met him again."

"You're right, that's hilarious. If you had no faith in us, why did you agree to train us?"

"You made a very good argument."

"And that was enough to convince you to waste our time and your own?"

She looked at him, then away. "There are some things that can't be discovered through reason. Maybe I wanted to help you because even though I didn't believe you could do it, I *wanted* to think that that you could."

Blays strolled into the square, waving at them. Out of deference, he hadn't been carrying his swords around the Silent Spires, but he was wearing them now. "Hello! Are we off to participate in something horrible?"

"It's about time, isn't it?" Dante said. "I don't think we've committed any war crimes in weeks."

Volo and Gladdic arrived soon after. Dante filled them in. As he spoke, servants showed up with tightly-packed bundles of provisions, blankets, and tools. It looked like more than they needed. As Dante was about to object that it would slow them down, hooves clopped into the plaza. Dante turned in confusion

—he hadn't seen any signs of horses the whole time they'd been at the Spires—and was utterly baffled by the team of dappled animals brought forth. They were the size of ponies, but they had the horns of goats. And the beards of goats. And the snouts, ears, and eyes of goats.

Dante wrinkled his brow. "What on earth are those?"

"What do they look like?" Ara said.

"Goats. Really big ones."

"Congratulations, you didn't need to ask me after all. You should apply this lesson to more of your questions in the future."

"But what are the really big goats *for*? Eating your really big piles of trash?"

Ara sighed. "What does it *look* like?"

"They're...wearing saddles. With stirrups. Lyle's balls, we're supposed to *ride* them?"

"I'm guessing you'll find that much more comfortable than letting them ride you."

Gladdic wandered forward, waving his left hand about before him. "I had wondered how your knights were able to cross the Hell-Painted Hills without dying. How fast can these beasts travel?"

"Would you rather I tell you? Or would you rather experience the joy of finding out for yourself?"

"Don't tell us!" Volo jogged over to a black goat with white ears and chin. "This one's mine. What are they called?"

"Lan haba. 'Strong-foot,' to you worthless barbarians."

Blays approached one of the animals, a brown-furred giant dappled with white spots. It gave him a sideways glance. "Any trick to riding them?"

"Sure," Ara said. "Don't fall off." She moved next to one of the lan haba and patted its well-groomed flank. "Given the circumstances, and the fact you've already felt the impact of the Hills for yourselves, I doubt I need to tell you not to delay. Fortunately, the animals are as strong as they look."

Dante turned to regard the fiery patterns splattered across the Hills. "They turn you into Blighted, don't they?"

"Not a pleasant fate. And not easy to come back from. Much easier to kill you." She flashed a grin. "Like I said. Don't delay."

The servants were already loading the beasts with provisions. There were eight lan haba in all: four for them, two for their guides, and two spares. As Dante waited for the final preparations, he gave thought to creating a loon linked to himself and Ara—both to keep her apprised of what was happening, and to continue their training as they traveled—but there were two problems there. First, even at a time like they presently faced, he didn't want to spread the loons to anyone he didn't have complete faith in. Not when they could be used by warlords and corrupt kings to do such harm.

And second, making a loon required parts of a dead animal. There *were* no animals in the Silent Spires, aside from the lan haba, which he was confident the Odo Sein would never let him kill. Although there wasn't any reason that a newly-killed *human* couldn't be used to make a loon, was there? Dante found his gaze resting on one of the older servants as the man shuffled across the plaza. Judging from the short, stuttery steps the man was taking, he wouldn't be useful for much longer anyway. Then why not—

Dante shook his head hard.

As soon as the animals were ready, Blays jumped into the saddle like he'd been riding giant goats his entire life. Dante brought himself beside one of the beasts, letting it accept his presence. He stuck his foot through the stirrup, pushed off, and swung into the saddle. The lan haba was a little lower to the ground than a typical riding horse but thicker through the middle. It smelled thoroughly goaty.

Ara moved to stand across from them. "Remember our deal.

Even if you kill the lich, if you don't come back to found the library of the Silent Spires, we'll make you wish the Eiden Rane had stuck you on his spear instead."

Dante laughed. "Is that right? You can't even leave this place. How do you think you'd come find us?"

"Our knights would."

"Yes, I bet they'd turn against the people who finally killed the monster who was bent on destroying your entire nation. Be seeing you, Bel Ara."

He nudged the lan haba's flanks. As the animal turned away, Dante spotted a smile on Ara's face.

Their two guides were a man and a woman dressed in airy white robes with masks that could be drawn over their mouths and noses in case the winds got too dusty. Both of them had the stoic and silent bearing of those whose duties endanger their lives on a regular basis. They brought the four outsiders to the southeast perimeter and stepped from the living oasis into the blasted slag of the wasteland.

The goats stepped from rock to rock with total surety. They weren't half as fast as a galloping horse, but the ride was much smoother. And compared to how slow Dante and the others had been on their way to the Spires—struggling up inclines, worried about their footing at all times—they were racing along.

"This won't take us a full day," he said in mild wonder. "According to what Jona told me, even if the White Lich pushes as fast as he can, we'll beat him to Aris Osis by as much as a day and a half."

Blays put his fist to his mouth and yawned. "What kind of defenses are we looking at mounting?"

"Jona thinks the Tanarians can field at least three thousand half-decent soldiers. Maybe as many as a thousand more, if they can arm some of the people who've been trickling in from the swamps. We'll still be outnumbered—two-fold, if not three—but the core of Aris Osis is nothing but towers. They'd need ten times as many to dislodge us."

"Unless, say, they had the help of the world's most powerful sorcerer to act as a siege engine."

"If he comes close enough to start knocking down towers, he'll be close enough for the knight to shut him down. Then it's just a matter of breaking through to the prime body."

"Think he'll bring it to a protracted siege instead?"

"I don't think he has a choice. But I'll send in my little flying spies before he's within twenty miles of the city. If he leaves the prime body behind, we'll find it."

This was the last significant conversation they had for several hours. Dante kept watch on himself and the others for signs of oncoming Blight, but the way the lan haba were steadily stepping forward, he doubted whether they'd feel any ill effects before they were out of the Hills.

The direct sunlight was brutal, but it turned out the servants had packed extra traveling robes. As to why they hadn't informed Dante and the others about that to begin with, he could only guess that it came down to the Spires' pervasive obsession with making everyone figure everything out for themselves.

The guides pushed onward into twilight. When Dante raised concerns about the beasts tripping, the woman grunted something about the lan habas' superior ability to see in the dark. They didn't call a halt until full darkness lay upon them. They camped in a valley that was deep enough to protect them from the wind but not so steep to have to worry about rocks falling on them in the night.

Sleeping in the Hills was never easy, but at least they had proper blankets. Even so, everyone was up before the sun. The guides had them on their way while the eastern crags were still turning gray. Dante passed the time fiddling with the stream. When this grew tiresome, he thought for a long time about the story Ara had told them about the founding of the Odo Sein. He was halfway through blurting out a question about it to Gladdic when he remembered Ara had sworn them to secrecy and they were in the presence of two Odo Sein soldiers with absolutely nothing to do except listen to every word the outsiders said. The thought that he'd almost exposed Ara made his back stiffen.

With the sun nearing eleven o'clock, they topped a ridge and looked down on a sprawl of green-black trees. Ribbons of water glimmered from the gaps in the canopy. Descending to the boundary, the smell of plants and half-stagnant water enveloped them like a mist.

"There it is!" Volo pointed downhill to where her canoe rested upside-down on the grass. "I was sure someone would take it. I'd steal it if I saw it lying around like that."

The guides brought them down to the swamp's edge, crossing into the grass of the living land; they would remain there for a day in order to let the corruption of the Hills fade from their bodies before returning to the Silent Spires. Dante thanked them. They nodded, saying nothing.

The four outsiders loaded up the canoe and got on their way, heading southeast toward the coast and Aris Osis.

With Volo paddling, Blays turned for a last look at the Hills. "That was a surprisingly uneventful trip, considering that it kills everyone else who passes through it, and your death can only be avoided with the aid of magical giant goats."

"There was nothing magic about them," Dante said.

"But they *were* pretty giant."

The canoe coasted along through the trees. Dante felt a fly land on him and smashed it with a scowl. "Gladdic, I never had the chance to ask you. What's your take on the story Ara told us about the founding of the Odo Sein?"

"I believe," the priest said, "that the Odo Sein have created a grand history for themselves. One which can be used to explain why they are special, and hence why they are justified in committing whatever crimes the Drakebane commands them to enact against his own people."

"I was actually wondering if you thought Shan could be right about the stream but wrong about the past, but I suppose that's also an answer."

"It is not a criticism unique to the Odo Sein. All of those who proclaim that only they know the truth are guilty of the same sinister motives."

"Including you and me?"

"If not, then we would be exceptional indeed."

"Do you need to turn yourself into the Mallish authorities? Because you're starting to sound like you don't believe in the gods at all."

"I believe," Gladdic said. "But I begin to wonder if I should."

"You know what's interesting? If you think about it, their story doesn't preclude ours from also being true. The gods could have created the world just as the *Cycle*—or your *Ban Naden*—says they did. And *then* the nethermancers might have enslaved four-fifths of the populace, leading to a revolt against them which they tried to stop with a weapon that destroyed all human culture. And then a long, long time later, after civilization returned, the mortals in the *Cycle* did all the things it says they did."

"That is logically possible. But it seems more likely that you're deluding yourself. If Shan's story is correct, and everything was destroyed—all knowledge, all records—then how do we still know of the gods?"

"Easy. The gods told their story to our ancestors, inspiring them to write the *Cycle*. If you'd created the entire world for people to live in, wouldn't you want them to know about that? I would. And I wouldn't let them stop them from knowing just because a group of morons screwed everything up tens of thousands of years ago."

"Yet the gods never correct us when we are wrong about them today."

Dante swatted at another fly. "Maybe it's enough that the story is known by some people."

"And maybe you rationalize, because it is more comfortable to be swaddled in lies than to face the cold truth with naked skin."

"That's enough," Blays said. "Of all the atrocious things you've done, by far the worst is making me imagine you naked."

Dante frowned. Now that the Silent Spires were behind them, Ara's claims felt flimsier, less authoritative. Yet something about the story of the Odo Sein remained compelling. Specifically, the idea that it *could* have happened, or at least that the history of the world *could* be so ancient, and they'd have no way to know it. Dante knew firsthand how much could be destroyed within a single century. With a thousand years of erosion, entire peoples and disasters were washed from the shores of time.

As long as they were, a century and even a millennium were still relatable enough spans of time that people had words to express them. Yet there was no word for a length of ten thousand years. Ten thousand years ago was so distant that not a single name, word, or deed from that time was remembered today.

And if, as Ara had implied, the time Shan had seen was closer to a hundred thousand years ago? Then time was a black pit, bottomless and without end. When your life came to a close, you were flung down that pit, and though your screams might echo to the surface for a while yet — until everyone who had known you died as well; and perhaps a few hundred years beyond that, if you were exceptionally famous — over a long enough period of time, you *would* be forgotten. Then you would be alone, damned to fall forever in darkness, punished eternally for having dared to exist for your flash-brief span of years.

This was deeply unsettling, so Dante turned to the purpose of improving their immediate security, which was all he could hope to control. He killed a half dozen dragonflies, sending two ahead, one behind, and three others in the direction of the lich's armada.

Their team passed the remainder of the day swapping between paddling and practicing with the stream. Dante checked in with Jona that night and was informed that the White Lich was now heading straight for Aris Osis. Even with all the speed of the Blighted, however, it would be two to three days until the enemy arrived at the city. It might even be long enough that Dante would be able to raise strategic ramparts with enough time to fully recover the nether before the battle.

They made camp on an island. After the quiet of the Spires, the cacophony of birds and bugs was almost overwhelming. Summer was near and brought the dawn early. They sailed on. Dante spent time with the stream, but in the middle of a bout of Forest, he found himself thinking of Ara. He'd promised to return to the Spires, and he hoped he'd be able to keep his word. Otherwise, she was confined there, and he'd never see her again.

They were still half a day out from Aris Osis when Dante's loon throbbed.

"Lord Galand," Jona said. "I bring urgent news. News that won't make you look at me with any fondness."

"The sooner you tell me it, the sooner I can figure out who actually deserves my anger."

"It's Aris Osis, sir. The enemy is much closer than we knew. They'll be upon the city in a matter of hours."

"That's not possible. Your scouts have been shadowing the lich this whole while. Even if he'd somehow slipped around you, he'd still be at least a day out from Aris Osis."

"You're not wrong, lord. The problem is that the enemy who's closing on the city isn't the White Lich. It's the Monsoon."

11

"The Monsoon?" Dante began to get to his feet. The rocking of the canoe reminded him this was extremely bad form. "How many are there?"

"Hard to be certain, sir," Jona said. "We've only had one scout come in yet, and she didn't stick around long enough to tally a good count. She claimed the enemy had no fewer than two thousand, but that it could easily be much more."

"Two thousand wouldn't be nearly enough to take the city. Ten thousand might not do it."

"Aye, Lord Galand. Captain Naran raised that same point, and suggested they will lie in wait to attack alongside the lich. But he also thought the Monsoon might strike first."

"Locking Aris Osis' defenders in place. Allowing the lich to maneuver freely."

"And perhaps to identify in advance where it's keeping its most vital defenders."

"Such as any remaining Knights of Odo Sein."

"That was the captain's thinking."

Dante gritted his teeth. "How did the city's scouts miss the fact there was a second fleet on the way?"

"The swamp is a dark place, lord. With so many of our eyes on the lich, we didn't spare enough to watch the rest of the wilds."

"I'll have eyes of my own on the lich soon enough. I'd like for you and Naran to withdraw to the city."

"Will you arrive before the Monsoon?"

"I doubt it. That's why I need your eyes there. That way, you can tell me exactly where to land the hammer-blow to break the siege."

Dante silenced the loon. The others had heard his side of the conversation and he needed no more than a few moments to deliver them the rest.

"The Monsoon will attack first," Gladdic declared. "To the Eiden Rane, they are wholly expendable. Just as Naran suspected, the lich will deploy them to press for weaknesses and to identify any elements who could pose a threat to the lich himself."

"Such as us," Dante said. "Which raises the question of whether we should intervene against the Monsoon at all."

Blays cracked his knuckles. "So your daring proposal is to race into Aris Osis as fast as we can, then boldly sit on our thumbs while its citizens are slaughtered?"

"The White Lich wants us to show our hand. If we hang back, we retain the element of surprise."

"But we can absolutely demolish the Monsoon. We'll shred these guys so bad there won't be enough of them left to wipe our asses with. Which I would recommend against, as it might turn out you're using a piece of *their* ass."

"The priority must remain upon the lich," Gladdic said. "If leaving the defenders of Aris Osis to fend for themselves enables us to bring the Eiden Rane down, then that's what we must do."

"When you break the point of the spear, you blunt the weapon. By crushing the Monsoon, we can smash the lich's campaign while saving thousands of lives."

"Those lives are inconsequential beyond their use against our foe. We have been forced beyond the bounds of conventional morality. Anything and everything may be sacrificed to the cause."

"I'd say that's been your motto all along. Aris Osis is your chance to get a little less in the red on the life-ledger."

Dante silently commanded one of his forward dragonflies to beeline toward Aris Osis and determine how far they had left to travel. "I think we have to play this one by ear. If the defenders are holding their own, there's no need to intervene. It would only reveal us. But if Aris Osis is in danger of falling to the Monsoon before the lich even gets there, we have to get involved. Otherwise he'll have the city without exposing himself to us. And that's the end of that."

Everyone except Gladdic took up the canoe's three paddles, driving themselves forward as fast as they could. When they wore down, Gladdic used the nether to remove the weakness from their muscles. Their pace was strong, but the path through the waterway was crooked and winding, fouled with brambles and dead trees. Dante's dragonfly spotted the towers of Aris Osis after an hour of flight, implying it was as little as thirty miles away, but he expected it would be six hours until their arrival.

The city still bore evidence of the attack led by the lesser lich the week previously. The outlying crops had been torn down and burned, and some of the house-raft neighborhoods had been scattered. Like a furrow left by a great plow, a trail of ash and devastation marked the pathway the lesser lich and his army of Blighted had carved across the islands on their way to the city's core. There, the towers of two islands had been knocked into rubble, broken stone jutting from the canals. Several other towers bore damage heavy enough to render them unstable. Repair efforts had been made at their bases, but these had clearly been suspended in the face of the second attack.

Their efforts were now being spent to buttress the defenses.

Aris Osis featured a unique challenge in that regard: each island was separated from its neighbors by a wide canal, and sported two to five towers, rendering them difficult to take through conventional means. However, this same separation meant that if the neighboring islands could be taken, the defenders would be completely cut off, without any means to retreat.

Furthermore, that lack of mobility meant that if the enemy could break a hole in the defenses, they could penetrate straight through to the citizen population. Not good news when the lich could convert every captured citizen into a new member of his own army.

To work with all these considerations, the people of Aris Osis were stacking their defenses on a peninsula of islands that extended into the protected bay of the port. To fend against the Blighted, who could bypass the chokepoint by walking straight through the water, the defenders had piled up dirt and rubble into ramparts on the shores of the island. Wooden stakes thrust outward from the shorelines and the tops of the ramparts. Soldiers drilled in war canoes, maneuvering between the canals and the bay. Laborers extended the hasty earthworks.

On the side of the peninsula facing away from the city and out to the ocean, a huge cluster of rafts and canoes bobbed in the gentle currents of the bay. If the defenses were overwhelmed, the people could hypothetically strike out to sea. But this struck Dante as a very desperate last resort. Few of the vessels were seaworthy, and he doubted there were enough to carry the thousands of people packed into the towers.

Still, it looked like more than enough to deal with the Monsoon. Dante ordered the dragonfly to gain elevation and head east-northeast in the direction of the incoming rebels. In less than half an hour of flight—a dozen miles, perhaps—his scout spotted the canoes slicing through the swamps. He lowered it through the canopy to skim over the length of the convoy.

Once he was done reviewing their troops, which took longer than he was happy about, he pinged Jona's loon. "I just got a look at the Monsoon's ranks. Your scouts must have been observing with one eye closed, because I see closer to four thousand."

"You'll have to pardon the men," Jona said as mildly as ever. "They weren't expecting to see any armies at all, let alone one of them."

"The Monsoon's traveling with some weird boats, too. Bigger than you typically see in the swamps. It could be logistical, but I have a bad feeling it's siege equipment."

"We're right about to enter the city, my lord. I'll pass your findings along. But I have a question, my lord."

"Yes?"

"If you can spy on them better than our own scouts, why weren't you doing so from the start?"

"My gods, you're right, Jona. Why didn't I think of that until right now?"

"This falls under the category of things I don't understand, doesn't it?"

"Even the nether has limits. Expect us in four hours. Until then, I'll be watching over you."

He sent another pair of dragonflies toward the city, leaving the first behind to follow the Monsoon. Two boring yet strenuous hours later, the Monsoon still hadn't deviated course or broken pace. Dante looned Jona to expect an attack in as little as twenty minutes.

Unlike most Tanarian cities, which were ringed by nothing more substantial than two sets of nets, Aris Osis was enclosed by a stone wall—the same one Volo had smuggled Dante and Blays through when they'd first come to Tanar Atain in search of Naran. Though the defenders were concentrating the bulk of their forces on the peninsula, they'd decided to make an initial stand at the wall, deploying four hundred soldiers along it, archers mixed with a few spearmen. In the event they were over-run, a long road consisting of both docks and small islands ran directly into the heart of the city, providing a fast means of with-drawal.

Other than the soldiers along the wall, the swampward reach-es of the city had been emptied out except for a handful of run-ners. The waters of their canals were so still that Dante could see the ripples of the fish breaching. As the first of the Monsoon's ca-noes broke from the treeline and into the clear outer ring of wa-ter on the north end of the city, one of the runners lit an arrow, tilted back his bow, and fired it into the air, leaving a thick band of reddish smoke in its wake.

The man hopped into a canoe and paddled like mad toward the interior. The Monsoon crossed the waters without resistance, a chevron of over six hundred boats. Most were simple canoes, but one in eight were larger double-hulled war canoes with a simple bridge, and one in twenty were wide, covered barges that resembled lumbering turtles. Rather than being oar-driven, they were propelled by a pair of objects that resembled mill wheels, one wheel affixed to either side of the hull. The exteriors had been painted black with red lines sectioning the design into plates, furthering the resemblance to a turtle, and seemed unusu-ally shiny, as if they'd been lacquered.

The armada came to a stop just outside of effective bow range. A lone war canoe detached from the mass. It bore the white flag with the two blue circles of the Monsoon.

Its captain climbed onto the top of the war canoe's bridge and made the typical demands for the city's defenders to lay down their arms and surrender. The defenders, aware that "surrender," in this case, was shorthand for "wait for the lich to turn you all into raving Blighted," responded with voluminous obscenities.

The war canoe returned to its ranks. There was a short pause as orders were relayed via shouting and semaphore. Ten of the turtle-boats detached from the armada, wheels churning as they advanced ploddingly on the wall in a loose line. A score of canoes followed tightly in their wake. The defenders loosed arrows that struck the sloped hulls of the turtle-boats without dealing any damage at all.

Flames lit up along the wall. A hail of burning arrows arced through the air, half landing on the boats while half sizzled into the water. Yet rather than flaring up and spreading to the hull, the oiled rags flickered dimly; the shiny surface of the boats had been applied to stymie this exact tactic.

A Monsoon officer bawled an order. Slots opened in the front and sides of the turtle-boats. Arrows whisked forth, sending men toppling from the walls. The armored boats advanced inexorably, suffering not a single casualty as they inflicted a dozen on the four hundred soldiers holding the walls.

A runner sprinted along the wall, handed a bundle of arrows to an archer, then ran on to deliver a second batch. The first archer nocked one of the new arrows, the tip of which bulged like a sack. As Dante realized it *was* a sack, and that he'd seen the Monsoon deploy ones just like them before, the man loosed his missile.

It had counterweights at the back to steady its heavy tip, and to compensate, the archer launched it in a steeper arc than the conventional arrows, lofting it into the air before it peaked and swooped down on the closest turtle-boat. It struck the ship on the port side. Light flashed; flame and smoke erupted from the boat, accompanied by a rolling boom. The ship stopped in its tracks. The wheel on its port side had been smashed to pieces and thrown across the water, the hull cracked and smoking.

A second arrow flew wide of its mark, but a third landed square, blowing open the nose of a second boat. It foundered, water pouring inside.

The surviving ships pressed hard forward, canoes darting from behind them to harry the defenders with arrows. A second contingent of turtle-boats detached from the fleet to trundle after the first wave, but there was no need; lacking more than a few of the explosive arrows, the defenders were only able to stop three of the first ten vessels from reaching the walls.

Arrows flew back and forth like hornets, but the defenders soon fell back. Hatches opened atop the turtle-boats. As the first attackers raced up ladders to claim their portion of wall, fellow soldiers scrambled from the canoes to follow them up top. A second wave of canoes was already on its way to reinforce them.

Now that the Monsoon had emerged from their shelters, they began to lose people as well, but they advanced steadily, pushing the Arisians back under a withering storm of arrows. Within a span of fifteen minutes from when the Monsoon had launched their attack, they'd driven the defenders to the center of the wall. The Arisians dashed down the steps to the long roadway leading back into the city.

Dante moved the closest of his dragonflies in for a better angle. As he did so, his connection to it snapped like a dry twig.

His heart froze. He sent his second dragonfly on the scene soaring higher and pulsed Jona's loon.

Jona answered with the crisp readiness he displayed while at sea. "Yes, lord?"

"Before you withdrew to the city, were you certain the White Lich was still with his army of Blighted?"

"Yes, sir."

"*How* certain?"

"Unless he's got friends who are also ten feet tall, with skin as white as snow, and eyes of every shade of blue, I am extremely certain he was still there, lord."

"You have to get the defenders off the bridge," Dante said. "The Monsoon has brought — "

Darkness flashed from atop the wall, streaking over the heads of the Arisians and smashing into a section of dock ahead of them. The wooden planks exploded into splinters, cutting off the defenders' retreat. The Monsoon charged forward, archers pelting the Arisians from atop the seized wall. The two sides clashed, corpses tumbling into the waters to both sides of the dock. After a minute of ferocious fighting, the beleaguered Arisians tried to drop back, but constrained by the tightness of the road, their retreat degraded into a chaotic mass. The scrum pushed dozens into the water. As those at the front were gashed down by Monsoon spears, other defenders leaped into the water, attempting to swim away.

Canoes swooped in to scoop them from the water. The Monsoon soldiers beat the prisoners into submission and carried them back to the fleet's reserves. Fresh recruits for the Blighted. Before the slaughter of the Arisian's front line of defense could be completed, the last hundred men surrendered.

"You just lost a tenth of your people," Dante said through the still-open loon. "And they've brought nethermancers."

The Monsoon had already cranked open the gates. Scores of canoes patrolled into the city, followed by the wallowing turtle-boats.

"Do you have orders?" Jona prompted.

"We're nearly there, but you have to delay them as much as possible. If they bring their nethermancers to bear on the towers, they can topple your entire defense within minutes."

"We'll do as we can, sir."

The Monsoon took several minutes to regroup, ferrying more captives to the back while the turtle-ships moved to the front. As soon as they renewed their advance, small teams of defenders popped up on both sides of the canal and fired a volley of arrows from their compact Tanarian bows. As soon as the arrows were in flight, they turned and ran, scampering across the narrow stone bridges leading to the next islands. The enemy's return fire landed on empty ground.

The city's islands and bridges, so quiet before, erupted into activity. While archers harried the Monsoon's advance, including with the occasional explosive arrow, teams assembled further down the canal to dump barrels, furniture, and anything else that would float into the waters. Others poled rafts together to clog the way forward.

With the Monsoon slowed to a crawl, Arisians rushed from the south to seize the chokepoints, provoking hot spots of gruesome urban warfare. Inflicting heavy losses on the Monsoon, the defenders might have been able to hold these positions for hours, if not indefinitely—but each time the advance stalled out, shadows streaked from the Monsoon nethermancers, murdering the defenders a dozen at a time.

Each minute gained was to be celebrated, but the outcome was inevitable. With Dante and the others still four miles from the city, the Arisians withdrew their battered squadrons to the crescent of islands that marked the entrance to the peninsula.

And their last defense.

The Monsoon regrouped again, sending scouts into the islands surrounding the point of entrance. Soldiers in white uniforms gathered across from the outermost of the defended towers. Arrows jabbed back and forth. A ball of nether looped from behind a short tower and crashed into the base of the defenders' outpost. It was followed by a second. Chunks of stone spun through the air.

Arisians sallied from the tower—presumably so that they wouldn't fall to their dooms when it was knocked down—and took cover behind whatever they could find. A few flung themselves into the water, followed by a trickle of them, and then a stream. A fourth ball of nether rocked the tower, making it lean like a man trying to see the soles of his boots without lifting his feet.

The sixth sent it crashing down.

Stone blocks slammed into the water, jetting spray dozens of feet into the air. Other parts landed on the island with rattling thuds. Dust spewed inland, aloft on the coastal breeze.

As it settled, a woman emerged from the Monsoon-held island. She wore a jabat long enough to be a dress, the white cloth emblazoned with circles of two different shades of blue. She looked on her work and smiled.

Three canoes shot from around the island where the tower had fallen, fighting their way through the still-choppy waters. They loosed arrows, but the turbulence sent the missiles flying wide of the sorcerer.

She snarled and summoned two gobs of shadows to her hands. She thrust forth her palms at the oncoming boats.

Before she could deliver it, the nether dropped from her hands as if it had died. She blinked in surprise.

A man in gleaming black scale armor arose from the neighboring island. He drew a long sword, the blade crackling purple as he pointed it at the sorcerer. "Death to the defiler! Death to the servant of the Eiden Rane!"

The Monsoon's archers fired on the canoes and the revealed Knight of Odo Sein, but the defenders' boats rushed onward, joined by others. The sorcerer turned and ran. An arrow pierced her right shoulder. She dropped, struggling to get up. The Arisians made landfall, hurling spears at the nethermancer, ignoring the incoming arrows even as the soldiers around them fell bleeding. As a Monsoon soldier helped the woman to her feet, a spear lanced through her chest, slamming her to the ground.

"What," Dante said, "is the knight doing in the middle of the battle?"

"Had no choice, lord," Jona said. "You said yourself that if their sorcerers brought their might against the towers, all the city was doomed."

"Okay, extreme circumstances and all, but why is he wearing his *armor*? And you can see that sword from Mallon! He's too obvious a target. At least show some *sense*!"

"Would you like me to—"

Jona cut off mid-sentence. The ambient noise from his side was gone, too. After a moment of shock, Dante understood: absorbed by the events of the battle, he'd left the loon open all the while. It had used the last of the nether bonding the two pieces together, and was now dead for good. Swearing violently, he tore the loon from his ear and hurled it into the swamp.

He watched through the dragonfly as a pitched battle erupted between the two contested islands. The Odo Sein attempted to withdraw, but a new blast of shadows forced him to remain at the island's edge. He raised his shield, deflecting an arrow.

Dante's last dragonfly went dark, struck down by a Monsoon sorcerer, or possibly by the Odo Sein knocking down every scrap of nether in the area. He cursed again, startling a possum hanging from a tree. Acutely aware that it was chipping away at his reserve of shadows, he killed and reanimated a single passing dragonfly, sending it whirring toward the city.

With Blays and Volo paddling as hard as they could, Dante recapped everything he'd seen, briefing them on what they could hope to expect. "It will be our job to neutralize any remaining nethermancers. If they're removed from the picture, the Arisians are more than capable of holding off the soldiers. Volo, is there another way into the city besides the front gates?"

She shook her head, black hair swaying. "Nope. Not that they ever told me."

"The Monsoon's still got a reserve force outside the gates. We'll need a disguise to get past them."

Gladdic made a murmuring noise. "And if they see through

it?"

"Then we'll need a crew of frighteningly effective murderers. Does anyone know where we can find such a thing?"

Blays blinked sweat from his eyes. "Sure, we *could* disguise ourselves as fellow Monsooners who just happened to fall behind, and who totally shouldn't need to answer any questions about that and definitely shouldn't be punished for it. Or you could just open a hole in the wall for us to sail through."

"I have a better idea: we do exactly what you just said."

Volo corrected course to bring them toward the western arm of the wall closest to where the battle for the peninsula was unfolding. Dante's dragonfly arrived at the city two minutes later. He sent it hundreds of feet into the air, too high to draw notice from enemy nethermancers or get caught up in the Odo Sein's sphere of negation.

The western wall was quiet, but a massive brawl was ongoing at the entrance to the peninsula. There, a second tower had fallen into the canal, forming an uneven bridge between two islands. Arrows zipped about, though less heavily than before; both sides were running low, resulting in clashes of spearmen battling for control of the bridge of rubble. On the water, squadrons of canoes hurtled toward each other, soldiers stabbing out as their boats clipped past each other. Nether flickered on the eastern fringe, slaying a team of Arisian archers who'd been punishing any Monsoon canoe that tried to enter the canal there.

To the west and center, there was no sign of sorcery. At that very moment, the Knight of Odo Sein, obvious in his demonic black armor, charged toward the eastern flank.

Before their canoe, the trees thinned, then vanished. They were spat into the brackish waters surrounding Aris Osis. Three Monsoon canoes were stationed near the wall a half mile to the north, but if they took any notice of Volo's canoe, they didn't show it.

They skimmed toward the looming wall. A pair of Arisian sentries stood from their posts, drawing bows. "Stay back or be fired upon!"

"We're friends!" Blays hollered. "Trust me, you'll really like us!"

"I said stay where you are!"

Volo glanced at Dante in confusion, still paddling. On the wall, the sentries sighted down their arrows. Gladdic flicked his left hand. White light shot toward the wall. Both men fell from sight.

Blays gawked. "Did you just kill them?"

"They were about to attempt to do the same to us," Gladdic said. "However, as a man of superior morals, I did not stoop to their level. I merely disabled them."

They rushed toward the wall, the wind whooshing over their faces. As they neared, Dante nicked his arm, then reached into the stone barrier. He softened it and drew it back, opening a hole there — one that, in the interest of preserving shadows, only ran a foot below the waterline, and was a mere three feet in width and height.

"Floating *shit*!" Volo squeaked. "We'll be smashed!"

She pulled in her paddle. Everyone ducked. They shot through the passage without a scrape. Volo laughed wildly, paddling hard. Dante guided her east, keeping two rows of islands between themselves and the fighting. Bodies bobbed everywhere, along with splintered wood, obliging Volo to weave through the flotsam like a shuttle on the loom.

Dante lowered his dragonfly closer to the eastern fighting. It was such a mess of tussling bodies that his search felt hopeless, yet he spotted Naran and Jona in moments, their foreign dress and features standing out from the Tanarians like a stain on a clean shirt. They stood on the southern face of an island connected to its northern neighbor by an arched stone bridge. At that moment, the Knight of Odo Sein stood on the southern foot of the bridge, rallying the defenders to retake control from the Monsoon. At a glance, five hundred soldiers were involved in the melee for the two islands, with reinforcements pouring in from both sides.

Volo slipped into a canal only to find the approach to the southern island blocked by an irregular line of stone rubble and shattered rafts. She craned her neck, hunting for a way around it.

Dante shook his head. "Faster for us to continue on foot. Volo, stay here with the canoe."

She tipped back her chin. "But I can help you."

"If the flank collapses, we'll need to get out of here in a hurry. Watch the boat and stay ready to go."

Sparing no more time for her arguments, he climbed out onto the broken rock of a fallen tower. Blays jogged behind him, not yet drawing his Odo Sein swords. Gladdic brought up the rear. Spotting them, Jona lifted his hand.

Dante ran to meet them. Naran grinned, clasping his hand. "I wasn't sure that I would see you again." His gaze moved to Gladdic. "In your case, I hoped that I wouldn't."

"We can resume internal hostilities after we've finished the external ones," Dante said. "Right now, our job is to get the Odo Sein off the front lines!"

Naran drew him close and lowered his voice. "The man in the armor is not the same man who earned it. He's merely a decoy. And a highly effective one at that. The Monsoon is throwing away countless lives in their effort to kill him."

"You dressed a soldier in the knight's armor? What happens when a nethermancer comes for him and he can't stop them?"

"The true Odo Sein remains close enough to neutralize their sorcery."

"That," Dante said, "is extraordinarily clever."

He took a moment to absorb the scene. The false knight was

providing a rallying point for the defenders, but he was also hanging behind the front lines. If a nethermancer came at him, it would be at grave personal risk. Dante was tempted to wade in and start blasting the Monsoon to shreds, but with their nethermancers neutralized, they seemed to be doing a pretty good job shredding themselves against the city's defenders.

"I say we watch and wait," he said. "There might not be any call to reveal ourselves today. For now, our single priority is to keep the real knight safe. Where is he?"

"Secure on the previous island we seized." Naran turned to the west and nodded to the glob of land on the other side of the rubble they'd crossed on the way in. His eyes flew wide. "Mother of storms!"

"*That* island?" Blays pointed. "The one in the process of being completely overrun by the Monsoon?"

Naran nodded, stone-faced. On the southwest shore of the island, which was separated from them a couple hundred feet of open water and most of the island itself, a horde of white-uniformed Monsoon were cutting their way through the Arisians, pushing toward a pillar of a man dressed in lacquer armor and laying about himself with a stout spear and a tall, rectangular shield. Cut off from the shore, the Knight of Odo Sein bellowed for aid.

"To him!" Dante took off at a run. "To the knight!"

He sprinted toward the debris, calling the nether to his hands. Before he could release it, the power of the Odo Sein clamped down on him. Hopping onto the broken rubble, he yelled to the knight, but the man was fighting for his life, lost in the helter-skelter of weapons and armor colliding and soldiers screaming in rage and pain.

Dante retreated past the spot where the power had afflicted him, but the nether remained inert. Gladdic cursed, the cords of his neck straining against his wrinkled skin as he fought to bring either the shadows or light to bear.

Blays ran ahead of them toward the canoe, skidding to a halt on the pebble-strewn rubble, staring at the spot where they'd left Volo. The canoe was gone. Almost halfway to the other island, Volo paddled with everything she had. Meaning to snatch the Odo Sein up and ferry him away to safety.

Dante made his way to the edge of the debris field, standing on a column of broken tower. Naran waved his hands over his head and yelled to a friendly canoe past the southern end of the rubble, convincing them to swing about.

On the western island, most of the Odo Sein's fellow soldiers had been knocked to the ground to bleed away their last. Catching a glimpse of Volo's canoe streaming toward him, the knight lashed about with redoubled vigor, fighting his way toward the shoreline. Volo cruised onward, reaching the shallows where reeds and grass grew.

Around and behind her, dark shapes broke the surface of the water. At first, their rounded tops resembled the backs of an army of turtles, but they continued to rise, the shapes flaring out like hideous pale mushrooms. Shoulders and arms emerged from the depths. With their upper bodies freed from the water, the Blighted stampeded toward the island.

Volo froze, retracting her paddle from the water. The wake of the Blighted's frenzied charge rocked her side to side. They ignored her for the moment, bent on the destruction of the Odo Sein. Seeing their gnashing faces, the knight pushed his way back up the slope, enemy spears knocking against his broad shield. The first row of Blighted hauled themselves to dry ground.

Dante cupped his hands to his mouth. "Drop the Odo Sein! Drop it now! For the love of the Silent Spires!"

Unhearing, the knight tried to bull his way onward. A spear slipped around his shield and pierced his right side. He fell to one knee, planting his spear hand in the muck. Two Blighted flung themselves at him from behind, yanking at his armor to expose his back and sinking their teeth into his skin.

The nether unlocked. In the blink of an eye, Gladdic punched his hand forward. A sheet of ether streaked away from him, expanding as it went until the glare on the water was so bright Dante had to shield his eyes. The ether sliced into the backs of the rearmost Blighted, exploding more dazzlingly than the Tanarians' special arrows.

Dante blinked, clearing the spots from his eyes. Dozens of half corpses sloshed about in the water, cut across the hips, gut, or ribs, depending on how far each Blighted had managed to climb from the water before being hit by the light. There was no sign of Volo. Her canoe bumped into a torso, stopping ten feet from the island.

On the island, the Blighted lay dead. So did many of the Monsoon soldiers. But the Knight of Odo Sein stirred, pulling himself away from the remainder. His shield arm dragged behind him, broken.

"Did you kill her?" Blays said. "Did you kill Volo?"

Gladdic worked his throat. Before he could answer, nether forked from the island they'd left behind, plowing into the Arisians at the center of the bridge and toppling them into the water.

"Save the knight!" Gladdic barked at Dante. "I will wreak our hell on those who wage war on the world!"

The canoe Naran had hailed swung up to the ruins. Dante rolled over the gunwale, accompanied by Naran and Jona. The oarsman shoved off toward the western island. There, a few of the surviving Monsoon soldiers were shaking off their daze. As they moved to pick up their dropped spears, Dante brought the nether to him. The triumph of its presence felt like standing from bed after a long illness.

He drew it into killing bolts, hurling them over the water. The Monsoon soldiers converging on the wounded Odo Sein didn't so much as look up as the shadows punched through their torsos in cloudbursts of blood. Dante sent a second volley behind the first, aiming them at a squadron of Monsoon charging in from the ruins. Seeing the black missiles, the soldiers scattered, throwing themselves toward cover. Dante guided the nether after them, ripping through their skulls and ribs. Later, the joy of the wrath he felt at finally being able to act would be shameful. For now, it burned inside him like sweet liquor.

Behind him, men screamed. People had been screaming for some time now, but this was something new: the shrieks of people seeing a death far worse than they'd imagined would take them. On the southern of the two contested islands, a pair of Andrac loped toward the bridge, twice the height of a man, long claws extended from their sides. The Arisians scrambled away as well, tripping over rocks. Sometimes they dropped their weapons and left them behind.

The Monsoon soldiers who'd taken the bridge shook off their paralysis and turned to run. Too late. The two Andrac overtook them in great bounds, slashing them into thick slabs of meat.

Naran grabbed the gunwale. "I feel sickened."

"I possess a simple solution," Dante said. "Quit looking."

"That is my paradox. I don't *want* to look away. The deaths of these traitors to humanity gives me more pleasure than starting or ending a long voyage."

"If you expect me to say that such feelings don't reflect your true self, or something else meant to reassure you of your basic civility, you're going to be disappointed. We're not a very good species, Naran. We're violent and we want to see our enemies fall. In good times, we can pretend to be better than that — but good times rarely last for long."

The Andrac continued their wholesale slaughter of the Monsoon. Nether flickered from the north island, crashing into the bridge. It gave way with a groan and clack of rock, landing with thunderous gouts of water, the two demons dumped into the canal with it. Blays, a purple sword snapping in each hand, sprinted past the ruins and vaulted far over the canal separating the two islands. As he cleared the apex of his jump, he disappeared from sight. There was no splash.

A pale torso spun in the current to Dante's right. He turned about, scanning the waters as the canoe passed through the bobbing carcasses. They passed Volo's black boat, which was dinged up but intact. It was empty. The canoe scraped to a soft halt in the grass and mud at the edge of the island.

Dante threw himself out, sandals squelching. Naran leaped out behind him. To Dante's right, a slim body lay on the shore. Volo's eyes were closed and her soaked hair clung to the side of her face. Her blood had trickled into the silt and he couldn't tell at a glance whether she was alive. He hesitated, aware that Naran was staring at him, then ran on toward the Knight of Odo Sein.

The man lay on his belly. His left arm was bent at the forearm, broken by his own shield when the blast of ether had knocked him over. Yet he showed only a few surface burns of the bluish variety caused by hostile exposure to the light. Somehow, Gladdic had managed to almost entirely avoid hitting the man with the ether straight on.

Even so, where his lacquered armor had been ripped away, the man's ragged jabat was stained red. Blood leaked from spear wounds and bites deep enough to have torn away flesh. More than one looked potentially fatal. Though the bites were more viscerally disturbing, Dante homed in on the nastiest of the spear wounds, a deep slit on his upper chest that had likely punctured a lung. Nether poured from his hands into the wound, sinking into its depths and sealing severed tissue back together. Pink, bubbly blood—the sign of lung trauma, though the nether had already confirmed that for Dante—was forced outward, dribbling down the man's chest like a clutch of frog's eggs.

As soon as that wound was treated, he moved to the next. Naran stood between him and the top of the low hill, wary for another attack. Dante finished the second wound and shifted to the third, a jab to the liver that would have killed the man in twenty minutes.

The knight gasped, eyes popping open.

"Warlock!" He grabbed the front of Dante's jabat. Golden sparks lit the man's face, spinning in tight patterns around his hands. The nether slammed closed. "Let me go!"

"*You* stop it with the Odo Sein! I'm trying to help you, you ass-brained moron!"

The man struggled to drag himself away. As he planted the palm of his broken arm against the ground, he gasped again. His eyes rolled back, face paling to nearly the same shade as the Eiden Rane. He collapsed.

The knight's power fell away, releasing the nether. Muttering curses, Dante drew the shadows back to him. The remaining stab wounds didn't look overly serious, so he turned to the bites taken from the flesh, which were gruesome and bleeding badly. Stilling his mind to an empty chamber, he waited for the ether to fill him, then directed it to the largest bite, which filled with a semi-opaque substance. It sealed over with new skin that was a perfect replacement of the old.

With that single action depleting almost half of the ether he could bring to bear, Dante opted to reserve the rest for the time being, patching the other bites with nether. Not as elegant, and it might leave scarring—Dante was rushing it—but the man would live.

That left a broken arm as the only serious wound. Sensing some serious triage in his future, Dante was tempted to leave it be. But with the White Lich close enough to fall upon the city in as little as a day, they'd need the knight at full strength. Dante knitted his bones back together, then closed all but the most superficial of his remaining cuts.

He shot to his feet and motioned to Naran. "Watch over him!"

Only then did he turn and sprint back to Volo, turf flying from his feet.

She lay in the same position as when he'd first seen her. She was still alive, but she had deep gouges in her back, the fringes of her skin blue with ether. The shallow angle of entry suggested she'd ducked as the light ripped over her, or even that she'd attempted to fling herself into the water.

She had bites taken out of her, too. Mostly the arms and shoulders. One had also been inflicted on the right side of her jaw, the skin dangling in a flap.

Dante placed the nether on the ethereal slices in her back. If you didn't know what you were doing, damage caused by ether could be hard to undo, but Dante had treated countless cases over the years. First, he used the nether to snuff out the light remaining in Volo's wounds, and only then closed them up.

He did the best he could to smooth out the skin on her jaw without leaving any marks behind. With the other bites, he filled in the flesh and covered them with new skin, but did little to deal with the cosmetics. She would have scars. Big and strange ones.

But she'd be all right. He wasn't yet sure the same could be said of Aris Osis.

He got to his feet and looked around him for the first time in several minutes. There was some skirmishing going on to the northwest, but it looked to mostly be an interference action.

The real battle was unfolding on the northern of the two islands Blays and Gladdic had gone to assault. There, shadows and light crashed together in storms of black and white motes.

Men hurled spears back and forth. One of the Andrac was staggering back from the north shore, bleeding nether like a smoking chimney. For a moment, Dante was taken aback that the enemy had found a way to hurt the demons so quickly, yet it shouldn't have been much of a surprise. The demons had first been created in Tanar Atain. Its sorcerers would also know how to destroy them.

The battle looked far from decided and he itched to join it. Yet the first priority was to remove the knight from harm's way. Could send him deep into the peninsula, but he'd have to accompany them all the way to safeguard against ambushes such as the one sprung by the Blighted. That would prevent him from joining the battle for at least fifteen minutes.

He took a quick look around, confirming there were no enemies nearby, then reached out to the nether on all sides. Didn't seem to be anything lurking or spying. He picked Volo up and slung her over his shoulder, grateful that the Tanarians were lightly built, and brought her over to a chunk of broken wall close to the knight.

"Help me carry him." Dante grabbed the knight's feet while Naran took the shoulders. Dante guided them toward Volo and set the knight beside her.

Naran set his hand on his hip. "Have you forgotten that the canoe is over there? In the water?"

"No time." Dante sank the ground beneath the two wounded, hollowing out a pit, then liquefied the stone wall and drew it over them, concealing them within a space the size of a small room. He left an air hole open on one side, slanting it so that no one could see or shoot into the space. "There. That should do it until we get back."

"And if you die in the field?!"

"Then you'd better make sure *you* don't." Dante scratched an X in the dirt with his sandal. "You're a pirate, aren't you? This should be fun for you."

"I am an honest merchant. I am only a pirate when a dishonest government declares me one."

Dante was already running for the canoe. He got in and ordered the sailor to make for the southern shore of the northern island.

The crewman slung out his lower jaw. "You mean the island being smashed to bits by sorcery and demons?"

"Yes, that's the one."

"Just checking."

The man shoved off, cutting across the waterway. Dante probed the nether beneath the surface, hunting for Blighted, but he didn't feel anything bigger than fish. To the north, two fleets of canoes rammed into each other, the sailors stabbing at each other with spears.

Under normal circumstances, the peculiar naval action would have been exciting. On the northern island, however, the wounded Andrac had gone as translucent as mist. The nether in its body streamed toward the northern shore, gathering around the hands of a man dressed in a piece of clothing that was difficult to correctly identify, as it had recently been on fire. The nethermancer formed the shadows into slender spears and whipped them into the front line of the Arisian defenders. A low stone wall blew apart, five soldiers tumbling away in pieces.

Gladdic was watching the man from forty yards away, light and darkness orbiting his left hand. Yet he did nothing as the enemy nethermancer lashed out at the Arisians a second time. The half-burned man raised his hands high in anger, sucking the last of the nether from the dying Andrac, and fired it at Gladdic in a shuddering wave. Gladdic met it with a torrent of shadows and a column of light, hazing the field with black and white sparks.

The air shimmered behind the nethermancer. Two rods of light blazed in the air, purple and black. The figure holding them coalesced the next instant. Blays drove one sword through the nethermancer's back and the other into the base of his neck, then yanked the upper blade to the right and the lower one to the left. The nethereal weapons shredded the man like wilted cabbage.

Arrows zipped toward Blays. He disappeared from sight. Gladdic strode forward, spraying nether into the Monsoon archers.

The canoe hit the shore. Dante vaulted over the prow and onto dry land with such skill he was annoyed that Naran and the crewman were the only ones to see it. He drew his Odo Sein blade, as did Naran, and ran up the low incline. With the nethermancer dead, the Arisians stood and charged. They hammered into the Monsoon lines with the clunk of spears on shields.

Dante was fifty feet from the front lines when Blays reappeared next to him, causing Dante to nearly dampen the front of his jabat.

"Did you find her?" Blays said.

"She's alive. But she's unconscious. She got hit hard."

"I saw. What about the knight?"

"Same with him."

"So everything's in order?"

"Hard as it is to believe, I'd say yes."

"Imagine that. Want to go win a battle, then?"

They joined the front lines, laying about with their Odo Sein weapons while Gladdic pounded at the attackers with both darkness and light. In less than a minute, the Monsoon began to fall back in an orderly retreat, taking to their canoes as others hunkered behind cover, loosing their remaining arrows to prevent the Arisians from overwhelming them. The surrendered field bore as many as three hundred bodies, a mix of dead from both sides.

Gladdic struck out at the archers only to be met by a wall of shadows cast from somewhere out in the water. At a command from an officer, half of the Arisian defenders got up and ran south. Dante was about to shout at them not to be cowards when he realized they were going for their own canoes.

Gladdic limped over to meet them, his face covered in sweat and ash. "We should join the pursuit."

"The Monsoon is broken," Naran said. "The city has already lost more people than it can afford. Perhaps it's better to let them run."

"They have taken hundreds of captives. If we do not reclaim them, the next time we face the lich, we'll be fighting them as Blighted instead."

"The Arisians can't do this themselves," Blays said. "Not as long as the Monsoon's got another sorcerer out there." He slammed his sword into its sheath. "We're bringing the prisoners home."

He turned and ran for the boats. At the shore, Naran grabbed two paddles left behind there. The four of them piled into the canoe that had brought Dante and Naran to the island and joined the swarm of Arisian vessels giving chase to the Monsoon. The three of them that still had two arms took up paddles and thrashed the water for all they were worth. Aided heavily by their crewman, who was fresh-armed while most of the others had recently been in battle, they slowly moved to the front of the chase.

Watching the enemy fleet, Naran counted under his breath, stopping after ten seconds. "We're not gaining quickly enough. They're leading us away from our defenses and toward their reserves. If we extend ourselves all the way to the gates, they will rejoin the remainder of their force and smash us."

Dante had lost track of his dragonfly during the intensity of the healing and fighting. Discovering that it was still flying in slow circles over the southern portion of the city, he brought it speeding forward. Through its eyes, he scouted the route ahead.

He tapped the sailor on the shoulder. "Get us as close as you can. Gladdic, watch for their nethermancer."

He sent a burst of nether into the crewman's muscles. The man grunted and paddled harder yet. They were outpacing the rest of the Arisians, entering the open gap of water between them and the Monsoon. A few arrows sailed toward them, splooshing into the water. Gladdic used a prong of ether to deflect one that appeared to be coming too close.

The Monsoon's armada had initially been strung out in a long line, but had condensed its formation on the move. They were presently streaming through a district of mixed islands and long public docks of merchant stalls. Dante watched closely as they skimmed past one of the docks and entered a watery square where two canals intersected. They paddled through it, entering a tight strait between two islands.

He felt down through the water and into the ground beneath it. A hearty layer of silt rested on top of a bed of clay. Dante moved into the clay, drawing it upwards in a great sweep. It broke the surface of the strait and rose to a height of four feet, cutting off the fraction of Monsoon vessels that had already cruised past it from the bulk of the boats behind them.

Canoes rammed into the wall with hollow thuds. Others back-paddled hard, showering the air with spray. Officers yelled out contradicting orders. One third of the fleet broke to starboard while the larger portion swerved to port. Dante reached into the clay again, ready to block the Monsoon a second time, but the city's defenders were already pouring into the intersection before the strait. They tore into the confused enemy before the Monsoon could escape.

The fight was short but brutal. Though the Monsoon were fellow countrymen—some of whom, most likely, had even grown up in this very city—the Arisians showed them no quarter, skewering them on spears and stabbing them over and over, faces contorted with an anger as red-hot as that of the Blighted. The crime the defenders were punishing them for was much more than rebellion against an emperor. Instead, it was for the treason of selling themselves to a conquerer who would not only take the land, but consume its people.

The handful of prisoners taken were beaten hard, tossed in the bottom of the war canoes, and hauled off for interrogation. The Arisian captives were shuttled south toward the peninsula. The defenders regrouped and headed for the gates. Dante and the others accompanied them, but the Monsoon had already departed north into the woods, taking with them hundreds of citizens and soldiers captured earlier in the fighting. A heated argument broke out between the defenders about whether to give chase.

Dante turned their canoe about and directed them back through the damaged city to the rubble-strewn island where he'd left Volo and the Odo Sein. Except for the dead, the island was deserted. Dante jogged to the smooth rock he'd shaped earlier. The nether was markedly slow to answer his call, lagging resentfully as he used it to open a passage in the side of the rock.

Volo was still unconscious, breathing deeply and slowly, twitching with occasional shudders. The knight moaned as they picked him up and carried him to the canoe. Rather than climbing in with the others, Blays got in Volo's black canoe, which had come to rest a short ways down the shore, and followed them to a tower made of bright orange bricks.

They were greeted by a gray-haired woman named Kina, who thanked them so profusely for their aid that she didn't even remember to insult them for being foreigners. Dante asked for and was granted three rooms, including one that would serve as a hospital. Staff helped put Volo and the knight to bed. Dante observed the two of them for a few minutes, using some of his dwindling supply of nether to heal three wounds that were worse than he'd initially assessed.

Done, he sat back, feeling a headache coming on. "Shall we retire to the other room?"

Gladdic quirked an eyebrow. "For what purpose?"

"To discuss what in the million hells we're going to do now that the White Lich knows we're in the city?"

"I do not question the discussion. I question us leaving this room. Until our task is complete, we should not leave the Knight of Odo Sein alone for a single second. We cannot allow him to come to harm under any circumstances."

"What a wonderful sentiment," Blays said. "Too bad you don't apply it to *your own fucking friends*!"

Gladdic looked him in the eye. "You are referring to young Volo."

"No, I'm referring to the fish we ate for breakfast. We're lucky she's alive, you son of a bitch! What were you thinking?"

"My thinking was very simple: that if I allowed the knight to perish, then I would doom everyone in the city. A state of being that would also include Volo."

Blays stalked forward, sandals landing heavily. "Go on and tell me how it had to be done because the greater good and also I'm not looking at the big picture *and* my head is so soft that you could spread it on a slice of bread. I've heard it all a million times before. You can go ahead and stroke yourself off for being such a decisive leader who's not afraid to make the hard decisions.

"You know what you can't do? *Sacrifice your own people*. When they're gone, they're gone. They don't get to come back. You don't get to betray them just because you're too fucking stupid and gutless to come up with a better solution. When someone's fought by your side all the way, and they've bled for you and you for them, that forges a sacred bond. When you break it, you forfeit your soul."

Gladdic smiled thinly. "You rage for the sake of poor Volo.

Yet if I had slaughtered an innocent soldier to save the knight's life, you would congratulate me on my quickness of mind."

"Are you seriously trying to call me a hypocrite? Of course I don't care about a stranger! But Volo's no stranger, is she? She's one of us. If you're that ready to kill one of us, then you should-n't be here!"

"I have explained this to you more than once. If that is what is required to dispense with the lich, I *am* ready to sacrifice any one of us. Including myself."

Blays gripped the hilt of his sword. "Would you like a hand with that? I promise it'll somehow slay the White Lich, too."

The old man narrowed his eyes to slits. "You do not argue this from the mind, as the Odo Sein would train us. Rather, you argue it from the guts, the angry spleen and the festering bowel. What lies at the core of this?"

"The crazy idea that you don't murder your own friends!"

Dante had been taken aback by the heat of Blays' fury—he was fond enough of Volo, but he considered her more of a useful ally than as a close friend like Naran—but the answer lit up like a torchstone. This wasn't about Volo.

It was about Lira. The woman Dante had sent to her death in order to save the city of Narashtovik.

"It wasn't a perfect call," Dante said. "But the point wasn't to kill Volo. She was in the wrong place at the wrong time."

Blays tossed up his hands. "Because she was trying to save the knight herself!"

"And then got taken by surprise. The same way we all were. If Gladdic hadn't acted, both the knight and Volo would have been ripped apart by the Blighted. Instead, they're both alive."

"Through sheer luck for both of them! Why are you defending this?"

"It turned out okay, didn't it? So it can't have been *quite* as bad as you're saying."

"You agree with him, don't you? You probably would have done the exact same thing." Blays eyed him, face reddened, a blond lock stuck to his brow. "I bet that when you healed them, you healed the knight first."

Dante sputtered, then opted for the truth. "I had to! He's the only Odo Sein left in Tanar Atain. As soon as I was done, I healed Volo, too."

"But you couldn't know she'd last that long. Why is this so hard to understand? We don't sacrifice each other! We stand together at all times, no matter how bloody and dark they get! That's why we always win!"

"What else was I supposed to do? Everything hinges on the knight. I'd have resurrected my own dad and killed him again if that's what it took to save the Odo Sein."

"Are you lying to me? Or to yourself? If the knight died, we could have gone back to our training. Just like we already planned."

"There's no guarantee we'll ever learn. Not before the lich is beyond our means to stop."

"Yes, that's what everyone says, isn't it? But they don't know a gods damn thing. Yet for some reason, we keep swallowing their every claim. And look where it's gotten us."

The disgust in his voice was so thick Dante fell back half a step. Blays strode from the room, slamming the door behind him.

Dante moved to the door and opened it, but he didn't bother to chase after Blays. Instead, he motioned to a servant standing at attention down the hall. "He'll be looking for beer. No, that's wrong. He'll want something much stronger. For everyone's sake, you should see that he gets it."

The servant pushed off from the wall and trotted after Blays. Dante reentered the chamber.

Naran cleared his throat. "He's walked out on us? Do you believe it'll be temporary?"

Dante flung himself down on a seating pad, wishing more than anything for a gloriously massive stuffed chair. "He won't give up after we've come this far. He just needs to blow off some steam. Fortunately, he's even better with that than he is with a sword."

"The rest of us do not have the luxury of taking time for ourselves," Gladdic said. "The Eiden Rane could strike as soon as tomorrow. We require a credible strategy."

"That depends entirely on whether the knight wakes up, doesn't it? If he's still unconscious when the enemy gets here, our 'credible strategy' will consist of 'running for the nearest canoe and paddling away as fast as we can, secure in the knowledge that no one will survive to tell anyone of our cowardice.'"

"Are you certain you healed him correctly?"

"I made what was bleeding not bleed and made the stuff that was broken quit that too. If you think you can do better, you're welcome to try."

Gladdic crossed the room to the pallet holding the knight. The man was in his forties, but he had the build of a soldier ten years younger. Even in his sleep it looked like the muscles of his face had been pulled tight behind his head. Gladdic kneeled beside him, muttering. A film of ether came to his hands. He dispersed it over the unconscious knight.

"This is a deep but normal sleep," Gladdic declared after a short observation. "As can be proven."

He reached out and pinched the man's nose shut. The knight jerked his head to the side. He made a muffled groan, then blinked, taking a hard breath through his mouth. The nether and ether closed shut to Dante as hard as Blays had slammed the door on his way out.

Dante rolled his eyes. "At least we know he hasn't lost any of his abilities."

"You are among allies, Knight of the Odo Sein." Gladdic's voice was almost gentle. "I am Gladdic, once of Bressel. That is Dante Galand, leader of Narashtovik in the north. The good Captain Naran has told us of each other."

The man tried to speak, then bent over coughing. Naran poured water from a pitcher into a cup, both objects made from exceedingly well-wrought glass, and handed it to the knight.

The knight drank, then tried again. "I'm alive?"

"And well," Gladdic said.

"But the Blighted. They were—eating me."

"They were," Dante said. "We thought that was rather rude, and asked them to stop. The request was phrased by chopping them in half. Then, as long as we were in the neighborhood, we decided to fix you up."

The knight stared at him blankly. "Your friend said you were my allies. But you talk like you're mocking me."

"It's been a long day, we've just scored our first real victory against the White Lich, and my other friend is off getting drunk without me. I'm not in the most formal of moods."

"It's a strange time for us all. My name is Bek Olan, Knight of Odo Sein and Sworn to the Drakebane."

"Glad to meet you. We've got a lot of work ahead of us, so excuse me for cutting to the chase. Do you still promise to help us kill the White Lich? By the way, and I mention this again for no reason, we did just save you from getting eaten alive by Blighted."

"Did you also save the city?"

"It took a beating. But the one we gave the Monsoon was far worse."

Bek laughed slowly. "Hari are helping to save Tanar Atain while the emperor forsakes it? This must be the end of the world, because everything is upside down."

"Yes or no, Bek?"

"My decision hasn't varied since the moment I made it. My entire life was spent training to die fighting the Eiden Rane. That's what I will do now."

"Perfect. The gods must be impressed with your devotion, because they're going to give you the chance to die to the lich within the next two days. Sleep now. We need you ready."

The chamber included two glass doors that opened onto a balcony. To let the wounded rest while being able to keep an eye on them, Dante brought Gladdic and Naran outside.

"We have the assets and the knowledge to kill the lich," Dante said. "If we can find the prime body within his army, and bring Bek within Odo Sein range, one good stab will end this. The problem is that, after today, the lich knows we're here and that we've got an Odo Sein with us. There's no way he hasn't guessed our plan."

Gladdic moved to the balustrade, resting his hand on the railing. It was well into the afternoon and the sun shimmered from the canals and the bay. "The intention of today's attack could not be more transparent: to assassinate the Odo Sein and leave us impotent to stop the Eiden Rane from absorbing the city. Since his effort failed, it would be foolish to assume the lich's next strike will be in person. More likely he will send another army led by one of his lieutenants."

Dante's skin prickled. "Or he won't send an army at all. Can the lesser liches travel underwater like the Blighted can?"

"Likely so. Though more intelligent, they share many traits with the Blighted, and are not subject to the same rules of mortality that we mortals face."

"Then we could be in deep shit. Although that might actually solve our problem, since an under-lich might not be able to walk through it."

It took Gladdic a moment. "You believe the Eiden Rane might send one of his lieutenants through the canals."

"That's what *I'd* do. We have no way of watching what's beneath the surface. One of his pet sorcerers could sneak up and
assassinate Bek before we knew what was happening. He could
even combine it with a frontal attack, then ambush us with a
lesser lich as soon as we step out from safety."

"He has already proven the concept with the Blighted. I believe this is eminently plausible. We must treat it as though it is a
part of his plan or risk being ruined by it."

Dante pinched the bridge of his nose. "The reason it's such a
good plan is that we can't really stop it. When he attacks again,
what are we supposed to do? Hole up in the top of a tower and
let the citizens get massacred by the Blighted until the White
Lich himself shows up? Or do we leave Aris Osis altogether?"

"Neither, because your premise is wrong. I *can* stop a lieutenant from infiltrating the canals. The ether can be applied to
dry land to determine whether it has been recently disturbed by
footsteps — and the same may be done to water."

"That's very clever. But there's no way you can watch the
whole city."

"Again, your premise is flawed. I only have to be able to observe the waterways closest to this island. I believe the roof of
that tower would provide an appropriate vantage." He pointed
to the tallest tower in the city, a black spire located a couple of islands away that stood a good sixty feet higher than the peak of
the one they were currently inside.

"You're just going to sit up there? And watch?"

"Indeed. That will provide *you* with the security necessary to
locate the Eiden Rane, surveil him, and deduce his next move. In
doing so, we might even craft a way to strike at him before he is
able to follow through with his plan."

Dante glanced around for any insects he could use as scouts.
"I'll start at once."

Gladdic nodded and turned to go.

Naran gave them a skeptical look. "Aren't you forgetting something? Such as coordinating with the city leaders who we will be relying on to provide a large-scale defense?"

"You've already been working with them, haven't you?" Dante said. "Let them know we're expecting another attack soon. And it's likely to be much worse than the one we weathered today."

"I'll do that. And I'll see about securing a new guide in case we need to move out while Volo remains incapacitated."

Naran and Gladdic departed the balcony. Seeing no bugs about, Dante did the same, exiting into the garden outside the tower to gather up a half dozen moths and large flies. As he sent them flying up to the balcony while he climbed the stairs, he felt a pang of resentment toward Blays. His input was always invaluable; even when his suggestions were too ridiculous to try, they tended to push Dante toward more creative solutions of his own. Dante knew as well as anyone that it wasn't always possible to throw aside the stresses of battle like a well-gnawed chicken bone, but would it have killed Blays to wait to explode until *after* they were out of immediate danger of being overrun?

Back in their quarters, Bek had fallen asleep again, snoring lightly. Volo remained deeply unconscious. On the balcony, Dante made himself a comfy seat of blankets and pads, then sent his tiny scouts soaring north from the city, directing the faster flies higher to hunt for the White Lich while the moths followed the largest "road" exiting the city to the north.

Movement on top of the black spire drew his eye. A tall, thin figure crossed to the edge of the spire's roof, attended to by a pair of servants. Gladdic settled into his perch, ether twinkling on his hand.

The moths spotted the retreating Monsoon after an hour of flight. The armada moved along beneath the trees at a steady clip. It had been diminished, but remained imposing in size.

Dante kept one moth steady in the air high above them while sending another to dip below the canopy. The Monsoon still fielded at least one nethermancer, possibly more. If he could identify them—

A tendril of awareness moved through the nether, questing toward the moth. Dante drew back to passive observation, leaving the insect to its own devices, but the alien presence continued onward, hunting in a wide spiral that soon tightened closer and closer around the thin cord connecting Dante to the moth. As the presence snapped down on the cord, Dante severed it.

Troubling. Either the nethermancer was extremely skilled, sensitive to any disruption of the shadows, or the White Lich had warned them to be on the lookout for such things. That the Monsoon had any nethermancers at all was even more troubling. The rebels hadn't seemed to have access to sorcerers back when Dante and Blays, in their ignorance, had been working alongside them. Either they'd been keeping some of their strength hidden, or they'd only recently found (or convinced) the nethermancers to join them.

But why *would* the nethermancers help them? Surely they had to understand that the Eiden Rane wouldn't allow people of their power to continue to exist without ensuring their absolute loyalty to him. Was that the very reason they were allying with him? To be made under-liches? Still slaves, yes, but at least thinking ones, whose lifespans would last for centuries. If Dante reached the point where he knew that victory against the lich was impossible, would he make the same decision?

The Monsoon wasn't doing anything more interesting than retreating. He couldn't get spies close enough to them to overhear their talk, and his flies were likely to take another few hours to reach the White Lich. With the western sky reddening and his stomach emptying, he got up to see about food.

In the inner chamber, Bek remained asleep. But Volo was sitting up in her bed, staring blankly across the room.

"Volo!" Dante ran to her, slowing as he neared. She didn't turn her head. "Volo? Are you all right?"

She didn't speak or look at him. He took a step closer. "Volo? You were hurt very badly. But you're okay now. Do you understand?"

Again, she gave no sign of having heard. Her eyes gazed right through him. Frowning, he waved a hand in her face, then drew back his elbow and threw a punch at her nose. He stopped it three inches from her face, which was good, because she didn't even flinch.

With a sinking feeling, Dante reached into the nether within her. As far as he could tell, her brain appeared intact—it wasn't bleeding or swollen—and the rest of her, while still showing some healing to do, was in relatively fine shape. He decided against summoning Gladdic away from his duties in favor of leaving her be and seeing if she snapped out of it on her own.

Dante stuck his head out in the hallway and asked the servant there for a meal. The servant went downstairs without a word. Ten minutes later, he knocked on the door and delivered a plate of fish, greens, and fried bananas.

"Thank you," Dante said. "I don't suppose you've heard any gossip about where my friend Blays has gone off to?"

"I have," the man said with some satisfaction. "Friend of mine said the hari is down at a pub on the docks with some of the soldiers. Word is your friend is trying to see which can hold more liquid: the bay, or his stomach."

After eating, Dante took a quick nap to replenish his dwindling command of the shadows. When he woke, he went back to close observation through his spies. The sun set. Lanterns glowed from shores and towers. The streets filled with the sounds of rowdy singing, drunken laughter, and boisterous, free-wheeling insult competitions that drew crowds by the score.

It was the liveliest Dante had seen Tanar Atain since before the revolution. He felt a small measure of pride in having helped restore it, however briefly it might last.

The White Lich and his army of Blighted didn't need lanterns or cook fires, and spotting them in the middle of the night might have proven exceedingly difficult if not for the fact there were many thousands of them in many hundreds of boats. That, and the fact that the White Lich glowed like a star descended to earth.

They had advanced over the last few hours and their camp was roughly thirty miles north of Aris Osis. Close enough to fall on the city within half a day. But the lich would be waiting for word from the Monsoon, pushing the timeline back to at least a full day. Cold comfort.

Keeping his distance from the lich, Dante dropped two flies through the canopy, gauging numbers and hunting for the prime body, which was probably being kept in an armored boat of some kind. As he sent a fly over a formation of Blighted, his connection to it was severed so abruptly that Dante uttered a startled "Hey!"

He commanded the second of the low-elevation flies to go still. Yet the presence that swept toward it was as inexorable as a rogue wave. Though Dante hadn't given it any orders, the fly began to move. He commanded it to stop. An iron grip clamped down on the insect. Dante grabbed hold of it with all his strength, yet it was like trying to stop a horse cart by grabbing hold of the rear gate and digging in his heels.

The fly buzzed downward, passing over the heads of the Blighted as they stirred restlessly in their undecorated canoes. The lich stood ahead, radiating faintly beneath the cover of the trees. He grew larger and larger until the fly could see nothing else, his eyes holding perfectly steady even as the color within them cycled from one shade of blue to the next.

Dante tried to sever the link to the fly, but it was like trying to cut through a wad of cotton with a block of wood.

The lich shook his massive head. "You are no more than this pest. No more than the fleas that feed on your weak meat. Everything is mine, sorcerer. And when you bend the knee to me, you will weep tears of joy."

The lich crushed the connection in a vise of nether.

Dante had sent two other flies there as well, which were currently circling high overhead, seemingly beyond detection. Yet they were so high up that they couldn't catch more than spotty glimpses of the Blighted through the canopy. He'd be able to follow the army's movement, but if he spotted the prime body, it would be through sheer luck. Even that felt highly unlikely. With the lich aware that he was being watched, there was no chance he'd let his vulnerability be seen.

A scream slashed across the night. Dante jerked his head up. Light fell from the black spire—a streak of ether. It silhouetted Gladdic as he hurtled toward the ground two hundred feet below. Dante shot to his feet. He grabbed at the shadows, but there was nothing he could do.

With a flash of pale light, Gladdic struck the ground.

12

Dante ran down the tower steps. Each second felt long enough to compose, seal, and deliver a letter, yet no time seemed to pass at all as he threw himself into a canoe, thrashing madly to the island hosting the black spire.

He'd been too far away to mark the exact spot where Gladdic had landed, but all he had to do was run to the cluster of servants and onlookers circled around the body.

Dante slid through the grass to kneel next to Gladdic. "Get back!"

The crowd retracted two steps, leaving him alone with the broken figure. It was both better than Dante had expected yet entirely gruesome: bones poking from the right shin, hip turned strangely, blood staining Gladdic's jabat and leaking from his lolling mouth.

Dante had already cut himself as he'd run across the island. The nether was everywhere, falling on him before he called to it. He sent it into Gladdic's form. The old man wasn't breathing. His heart was still. Yet the nether still circulated within him. Pulsing in confusion. Dante had seen this before: it was the state in which the body wasn't dead in the full sense, the shadows within it not yet certain that they were supposed to flow from the corpse to rejoin the world as a whole.

He drove the nether into Gladdic's heart like a black dagger. Blocking out all other thoughts, he churned the nether in a circle to mix with the unsteady shadows that were already there. Once they were thoroughly emulsified, he expanded the nether, contracted it, and expanded it again, slowly at first, then quicker and quicker with each cycle. Until the frantic pace matched the thrum of his own heart.

He held the pace for twelve seconds. Feeling woozy, he removed himself from Gladdic's heart. Yet it continued to beat on its own. Gladdic coughed bright red blood, groaned, and lapsed back into unconsciousness.

The crowd erupted into gasps and chatter; someone gave a short scream. A young man with ragged hair fell to his knees and lowered his face in supplication. "You brought him back from the dead!"

Dante shook his head, too focused on his task to try to explain that Gladdic hadn't really been dead — and aware that, even if he tried, it would do nothing to quench the ridiculous stories the locals would be telling about it later that same night. He cleared his mind of thoughts, waiting with forced patience while the ether filled him. He sent the light to Gladdic's shattered shin, making it whole, while at the same time applying the nether to the priest's numerous and catastrophic internal injuries.

Bad though these were, Gladdic had fallen more than two hundred feet. The impact should have burst him apart. The flash of light Dante had seen at the end must have been some trick of ether Gladdic had used to save his life.

Dante hadn't had the time and rest to recuperate all of the nether he'd spent during the battle and he ran out before he'd finished undoing the damage to Gladdic's body. It would have to be enough for the time being. A team of soldiers arrived with a stretcher. They gathered Gladdic up and transported him to the tower where Volo and Bek were currently recovering.

Dante tilted back his head at the spire. Some loose masonry was scattered across the island.

He turned to the crowd. "Was anyone with him when he fell? Did you see what happened?"

A servant took a step forward, bowing his head. "I was on the roof. He was near the edge, muttering to himself and casting his weird spells. Then he cried out and slipped over the edge."

A woman dressed in the green and white of the Drakebane's soldiers nodded. "Saw the same. Ledge crumbled under his foot. Had warned him it'd been damaged in the fighting, but he didn't listen."

No one had anything more than that. Dante got the name of the soldier and the servant who'd witnessed it, then paddled back to the island where they'd set up their private hospital, which was getting disturbingly full. A pair of soldiers had been posted outside the hospital quarters. Inside, Gladdic was unattended. Dante wasn't certain if that was because local physicians had decided they couldn't do anything for him, or if they refused to touch dirty foreigners.

Gladdic was breathing deeply and evenly. It didn't seem like the kind of sleep he would soon wake from. Volo had curled up to face the wall. Dante called to her softly, but she gave no sign she'd heard. Bek, at least, seemed reasonably healthy, given what he'd been through, although obviously weak.

The door banged open, vomiting Blays into the room. His eyes were bleary and he was missing one of his sandals. Naran entered after him, looking annoyed yet grave.

Blays staggered over to Gladdic, taking a route that was wriggly enough to seduce a snake. "What happened to him?"

"He fell from a tower," Dante said.

"A tower? Are you sure it wasn't his high horse?"

Dante explained what little he knew. "He'll live. I think."

"Hardly a surprise, is it? Devils never die easy. If he was going to fall on something, why couldn't it have been a field of whirling blades?"

"Are you that drunk? Or just that stupid? He could be out for days. If the White Lich shows up and Gladdic's still unconscious, that means no Andrac. We'll be down to a single sorcerer."

Blays crossed his arms and made an attempt to nod, though his head was swaying side to side as much as up and down. "Yeah, well, he's still a bastard. And I'm tired. Wake me up if he dies, will you? Just make sure to bring beer."

Blays shuffled toward the other room, ramming into the doorway and half-collapsing inside. Even with the door closed behind him, the racket he made unfolding his bed from the wall was enough to wake Bek.

Naran shook his head in disgust and indicated the balcony. It was hours past sundown and the offshore breeze had died away to nothing, leaving the night humid and warm. Most of the revelers had gone off to bed, but isolated shouts and cackles rang through the darkness.

"We're dead," Dante said. "With Gladdic in this state, a lesser lich could sneak up on us at any moment."

Naran pinched his chin. "In that case, I would recommend the use of a little-known asset known as 'guards.' It is admittedly primitive when compared to sorcery, but some have found it effective."

"Yes, all right, maybe it's not the end of the world in and of itself. But this isn't our only problem, is it? Volo's catatonic. I don't even know if she can hear me. Gladdic might be in a coma. Even if he snaps out of it in time, Blays can barely stand to stay in the same room with him. Everything's falling apart, and it's at the worst possible time."

"Given the frequency that you find yourself in such conditions, I had come to think that you enjoyed them."

"I don't know if we can rely on our original plan to take out the lich. I need to think of something else. Some way to hit the lich before he comes close to the city and puts his guard up."

Naran nodded, gazing across the dark towers. "As before, I don't know what help I can be to you. But I'll offer whatever I can."

"I suppose you can help me keep an eye on the city. We should set up patrols to look out for more Blighted. The attempt they made today was too good not to try again."

They went to the ground floor to speak to a woman named Sal Dan, who had been acting as Naran's liaison since the first threats had arisen against the city. She sent runners out to bring more soldiers to the island for instruction.

While they waited, Dante asked Naran to step outside. He moved a short ways from the tower, checking to ensure they were alone. "The loon I gave Jona broke when we were on our way here. I'm going to replace it."

"Do you anticipate that we'll be working separately again?"

"It's possible I'll need to venture outside the city for recon. Besides, if you're out on patrol and you bump into a lesser lich, I doubt you'll want to wait for a runner to inform me that you're currently shitting your pants."

Dante waited until a pair of the city's innumerable rats wandered by, then slew them with one of his few remaining dabs of nether. He picked up the bodies and brought them upstairs, where he severed their heads and rapidly cleaned them of flesh and brains, a process that had become second nature to him.

Naran clamped his hands in his armpits. "Is it *required* that everything involving your art must be disgusting?"

"You sound like Blays. As the saying goes, if you want to make a loon, you have to break a few rats' skulls."

Dante cracked the skulls into the component pieces that would form the loon and bound them together with some Tanarian thread that was strong enough to use as fishing line.

He cut his finger and Naran's and they each added a dab of blood to the two parts, forging the connection between them. They tested them to confirm they worked, then returned downstairs, where Sal had assembled thirty soldiers. After Dante briefed them on the previous Blighted attack, they took to canoes and dispersed through the city canals.

Feeling moderately better about the state of things, Dante returned to his balcony, shifting his attention between the White Lich, the retreating Monsoon (who'd made camp in the swamps miles north of Aris Osis), and the city's innumerable canals and waterways. The revelry had finally ended, citizens exhausted by the battle trundling off to their beds, aware they might have another fight on their hands all too soon. Having had an awfully long day himself, Dante propped his back against the wall.

He woke with a start, heart pounding. It was still dark, but the stars had jumped close to two hours. Two hours that Dante had neglected to keep watch on the vulnerable city.

He activated his new loon. Naran didn't answer. He was probably asleep, too, leaving the patrols to better-rested Tanarians. Dante sent his nearby bugs on a quick sweep of the skies. The city seemed at peace, but that could be true right up until the moment ten thousand Blighted jumped from hiding in the waterways.

He jogged up the stairwell to the rooftop, emptying himself of thoughts. In the stillness, the ether arrived, coming freely, most of his ability restored by sleep and the long hours since he'd used it. He pushed open the hatch to the roof. He was two hundred feet high. Enough to see a good portion of the city at once. Gathering up the ether, he sent it down to the canals. Not to the surface, which would likely be painted with the disturbance of any number of vessels even at this late hour, but below it. Faint, small lines appeared, the trails left behind by cruising fish.

He cast his net further and further, working in an outward

spiral. Knowing he had limited light to work with, he gave each segment of canal no more than a dusting, hoping that it would be enough to catch the trail left by anything human-sized.

As he neared the western wall, the dust lit up like white fire, illuminating dozens of tangled strands. Dante's throat caught. He sent a dragonfly screaming toward the site, but it couldn't see past the murky surface of the canal.

Dante flung himself down the steps, pausing only to inform the guards stationed outside their quarters that he was going to check on a possible disturbance. As he ran out the doors, he pulsed Naran's loon again, but there was no response.

He hopped in a canoe, stirring the scent of brackish water as he paddled toward the western wall. There had been something like thirty or forty trails through the water. If they were all Blighted, that wouldn't be a problem; the shadows were starting to come easily again, and would rip apart the undead in seconds. If they were Blighted led by a lesser lich, it might be more of a challenge, yet he fully expected that he'd still be able to destroy them by himself — or at the very least retreat and rally at one of the towers.

Besides, with most of his team injured, or passed out in bed, what other choice was there?

He came to the southern tips of the silvery trails, which were already fading away. He tracked them north, the light strengthening as he went. After a few hundred yards, it was blazing under the water, and seemed to be intensifying at a sluggish walking speed. One that would match that of bodies slogging along underwater.

Dante brought the canoe in to land. Nicking his arm, he summoned the nether to his right hand. He dropped a good chunk of his ether into the water, asking it to glow as pure light.

Pale rays shot through the water. On the canal bed, illuminated despite the murk, forty Blighted threw their hands over their eyes against the intrusion of the light.

Dante didn't have much experience with using the nether to blast things underwater, so he sent a single bolt as a test case. It moved more slowly than it would through open air, but struck the target forcefully enough to punch a hole through the man's chest. He staggered, a cloud of blood wafting through the water.

The Blighted took off to the north at what passed for a run. Dante only had to walk to keep up, striding alongside a retaining wall. He plowed a half dozen shadowy missiles into the water. All struck their targets, but only three did so with enough damage to kill. Could he force or lure them from the water somehow? Or was there a way to work with the water to reduce the energy he was spending? Because while it was likely that it would be at least another day before the White Lich arrived —

He passed the corner of the retaining wall. A shadow flew toward him, robes flapping behind it. Dante thrust at it with the nether, but the nether was already coming at him, battering past his defenses, enfolding everything in darkness.

Cold tingled over him. He smelled ice. It felt like some time had passed. He opened his eyes.

And stared into those of the White Lich.

Dante kicked his feet against the stone ground, trying to slide away as he snatched out at the nether. The lich lifted his index finger. Dante's feet and hands seemed to freeze to the floor. A whip of ether dashed the shadows from his command.

"You will stop that." The lich's metallic voice grated like flint drawn down the side of a copper bowl. "Or I will hurt you until you learn to stop."

Dante bit his teeth together hard enough to strain his jaw. He made another grab at the nether. The ether whipped out again, dispersing it. A second whip of ether lashed at Dante. Pain launched up his spine. Every muscle in his body went as stiff as a tile. He heard himself scream.

He was gone for a while. The coldness returned. He opened his eyes. He'd pissed himself.

He was lying in a stone chamber. The walls were covered in glyphs and the air smelled damp and somehow old. The White Lich stood fifteen feet from him, the light emanating from the sorcerer's skin making his outline indistinct, like a vision from a dream. He barely had room to stand without scraping his head on the ceiling.

Dante found he was able to tilt his head to meet the lich's gaze, but the rest of his body was bound in place by implacable strands of ether. "Why not kill me?"

The lich's expression barely changed, yet he was somehow able to exude a sense of pitying contempt. "You are smarter than most, sorcerer. Don't beg me for answers that you can find for yourself."

"You want me for something. Information. Or to turn me into one of your slaves. Or both."

"Think more deeply yet."

"Except for the fact that other nethermancers seem to be of use to you, and that you're completely insane, I know almost nothing about you."

Only the lich's lips moved. "We are not always rational. Not everything is done in the service of securing resources. Sometimes we act for satisfaction. Maybe I just want to hurt you."

Dante's scalp tingled. "Do you?"

"Yes," the lich said. "But I do not think that I will."

"How did you get to me?"

"You already possess the answer."

Despite his half-terror, Dante nearly rolled his eyes. Then he frowned instead. "After you ambushed us with the Blighted, you knew we'd be on the lookout for further incursions. So you gave us one. When I went out to investigate, your lieutenant attacked me from the shadows."

"Yes."

"Why not just kill me, though? What if I'd been able to fight off your lieutenant? Or woken up while he was still taking me to you, and destroyed him?"

"You oppose me. You would give your life to stop me. Do you even know what it is that you fight?"

"Well, yes. A madman bent on conquering everything."

"*Why* do I do what I do?"

"Power. You want to rule everything. And remove all threats to your life."

"Those are lesser goals. What is the main one?"

Dante thought for several seconds, then shook his head. "I don't know. You forgot to send the manifesto around."

"How long have you humans lived on this land?"

"It isn't entirely clear. I was taught that the gods gave us life about two thousand years ago."

The lich's mouth budged into the suggestion of a smile. The light in his eyes danced. "You are taught wrong. Your knowledge is as shallow as this swamp. The truth is as deep as the seas that lie beyond the land."

"You're talking about the uniquely Tanarian idea that we've been around much longer than that. At least twenty thousand years. Maybe as much as a hundred thousand."

"This interests you. I see it in your face. Yet you deny it?"

Dante would have crossed his arms, but as they were currently locked in place beside him, he settled for crinkling his brow. "Can I say that I find it excessively odd that you, the all-feared Eiden Rane, have kidnapped me in order to deliver me a history lesson?"

"I do not fear when birds caw or frogs croak. Speak as you will. Do you know how the old world was lost?"

"The sorcerers built a beautiful world, but they did so on the backs of their slaves. Eventually, there was a rebellion. Apparently one so big that the entire *world* got smashed up, which I find difficult to believe logistically. As the sorcerers were on the brink of defeat, they unleashed a race of demons they'd created. Ones that hunted people. The demons slaughtered almost everyone. Drove the survivors into hiding. After a long while, the demons died out, but it was tens of thousands of years until people began to build cities and nations again." He crooked one eye. "Supposedly."

Effortlessly, the Eiden Rane drew the ether to him, the light scintillating and jagged. If Dante hadn't already pissed himself, he would have done so then.

The lich spread his hands wide. In the air between them, a vision formed, as crystal clear as existence itself. A great city. Towers like blades of glass. Gleaming streets. Horses as proud as victorious warriors. Then, in a mad rush that somehow remained comprehensible to Dante's eye, those clean streets filled with rebels. Towers burned and fell. Light and shadow smashed whole neighborhoods into craters.

As the last of the towers was set to be taken, creatures flowed from its base. Humanoid, but their arms ended in long claws, their hairless bodies hard and lean. They crossed the rubble in great bounds, the fangs of their long jaws stained with blood. In the sped-up vision, they tore through the remains of the city in a blink, then spread outward, multiplying as they went, devouring whole towns, cities, everything.

Until there was no more smoke. No more farmers driving their flocks, or children playing in the fields. No more anything but the wind in the grass.

The lich lowered his hands. The vision faded, leaving them in the dimness of the chamber. "This is what once was."

"How do you know it looked like that? You weren't *there*, were you?"

The giant laughed, a surprising sound like the ring of steel bowls clapped together. "No. But I have seen it."

"You aren't Shan, are you?"

"Shan is long dead, and I am not. What I've shown you is what was. What must be prevented from ever happening again."

Dante sputtered. "Your plan is to save the world from being destroyed by destroying the world?"

"It will not be destroyed."

"But it won't *be* anything. It'll just be you sitting on a mountain of bones getting worshipped by a pack of murderous half-zombies."

"You deride the Blighted as mindless slaves to their hungers and hate. How is that so different from when they lived as humans?"

"The Blighted can't even put their pants on the right way. Which won't be much of a problem, as the Blighted are too stupid to make new pants, and will soon all be naked. Enjoy looking at *that* for the rest of eternity."

"The Blighted are one tool. A craftsman needs many. Some, like you, will retain your intelligence."

"So you're going to make me one of your under-liches. I'll wait to thank you until I have no free will. Then you can make me thank you as much as you want. Incidentally, I'm sure your generosity toward elites like me will be of great comfort to the Blighted."

"Don't speak like you have any care for them," the lich said. "You kill them like roaches. And that is appropriate. Once the plan is complete, there will be no more need for them."

"What will you do with them then?"

"I have chosen not to decide yet. Perhaps I will destroy them. Perhaps I will remove them to their own land until their bodies wear out. It does not matter. They will be happy with whatever I decide."

"Then what? You, me, and the handful of other slave-sorcerers who survived the global extermination spend the next eternity getting drunk and remembering the good old days when the concept of 'days' mattered?"

"Then," the lich said, cupping his hands and gazing into them, "a new people will replace them."

"To worship you, I suppose?"

"In part. And why not? I will have the power of a god. In some ways more, for I will have done more for them than any of the gods ever has."

"But that isn't the main reason?"

"Vanity drives men to make accomplishments because they know they will die and be forgotten. I face neither fate, and have thus set vanity aside. Do you know what the centuries have shown me? That all people of all times yearn to kill one another. To destroy everyone that is not of their kind. That they have not done so is not out of their goodness, but only because they have lacked the means. So I will stop them before they achieve that end. By binding them to me. And by making them all as one people, united, with no urge to fall upon one another even if the day comes that I pass from this world."

Dante took a moment to attempt to conceive this. "Just everyone the same, from one shore to the other? In the mountains and the deserts and the coasts? On every continent of the world?"

"Is it not worth it for peace? For harmony? A single religion, a single mode of thought, all of the world united at last. The gods have cursed us with differences. With so many ideas that a mind can never hold them all, and shatters beneath their contradictions, trying in vain to make sense of what is around them. I will liberate them from the burden of thought. For all will be answered, and people may at last move forward in serenity."

"But you can't just demand they all think the same thing. The struggle toward truth is the core of what makes us human."

"What happens when all questions have been answered and all truths delivered? The righteousness lies not in the struggle, little sorcerer. Why do you resent the thought of others living in enlightened unity? Is it because you hold yourself superior to them? Do you believe that only *you* have the clarity of mind to seek and discover that which is right? What flaw in you makes you yearn for others to suffer?"

Dante shook his head, but all he found inside himself were simple denials, devoid of any conviction. "I just don't like the idea of making people think a certain way. Let them follow their own paths. In some ways, the journey's more important than the conclusion."

"It is for their own good, and they will be happier for it." The lich tilted his massive head. "Do you not understand? You find this idea so dangerous because it is so beguiling. You claim to seek truth, yet when it stands before you at last, you reject it."

"Why are you even trying to convince me of this? *You* don't have any doubts about it, do you? Once I'm under your power, neither will I. So why not just be-lich me already so that I'll agree with your every word?"

The White Lich laughed again, the icy planes of his face looking like they might crack away. "Because there is so much more pleasure in bringing you to understand that you have been fighting for the cause of suffering and extinction. Abandon it now. Pledge yourself to the glory of peace. Let your last act as a mortal man be the first moral choice of your existence. That is my gift to you."

For just a moment, Dante didn't know what he would say. Then it burst forth in a torrent. "You claim you'll bring them peace by making them all one people. But even that isn't good enough, is it? Because within that people, they'll still be *individuals*, pursuing their own goals and dreams. Which means there will be struggles. Conflicts. Maybe even wars. So the only way to solve *that* is to take away their ability to *be* individuals, with their own minds and mouths, their own thoughts and speech.

"But it goes deeper than that, doesn't it? You don't only want to silence them to stop them from hurting each other. You want to shut them up because you're afraid that if they get the chance to speak, they'll prove you wrong. And then your whole great quest collapses into ashes." Dante smiled bitterly. "You say you'll bring them peace. Harmony. Unity. And in exchange, all they have to give up is everything."

The giant didn't look the slightest bit upset by Dante's rebuke. "We have spent enough time on words. It is time to put you to use. I have thought about sending you to kill your friends. That would be amusing. But I want them gone, and your victory over them would not be assured. Instead, I will send you away and see if they follow you. They might not care to, and that would be amusing in its own way, but I think that they will. In doing so, they will abandon the city of Aris Osis to me. And once I have absorbed its people to myself, it will no longer matter what your friends do—although I expect that they will have already died fighting you."

"You can't do this." Dante activated his loon.

"Yes?" Naran answered at once, sounded urgent. "Dante, where are you?"

"You may have captured me," Dante said to the lich. "You might turn me into one of your pet nethermancers. But my friends will find you. They'll kill you. And whatever you try to do to me, I'll fight back. I'll break free. I'll—"

The lich lifted his left hand, curling his fingers. Light seeped through Dante's skin in little droplets, pooling there and then streaming toward the lich in white threads. Dante's body went ice-cold. He was still breathing, but he didn't seem to be getting any air. Sound roared in his eyes, drowning out the beating of his heart. He grasped at the nether, but he might as well have been trying to grab a cloud.

For as much as he was afraid, he was just as surprised. Somehow, until that very moment, he had assumed that he'd find a way to escape, or resist, or even talk the White Lich out of it. In the bedrock of his soul, he had always told himself that he would never let himself be made a slave.

He had been wrong.

13

Blays awoke to two sensations, neither of them pleasant. The first was a most violent hangover, which he recalled being extremely well-earned. And the second was that of being shaken about by some utter prick who was about to learn that he who wakes a hungover man is he whose balls are about to be booted up into his body cavity.

He slapped away Naran's hand. "Naran, you monster. Unless the White Lich himself is here to defile my soul, you can stuff it up your ass and keep it there until noon. On second thought, make that four o'clock."

"Get up," Naran said. "I don't care how much pain you've put yourself in. *Get up*, Mr. Buckler."

There was a shakiness to the captain's voice that made sweat pop out across Blays' body. Something had gone wrong. That in itself was no cause for alarm, to say nothing of rousting a man from bed like a brute. Over the last fifteen-odd years, Blays had experienced enough things going wrong that he now considered it unusual when things *weren't* falling to shit.

But he knew at once that this was very, very different.

He sat up, wincing at the brightness of the sunlight through the windows. "What is it?"

"Dante has been taken."

"What? *When?*"

"I believe it happened last night — he went missing then, and I couldn't contact him. But I didn't know what had happened until just a minute ago."

"Why didn't you tell me about this hours ago?"

"I made an attempt to wake you. It failed, as someone was too drunk. I don't believe it was me."

Blays had fallen asleep in his clothes, meaning he only had to find his sandals and swords. The blades were leaned against the head of the bed in easy grabbing range, the same place he always left them — it was good to know that even after a solid gallon of what passed for Tanarian beer, he was still able to remember what was important in life — but one of his sandals was missing. He moved toward the other room, meaning to steal one of Gladdic's.

"Who thieved him? The Monsoon?"

Naran trailed after him. "That's possible. But whoever took him, he's now in the hands of the White Lich."

Blays froze with Gladdic's sandal halfway onto his foot. "Naran. Please tell me you're joking. And that this is a well-deserved punishment for my dereliction of duty."

"Last night, Dante forged a new loon so he and I could keep up with each other's patrols. Since last night, I've tried to contact him repeatedly, without success. Not five minutes ago, he pulsed me. It was clear that he was talking to someone else, but that he wanted me to hear their conversation." Naran described what he'd heard. It wasn't much. "There can be no doubt that he was speaking to the Eiden Rane — and that the enemy meant to convert Dante into a lesser lich under his command."

A wave of immense smallness passed over Blays. "Do we know if the lich has succeeded yet?"

"Based on the last noises I heard before the loon went dead, I would assume he's enacting the process right now."

"Then we have to go stop him."

"The lich is likely to be hours away from here. The transformation of the Blighted is nearly instant. I'm afraid there is no way to get there in time."

"We still have to try!"

Naran kept his voice low. "We don't know where he is, Blays. Even if we did, we'd have to face off against the White Lich — and this time, we would do so without Dante's help. Or Gladdic's. The two of us wouldn't stand a chance."

Blays sank to a crouch, hands pressed to the sides of his head. A hundred ideas swirled across his mind, but most of them were stupid, or useless visions of cutting the White Lich's fat stupid head off. Except the lich bled this ghastly white stuff, it wouldn't even spray in a properly satisfying —

Blays jerked up his head. "Dante made a loon for you?"

"To replace the one he and Jona had been using, which broke yesterday."

"Your loon has his blood on it." Blays sprinted into the other room. Gladdic was asleep or unconscious in his bed, his pale shins looking like the trunks of birch saplings. "Gladdic! Wake up, you old son of a bitch!"

Naran glared at him. "He is recovering from his fall. Show some decency!"

"If he doesn't get up, the only thing I'll show him is the back of my hand. Gladdic!" He grabbed the old man's jabat, which was perfectly clean, having replaced the blood-stained one he'd been wearing during his topple from the tower, and gave him a good shake. "Open your eyes, you prick! Wake up and do some good for once in your miserable life!"

Gladdic's head lolled, then snapped forward. He opened his eyes, the whites of which had gone faintly yellow. He made a clicking noise in his throat.

Blays kept a tight grip on the front of his jabat. "Gladdic? Are you in there?"

"I...live."

"Yes, and we're all very upset about that. Do you remember what happened?"

"The tower. I was on top of it. Watching over all of the world. And then..." He narrowed his eyes to slits, then bared his teeth and shook his head. "I cannot remember. Everything is blank." His mouth fell open. He fixed his eyes on Blays. "Wait. There is more!"

"Yes?"

"I was fishing!"

Blays gave a grunt of laughter. "I think you cracked your skull. You weren't fishing, you were falling. The difference is that fishing involves a line and some fish, whereas falling involves breaking parts of you, and the occasional splattering."

"I was at Ordimer Stream. Outside of Fallhedge. That is the village where I spent my childhood. I was at the stream and it was vital that I catch enough trout, for my father was sick in bed and my mother had died the year before, and my younger sisters would have no dinner except what I brought home. It was close to winter and the leaves were falling in the water, and the sun was about to go down and I was cold, but I stayed until I caught my fourth fish and then I walked home, and although it was dark and I was frightened, I was proud, too. Because that night, my sisters would not go hungry."

"What's this? A memory of yours?"

"It was more than a memory. I experienced it in perfect clarity. As though I were living it anew. Do you not see?"

Blays snapped his fingers. "You died, didn't you? What you saw was the Pastlands."

"I believe so. Yet if I was dead, how can I be here now? Breathing? Speaking? Questioning?"

"Because apparently Dante is a miracle-worker. You'll have to thank him for that. Except you can't, because the White Lich took him."

Gladdic's mouth fell open again, eyes gleaming in horror. It was an expression Blays wouldn't have thought him capable of. "But how?"

Blays and Naran explained what little they knew. During this, Gladdic closed his eyes. Winky little pieces of light flowed down his body. When he finished and opened his eyes again, his face looked somewhat less haunted, meaning it appeared to only be housing four or five ghosts instead of a full dozen.

Blays' head hurt, but he hardly felt it as he paced about. "The lich might have stolen Dante. But we can find him. We've got some of his blood. We need you to open a connection between it and the rest of the blood sloshing around in his body and use that to track him down."

"And then what? If he has been converted into lichdom, he will be utterly loyal to the Eiden Rane. He will attempt to destroy us on sight."

"When we left, Ara said that there's a way to reverse being Blighted. Maybe there's a way to de-lich somebody, too."

"You are suggesting we return to the Silent Spires, learn if there is indeed a method to undo what has been done, then chase Dante down and apply this method to him?"

"Unless you think we can slap it out of him."

"You are made foolish by your passions. You don't understand what this course of action will lead to."

"Saving our friend from being used against us, teaming up with him to rip the lich into glowing white confetti, and then being thrown a country-wide party by the grateful locals?"

"It is three days from here to the Hell-Painted Hills. Then one to two more days to reach the Silent Spires. Even if the lore you seek is real, and can be conveyed to us instantly, it will be five to seven days before we can even begin the hunt for Dante."

"I think he'll forgive us for not being able to violate the laws of nature and time to get to him sooner."

Gladdic had been seated on his bed. He stood, pre-wincing and then looking mildly surprised at the apparent lack of pain. "During that timespan, short as it seems, the Eiden Rane will invade Aris Osis. We will not be here to defend it, and it will fall. In a single stroke, the lich will double both the size of his army and his personal power. After that, there will be no fighting him."

"I don't care. We're going to find Dante. And we're going to save him."

"This might well be the Eiden Rane's very plan! Entice us to depart the city, and then claim it once there is nothing left to threaten him. We cannot fall into his trap!"

"We're not going to fall into any trap. We're going to *jump* into it."

Gladdic shuffled to the glass door and flung it open to the balcony. He swept his hand across the towers of the city. "You would sacrifice all of these people for this? Along with our only real chance to kill the Eiden Rane—a chance we have spent everything preparing for? That Dante was fighting for? And you would do all this on the *possibility* that we might learn a way to undo what has been done?"

"Yes! Yes, gods damn you, I would!"

"But what is the point? You would save your friend only to lose the world! How can we kill the lich if we give this up?"

Blays crossed to him in a blink, jabbing his finger at Gladdic's face. "Do you know how many times he and I have done the impossible? I don't, because I stopped keeping track after it hit triple digits. We'll get him back—and we'll find a way to win. Just like we always do."

Gladdic looked away with a grimace, exposing his worn teeth. "How can you throw so much away like this?"

"Because he would do the same for me."

The look that came to Gladdic's face contained a blend of sadness, envy, and resolution. "Very well. We will abandon the city and travel to the Silent Spires. But I ask one thing of you."

"What's that?"

"Pray that we are making the right decision."

Blays clapped his hands and dashed into the other room to gather up his things. He was getting his pack laced up before he understood what he was feeling: gratitude. Toward Gladdic.

Giving a hard boot to such unwelcome thoughts, he walked over to the old bastard, who was searching about for a second sandal.

Blays jerked his thumb toward the other room. "Have you given any thought to Volo? I'm not sure if she's well enough to travel. Think we're better off leaving her here?"

A fleeting look of pity crossed Gladdic's face. "You still fail to see the consequences of your course. If you leave young Volo here, she will die along with all of the others at the lich's hand."

Blays rocked back on his heels, swearing loudly. "Then she's coming with us."

"And if she is still unable to care for herself when we reach the Hills? For the sake of our own lives, we cannot allow ourselves to be slowed down."

Blays met the old man's eyes. "I know what you're trying to do. Do you think I'm a newcomer to hard decisions?"

Gladdic watched him a moment, then smiled and returned to his search.

Consulting with Bek, they decided the knight was sound enough to travel with them and would also be better off stashed away at the Silent Spires. While they saw to their arrangements, Naran dashed off to the docks to warn Jona and the *Sword of the South* to be ready to flee the city at the first sign of invasion.

All told, they were ready to go in less than an hour. Knowing that it would only touch off a ruckus, Blays almost left the tower without telling a single Tanarian soul. At the end, though, he wrote a simple note and left it in their quarters. He included the suggestion that the Arisians might flee the city and scatter in all directions. He doubted they'd take his advice.

The five of them assembled on the shore. Volo could walk on her own, as long as you sort of prodded her along as you went, but she needed help getting into the canoe, and was obviously not going to provide any help navigating, obliging Blays to take the seat in the fore. He took them west toward the hole Dante had opened in the wall the day before. It was early enough in the morning that the laborers were just now showing up to patch it up with boards.

Blays smiled and waved politely as they passed through the gap. "This isn't the first time I've said this, but this time really isn't our proudest moment."

Naran lifted an eyebrow. "They're probably all about to die, and you're joking about it?"

Blays tightened his grip on the paddle.

"If it is any consolation," Gladdic said, "most of them will not die. They will become Blighted."

Blays frowned. "I think you may have discovered a new form of anti-consoling."

As they neared the end of the clear water, the forest rising before them, he turned around for a last glimpse of Aris Osis.

Gladdic leaned forward and touched him on the shoulder. "Do not look back at it. It is already gone."

The pleasant thing about the swamp was that if you wanted to put a city behind you, all it took was a few minutes of boating into the trees.

The unpleasant thing about the swamp was that as soon as you got away from the city, you were faced with nothing but a lot of fetid muck, swarms upon swarms of flies, and long squig-gly things that seemed personally invested in killing you.

Nobody said much for the first two miles. Blays had noticed that was very common at the start of trips: initial silence, as though no one wanted to disturb the extremely sensitive busi-ness of repeatedly shoving a paddle in the water or letting your horse trot along or what have you, followed by the realization of just how *long* you were going to be out there, and that if you did-n't fill some of the time with talking, you would probably soon be murdering each other instead.

After a bit of discussing directions with Bek, Gladdic lifted his head. "Where is the object that contains Galand's blood?"

Naran unclipped his loon from his ear and handed it over. "It lies within this."

Gladdic turned the hunk of bone jewelry in his hand. "One of his foolish ear rings? Why would he bleed on it?"

"He bleeds on *everything*," Blays said. "Haven't you noticed I don't like to stand within three feet of him?"

"I had assumed that was because he had noticed your odor, and ordered you to keep your distance."

Despite himself, Blays snorted.

"My blood is on it as well," Naran said. "In case that's rele-vant."

Gladdic eyed them as if he found them unspeakably barbaric. "This is a nethereal object, yes? And not merely a piece of shad-ow-worshipping degenerate iconography?"

"It doesn't matter," Blays said. "Now get your face into that blood and get to work."

He could feel Gladdic bringing the nether to him, manipulat-ing it in a cold way that was practical yet elegant. Sometimes the old man whispered to himself, as if he'd forgotten where he was, or was too mad and senile to care.

After twenty minutes of this, and entirely without warning,

Gladdic shot halfway to his feet, crying out in pain.

Blays ducked lower to stop the boat from rolling back and forth. "What are you doing, you crazy idiot? Looking to feed the ziki oko?"

Gladdic rubbed his forehead with his palm. "I believe I have discovered how this process works. With its aid, I have success-fully located Captain Naran."

Blays chuckled, swooping his paddle through the water. "Then you possess the eldritch power of 'sight'? At last I under-stand why Dante was so eager to team up with you."

The priest returned to his whispers. In less than a minute, he snapped his fingers. "I have found the correct signal. Dante lives."

Relief warmed Blays' veins like a good stout. "How far away?"

"As my prior experience is limited to locating a man seated immediately before me, I cannot say. The signal is not terribly strong, but it points somewhere to our northeast."

"Keep an eye on it, figuratively speaking. We'll want to know if the lich sends him off somewhere else."

"Such as after us."

That thought hadn't occurred to Blays. He didn't like it.

He paddled until he'd sweated off his hangover, then passed the tool over to Naran and took a nap. It was a muggy day with little wind and Blays was happy when it came to an end. They found a nice little island, where Blays helped lift Volo from the canoe. He thought he saw a glimmer of light in her eye, but it was gone so fast he couldn't be sure.

The trees fell away. The Hell-Painted Hills lifted before them, threatening and stark. The swamps, for once, had been perfectly uneventful. Over the last two and a half days, Dante seemed to have been traveling slowly northwest, but Gladdic had no way to know how far or for what purpose.

After taking a long look around to get his bearings, Blays headed north, meaning to find the exact spot where they'd crossed the border before. He found the location a mile later, but his self-congratulations on bringing them to it were short-lived. The goat-like lan haba where nowhere to be seen.

He beached the canoe on a grassy shore connected to the barren hills, silently cursing Dante for not having thought to give Ara a loon. Then again, Dante would have still been in possession of that loon, leaving them stuck in the exact same position.

He jerked his chin at Gladdic. "I don't suppose you have any neat tricks to get ahold of Ara and ask her to please send out the giant goats?"

Gladdic's eyes shifted back and forth as he surveyed the slagged countryside. "None that would work."

"You can't send a dead pigeon with a note tied around its neck?"

"It would not be delivered. When Dante sent his minions toward the Spires, they ceased to function as soon as they crossed the borders, felled by the Odo Sein."

"You could send pigeon after pigeon until someone sees one falling and wanders over to check on what's going on with all the suicidal pigeons."

"Even if successful, it would take longer than we would on our own. There is also the matter that none of the people at the Spires can read."

"I never thought illiteracy would come back to bite anyone in the ass." Blays planted his hands on the small of his back. "Bek, are you any help here?"

The knight shook his head. "I've only traveled through the Hell-Painted Hills twice: once to begin my training, and once to end it."

"Then it sounds like we're traveling by foot-wagon." Blays

clucked his tongue. "Volo? How's that sound, hey?" She didn't so much as look his way. He sighed. "Guess we'll have to carry her."

"We shall do no such thing," Gladdic said.

"What? You think we're better off trying to roll her? In the state she's in, she can hardly walk down a paved road by herself. She could never make it through the Hills."

"Then she is a burden we cannot allow to slow us down. You sacrificed the city of Aris Osis for this, Blays Buckler. You may have sacrificed *everything* for it. I will not endanger our mission for the sake of a single soul."

The two men stared at each other. Blays had that feeling where you really wanted to pick something up and hit something else with it, which was never a great indicator of the rightness of one's position. Even with help from Naran and the still-recovering Bek, would he really be able to carry Volo all that way? Up the slopes? Over the crags? All without slowing them down and risking being Blighted themselves?

"We could leave her here for now," he said, hating the words and himself. "I don't think she's in any danger of wandering off."

Naran gaped. "Are you mad? She may not wander off, but she won't feed herself, either. Nor defend herself from attacks by people or animals."

"We can hide her. If we send someone back with lan habas the instant we get to the Spires, she won't be alone more than three days."

"She won't be alone at all. Because I will stay with her."

"We should have sent her with the *Sword of the South*," Blays muttered. "But I kept thinking she'd get better."

"There is no hand waiting to pull us from the depths of our troubles," Gladdic said. "No guarantee of progress, nor better days. The Eiden Rane may be the only one of us whose fate is not the slow disintegration of the body and mind."

"With inspirational sermons like that, I can see how you went so far in the priesthood." Blays shook Naran's hand. "We'll send someone for you as soon as we get there. If you haven't heard from us in a week, you should probably assume Bel Ara got fed up with our endless problems and fed us to the goats."

"I will find my way," Naran said. "Good luck on yours."

Without ceremony, Blays, Gladdic, and Bek hiked up into the hills. The heat of the day glowed from the rocks. If not for the steady wind blowing off them, it would have been unbearable. At the top of the first ridge, Blays stopped to look back the way they'd come in, shielding his eyes. Naran and Volo were seated beneath a tree. Blays had a sudden pang that he wouldn't see them again.

He turned around and hiked on.

He soon learned that Bek wasn't much for talking. Gladdic certainly was, but Blays was not especially interested in hearing what he had to say, as Gladdic seemed afflicted with such an exuberance of bile that he couldn't open his mouth without disgorging a stream of it.

This was unfortunate, as it left Blays alone with his thoughts. Such as the idea that Ara might not know how to reverse Dante's condition. Or that she would claim there *was* no way to reverse it. In that case, where could they go to find that knowledge? Bressel, Narashtovik, or the Houkkalli Islands would be the usual bets. All were centers of scholasticism, and he knew exactly where they were.

But these were also places where lich-craft was, as far as he knew, unknown, and hence would be unlikely to know fuck-all about it. What was the alternative? Race off in a random direction in the hopes that whoever they ran into over there would know what to do? How much time would they have to search for answers before the White Lich just sort of consumed everything?

Blays had a strong tan going, but he'd have been burned into cinders if not for Gladdic's regular applications of ether, which restored their skin to its previous state. Night fell and they marched on, aided by a floating ball of light and the nether that kept their muscles fresh.

They slept through the deepest part of the night, only allowing themselves a few hours before continuing on. A summer storm blew in around noon. The hiss of the rain on the rocks was a welcome break from the heat, but it was not so welcome that the rocks were now all slick and wet, happy to fling the three occupiers down their skin-removingly hostile slopes. Steam rose like a pot of boiling water.

In a way, the wet landscape reminded him of the Fingers of Pocket Cove, except the Hell-Painted Hills didn't even have moss and shrubs to break up the monotony of blank rock. It was odd that his memory of the Fingers made him smile, considering the time in question had involved dodging three-foot-long centipedes while he'd been completely naked as part of a bizarre nether-training exercise. Yet it seemed as though the addition of time transformed many of the bitter periods of his life into his better memories.

Such as when he and Dante had first fled Bressel while being chased by lunatic Arawnites. Not so much fun when it had been taking place, but in hindsight, they'd mostly just caught and eaten a lot of fish and nothing particularly bad had come of it. Or when the two of them had tried to convince the maddeningly obstinate norren to quit fighting each other only for those same norren to trick them into that ridiculous quest for the Quivering Bow, manipulating him and Dante into freeing their enslaved friends. The ruse had infuriated Blays at the time, but he now found it hilarious, and related the story wherever he went to gales of laughter. He was already beginning to regard the deceit that had brought them to the Plagued Islands in the same way.

Easy times were pleasant in the moment, but left little dent on the memory. It was the times when you struggled that seemed most vibrant in retrospect, the most important toward the telling of the story of your life.

Yet they could only be *good* if you came out the other side intact and well. Blays wasn't sure that this time would be the same.

Late that day, the seven towers of the Silent Spires speared toward the pregnant clouds. And none too soon; all three of them were drenched, nauseous from their time in the Hills, and eagerly anticipating the moment when they could collapse. Someone from the towers must have been watching them — Blays supposed they had damn little else to do — because their trio was met at the border of grass and trees by a host of soldiers bearing long spears.

The soldiers parted, Bel Ara striding past them, the hem of her robes dampened by the rainy grass. Normally, she carried a solid dose of smugness around with her, which was probably why Dante liked her. And Blays might have as well, except that being married seemed to clear your vision toward those who were no longer potential partners, allowing you to see in great detail the foibles you would otherwise blind yourself to as you pursued them for romantic or sexual ends.

But on that afternoon, Ara didn't look smug at all. She looked like she was trying not to look scared.

She stopped across from Bek. "Bek? I never thought I'd see you again."

The knight bowed at the waist. "As always, Bel Ara, I can't tell if you would consider that a good thing or a bad thing."

"Let's just leave it as a thing." She turned her fetching face to Gladdic, then Blays. "Where's the other warlock? The one who's so fond of demanding answers he doesn't deserve?"

"We should get out of the rain," Blays said. "We have a lot to talk about."

"Are you afraid of the sun getting sun on you? The wind getting wind on you? What makes you afraid of a little wetness?"

"Dante was taken by the Eiden Rane. Who turned him into a lesser lich."

Ara's gaze drifted down and to the left, then snapped back to Blays. "You saw this yourself? You didn't, did you? Otherwise, you wouldn't be alive."

"We weren't there, but Dante has ways of communicating with us across distances. Warlock things, you know how it is. He told us what was happening. We haven't heard from him since. That was four days ago."

She reached out to the side, but there was nothing for her to hold on to. "Locked into slavery at the hands of the tyrant you were trying to cast down. And made to love every second of it. The Eiden Rane is a sadist."

Seeing her aggrievement, Blays felt mildly bad for hitting her with it so bluntly. Then again, she'd asked for it. "The good news is Gladdic can tell that Dante's still alive. Again, warlock things."

Ara was already composing herself. "How did Dante let himself be taken?"

"I was meaning to ask the White Lich the same thing next time I saw him, but we haven't bumped into each other yet. For all I know, the lich snuck into Aris Osis, and knowing that Dante can't stand to lose anything, promptly challenged him to a getting-kidnapped contest."

"You speak nonsense like it tastes good on your tongue. But you were right about one thing. Let's get out of the rain."

She brought Blays and Gladdic to the tower they'd been staying in before. For reasons Blays didn't understand, which probably meant they were arbitrary customs, Bek had to go to a different tower. Servants brought them dry jabats. They changed, then met Ara on the balcony. She insisted on hearing everything that had happened since their return to the swamps, which Blays found somewhat hypocritical. He didn't say this out loud, what with depending on her help and all, but he made a mental note to say as much to Gladdic later, if only so that bit of cleverness wouldn't be lost to the world.

After a few minutes, they finished their story. Ara clasped her hands in front of her waist. "Is that everything?"

"I think it's too much as it is," Blays said.

She scooped a small glass flowerpot from the balcony and hurled it at him. He tucked his chin and covered his ear, the pot bouncing from the top of his shoulder and shattering against the wall.

As she bent to pick up another pot, Blays closed on her, threading his right arm through hers and bending it behind her back. "Hey! What is wrong with you?"

She pivoted to the right, trying to extract herself from his lock, but he grabbed the collar of her robe with his right hand and her wrist with his left.

"Let me go!" Ara tipped her head forward. As she swung it back at his face, meaning to bash out his teeth, Blays swept her foot from beneath her, holding tight to her robe as he guided her to the ground.

But not *too* gently. He landed on her with just enough force to knock the wind from her, granting her half a minute of hitched breathing to think about the repercussions of her actions.

"Bel Ara, you appear to be upset," he said. "If you'd like to explain why, I'd be happy to listen. But if you dislike my company that much, I'll be just as happy to toss you off the balcony so that you can make friends with the ground instead."

"I'd let you. I'd be better off." Her voice was tight and scratchy from the struggle to regain her breath. "Except then I wouldn't be able to see your face when I tell you what an idiot you are."

Slowly, he removed his weight from her, unfolding his arm

from hers. He got to his feet, pushing the flower pot behind him where she couldn't get at it. Ara stood. Her hair and robes were disheveled, but her athlete's build and the smolder in her eyes provided her with a dignity that couldn't be taken from her if she were thrust into jester's clothes and shoved down a muddy hill.

"You *fools*," she spat. "You should have stayed in Aris Osis!"

"To get murdered by the White Lich and my best friend? I'm sorry, but in your country, is dying pointlessly considered a virtue?"

"You still had a Knight of Odo Sein at your side! But you turned and ran like cowards. Are you that helpless without Dante?"

"Cowards? Helpless? *You're* the ones whose fearless leader abandoned you to get ravaged by undead cannibals. We'll figure some other way to come at the lich."

"No you won't. You should have fought for Aris Osis, and taken your shot at the Eiden Rane. You know I can't tell you a word about how to help your friend. You came here for nothing, and now everything is lost."

Blays furrowed his brow. "Wait. Wait. Wait until I tell you that you can stop waiting. You're not pulling that 'figure it out for yourself' crap on us right now, are you?"

"Maybe you don't understand, since your ears only have space for what you want to hear, but that's what my faith demands of me. I can't tell you how to un-Blight your friend. You *do* have to figure it out for yourself."

"Do I, though? Because it would make so much more sense for you to simply tell me."

"You ask me to break with my faith. To give up everything I believe in."

"You're not giving it up. You're temporarily setting it aside. Or forgetting that it's there. Or overruling it for being so damn

THE LIGHT OF LIFE

demanding. Faith is supposed to serve the people who hold it. Right now, yours is only hurting you."

Ara flexed her jaw. "And if I strolled into your temple and demanded for you to forsake your gods for your own good, you'd hop right to it?"

"Denying the gods is great! I do it every day!"

"You only deny them on things that don't matter. But what about when they tell you not to murder the innocent? Or forsake your wife for other women? Is it still fun for you to defy them then?"

"Do you know how often I have to betray what *I* believe in? How many times I've had to kill people who didn't deserve it? How often I've hurt people because not hurting them would be even worse?"

The priestess looked him up and down. "If you betray your beliefs that freely, in what sense can you be said to hold them?"

"It's what I have to do to save lives and stave off chaos, Ara. Even though I hate it. Even though it kills me. Just this once, be strong enough to throw aside your beliefs. Otherwise, we're all dead."

"This is a very strange argument." Her voice was soft now, all her anger gone. "Our beliefs are the only thing that makes us good."

Gladdic bowed his head. "Then don't simply hand us the answers on a gilded plate. Rather guide us to them, so that we might deduce them for ourselves."

"That's cheating."

"It is not as bad as it could be. To my understanding of your theology, it may even be possible to argue that it is acceptable practice, so long as you are careful in how you guide us."

"A compromise that lets me flaunt the laws that give us strength while pretending to be a virtuous and humble servant. The two of you, I don't think, are the best of people."

"Gladdic might be a sack of shit," Blays said, "but I am a respected and well-liked figure in all kinds of different lands."

Gladdic grunted. "Only because you happened to be on the side of victory. Had you lost in the Plagued Islands, for instance, you would be seen as meddlesome warmongers whose unwanted interference caused thousands of unnecessary deaths."

"To apply some Odo Sein logic here, maybe I keep winning because I'm so damn right all the time. In any event, we'll work with you on this however it needs to be done, Ara. What do you say?"

She moved to the balcony, resting her palms on the rain-slick railing. The bleakness of the Hills rolled away before her. "I say that it isn't much of a compromise. I can deny it to the others, but I'll still know I betrayed our order."

"But if you don't—"

"Shut up. If I have to hear you say 'But we'll all die if you don't' one more time, I'll throw *myself* off this balcony. Yes, I'll help you. And I'll learn what it feels like to hate myself."

Blays thought that was rather heavy on the guilt, but then again, it wasn't every day that he converted someone into a heretic. He would have liked to start right away, but his body reminded him that after the sickness of the Hills, not to mention the almost total lack of sleep they'd gotten while crossing them, starting right away would ensure that he'd never be able to finish, as he would shortly drop dead.

Instead, they ate, then were ushered to the same room they'd occupied before. Blays swung his bed down from the wall, punched the mattress around, then climbed onto it.

"Funny," he said. "We were barely gone for a week. It even smells the same. But it feels so different."

Gladdic shuffled to the candle made of plant wax and blew it out. "That is because it is not the place itself that makes it feel as it does, but rather the people who are there with you in it. And many of our people are now gone."

"Doesn't it ever get tiring?"

"What is that?"

"Looking at everything through shit-colored lenses."

Gladdic didn't answer right away. "Sometimes, it is exhausting. But at least, and for the first time in my life, I think I might be seeing the truth."

Blays rolled over and slept. He dreamed of a figure in a black cloak breaking through the Hell-Painted Hills, a storm of darkness in each hand and a smile on his face. The figure was just as he'd always been, except the face was wrong: so pale, and more gaunt even than Gladdic, without the slightest trace of mercy.

Blays tried to draw his swords, but they felt glued into their sheaths. Clouds of shadows blocked out the sun, streaming across the sky as if they were erasing it. He might have tried to run, but he knew there was no point.

After all of the tedious morning wake-up business — the Tanarians, being savages, declined to serve any kind of liquor with breakfast — Ara brought Blays and Gladdic to the edge of the field downwind from the seven Spires. She was alone and looked like she hadn't slept more than half the night.

"What are you staring at?" she said croakily. "Let's get on with this before I change my mind."

"Right," Blays said. "I guess we should start with the biggie. *Is* there a way to undo getting turned into a lich?"

"How would I know?"

"You said you knew how to cure being Blighted!"

"Spinning gods. Do you even listen to yourself? Or do you just let the words fall from you, like animals fertilizing the fields with their own waste?"

"Let me guess. The Blighted, by virtue of being Blighted, are not the same thing as being a lich?"

"Very good. If you've got that down, maybe you're ready to

explain to me why a rake isn't the same thing as a swamp drag-on."

"But liches and Blighted aren't *that* different. From what I've seen, they're actually pretty similar. Maybe reversing the two conditions is like being a physician, where if you can cure the red fever, then you can cure green fever as well."

"I don't know about your disgusting northern poxes. But I get the point. You're probably correct. The way you remove the lich-ness from somebody is probably similar to or the same as the way you remove the Blight."

Blays clapped once. "Progress! So how do you remove the Blight?"

Ara glanced away, sighing through her teeth. "You're going to have to do so much better than that. What you should be asking yourself is what it means to be Blighted."

"To be an unpleasantly angry eater of people?"

"You can take my heresy more seriously, or you can watch your friend serve your worst enemy as everyone around you dies."

Gladdic leaned forward. "To be Blighted is to be converted into something not fully human."

"Wrong," Ara said. "You've confronted the lich before. Have you seen him make any Blighted?"

"Yes."

"What did you see?"

"He drew something from them." Gladdic jerked back his head. "To be Blighted is not to be converted into something inhu-man. Rather, it is to have something human taken away from you."

"What might that be?"

"It resembled ether. More than that—it *was* ether. I am sure of it."

"And when it left them," Blays said, "they weren't really alive anymore. They weren't afraid of anything. Didn't even have to breathe. I might be talking crazy here, but what if it's the ethereal version of a trace?"

Gladdic lifted an eyebrow. "What if indeed, Ara?"

She lifted a dismissive hand. "What if you'd quit your foreign babble and speak real words?"

"Though we all have nether flowing in and out of us, each of us also possesses a portion of nether that is fully unique to every individual. It is called a trace, and it might be thought of as a nethereal embodiment, or perhaps expression, of the soul. Since learning of it, I have suspected — or if I am to be honest, I wanted to believe — that there was an analogous form of ether. Only I could never find it. But the Eiden Rane has done so, hasn't he?"

"You've seen the Blighted. You've seen the White Lich. You've seen the White Lich create the Blighted. Does your theory fit with everything you've seen?"

They'd been seated, but Gladdic was so excited he couldn't help himself from pushing himself to his feet and pacing about the grass. "The White Lich steals the ethereal traces from the people. This, in turn, converts them into the Blighted. While at the same time, he absorbs this substance — this light of life — into himself, enhancing his own strength. Am I correct?"

"That all sounds very seamless."

"Indeed. It fits together like the joinery of a master carpenter. Yet I still do not *know!*"

Ara looked down at the grass. "What do you know of me? Am I the type to listen to stupidity without calling it such? Without laughing at you? Without mocking you for having brains no better than the contents of a gecko's stomach?"

Gladdic chuckled lowly. "Surely you are not of that type, Bel Ara."

"Am I laughing and mocking you right now?"

"No, Bel Ara. You are not."

"Well that's cleverly done," Blays said. "How do you remove the Blight, then? By giving the poor fellow's ether-trace back to him?"

Ara eyed him levelly. "How would you do that when it's become a part of the Eiden Rane?"

"By carving it out of him? Could you even do something like that?"

"It does not seem likely," Gladdic said. "When traces are mingled together to form an Andrac, they cannot be unmixed afterward. I would assume the same would be true when the White Lich mixes the ethereal traces within himself."

Ara plucked up a sprig of grass, letting the wind scatter it across the boundary into the wasteland. She pointed to the golden sparks circulating near Gladdic's left shoulder. "If those are any indication, what you're saying makes a lot of sense."

Gladdic paced some more. "To be able to think clearly about this phenomenon, we must first give it a name. 'Ether-trace' is too clumsy, and renders it secondary to the nether, an incorrect stance to suppose. Might we simply call it the light of life? Perhaps, but the phrase hits my ear as too grandiose."

Blays rolled his eyes. "You'd be the expert on excess grandiosity."

"As a source of our inner light, we might call it the spark, or perhaps the ember. But I believe these words are also too noble, for each one only serves the span of a single life, spending the rest of eternity as no more than a marker of the human it once imbued. In that case, much as we call the trace a trace, I propose we name this substance a 'remnant.'"

"For all I care, you can call it a gibbery woo-light. Can we get on with it already?"

"Very well. So if the original remnant cannot be returned to the victim, that leaves two possibilities. First, that a new remnant can be created for them from scratch. Or second, that a part of an existing remnant might be transferred to them." He made a fist of his hand and brought it close to his mouth. "I can think of no way to deduce which possibility must be false and which must be true."

Blays scratched his head. "Any idea which one would be true if you were talking about traces?"

"I do not. But I see a path toward discovering the answer. I could attempt to remove someone's trace, then attempt to restore it through both methods, and see which succeeded."

"You want to take out someone's trace? The way the lich is taking out people's remnants? Wouldn't doing that risk turning the victim into some weird ether-Blighted?"

"I would think so. That is why I will perform this experiment on an unskilled servant, or perhaps someone who is too old to be of use, and no longer has purpose. Ara, who here might I use in this way?"

She blinked at him. "Are you serious?"

Gladdic gazed back. "If that is what it takes, yes. I have reached the edge of where pure reason can bring me. I stand on a ravine; the only way across is to build a bridge of experimentation, and see what lies on the other side."

Ara rose to her feet, running her hands over the sides of her head, which were clipped short in Tanarian style. "Sometimes I'd swear I can see the future. And it's a curse."

"My lady?"

"You want me to hand you the answers. Otherwise, you'll be *forced* to do something awful in order to get them. Which, as intended, tempts me to bend even more than I already have. To the point of breaking my vows altogether. This is exactly what I was afraid would happen. You compromise yourself once, telling yourself it's for a good cause. But if it turns out that isn't enough, what then? If it made sense to betray your beliefs the first time, and you do so but the problem's still there, it only makes sense to compromise yourself again, doesn't it? It would be illogical to do otherwise. Because if it was right once, it must be right again; either that, or it was *never* right."

She had been lecturing in the direction of the Hell-Painted Hills. She turned now to Blays, and though it seemed impossible, one of her eyes burned with wrath while the other brimmed with sorrow.

"If it made sense to betray yourself the first time, and the second, why not the third time? The tenth? *Every* time? Where does it stop? How many steps can you take away from your center before you become lost for good?"

In any other place, the question would have been rhetorical. In the maddening land of Tanar Atain, however, they expected answers to their impossible questions. And if you couldn't provide those answers—which they couldn't either, otherwise they wouldn't have had to ask you in the first place—then *you* were the idiot.

"Someone like Gladdic would tell you that there *is* no end," Blays said, making it up as he went along, because that's what everyone else seemed to be doing all the time. "He'd say that if the outcome leads to more good than the bad it takes to get it done, then the evil man is he who lacks the moral courage to do what needs doing."

Ara smirked. "Is that true, Gladdic?"

The old man shrugged. "It is close enough that I feel no need to argue."

"By contrast," Blays went on, "someone like Dante would go on about how everybody thinks they've got one set of morals, but they've actually got two. One is what you'd call conventional morality. I don't think he's ever stuck a label on the second kind, but I'd call it emergency morality. Now, your conventional morality is for conventional times. When things are normal, you don't just go about stealing things and killing people. Why, that would just be wrong.

"But when an emergency strikes, things change. If you're starving, there's nothing wrong with stealing bread. If you're in the middle of a national uprising, there's nothing wrong with executing the rebels — or, if you're a rebel, the loyalists. But even then, you've still got standards of right and wrong. If you're starving, stealing bread is one thing, but it's quite another to steal an honest man's purse because you want to buy some pretty clothes. In a rebellion, you wouldn't murder a rebel's *children*, or slaughter his whole town. You still have values, but they're more flexible. More suited to the circumstance.

"Now, most people don't know their emergency values too well, because they don't spend much time in emergencies. Lucky for them. But those values are still there inside you. And as long as you don't violate your conventional values when you're in conventional times, or your emergency values when you're in emergency times, there's really no violation at all."

"An interesting perspective. If awfully wordy." Ara watched him closely. "And you, yellow-hair? What do you say?"

"I say you don't have to ask when you've gone too far. Your heart will let you know."

She tucked down the corners of her mouth. "There's no reason in an argument like that."

Blays burst into laughter. "If you think we're beings of pure reason, you need to get out of the Spires and go watch a married couple discuss money. We have brains, but we've got souls, too. It's harder for us to hear them, but they'll speak to you, if you know how to listen."

Ara lifted her eyes to the sky and shook her head. "You can't remove the Blight by getting a person's inner light — their remnant, as you want to name it — back from the Eiden Rane. You can't build a new one for them from nothing, either. Not so much as I know, at least, for I'm glad to say I'm not a devil-siring warlock. But what you can do is give a Blighted person a piece of your own remnant."

After so much time hunting, snuffling, and hustling for every scrap of conjecture they could find in the attempt to cobble together the most basic knowledge of the Odo Sein, hearing Ara flat-out state the facts felt as alarming as it would to watch Dante burn a pile of copies of the *Cycle of Arawn*.

Gladdic sat up even straighter than normal. "How is this transfer accomplished?"

"I can't believe I'm telling you this. But you know what? If the other bels find out, and want to pitch me from the top of a tower, I'll laugh all the way down. Because while they were following their rules, I was saving our country."

Ara plopped down in the grass, looking infinitely more at peace with her decision than a moment earlier. "The method's achieved by using the Odo Sein to open a connection between yourself and the Blighted that you want to restore. There's a little more to it than that, but not much. And don't ask me why, if it's that simple, we don't just do this to all the Blighted. When you give part of your light to one of the Blighted, it doesn't come back. And it takes a *lot*. Most people only have enough light in them to reverse a single Blighted. A handful can do two. And some don't have enough to even do it once. They try and boom, they drop dead and the other guy's still Blighted. In almost every situation, the life of a Knight of Odo Sein is more valuable than the person they'd try to save."

Gladdic creased his brow. "Why should an Odo Sein be able to perform such an act while a sorcerer would not?"

"I don't know. Maybe you can, if you'd bother to figure it out for yourself instead of asking for a mental handout. But part of the reason you're asking that question is because you misunderstand the Golden Stream. All of you do. Including the dolt you're trying to rescue. When we stop you from using the light or the shadows, how exactly do you think we're doing that?"

"If you ask me for specifics, I have none to offer. But as a general concept, you lock or freeze the powers in place, rendering us unable to make use of them."

"Wrong. We cut each of you off from the shadows *as individuals*. I could stop you, Gladdic, from accessing them right now, while leaving Blays free to do whatever he wanted with the nether. Don't bother questioning me on this. I'll show you." She concentrated, golden flecks of stream condensing around her, then motioned to Gladdic. "Go ahead. Try me."

Gladdic splayed out his hand, then shook his head. "It is as though the nether is trapped beneath a block of stone."

She pointed to Blays. "Now you."

Blays grabbed out at the nether and managed to convince a small portion of it to pay attention to him. He shaped it into a ball of blackness in his palm. "We've been wrong about this the whole time?"

"How is this possible?" Gladdic said. "And if it is so, why do you not employ both sorcerers and Odo Sein? With the power to negate enemy magic while wielding your own, you could seize control of the entire continent!"

"So we could live in your worthless dry lands filled with your useless dumb people? We have no interest in playing in the trash that lies outside Tanar Atain. And you know damn well why we would never work alongside sorcerers. Unlike the foul-minded slugs of the Righteous Monsoon, we know that sorcery is corruption. The Eiden Rane is proof enough of that. So is the history of Tanar Atain—and of the world."

"You won't work alongside sorcerers?" Blays said. "In that case, you might want to sit down, as I have some shocking news for you."

Ara rolled her eyes. "It's forbidden to train *Tanarians* as warlocks. But you outsiders are depraved and can't be expected to hold to our laws. On top of that, you'll be gone soon and we'll have nothing to worry about. Now would you like to continue critiquing your perceived flaws in our culture? Or would you like to learn how to deliver your friend from the Eiden Rane?"

"That one, please."

"Here's the truth you will try to deny, because it means you've been wrong about everything and couldn't even think of an alternative. All shadows are connected to all other shadows. All light is connected to all other light. It doesn't seem that way to you, because you can't see the connections, but through the Golden Stream, they become visible. That's how we can cut you off from them. That's how a trained knight can find the connection between his own remnant and the few sparks of the one that remains in a Blighted, and equalize the two, restoring the Blighted's humanity."

"I do not accept this explanation at face value," Gladdic said. "As it contradicts everything I have seen for myself."

"Yes, and under normal conditions, you wouldn't be questioning my explanation, since you'd be learning all of these things through your own efforts—or coming up with your own original system that proves *us* wrong. But we're in an emergency, aren't we? So shut up and take me at my word."

"Yes, Bel Ara."

Watching Gladdic roll over like a dog, Blays bit his cheek to quit from smiling.

Ara gave them both a moment, ensuring they were compliant. "If you give it two seconds of thought, you'd realize that in the same way our practice of the dana kide is built on the function of the Golden Stream, the connectedness of all light to itself and all shadow to itself is the basis for our belief in the Body. For we're all connected, too. All part of the same whole. No matter how great or crummy your role in the Body feels—whether you're part of the brain, the right hand, or the throbbing asshole

—without you, the rest of us can't function. And we all fall apart."

Bitterness stained her face. "That's part of what the Monsoon rebelled against. Not only did they think they held the one right answer, and that our quest for truth was nothing but an attack on that, but they resented that the Body split people up by their ability to do the task. So sure in their righteousness, they conjured a monster. One that will destroy us and enslave them."

"Not to interrupt your hatred of your fellow countrymen," Blays said. "But we've already got a way to find Dante. It sounds like all we've got to do to free him from the White Lich is bring Bek to him and transfer him a new remnant."

Ara smiled in a way that was either commiserating or condescending, depending on how irritable you were feeling. "If it were that easy, don't you think Bek would have told you so already, and saved you the trip here?"

"No no no. I refuse to acknowledge that this is heading the way that it's heading."

"Don't worry, my barbarian friend. There's only one more thing you have to do: travel to Dara Bode, sneak into the city, and break into the Bastion of Last Acts."

EDWARD W. ROBERTSON

14

He had thought the servants of the One would see the world in the same way that the world saw them: bleached-out, sickly and desperate, aching with a hunger that could never be filled. For surely such wretched creatures could see nothing good around them, and would want only to tear it down and devour it, to stomp it into rubble and burn it into smoke.

As in so many things, he had been wrong.

The swamp, once a dreary green-black mire choking with flies, spiders, snakes, wasps, and ziki oko, now looked like a defiant expression of life. Flowers of every color added depth to the greens of the trees and the murk of the water. Every scrap of land was colonized with trees, grass, brambles, and shrubs; even the trees weren't safe, festooned with mosses and vines, to say nothing of the birds and rodents tearing around their boughs. All of it thrived. It was a wonder.

He hadn't just been given new eyes. He'd been granted a new nose and ears, too. The sounds of birdsong and splashing fish were as beautiful as the bright pop of the flowers. The air flowed with the smell of ginger flowers and citrus. Even the background scent of decay was no longer offensive. Decay meant nothing more than that life had lived, finished its cycle, and was now replenishing itself. Just as it was meant to do.

Yet better than any of the things that had been given to him was the thing that had been taken away.

Fear.

He traveled north in a plain canoe, alone in the wilds of the swamps, but he didn't feel a single drop of fear. He had no fear of getting lost. No fear of getting hurt or sick. No fear of getting mauled by the animals, which either ignored him or actively avoided him, even the midges and mosquitos.

It was a lack that went beyond concern of his personal safety. He felt no social fear, either. No fear of being wrong, of insulting or hurting someone he cared about, of being judged, of failing. It was all gone. And it felt indescribable. Like the best dream he'd ever had. Like falling asleep in a lover's arms. It felt, paradoxically enough, like total freedom. With all fear fallen away, he could look on the world in wonder, seeing its full potential for the first time in his life.

And in it he saw the vision of the One, the White Lich, the Eiden Rane. He now understood how the world could be a single unified entity, where *everyone* was free from fear, and worked as one to build the eternal empire of paradise.

Dante paddled alone beneath the trees, traveling with purpose but without haste, noting the birds on the wing, the lizards leaping between leaves, the flash of scales beneath the water. He didn't seem to need to sleep anymore, and when night fought down the day, he traveled by the distant light of the half moon, frogs peeping and crickets whirring, like the guided hum of the earth meditating on itself.

He didn't know the name of the village, but the lich had given him a vision of its location. And the lich did not make mistakes. The settlement, when Dante came to it, was empty. Not surprising. Many of the people in the interior had been recruited or subjugated to the Monsoon. Many others had fled, either to Bressel to join the Drakebane, or out into the wilds where they might be hidden. Some had even taken their canoes to the coast, seeking other lands altogether.

Raft-boats sat vacant. The central dock was silent. Yet in one of the stands of bananas grown in the city's outer ring, several trees had been hacked down no more than a day or two earlier, the cut trunks still green-white and damp rather than brown and dead.

Casting the ether on the water showed no trace of the villagers, but the dragonflies found them easily enough. A few hundred people huddled within a dark grove, sleeping in their lashed-together canoes. When they woke, they spent their time fishing, picking berries, and staring fearfully out into the swamps.

Dante told the lich that he had found them, and the lich told him to wait for the Blighted.

He bided his time. He'd feared eternity might be boring, but with every sensation a wonder, every second was filled. When he liked, he contemplated everything that was to come, and the anticipation glowed as purely as ether.

"Little sorcerer." The copper-kettle voice in his mind was as clear as if he kneeled before the Eiden Rane in person. "We approach Aris Osis. I know you have no news, or else you'd have shared it with me."

"Correct, master."

"That is good. There is no sign of your friends here; they have abandoned the city to me. Do you think they fled due to cowardice?"

"I doubt that, master. They'll seek another solution. That's what we always did. Either they're working on a new way to strike at you, or they're trying to come for me."

"They are not as cunning as I gave them credit. They should have seen that when they handed me the city, they handed themselves their own defeat."

"We knew that would be the consequence of you taking Aris Osis. This turn of events must have made them irrational."

"It's no matter. If they come for me, I'll kill them. If they come for you, then you will do the same."

Dante gazed through the trees. "Master?"

"Speak."

"They are powerful people. If I'm of use to you, they can be, too."

"There is no need, little sorcerer."

"But I think they can serve you better than you know. Destroying useful resources is a mistake. It's better to—"

"*NO!*" The voice pounded through his head like an iron maul striking a cracked bell. "You may speak like a knight who kneels to his lord. But you will not argue as though we are equals!"

And then the fear rushed back over Dante, the same heart-deep fear he'd felt when yelled at as a child. He felt cold in a way that made it seem as though he'd never feel warmth again.

Seated in his canoe, he bowed until his forehead was level with his knees. "I'm sorry, master. I only mean to help."

"You might possess too much will. We will correct that in time. For now, be silent. My army has come to Aris Osis. I will allow you to share in my triumph."

Before Dante could ask how, the walls of Aris Osis filled his sight. Defenders lined the walls, spears flashing in the sunlight. The Blighted sat across the water from them, filling their boats by the thousands. And the Eiden Rane stood among them.

The vision was so intense that if Dante hadn't already stopped needing to breathe, he would have forgotten to. While somehow still being able to see the walls, where the lich called out his terms for the city's surrender, a second scene opened to his sight: the bay on the southwest edge of Aris Osis. Among the gentle blue waves, a fleet of double-hulled canoes, rafts, and small sailing vessels shoved off, making way for the exit between the two arms of rock that protected the port from storms.

A scowl crept over Dante's face. Thousands of potential soldiers were slipping through their fingers. In doing so, the citizens cheated themselves of the chance to serve as a brick in the great tower being constructed by the Eiden Rane. Yet surely the lich was capable of fielding a navy of his own. How could this possibility have been overlooked?

As the first of the vessels neared the gap, a team of Blighted emerged from the water on the tip of the western jetty. They dragged a heavy chain behind them. Nether flocked like birds; a lesser lich stood among them, pulling the massive chain taut—and revealing that it had already been secured to the eastern arm enfolding the bay.

The first of the fleeing canoes dashed into it with hollow clunks. Sailing vessels plowed into them from behind with a devastating crunch of wood. Yet the chain held fast. As the sailors yelled at each other, struggling to untangle their vessels, Blighted paddled in from both sides, throwing themselves over the gunwales and dragging the Arisians off to be bound in ropes.

Dante laughed out loud. He might have been relieved of the burden of fear, except when the One wanted him to feel it, yet he still carried the poison of doubt. He wouldn't lose faith again.

His sight shifted. At the other end of the city, Blighted boiled out of the water at the base of the walls, scrambling upwards. Defenders leaned over to fire on them with arrows. Across the open water, darts of light streaked from the White Lich's hands. Each one found its mark, knocking archers across the battlements or into the water below.

In less than two minutes, the Blighted took the walls and opened the gates. Guided by the Eiden Rane, their advance through the city was gradual yet relentless.

Aris Osis fell with only the barest flicker of sorcery from its foes.

It took hours to root out the towers and rafts. At the end, people lay piled on the docks like netted fish, squirming in their restraints.

The Eiden Rane debarked, considering the thousands of people arrayed before him. "Right now, you fear me. I would do the same. But in an hour, you will love me."

He lifted his heavy hands. A glowing fog lifted from the still-living bodies, condensing over the dock, ether crackling within it like a captive lightning storm. Streams of fog assembled in jarringly regular patterns, and seemed not to flow but to shine toward the lich.

He took nine-tenths of them. There were so many bodies that it was an hour before the process was done.

The tenth of them that remained were too exhausted by terror to do more than lie on the docks like they were already dead. The Eiden Rane nodded to the waiting Blighted. As they hurled themselves on the two thousand living captives, staining the bay red with blood, the lich seated himself on the seawall and gazed on his new land.

Later, his voice rang in Dante's mind, but Dante wasn't startled by it.

"Little sorcerer. The city is mine."

"I witnessed."

"I have considered your request. I will take Gladdic under my power. He is versed in both light and dark, and that is rare."

"Thank you, master. What about Blays?"

"I have no need of him."

"But he has abilities of his own. Just as rare as Gladdic's."

"They do nothing to impress me."

"That's because they're subtle. But when called for, they're extremely effective."

"I have decided, little sorcerer." There was the barest edge of menace in the White Lich's voice, but it was enough. "A man only needs so many tools to do his job. Any more becomes clutter. If the chance presents, I will take Gladdic. I have no need for your Blays."

"I understand. What will be done with him?"

"If he comes for you, you will kill him. If you wish, you may make it fast."

"Yes, master."

"Good. Now go and do what is tasked of you."

Dante was about to object that the Blighted hadn't arrived to support him yet, but before he could express a single word, black lumps rose from the water like the backs of small turtles. Their hairy scalps were followed by pale faces and hungry, haunted eyes.

He gathered up the Blighted, who willingly followed his orders but remained fully under the control of the Eiden Rane, and sent them under the waters surrounding the deep grove where the refugees from the village made their camp. Once they were in position, he paddled after them.

The villagers recognized what he was as soon as they saw him—a reaction that would, before his transition, have made him feel ashamed to be so monstrous. Now, their loathing only served to reinforce the notion that he had shed the weakness of humanity and become something more.

The humans piled into their boats, breaking in every direction. The Blighted caught most of them. Dante harvested branches and brambles to block the path of the few who were on the verge of getting away. A small portion turned back to fight. Dante wielded the nether to pound them into chum for the ziki oko.

The remainder he froze in place, using the shadows to lock their muscles down tight. The Blighted bound nine-tenths of them in ropes, then took the last tenth for themselves. The villagers screamed, but that was to be expected.

Once this was done, and the Blighted were sated (or at least as sated as the Blighted could get), blood drying on their cheeks and chests, they picked up the lich's share and loaded the prisoners into their undecorated canoes.

The Blighted shoved off, bearing their cargo toward the White Lich. For a fleeting moment, Dante felt pity for the terror the humans must have been feeling.

Yet then he remembered the glory that awaited them.

15

Seated in the grass across from Ara, Blays' mouth fell open. "You said we only had *one* thing left to do. In what world does traveling to the capital, sneaking into the city, and then busting into the palace count as *one thing*?"

Ara rolled her eyes. "Don't argue semantics with me. It's all part of the same task."

"And after we infiltrate the city, which is occupied by the enemy, and find a way into the Bastion, which is heavily occupied by the enemy, we do what, exactly? Steal something?"

"Assuming it's still there."

"*Assuming it's still there?*" Blays hopped to his feet, waving his arms around like he was juggling objects that were very wide and very invisible. "Call me entitled, but you could have told us about the massive complication *before* I got my hopes up!"

"You got your own hopes up."

"Then why didn't you stop me?"

"Do you know why you outlanders are so insufferable? Because you can't even take responsibility for your own feelings."

"In that case, I suppose it isn't my fault that I currently feel like you're being a giant bitch."

He expected to be slapped, cursed at, booted in the testicles, or all of the above while also being being put into a chokehold which she might even be able to pull off, given her build, but then she went and laughed in surprise.

"Maybe I'm wrong about you, hari. Mind you, I *doubt* that I'm wrong. But I'm now at least open to the idea that you could live in our country without disgracing yourself and your ancestors."

"If I ever reach the day when my crimes get me banned from all other nations, I might take you up on that."

"You two are as farcical as the task before us," Gladdic said. "What must we retrieve from Aris Osis?"

"Your sense of humor," Ara said. "Once you've got that in hand, you should also look for the Aba Quen."

"The Aba Quen? I was told that was a myth."

"Which is a damn good way to get you to think it's just a silly story that you'd be a giant idiot to believe, isn't it?"

"But it's said that the Aba Quen can be used to steal a man's very soul." Gladdic's mouth formed an O. "It *can*?"

Blays folded his arms. "If you're expecting me to fetch this thing for you, it might be useful for you to give me any idea what it is."

"The Aba Quen is an ancient and priceless carving. It is a small ivory statue of a lizard wrapped around a skeletal forearm."

Ara made a huffing noise. "Not just a *lizard*. The Laughing Gecko. He's said to creep through your windows at night while you're sleeping and steal your baby's soul."

"I apologize, Bel Ara. My knowledge of the legends of Tanarian reptiles is poor at best."

"Why exactly do we need this?" Blays said. "Because you can never have enough statues of baby-killing geckos?"

Ara motioned to Gladdic. "Remnants are new to you, but you have experience with the nethereal ones, don't you? Can you steal one from another person?"

Gladdic shook his head. "I have access to my own. But I cannot take one from a living person, nor even manipulate it."

"Same thing's true about the remnants. Excepting the Eiden Rane, obviously. A properly trained Knight of Odo Sein knows *how* to restore a stolen remnant, but that doesn't mean they *can*. That requires the use of the Aba Quen."

Gladdic rubbed the white stubble on his chin. "How might a statue allow one to manipulate another person's inner ether?"

"How would I know how you warlocks defile people's souls? All I know is that we used to have it and that's what it did for us. During the rebellion, the Monsoon stole it and took it to the Bastion. One of our knights got word to us as he was leaving for Bressel. From what he saw, they weren't even using it. They were just keeping it there because they could tell it was important."

"If it has such a power, why not deploy it against their enemies? Even the threat of its use could cause the Monsoon's remaining enemies to do whatever the Monsoon demanded of them."

"The rebels are too stupid to know what it does. We didn't exactly run around telling everyone about its awesome power. It's from a much older time, too. Some of us think the Eiden Rane made it himself, back when he was learning how to absorb remnants into himself. Others think he found it, and used it to teach himself the process."

"Perhaps that is one reason the Monsoon has recruited sorcerers to its side. They might have recognized the importance of the Aba Quen, if not its function, and endeavored to study it."

Blays stuck his tongue out from the corner of his mouth. "How long ago was it taken to the Bastion? Weeks? Months? How can you be sure it's still there?"

Ara shrugged. "I'm not."

"That's not very comforting."

"But it's true, which means I don't give a shit if it makes you uncomfortable."

"If anything, you should be getting snippy with yourself. You knew the almighty lizard was at the Bastion all this time, but you couldn't be arsed to do anything to get it back?"

"Do you see an army at our beck and call? I know this is the sort of unimportant triviality that's easy to forget, but do you remember when I told you we couldn't leave the Silent Spires or we'd die?" She'd been blustering, but she now retracted on herself. "We didn't see the point of risking an assault. Not with the emperor gone and the Eiden Rane on the rampage. Even though they've agreed to let me train you, most of the other bels don't believe you'll be able to stop the lich."

"Do *you*?"

She gestured out at the wasteland. "Who cares what I think? Go try to get the Aba Quen. If you pull that off, try to restore Dante. If you do *that*, go and see if you can stop the lich. Why should my *opinion* of what you might be able to do impact your ability to actually do it?"

"Well, when you put it like that it all sounds so simple."

Ara gave him a long and skeptical look, then laughed, breaking into a smile. "I can't believe I just told you all of this like it was nothing. It makes me feel so dirty."

"In that case, you're welcome."

Gladdic, like Dante, didn't seem to be able to travel further than the nearest privy without carrying writing supplies with him. He had Ara sketch the Aba Quen for them, which indeed looked like a lizard with a blunt head and round toes wrapped around a skeletal forearm.

After their night of rest in the Spires, Blays and Gladdic were perfectly healthy enough to journey back across the Hell-Painted Hills. Ara ordered up a team of lan haba, which assembled at the eastern fringe of the trees.

Blays swung into the saddle. He was more than used to the

smell of large furry animals, but after so long in a place where there were no mammals larger than a cat—and these tended to be tree-hopping carnivores that would gladly eat your face while you were still wearing it, meaning it was best to keep a certain distance—the scent of the oversized goats was almost dizzying.

Bel Ara was there to see them off, sweating lightly in the heat of the day. "Find him, will you? Bring him back."

Blays took up the reins. "I thought you didn't believe in us."

"He's our only chance, isn't he?"

"Having him with us gives us our *best* chance. But the rest of us know a few tricks of our own. Even if we can't turn Dante, we'll make the lich very annoyed at us before we're dead—and if luck likes us on the day we take our swords against him, we may even kill him."

She didn't look convinced, but he wouldn't say that she looked doubtful, either. They rode out into the maniacal hills. Blays carried a certain bravado along with him. He'd found that the mere act of saying words out loud could make you believe them. They made your feet lighter beneath you, too. Repeated often enough, and they had the power to make that belief in yourself permanent. It was almost like a form of magic, and though it was more subtle than the nether, it was just as real.

That day, however, the enchantment faded before they'd made their first mile.

Bek rode with them, as laconic as ever. Bit risky, bringing him with them to Dara Bode, but after they had the Aba Quen, they'd need his abilities to bring to bear against Dante. Assuming, of course, that they were able to find the Aba Quen, which Blays wasn't fully confident about. If it had been moved, the number of non-Bastion places it might be hiding in included the entire rest of the swamps.

He watched Gladdic from the corner of his eye. Then again,

even if it was gone, sorcerers had a way of finding things that wanted to stay hidden.

They arrived at the swamp just under a day after leaving the Spires. Naran emerged from the trees to greet them. He looked in fine shape, and after their ride, he was cleaner than they were, too.

Blays hopped down from the boat. "Volo?"

Naran gave a small shake of his head. "There's been no change."

"I'm not liking that."

"I doubt that she is, either."

That made things downright uncomfortable, so Blays launched into an explanation of what they'd learned in the Spires regarding their upcoming voyage to Dara Bode.

"As before, her condition will only slow you down," Naran said. "But I won't abandon her. I'll stay with her at the Spires, if they will allow it."

Their guides exchanged a look, then nodded.

"You're sure of that?" Blays turned back to the Hills. "I don't know how long we'll be gone. Stay there too long, and you might get trapped there."

"If you fail, it will likely be safest in the Spires. Until the end comes at last for them, too."

They made parting arrangements. As Naran helped Volo into a saddle, Blays, Gladdic, and Bek loaded themselves into the canoe. Blays and Naran waved to each other, then went their separate ways.

Blays dabbed the paddle in the water. "Which way is Dara Bode again?"

Gladdic and Bek pointed in two different directions. Blays split the difference, paddling at a pace that was more brisk than sustainable. When he got tired, they flipped the canoe about so Bek was in front, allowing him to take over duties.

Blays mopped his brow against the shoulder of his jabat. "Gladdic, how well did you get to know the layout of the Bastion while you were there? Or were you too busy torturing Naran to pay attention to that?"

Gladdic snorted. "I know it reasonably well. The most difficult portion will be crossing the moat unseen, but if you and Dante were able to do so, I don't see why we would be unable."

"Leaving the minor matter of finding a hand-sized figurine in the middle of a palace-sized palace."

"It will not be as challenging as you fear. For they will be afraid of having the Aba Quen stolen back from them, and when people are afraid, that is when they become most predictable."

"How so? That's when they're most likely to punch you in the face. Or call your mother names that would make *your* lanky old mother blush. Or offer to do vile things to or for you."

"Yet you know they will react in these ways, and will not be surprised when they live down to your expectation. In this case, their fear will cause them to keep the Aba Quen in those places they consider most secure: the peak of the Blue Tower, or more likely, in the Lower Vault. It will be little issue for us to penetrate these places without being seen — and even if we are, to dispense with those who have seen us."

Bek was a fellow fighting man in fair shape, but he was more than a decade older and his arms wore out sooner than Blays' had. Blays replaced him as head paddler and soon found himself wishing he hadn't. The part of the swamp nearest the Hell-Painted Hills was different from other parts in a way Blays couldn't fully put his finger on, but which certainly involved a thickening of the shrubbery and a tightening of the waterways.

Unlike Volo, who seemed to have a sixth sense for which routes would remain open, Blays more than once found himself faced with an impassible wall of growth. The first time, the blockage was thin enough for Gladdic to use the nether to gouge a hole through to the other side, but the next time they hit an ob-struction, Blays had to swing about, backtrack, and find a new path. The third time he came up against a crush of branches, he swore and smacked at the water with his paddle.

"Do you continue to lead us down dead ends on purpose?" Gladdic muttered.

"I'm just looking for the best one. It's the perfect spot to dump your body in."

"Have you not noticed that the dead ends are commonly pre-saged by the presence of dulia?"

"What-ya?"

Gladdic pointed to a vine wreathed through the brambles and dotted with small purple flowers. "They entwine themselves in the low, thick shrubs that most commonly crowd themselves be-tween the trees. Avoid entering the paths where they grow, and you will avoid these stoppages. Why do you keep ignoring the signs?"

Blays paddled them back toward the entrance. "How do you expect me to have known about them in the first place? Half the time we've been here, I've been busy paddling. The other half, I've been busy paddling for my life."

"Then consider yourself educated."

"Next time I'm messing up, why don't you consider educating me *before* I've made the same mistake twenty times in a row?"

"Because I don't know what I relish more: telling you that you are wrong, or watching you be wrong."

Between Blays and Bek switching off at the paddle, Gladdic wiping away their weariness with the nether, and the longer daylight hours, they had a plan to reach Dara Bode in as little as four days. However, no one had yet come up with a form of sor-cery to eliminate the need for sleep—and, honestly, Blays proba-bly would have strangled them if they did—and so as night neared, they turned the boat into an island, hid it within the grass, and made camp behind a screen of trees.

They still had some vegetables and pies from the Spires, but in dire need of fresh meat, Blays baited a hook with bits of potato and dropped a line in the water. In almost no time at all, he'd caught six fish, their silver scales speckled with iridescent pink spots. He cleaned them and tossed the guts into the water, which were immediately tended to by a boiling cloud of ziki oko, who were in turn dispersed by an influx of the orange catfish that preyed on them.

Finished, Blays brought his catch back to the center of the island.

Gladdic frowned. "What do you intend to cook them with?"

"I was considering using an invention I've heard stories about in our travels. I think it's called 'fire.'"

"We are presently in enemy territory in the midst of an effort to rob them of what could be the most valuable object in their entire possession. We can't light a fire!"

"Yes we can, because I want one. So if you don't want anybody to see it, you'd better drop a shadowsphere on it."

Gladdic lowered his brows. Before the priest could argue, Blays went off to gather kindling, which lay in great abundance about the island. He returned to find that Bek had dug a small fire pit in his absence. Blays arranged his materials, then snapped his fingers and lit it with a spark of nether.

Gladdic watched this unfold in disapproving silence. Muttering to himself, he dropped a wad of shadows over the fire. There was still plenty of smoke, but most of it was broken up by the trees. Besides, they were already in the very last of the twilight, and the smoke wouldn't be visible for long.

Cooking the fish over a fire he couldn't see was an interesting experience, but Blays could have done so by the smell of the crisping skin alone. Bek and Gladdic stayed close, gazing at the nether-shrouded fire with expressions that were entirely dog-like.

Once the meat was white and the skin was brown, Blays served it up on a bed of the oversized, teardrop-shaped leaves that grew on the banks. Using their bare hands, they tore into the meat with a ferocity that ought to have qualified them as honorary Blighted.

Afterward, Gladdic considered the remains of his meal, which consisted of little more than a skeleton and a few scraps of undercooked skin. "I have given it much thought. And I have decided this was, in fact, worth the risk."

Blays picked at his teeth with a needle-thin bone. "As I always say, the best offense against black times is stuffing yourself silly."

This was met by grunts of approval. Blays enjoyed the smell of the wood smoke for another minute, then kicked dirt over the blacked-out fire. Gladdic dispelled the shadowsphere.

Bek laughed softly. "After a lifetime training to destroy it, it's very strange to sit in the presence of sorcery. Even stranger to appreciate it."

"Personally, I'd rather stick to swords," Blays said. "But with all these cheaters running around, you have to fight them at their own game."

"And not only do you know magic, but now you're learning to use the Odo Sein."

"Not terribly well, as evidenced by your presence. Not to suggest it isn't anything but pleasant and enlightening."

"You foreigners waste so many words on politeness it's a wonder you have any left to get anything done."

"Yet in my land I'm considered rude. There's no justice anywhere, sir knight."

Bek smiled, then grew serious. Or at least as serious as a man can be when his face is covered in fish grease. "Stranger than any of this is the idea that two hari are learning the Odo Sein. Even hearing it from the bels themselves, I can't believe it. Would you show me what you can do?"

Blays and Gladdic exchanged first a look, then mutual shrugs. They seated themselves. Blays closed his eyes and lobbed himself into the practice that, with his typical callous disregard for all that was fun in life, Dante had dubbed "Forest."

After a couple of minutes of silence, Bek cursed and laughed. "Black streams! Even when I see it, I still can't believe it!"

Blays opened his eyes. In the dark of the night, golden flecks danced about in their curious patterns, neither fully orderly nor completely chaotic. "A miracle, right? Yet as miraculous as our powers may be, we haven't yet been able to, you know, *do* anything with them. What we can do is about as useful as having a painting of a steak."

"Remarkable," Gladdic said. "It has hardly been five minutes since our supper, yet you still frame everything in terms of food."

"I'd put it in terms of drink, except I don't want to think about how long it's been since I've had one." Blays flicked his fish bone at the mix of dirt and ash. "Then again, if we'd like to resume our efforts at not being so terrible, we've got a tried-and-true Knight of Odo Sein right in front of us, don't we?"

Bek beetled his brow. "What are you asking?"

"When you access the stream, what do you do? Any hot tips for us?"

The knight looked at him like Blays had asked him to regurgitate his fish and feed it to Blays like a baby bird. "It's no wonder you can't figure out how to use the stream. You're as dumb as a log-worm!"

"Assuming that a log-worm is pretty dumb, I'm inclined to agree with you. Now would you mind explaining *why* you think my head is a vessel of night soil?"

Gladdic sighed. "It is because you asked him to explain precisely how one uses the skill. Such a question defies the core virtue of the Odo Sein."

"At least one of you gets it," Bek said. "Was Bel Ara drunk when she took you on?"

"No," Blays said levelly. "She, along with the rest of your council, was convinced to teach us by someone who showed her how he could preserve Tanar Atain in two ways: in the present, by killing the White Lich. And in the future, by recording your country's past. All while standing to gain nothing for himself."

The knight darted a glance at Blays' hands, which weren't far from the hilts of his swords. "If I didn't know better, I'd say you're ready to take an apology from me—or to take a piece of my hide with your steel. But you're in our lands now. We have no idea what trifles you foreigners consider an insult, nor how much groveling it takes to make an apology for them."

"Go on, then, and hack at each other." Gladdic's words were pure scorn. "Then as long as we're betraying everything we came here to do, I shall run off to swear fealty to the White Lich."

The corner of Blays' mouth twitched. He wasn't sure if it was a smile. He hoisted his hands over his head and stretched. "I suppose if Bel Ara couldn't pound it through our thick heads, you're not likely to do any better, kind knight. For me, trying to get the stream to move is like trying to suck an apple through a reed." He swung his head toward Gladdic. "Hold on. Suppose there's a way to make a bigger reed?"

"If this is a metaphor, it is as cloudy as a syphilitic's urine."

"You have no idea how glad I am that I've already eaten. But follow me on this. Even for a skilled nethermancer, trying to get the shadows to do what you want without bribing them with blood is a lot harder than when you splash some of the red stuff around first. By using blood, you're making the reed bigger."

"The reed through which you are attempting to suck the apple."

"That's right."

"Which is a thing that has never been attempted by anyone."

"But you still understand what I'm getting at, so quit pretending you don't. Blood makes it easier to access the nether. Is there anything similar for ether?"

"You are incapable of using the ether. What does it matter?"

"Because I'm *trying* to figure out if this is something that exists with all the powers. Including the stream."

"Yes," Gladdic said slowly. "There is."

"Well, what is it?"

"A closely guarded secret. But you will next explain that knowing this secret will help you to determine a possible analogue for the stream, and although I would respond by insisting it would not, you wouldn't believe me until you could judge for yourself."

"That sounds pretty much how it would go. Except my side of things would involve passing more judgments about your mother."

"It involves the breaking of something delicate," Gladdic said. "A glass figurine or a shell are two favorites. Anything that is beautiful or the product of long labor works best, for the ether is agitated by the chaos of such an object being destroyed. It arrives eager to restore the damage, and then to correct further disorder around it."

Blays leaned back, swatting at something on his arm. "Nether's the stuff of the cycle of life. Of birth, creation, and death. Blood fuels it. Ether's the stuff of order and preservation, and gets riled up when you mess with that. Bit contradictory, isn't it? One's for it, one's against it. So if there's anything like this with the stream, it could be either something that promotes thought and reason, or exactly the opposite."

"Blood magic and totems," Bek said. "It's a wonder the people of your mad lands aren't sacrificing each other from sunup to sundown."

"The products of blood magic and totems were what saved your life in Aris Osis," Gladdic said. "And if the gods will it, it will be blood magic and totems that allow us to destroy the Eiden Rane and save your damned country. You were brought up to believe these powers are evil, yet even when evidence otherwise stands before you like a mountain, you still deny that it's true."

Bek's face flushed a rather incredible shade of scarlet. "These are desperate times. Everything's out the window."

"Indeed."

If Gladdic had pressed the obvious hypocrisy, Bek might have gone on the defensive. Instead, the old priest said nothing, letting the silence stretch to the breaking point.

"Damn you," Bek murmured. He had his head tipped back and was staring into nothing, making it unclear who exactly he was damning. He met Gladdic's eyes. "I shouldn't tell you this. Even if I believe it's true—and there's nothing I've ever seen to say otherwise—if I tell you what I know, it'll discourage you from finding out and proving me wrong."

"Which would be a loss for the Odo Sein. As you currently believe there is no such 'reed' to make the stream flow more freely."

Bek made the barest nod. "That'd be a reasonable conclusion."

Blays exhaled raggedly. "Gods, I hate having to think this much. Why can't I be right about everything on the first try?" He looked up. "Gladdic, those shells you're talking about breaking— they aren't shaden, are they?"

"Shaden's association with the nether renders them distasteful to the priests," Gladdic said. "Not to mention they are somewhat large. Any reasonably complex shell would do, although some argue that the most effective shells are prettier or bear more sophisticated patterns that make their destruction more offensive to the ether." He had been pacing as he spoke, lecturing. "Why do you ask?"

"When I learned to use the nether at Pocket Cove, we used shells, too. Not to generate more nether, but to make it easier to take the step from being able to touch the shadows to being able to actually use the stupid stuff. That's what idiots like me have to do, anyway. I think they typically take on a higher caliber of student."

"I have only heard rumors of Pocket Cove, and each one intrigues me more. I would like to hear more about them, along with their methods of training."

"Not tonight," Blays decided. "But maybe another time. What I'm interested in right now is whether there's anything similar to help students access the ether. Or the stream."

Bek swore under his breath. "That's too good of a piece of deduction to let go by."

"You're saying such a thing exists?"

"I'll say that if it *did* exist, I don't see any way you could reason your way toward determining what you're looking for."

"Me neither. So why not tell us? Other than your kooky religious beliefs that sound perfectly enlightened in most circumstances but are currently trying to kill us?"

"What need do you even have for it? Aren't I here to wield the Odo Sein for you?"

"That's the plan," Blays said. "But in my experience, plans have a habit of going to shit even when they're not being opposed by a malevolent demigod. In the event that something happens to you — wait, let me rephrase that in Tanarian terms. In the event the lich chops your head from your neck and uses your skull as his porridge bowl, it would be nice if one of us had also learned to use the Odo Sein. Because I'm not sure waving your dismembered remains at the lich will do the trick."

"I can't tell you what it is." Bek gazed at his hands. "But I'll watch for one of them on the way to Dara Bode, and if I see one, I'll get it for you. Don't ask me for more than that."

"No worries on that front." Blays rolled himself into his light-weight travel blanket. "As tight-lipped as your order is, I could ask you which way the sun rises all night and I still wouldn't know until dawn."

Of all the reasons Blays hated the White Lich, his third-highest reason—and making a serious charge at second place—was that he hadn't been able to sleep past noon for several weeks.

As usual, they got up way too damned early and resumed the tedious job of propelling themselves through the swamp. Check that: the *awful* swamp. They'd run out of Volo's bug-repelling paste while returning to the Hell-Painted Hills, and while Bek had provided them with a second method (chewing up a particular bitter-tasting leaf and rubbing it around your skin), it wasn't half as effective. While Blays was paddling, he wished he wasn't so that he'd be able to scratch his bites. When he wasn't paddling, he wished he was so he'd have something to distract him from the itchiness.

Once upon a time, there had been incidental boat traffic everywhere but the fringes and deepest reaches of the swamp. These days, the waterways were all but empty. Later that morning, when Gladdic warned them of an approaching vessel, Blays pulled them behind a patch of thorns. He wasn't surprised in the slightest when the boat that advanced into view was a Monsoon war canoe. Gladdic held the nether in hand, but the boat passed without noticing them.

At noon, they stopped for a quick break to stretch their legs and deflate their bladders.

"Dante is moving eastward," Gladdic announced to Blays, holding his hand to the side of his head. "If he holds course, his path should take him just north of Dara Bode. He could easily deviate to the capital. Do you think his path is coincidence?"

"It has to be. There's no possible way he'd know where we

were going."

"Unless he's left his eyes upon us."

That was a troublesome thought. It turned out to be the pernicious variety that sounded ridiculous at first but wormed its way deeper and deeper into your mind the more you thought about it. Blays spent an uncomfortable chunk of the afternoon dwelling on that possibility before moving on to a more generalized malaise. What if he hadn't gotten so drunk that night? So angry? If he'd been there, Dante wouldn't have gone out on patrol alone. And while it was possible that, had they gone out together, they both would have been taken, Blays didn't think that's how it would have turned out.

Now, their only hope lay in finding some foolish lizard statue, tracking Dante down, unleashing the statue's power on him, and praying that it worked on lesser liches the same way it did on the Blighted. Oh right, and also they needed to survive the encounter with Dante long enough to use the Aba Quen in the first place, which Blays had more than a few doubts they'd be able to do.

If Dante had been with them on a similar mission, he wouldn't have felt half as worried. As he'd said before, like alchemists of chaos, the pair of them had a way of transmuting disorder into opportunity.

For obvious reasons, however, Dante was not there. His role was currently being filled by Gladdic. And Blays was still a long way from sure about Gladdic. Granted, the old man had abandoned the immediate fight against the lich to pursue this line of action, which was a point in his favor, but there were still about nine thousand other strikes against him. Like the Plagued Islands. And the campaign against the Collen Basin. And Volo, who was looking more and more like she'd be dazed forever — although that act *had* maybe saved Bek's life, who was vital to the current process of saving Dante's life, and without Dante,

Blays pegged their chances of stopping the White Lich at somewhere between "laughable" and "fuck-all."

It was all very confusing. The kind of confusion that could only be distilled with a long night in the company of brown liquor, which Blays didn't have any of. What he had instead was the deepening conviction that they should have walked away from this a long time ago. Like as soon as they'd rescued Naran. Everything after that had been a rage-blinded quest for revenge. Against someone who had, quite unbeknownst to them, been working to fight the thing they were now *all* trying to stop.

Still, if you could pinpoint a single mistake to blame for their current straits, it had to be the decision to go after Gladdic rather than taking Naran from the Blue Tower and walking away. But after everything that Gladdic had done, how could they not have tried to bring him to justice? That angle of things was Gladdic's fault, wasn't it?

None of it made any sense. He was starting to fear that it never would.

Bek held up his right arm. "Stop."

Blays backbeat, then dragged the paddle in the water. "What've you got?"

"That inlet over there. You should take it."

The inlet was a barely-visible gap in the trees. Bek didn't appear ready to volunteer anything as to *why* Blays should take it rather than the quite clear path ahead, but knowing that asking would be fruitless, Blays brought them through it, ducking under a pair of outstretched branches guarding the entry.

After forty feet of tight travel, the way opened into a wide and roughly circular pool of water. This was hemmed in on the sides by dense growth and overhead by the canopy. The water was studded by small islands sporting short trees. It felt still even by the sluggish standards of the swamp.

Bek surveyed the area expressionlessly, then pointed to an island a third of the way across the clearing. "That one. Circle it. Slowly."

Blays brought them up to the island. It looked like any of the hundreds of other micro-islands they'd recently passed, if a little mossier than most. Bek kept his eyes locked on the shores.

Blays made a complete circuit, then brought them to a stop. "What are we supposed to be looking for?"

"You don't look," Bek said. "I look. You paddle."

He directed them to a second island. Blays circled it slowly.

Halfway around, Bek grabbed him by the upper arm and whispered, "Stop! Don't scare it!"

Blays dragged his paddle. He followed Bek's line of sight to the shore. "Scare what? The moss?"

"The crab. See it there?"

"No, but I'll trust that you do, because the alternative is that the last Knight of Odo Sein and our only hope of victory just went completely insane."

"There's a bearded crab right there. That's the object that will get you closer to learning the Odo Sein. Bring me in nice and slow."

Blays hesitated, then reminded himself that he'd been involved in any number of far stranger things over the years. Stealthily as he could, he brought them in toward the island, still utterly failing to spot the crab.

A long portion of the bank slid away from the island. The front portion of the slide launched into the air, hurling toward the canoe. Blays grabbed Gladdic by the jabat and yanked him into the bottom of the boat. The swamp dragon's head soared over them, teeth clapping shut in the empty space.

With a shout, Bek drew his Odo Sein blade, nether zipping down the dark steel. The canoe rocked madly. Ether blasted from Gladdic's hand into the swamp dragon's long neck, but the enormous lizards were nearly as hardened against sorcery as the kappers of the Wodun Mountains, and its scales dispersed the light like glowing milkweed seeds.

The dragon swung about in the frothy water, lifting its head. If it came down on the canoe, it'd smash the boat into a million small pieces. Even if the three of them weren't hurt or stunned by the attack, Blays doubted more than one of them would make it to shore without being eaten.

"Lie down!" He got to his feet, drawing one sword.

Gladdic had already complied. Bek crouched, blade held up for the incoming strike. He was still standing higher than Blays would have liked, but there was nothing for it. Blays slipped into the shadows. He dashed forward, his feet oozing into the surface of the water like it was thick mud, and launched himself at the dragon.

He took a passing whack at the beast's throat as he went by, but even with the nethereal weapon, trying to cut through the dragon's skin was like trying to chew through tanned leather. It didn't even seem to notice him. That being the exact opposite of his goals, he exited the shadows mid-jump, landing on the dragon's back and stomping down as hard as he could.

The dragon's back was half-coated in living grass, moss, snails, and what appeared to be small chunks of rock embedded among the scales, which were the color and texture of dirt. Blays drew his second sword and dropped his right knee, stabbing both weapons downward. One hit the scales and slid off. The other lodged momentarily, gouging a fraction of an inch into the chitin before stopping.

Blays yanked the weapon free and laid about himself in wild abandon, slashing and jabbing at the dragon as he worked his way toward the base of its neck. This delivered exactly zero appreciable damage to the monster.

But while hurting the monster would have been nice, Blays was more than satisfied by the result: the swamp dragon abandoned its intentions to belly flop onto the canoe and focused on him instead. The beast curled its head around, angling for a bite, but Blays simply circled around the back of its neck, giving it two more whacks for good measure. The lizard wrenched its head around to the other side, trying to catch him from the rear. He merely danced to the spot it had just vacated, leaving the animal snapping in vain, unable to stretch far enough across its own back to reach him.

He jabbed at its neck with everything he had. It snapped at him twice more, then exhaled hard, its back contracting, and dived beneath the surface.

Blays jumped into the air and into the netherworld. The water lit up with bright silver bubbles. The swamp dragon was a terribly long mass, bright black under the dull shade of the water.

As Blays began to descend, blindingly white ether poured from Gladdic's hand and spread across the surface of the swamp. With a series of hollow cracks, the water froze solid.

Blays landed lightly. Beneath him, the dragon headed for the canoe only to bonk into a wall of ice. It slammed its head into the wall, but the ice held.

Blays popped from the netherworld. He made way for the canoe, skidding on the ice.

"No!" Gladdic thrust his finger toward the shore. "Deliver the crab!"

"You've got to be joking!" Blays turned back to the island, certain it would be futile, yet his eyes latched onto the crab at once: a dark lump near the water's edge, pebbles stuck to its back, a beard-like plume of moss hanging from its chin.

Under the water, the swamp dragon took another bash at the wall of ice, cracking it with an eerie groan. Shaking his head, Blays dashed toward the island, squishing into the mud at its edge. The alarmed crab shuffled toward the water, left-hand claw opening and closing as it went. Blays maneuvered behind it and scooped it up. Its pointed legs scrabbled at the air.

The dragon slammed into the ice yet again. A crack shot toward the surface, opaquing it. Blays made a run for the canoe. When he was ten feet from the boat, the ice snapped underfoot, spilling him forward. He tucked the crab to his chest with one hand and reached out with the other, seeking the ground and guiding himself into a shoulder roll. The ice breathed cold through the thin fabric of the jabat. He came to his feet and hopped into the canoe.

Bek was paddling before Blays' butt hit the bench. The canoe sped away from the island and toward the narrow tunnel through the growth. Behind them, the swamp dragon crashed through the fragmenting ice, surfacing amid a turmoil of bubbles.

Gladdic wriggled his fingers. A ball of darkness enfolded the dragon's head. It shook itself, trying to free itself from its blindness, but under Gladdic's close concentration, the shadowsphere followed the beast's every movement.

They entered the passage through the trees. As Bek took them through a curve, blocking line of sight, the dragon was still thrashing its head in fury.

"I never thought I'd risk my life for a crab." Blays held the poky little thing away from himself. "Especially one I wasn't going to poach in butter."

In the aft of the canoe, Gladdic was twisted about, watching for pursuit from the dragon. "How did you know it would be there?"

"The flowers growing outside the inlet," Bek said. "The little yellow ones shaped like hands. The crabs favor the fruits the flowers grow."

Blays winced as the crab poked him with a foot. "How exactly is this supposed to help us reach the stream?"

"I don't know."

"I see. Remind me why I just risked getting bitten in half trying to grab it, then?"

"I don't know *how* the crabs help. I only know that they do. Thought is the bridge between your self and the world around you. The Odo Sein is what exists between these two realms. Existing between land and water, the crabs are a bridge as well." Bek paddled thoughtfully. "Also, their beards signify their wisdom."

"Are you being quite serious?" Blays held the crab up for a better look at the moss hanging from its face. "This thing is special because it's got a bit of moss growing where its chin would be if crabs had chins?"

"That's what I was told. If you don't believe me, you should try to prove me wrong."

"How do you use it?"

"How do you think?"

"Gods damn it, if I have to hear that one more—"

"There's no trick," Bek said. "Just keep it near you as you access the stream."

Gazing into the crab's beady little eyes, Blays was glad Dante wasn't around to witness what he was about to do. Finding the creature's constant jabs and tickles distracting, he set it in the bottom of his traveling cup, then started daydreaming about long-gone forests.

Once he had a few motes of gold making figure-eights near his right shoulder, he swooped down on them with the grace of a pouncing cat. Impressive though this maneuver was, the flecks of stream remained stubbornly unconvinced of his authority, failing to so much as twitch from their pattern.

Blays tried again and again until the last of his stream faded away. "I'm not getting anywhere. Are you sure this crab's beard isn't defective?"

Gladdic had been keeping one eye on Blays' efforts and the

other one out for patrols or other dangers. They all swapped roles, with Blays taking up the paddle.

Twenty minutes later, Gladdic shook his head. "I cannot see any difference at all."

Almost like it was an afterthought, Bek conjured up a thread of stream, drawing it to himself. "The fault isn't with the crab. The crab is fine."

Even though he'd just watched the knight seem to put the crab to use, Blays would have taken the whole thing for a bizarre prank played on gullible outsiders. Except for one thing: he himself had used a sea snail as a part of his own training in the nether. So why was it so ridiculous to think a crab might be able to do the same thing with the stream? Shaden were filled with nether. Kappers and swamp dragons were resistant to it. If humans could manipulate the light and shadows, why wouldn't animals be able to interact with them as well?

He picked up the cup. Earlier, the crab had been scrabbling at the smooth tin sides, but it now rested at the bottom, seemingly resigned to its fate. More than a few philosophers and farmers claimed that the ability to make peace with your lot in life was a virtue. Perhaps the highest one there was.

In that this idea made for the perfect justification to kick back and do nothing, Blays favored it. But he'd always been suspicious that it was little more than an excuse that the timid used to justify quivering behind locked doors when the day called for strong people to go forth and kick ass.

He set down the cup, closed his eyes, and got back to work on the stream.

They exited the woods, unveiling the lights of Dara Bode. Behind the sprawling raft-houses and docks, stone buildings and towers stood on hills that, despite rising no more than a few score feet high, were the highest points of land Blays had seen in

Tanar Atain other than the Wound and the Hell-Painted Hills. At the city center, the Bastion's spires lorded it up over everything.

They'd bided their time waiting for nightfall arguing about whether to approach the front gates or try to sneak in elsewhere on the perimeter, which wasn't walled, but which was enclosed by two separate fish nets and was heavily patrolled. Gladdic had eventually won out on the idea that if they tried the gates, there was at least the chance they'd be allowed inside without further issue. And even if they were apprehended, they could dash back into the wilds to hide, and then try another way in.

It sounded reasonable enough. Yet as they paddled into the light cast by the the sentries' lanterns, Blays' instincts cleared their throat and informed him that they had made the entirely incorrect decision.

The sentries were already standing up and watching them, spears planted beside them, meaning it was much too late to turn the canoe around without making themselves look extra guilty. Blays donned his best "I am but a stupid foreigner" expression, which he'd had many opportunities to perfect over the years, and removed his paddle from the water. Bek sat in the canoe's center. He was out of his armor, and as far as Blays could tell, he looked like your average, everyday Tanarian. Gladdic sat aft, back hunched and chin down, as if he was asleep.

"Travelers?" One of the sentries lifted his lantern, dousing the canoe in yellow light. "Identify yourselves."

"My name's Cren Nalen, of Raga Don," Bek said. "These are my two servants."

"What brings a villager to the capital in the middle of the night?"

"Raga Don was attacked. I've traveled for days, but the war is everywhere."

"The gates are closed."

"Sirs, the capital is the only place I can find safety. You have to let me in."

"Every village is given the chance to surrender," the sentry said. "If it didn't, then it was attacked with good cause. We owe you nothing."

"But we're countrymen!"

A second man laughed. "Not anymore. You want safety, then you'd best leave Tanar Atain, to slink away like your coward emperor."

Bek went very still in a way that almost always meant fists — or far more lethal weapons — were about to get flung around.

"Pardon me," Blays interrupted. "For I am but a worthless hari, and if not for the fact I'd be eaten alive otherwise, I wouldn't taint this boat with my presence, let alone your grand capital. Our master spoke at great length to convince the others to turn Raga Don over to the virtuous liberators of the Righteous Monsoon. By the end of his words, even a lowborn worm like myself was crying from my wormy little eyes. Even so, the other leaders didn't listen, and decided to fight you. But is their stupidity my master's fault?"

"Yes," the sentry answered. "Now fuck off."

Without a word, Gladdic splayed his left hand. Nether streaked through the night. The two sentries' heads snapped back, then rolled forward, spewing blood from the holes punched through their foreheads. They collapsed together.

Gladdic climbed out onto the dock. "Retrieve their uniforms. I will open the gates."

Blays clenched his teeth hard enough to snap something. He rolled out of the canoe, glanced down the docks, then peeled the white and blue jabats from the Monsoon sentries, doing his best not to get them too bloody. He tossed the clothes to Bek, then lowered one of the bodies into the water next to the canoe.

"What are you doing?" Bek whispered.

"Not leaving a pair of corpses in the middle of the front

gates." Sweating from the effort, Blays dunked the second body with a small splash.

The gates parted, swinging outward with no sound except the creak of ropes. Blays grabbed the two bodies by their wrists, dragging them along as Bek brought the canoe forward. Gladdic waited on a stone ledge on the other side. They gave him a hand into the boat.

They struck out from the gates and into the cover of the ring of crops cultivated between the fish nets and the outermost neighborhoods. The long leaves of banana trees fluttered in the weak breeze. Blays instructed Bek to take them to a cluster of trees, then stuffed the two corpses between the tightly-packed trunks.

Blays rinsed his hands, then gave Gladdic a tap on the shoulder that wasn't quite a punch. "Was that strictly necessary?"

Gladdic rubbed his shoulder. "To prevent them from raising the alarm so that the entire city might descend upon us? I thought so, yes."

"I told you we should have come in from the side. Then again, whoever could have guessed that the paranoid Monsoon wasn't going to let two hari into the city after nightfall?"

"We are now through the gates with two uniforms in hand. I know that you are so fond of criticism that you would denounce your own mother's methods as she gave birth to you, but in this case, you are mistaken."

Blays' hair and features were too obviously foreign to pass as a soldier, so Bek and Gladdic changed into the uniforms instead, which turned out to be a tricky maneuver to execute while inside a canoe. Once they were dressed, Bek paddled onward, exiting the agricultural district and entering a neighborhood of raft-houses.

Before the coming of the Monsoon, these had been raucous with laughter and debate. They were now almost entirely quiet, the inhabitants keeping themselves indoors, murmuring too softly for their neighbors to hear. Blays found himself angered by the silence. He'd always measured a society's virtue through how much cheer, arguing, and all-around rowdiness it could produce without also producing violence and riots. Apparently the Monsoon was incapable of any spirit whatsoever.

On the plus side, this deadness of spirit meant there were fewer people out wandering around who would be inclined to yell at them about what they were doing. They cut past the slums and into the canals separating the wealthy islands from each other. Within a span of minutes, they approached the short earthen rampart surrounding the moat which in turn surrounded the heart of the city.

Blays had seen a few moats in his day, but nothing in Mallon, Gask, or anywhere else he'd traveled could compare to the one surrounding the Bastion of Last Acts. It was a full bowshot across. Not some dinky little rabbit-hunting bow, either. A war bow. Also, the water was stuffed to the gills, so to speak, with ziki oko. Anyone who fell in, or attempted to swim it, would be treated to the rare opportunity of seeing what their own skeleton looked like, which would give them quite the interesting conversation starter once the ziki oko's ministrations sent them into the Mists.

In the middle of the moat, the towers and halls of the Bastion were your typical display of grandeur, of the sort that announced, "I will now work my people to death building enough walls to ensure that none of their descendants can ever step foot in this palace again." The only thing of mild interest about them was that they were built from pale blue granite, with the quite literal-minded Blue Tower looking as blue as a sky or the ocean or one of those other very blue things.

Bek brought them up against the edge of the rampart, which rose four-plus feet from the water and was held in check by a sheer retaining wall. They tied the canoe to a metal rod mortared into the bricks. Blays helped boost Gladdic to the top of the retaining wall, then followed him up, lying flat on the short grass.

Prone beside him, Gladdic was already gesturing away, weaving his hand through a series of snaky gestures and muttering to himself. A dark spot materialized on the ground near him, as black as the Blue Tower was blue.

A bit more mumbling and weaving, and a second spot appeared, then a third. Traces. Blays was pretty damn curious how Gladdic was able to find and expose them without shadowalking into the netherworld, but he had a feeling that would be one secret the priest kept to himself.

Two feet from the ground, a child-sized silhouette unfurled. The miniature Andrac spread its claws wide and tipped back its head, white light burning from within its throat. Gladdic made a cutting motion and the demon closed its mouth, extinguishing the light before it could be seen from the fortress.

"You will find the Aba Quen," Gladdic breathed. He described the statue, as well as the most likely places he expected it to be kept. "Now go. Do not be seen."

The pint-sized Star-Eater nodded its head and dropped into the water without a splash. The summer night air was alive with crickets and smelled like fresh water. A minute later, a shadow slipped from the moat onto the dock that fronted the Bastion's doors and slipped inside.

"Not a bad spy," Blays whispered. "Although I think Dante's moths are subtler."

"We each have our own style." Lying on his stomach in the grass, Gladdic motioned to the moat. "Have you considered how we might cross this?"

"We're going inside? I thought your little pet would just fetch it for us."

"How may a shadow pick up that which is real?"

"Let me get this straight. You brought us here fully aware we needed to break into the Bastion. And you didn't give a moment's thought to how we were going to *get* to it?"

"You and Dante had no troubles crossing it when you came for Captain Naran. Why not use the same trick now?"

"Because Dante did it all and he can do a lot of stuff you can't."

"Ah," Gladdic said. "That is a fairly good reason."

Blays spent the next several minutes thinking about how they might lift the canoe up to the top of the earthworks without a) making gobs of noise and b) breaking themselves. Other than smashing their boat into pieces, bringing the pieces up top, then reassembling them into a solid boat—a plan they didn't have the tools or ability to pull off—he didn't see a way.

Bek didn't offer a single bit of insight. In fact, Blays got the impression the knight thought it was somehow improper to sneak into a lord's castle and rob the place of its most valuable possession.

Fifteen minutes after it had departed, the Andrac climbed onto the rampart in front of them, nearly causing Blays to evacuate into his jabat. The demon crouched in front of Gladdic, communing noiselessly.

The old man smiled. "The Aba Quen is here, held within the Lower Vault. Just where I suspected it would be."

"That's a welcome bit of news. Now don't disappoint me by telling me we still don't have a way across the moat."

"I have thought about it. And I have concluded that I do not know how."

Blays sucked his upper teeth. "How far is the Lower Vault from here?"

"I imagine it is the same distance as the fortress we are currently staring at."

"But how long would it take someone to run to it from here?

Assuming they were a talented and handsome individual who wouldn't have to slow down for any doors?"

Gladdic tapped his chin. "Three minutes? Perhaps four."

"I'll go by myself. Your little friend can show me the way. I'm going to be tight on time, though, especially if I run into any trouble. But if we had a way across — "

"Then it would all become much easier. I am painfully aware."

"You know, this would be extremely simple if you could harvest us a second canoe. But nooo, you were too busy pitting the Plagued Islanders into war with each other to learn anything from them."

Gladdic was rubbing his temples, stretching his wrinkled skin. As Blays finished speaking, his left eyebrow bent upward. "I cannot make us a vessel made of wood. But which god declared that a boat must be made from trees?"

He crawled to the inner edge of the earthworks. As the first light of ether glowed from his fingers, he smothered it in a shadowsphere. A pale line appeared in the water below, bobbing to the surface: an arm of solid ice. With deft, precise movements, Gladdic expanded it on both sides, curving the edges upward and curving the nose into a point. In a matter of seconds, an icy canoe rested on the water, mist curling from its frozen flanks.

Blays laughed softly. "Neat trick. But I think I'll stick with a wooden paddle."

He lowered himself down the outer edge of the wall and snagged a paddle from their original canoe. When he climbed back up, he found that Gladdic, Bek, and the little Star-Eater had climbed into the ice-boat.

"We will wait for you outside the walls," Gladdic said. "In case, as you say, there is trouble."

Blays kneeled in the bow, the ice stinging his bare legs, and paddled hard for the Bastion shores, shifting his weight from knee to knee to try to prevent them from freezing solid. As soon as the canoe slid onto solid ground, he jumped out and rubbed the warmth back into his legs.

"We will wait here for you," Gladdic said. "Good luck, sir Blays."

"Thanks, sir Gladdic."

Blays shrugged at the Andrac. It stared up at him, saying nothing. Interpreting this as demonic for "Why yes I am ready," Blays walked up to the stone wall and plunged into the shadows.

The night's gloom lit up with the moon-like eeriness of the netherworld. He crossed through the wall and into a sitting room. In the hallway beyond, the Andrac took the lead, dashing silently over the reed mat lining the center of the passage.

They'd hardly gotten anywhere before the glowing outline of a person appeared at the far end of the corridor. The Andrac stopped and sank into the wall. Ensconced in the shadows, Blays wouldn't have been noticed by the intruder even if he'd done a handstand with his jabat flipped over his head while blowing a trumpet. But he needed the Andrac, and it wouldn't do to have a servant run off shrieking about bumping into a child-sized demon. He didn't particularly want to kill an innocent resident, either. As he waited, he gritted his teeth, feeling each second trickle away from him.

The woman walked past. The Andrac detached from the wall, skimming down the hallway. Blays ran a step behind it. After another turn, the demon ran toward a closed door, vanishing through the stone wall beside it. Blays followed it into a stairwell. This was completely dark and at the speed they were going Blays would likely have found himself the proud owner of a broken leg if not for the dark shine of the nether to light the way.

The air took on the quality of dankness universal to all underground spaces with poor circulation of air. The Andrac exited into another dark hallway, doors flicking past on both sides. They were fed into a sprawling room. The skeletons of small animals lay arranged on tables. Other surfaces hosted candles burned to various lengths, along with glass flasks and small metal pots. Blays recognized it at once: sorcerer's den.

The demon ran to the far end of the room. There, a great iron doorway blocked the way forward, sealed with chains big enough to beat a bull to death with and padlocks that looked capable of choking a swamp dragon. Patterns and sigils of warding were etched across the entire surface of the door. The Andrac stepped to the side and walked through the wall. So did Blays.

The chamber beyond was a step lower and he fell six inches, uttering a small yelp of alarm. The room was narrower than the one before it, the walls to right and left standing twenty feet apart. The lower four feet of the walls were blank, with everything above that sporting cabinets and shelves loaded down with glassware, idols, and pieces of metal whose purpose was no doubt inscrutable to anyone but obsessive and crank-minded nethermancers.

The Andrac trotted past all of this, arriving at a group of display cases set on sturdy stands that, like the cabinets, were four feet high. The little demon stopped in front of one, nodding to it.

Even without the ivory gecko wrapped around them, Blays had spent more than enough time around Dante to recognize the bones inside the case: those of a human forearm.

He grinned at the demon. "For a being of pure evil, you do good work."

The case had a broad step in front of it to allow better access. Blays climbed it, then exited the shadows. The room was so dark he could barely see his own hand. The only light came from the Andrac's dim and slitted eyes.

"Point your face this way, will you? I can't see a damn thing."

The Star-Eater obliged, opening its eyes wider. Blays undid

the latch on the hinge panel on the front of the case and swung the panel open. He reached for the Aba Quen.

As soon as his fingers touched the smooth, cool ivory, he stopped. The room prior to this had absolutely, definitely been a laboratory for sorcerers. He knew what sorcerers were like. Suspicious creatures who imagined everyone else was as conniving and covetous as they were. He took hold of the carving, then moved into the shadows. Only then did he lift it.

With a metal clang, something shot up beneath him. Spears. Emerging from the step he was standing on. If he'd been wearing his normal meat-based body, he'd have been impaled, and one of the spears would currently be waving his dangly bits as a flag. He chuckled softly.

Heavy clunks sounded from all sides. He craned his neck in mild confusion — what next, machines that shot arrows at him? — then rocked back on his feet.

The entire room was flooding with water.

16

The water swirled across the floor in a foaming torrent. If he'd been your average non-shadowalking type, and had somehow avoided the spears, and had jumped off the step, he would currently be getting swept to the back of the room, either to be smashed into the back wall and drowned, or to be carried into some insidious nethermancer's trap to be held until authorities arrived — or possibly just to be held down for more effective drowning.

Either way, he very much doubted that his current situation had gone without notice.

He motioned to the little Andrac. "I take it from the attempt to flush us that it's time to leave. Might I suggest running?"

He tucked the Aba Quen into his jabat, ensuring it was secure, and leaped off the step. He landed on the eddying surface of the water with a small splash. Rather than yanking him from his feet and carrying him away, the torrent merely felt slippery, like wet clay, obliging him to proceed in careful, loping hop-steps.

The water appeared to be gushing from the lower front of the room, where it took a step down from the laboratory on the other side. Which explained why it was a step lower in the first place. And why all the cabinets and cases housing the nethermancers' valuables were elevated four feet off the ground. With an appreciative nod at their engineering, Blays galloped right through the wall.

The laboratory on the other side was bone dry; the roar of the water in the other room was now a muffled hiss. From the tables, the skeletons of the birds and rodents seemed to be watching him. The feeling was so strong that he stopped and peered at them, searching them for signs of nethereal animation, but a closer inspection revealed they were just your standard piles of dead stuff.

The little Star-Eater slitted its eyes at him. In the real world, the demons looked flat and unreal, but in the shadows, they were as vivid as a tree or a wolf. On a full-sized Andrac, the expression of impatience it was currently wielding on Blays would have been menacing. As this demon only stood to his mid-thigh, the look was comical instead.

Its impatience wasn't unfounded, however. Blays resumed running, heading across the long room toward the stairwell. As he entered the hallway, an awareness entered the shadows like a shark coming to a reef, questing about with predatory malice. Blays froze in place and tried to make himself very small. Three seconds crept by, then five, then ten. He still had more than half his shadows left in him, but if he had to wait much longer—

A presence hammered into his side, knocking him from the nether like a loose tooth. Swearing extensively, he drew a knife, nicked the back of his arm, and sprinted toward the stairs, drawing a sword in his right hand and a small hunk of shadows in his left. He pulled the stairwell door open and listened a moment for the smack of feet, then took the steps three at a time.

He came to the ground floor landing and reached for the door. It flew open before he could touch it. A soldier shouted out in surprise, jabbing instinctually with his short spear. Blays caught the haft with the edge of his blade, sliding it past him, and stabbed the man in the chest, the churning nether of the Odo Sein weapon parting the soldier's breastbone like boiled chicken.

The Andrac ran past the body and out the door. An instant later, a bolt of nether flicked into its side. This appeared to do nothing, but the spear of ether that followed it punched a hole through the demon's neck, spraying shadows across the hall.

Thirty feet down the way, a sorcerer in light blue robes stood with her feet apart and her hand outstretched. Tendrils of shadows extended from the Andrac as she drew the nether from its body. Blays spun about and ran deeper into the Bastion, the demon flying along behind him. He could feel the nether zipping down the hallway toward them. He flung himself down a side passage. The shadows pounded into the corner with a hail of stone.

"I don't suppose you know a way out of here?"

Blays looked to the demon as if he actually expected an answer and came to the realization that the chaos of the moment had driven him temporarily insane. With footsteps pounding after them, and another lance of nether bending around the corner, Blays blipped into the shadows and jumped to his left, taking a shortcut through the wall.

As soon as he was clear, he dropped back into the physical world, praying the action had been too fast for the enemy nethermancer to track. He found himself in a yawning and empty room. Windows shed light from above, but the openings were nearly twenty feet up and there was no way to climb to them.

The presence quested forth again. Blays wished it had a face so that he could punch it.

He glanced at the Andrac. "Well, little fellow. How would you like to collect your share of glory?"

The demon flexed its claws in anticipation, although Blays suspected it was less enthusiastic about potential valor than it was about the chance to rip a fleshy human into messy pieces.

He moved back to the wall. The presence circled closer, homing in on the Andrac.

And Blays homed in on it.

He pointed to a section of wall with his sword. The Star-Eater lowered its head and ran full-tilt through the wall. Blays bounced on his heel and followed after it, rolling into the shadows just before he was about to bash his brains out on the stone. In the hallway on the other side, the Andrac threw itself at the sorcerer, who jerked up her hands in surprise. Ether sprayed from her fingers in straight lines, raking tatters from the Andrac. It slashed at her leg, grinning at the sight of the blood flowing from her thigh.

Yet she was already sucking the nether from the Andrac's wounds and applying it to her own, the gashes fading as the demon became semi-transparent. Blays drew his second sword and charged. She backpedaled, the faltering Andrac giving chase and ripping at her shin.

The woman drew back her arm, yanking a fat gob of nether from the demon. They both stumbled. She fired a blast of nether at Blays. He held up the meager bit of it that he could command, waiting until her attack was almost on him before deflecting it.

He leaped through the shower of black sparks. She was already drawing more power from the small Andrac, which fell on its face, now-ghostly claws outstretched before it. Blays made an overhand slash toward the sorcerer's head. She threw up her right hand, which succeeded in saving her skull at the cost of sending her hand and half her forearm smacking against the wall.

She wailed in the particular kind of panic that overtook people when they watched themselves lose a limb. Shadows whipped around her head. Before she could think about doing anything with them, Blays stuck his other blade into her gut. She gasped, face going gray. He flexed his elbow and backhanded his first sword through her neck.

Her head landed a foot from her hand. Her mouth hung open, the eyes blinking at him dully. That reaction was one reason he wasn't particularly fond of beheading people, but when you were dealing with nethermancers, it was always best to chop too much rather than too little.

He turned to the Andrac. "Still with me?"

It didn't move. Except for the integrity of its body, which was collapsing on itself. Blays kneeled halfway down, intending to touch the demon on the back, then grunted at himself.

"I'll remember you, little one." He straightened. Wisps of nether curled away. The Andrac was gone.

Blays glanced up and down the hallway, trying to get his bearings after the chase. Even by the standards of stately castles, the Bastion was big. The wrong turn could find him utterly lost in hostile territory.

Then again, he had no need to follow the rigid confines of "hallways" and "rooms." He shifted back into the shadows. Felt a bit wobbly. Less than two minutes before he ran short, he thought. He aligned himself in what he thought was a southerly direction that would take him back to the others and ran as fast as he could, blowing through a wall. Heading in a straight line, he knifed through a second wall, only to blunder into something yielding yet smothering. It felt clothy. He ripped the tapestry from himself, cast it aside, and sprinted on.

Without warning, the bright darkness of the netherworld fell away, replaced by the dull darkness of an average room. Back in the real world, Blays immediately tripped over a kneeling mat, sprawling forward. He managed to tuck and roll as if that had been his plan all along, but with no one there to witness it, the victory felt hollow.

He pressed his palms against his eyes, wanting to groan. He hadn't run out of shadows. He hadn't been forced out by a nethermancer, either. Instead, it had been the locking-out of the Odo Sein. How had the Monsoon gotten their hands on someone with the power? Had they turned a knight traitor? Or, much like their current rash of sorcerers, did they have a secret training ground of their own?

As he took a well-deserved moment to mull all the ways that life was unfair, he spotted a silver lining to his predicament. The room he was in also had windows high up on its walls. Like before, they were too high to get to, but the moon was angling through them from slightly to his right. Given the time of night, that meant the windows were facing south.

Keeping one hand on the hilt of his sword, which he'd put away after dealing with the nethermancer, he jogged toward the southern wall. He cracked open the door and peeked into the hallway. Light glowed to his left, strengthening in intensity. A pair of soldiers ran down the corridor bearing a lantern. Blays let them pass.

Once the lantern faded around a corner, he headed the opposite way, turning right at the intersection to resume heading south. Footsteps scraped ahead. Two dim figures spotted him, jogging forward. Blays drew both swords. Their purple light illuminated the gaunt face of Gladdic and the warrior's frame of Bek.

Blays ran to meet them. "What are you doing in here?"

"Mitigating your incompetence," Gladdic said. "Did you find the Aba Quen?"

Blays sheathed his swords and removed the statue from his jabat. "Would you like to sing my praises now? Or wait until things calm down?"

Bek moved to touch the Aba Quen, then stopped himself, as if it was too holy. "That is it. The remnant that lifts the Blight."

"Then our work here is done. Let's get out of here like it's filled with people trying to kill us."

THE LIGHT OF LIFE

Gladdic turned about and jogged down the passage. Nether wreathed his hand.

Blays cocked his head at Bek. "Hang on, he can use the shadows, but I can't? Are *you* locking me out of them?"

The power slid from Blays' shoulders like a water-bearer's pole. Bek gestured behind them. "I didn't know it was you. All I knew was that a warlock was at play. I put a stop to everything I could feel."

"And nearly put a stop to my heart, too. You—"

Three soldiers spilled from a side room. Gladdic blasted them into giblets before Blays could draw his sword. He stepped over the bodies, blood sliding beneath his sandals. The next turn of the corridor took them to the expansive foyer containing the Bastion's front doors.

Though the room was the size of a small chapel, it was completely aglow with lanterns, which were borne in turn by a squadron of Monsoon soldiers. They raised their spears and small round shields.

Blays drew his swords and charged. Looking puzzled and contemptuous, the dozen-odd soldiers formed an inverted chevron, ready to tear him to pieces. Arrowheads of nether whipped past Blays' shoulders and thumped into the bodies of the soldiers. Every one of them fell to the ground at once.

"That looked like they'd practiced it!" Blays vaulted over a still-twitching corpse and threw open one of the oversized doors. There was shouting going on from within the Bastion, but the night was peaceful with the song of crickets.

They ran along the thin strip of land fringing the fortress. The icy canoe rested in the shallows, fog swirling about its edges. It looked a little melty, but Gladdic solved that with a wave of his hand, the ether solidifying the boat's underside. They climbed aboard and launched off, Blays paddling while Bek and Gladdic watched for threats.

"I was led to believe you were so good at stealing that you could filch a man's own shadow," Gladdic said. "Then why is it that we currently have an entire palace attempting to hunt us down?"

"Because those cheating bastards tried to stop me from taking their stuff," Blays said. "They used traps and things. Completely unsporting."

"One wonders whether—"

Gladdic was interrupted by a streak of nether hurtling toward them from the Bastion walls. Gladdic lifted his hand, meeting it with a wedge of ether. Blays had his back turned to the conflagration, but the light of the impact sparkled over the water. Gold specks lit up around Bek as he clamped down on the enemy nethermancer.

An arrow plunked into the water to starboard, followed by one to port. Blays risked a quick look at Gladdic. "Mind putting a stop to that?"

Gladdic forked his fingers, loosing nethereal missiles toward the battlements. Someone screamed. Gladdic cried out in surprise. Impossibly, a flock of shadows was flying toward them from the walls, in direct defiance of the Odo Sein. Bek's mouth fell open in shock as Gladdic released a barrage of ether toward the incoming attack. Bek gathered up motes of the stream, shaping them for use, but he was already too late. Shadow and light met in the air like a thunderstorm on a summer night.

Yet just as it looked like every piece had been countered, a followup strike of nether speared into the water, vanishing from sight. It punched through the bottom of the boat in a spume of water. With a series of cracks like a toppling tree, the ice canoe splintered to pieces.

Blays plunged into the lukewarm moat. He kicked hard for the surface, knowing it wouldn't help, that the ziki oko would begin eating him within seconds. His head broke free. Bek rose beside him, clutching uselessly at the remaining chunks of ice, which were far too small to try to ride.

They'd crossed most of the moat, but were still fifty feet from the earthworks. They'd be skeletons long before they made it.

Then again, he didn't have to swim, did he? Not when he could slip into the safety of the shadows and run across the water. He still had the Aba Quen safe in his jabat. All it would take to get out of the moat was to leave Bek and Gladdic behind.

He reached for the nether.

Chips of gold spun around his head, distracting him for half an instant; they felt closer than ever before, as if he could reach out and hold them in his hand. Lights flashed below the surface of the moat. At first Blays thought these were the silvery ziki oko converging on their meaty targets, but the lights were *too* bright, and rather than zipping toward the humans, they were plowing into the hand-sized shapes that had been coming toward the three of them. The ziki oko were ripped into clouds of scales and blood.

Gladdic couldn't possibly hit every single one of the fish, but the ones he missed were swerving course, chomping down on the gobs of raw flesh and sinking bone. The constant strobing of the ether seemed to confuse others, sending them wandering unsteadily away.

Gladdic emerged with a gasp. "Swim, you idiots!"

Blays kicked his feet, grabbing the paddle he'd dropped when the enemy sorcerer had destroyed their boat. Ether flew about on all sides like vengeful fairies that had decided to take to the water and make the fish pay for every bad thought they'd ever had. Swimming hard, Blays kept the nether in his hand the whole way, ready to roll into the shadows if the ziki oko broke through the melee of light, blood, and guts. It was all so distracting that he frowned in surprise when he reached out for another stroke and touched solid bricks.

He scrambled up the wall so fast he couldn't remember having done it. Bek looked to be all right, but Gladdic was having trouble getting up the wall. Blays lowered the paddle. Gladdic grabbed it and Blays pulled him up.

Back the way they'd come, pale hunks of fish bobbed so thickly on the water you could practically have walked across them. The moat began to boil as if the whole damn thing were suspended over a campfire, but that was just the ziki oko eating their own.

Their canoe was right where they'd left it, tied to the metal pin in the wall. They dropped into it and headed directly away from the Bastion. Horns were already sounding behind them.

"What is the matter with you?" Gladdic demanded. Blays half-turned, still paddling, but before he could defend himself, Gladdic gestured in Bek's face. "You were supposed to be neutralizing their sorcerers!"

"I employed my ability as I have been trained," Bek said. "That's never happened before. I must have missed one of them."

"Fine time for your first failure to occur right as we were sailing across a sea of monsters!"

"Berate me all you want. I did my duty."

Figuring that the gates would be aswarm with people disinclined to let them through, Blays cut south through the canals of the merchants and aristocrats, the steep-sided hills looming above them. Horns blatted from all about the city, summoning and directing patrols. Lanterns and candles flared to life across the islands. Blays paddled past the manors, water dripping from his hair and clothes after his dip in the moat, and entered a market district.

As they sliced past a dock, a man raised a lantern high above his head. "There they are! I see the hari—"

A black bolt whisked into the civilian's chest. He dropped on his rear, still holding up the lantern, face drooping like he'd just lost a bet.

But his cry was taken up by others, who poured across the dock, pointing at the canoe and yelling for guards. A high-pitched horn squealed from nearby.

"How curious," Gladdic said. "To them, their horn is a call to brave action. To us, it is a warning to flee for our miserable lives. Yet it is the same sound to us all."

"You should really write that down," Blays said. "I'd hand you some parchment, but I appear to be occupied with saving our foolish hides."

As they crossed an intersection of canals, a white war canoe rushed at them from their port side. Gladdic hulled it with a hammer of nether. Its crew yelled out in anger, paddling the wounded vessel over to the closest dock before it could sink.

Another couple of minutes and they were hustling along through the slums of rafts. The people there watched them glumly, but did so in darkness, unwilling or unable to waste a candle. A few of them even looked hopeful. The rebels might have taken the city, but the city hadn't necessarily taken to the rebels.

The way things had been going, Blays expected to reach the city's nets and come face to face with a full-fledged armada, but as they exited the clusters of banana trees, they looked out on open water. Gladdic sliced through the fish nets with a blade of nether. As Blays paddled them past, ether glimmered on the water, knitting the slashed nets back together.

He lifted an eyebrow at Gladdic. "How considerate of you."

"By mending the net, it will be more difficult for them to determine which way we went."

"And for a second there I thought you might want to save the city's poor from being gobbled by ziki oko."

Blays steered the canoe back into the wilds of the swamps. The city was lost to the trees behind them. They didn't see any sign of pursuit, but wary of enemy nethermancers tracking them down, they didn't pull ashore on a random island until well after midnight.

Blays shook out his arms, then handed Bek the carving of the gecko with its tail wrapped around the two bones. "Well? Does everything seem to be in order?"

The knight turned the figure over in his hands. Dots of stream materialized around him, disappearing as he put them to use. "It's the Aba Quen. And it's functional."

"And that's all you need? You can free Dante with this?"

Bek cupped the statue in his hands. "I can do as I've been trained. I can't promise it will work."

"Is the process of be-liching someone that much different than Blighting them?"

"If this was known, don't you think Bel Ara would have been the one to tell you?"

"Or *not* tell me while lording her knowledge over me." Blays knew Bek was right—in fact, he'd known the answer to the question before he'd even said it out loud—yet he'd felt compelled to ask anyway. Now that they had the Aba Quen in hand, nothing stood between them and Dante. Ostensibly speaking, this was a very good thing—but it also meant there was nothing left between them and potential failure. "Plan, then? Where's Dante?"

Gladdic closed his eyes and touched his brow. "He is presently some distance to the east. I would estimate fifty miles, and perhaps more. He has been traveling that way for two days now."

Blays tilted back his head, envisioning the lay of the land. "Not a whole lot over that way, is there? Other than the odd village?"

"Perhaps the Eiden Rane is using Dante to collect more souls from the hinterlands while the lich sees to the larger populations." Gladdic lowered himself to his bedroll. "We will begin our pursuit in the morning. We may talk as we travel."

Reasonable an idea as this was, Blays couldn't get to sleep for a long time. Even then, he couldn't tell if he was awake or dreaming of being awake. He got up at first light feeling impossibly groggy, but he knew getting the paddle going would get his blood moving as well.

Besides, now wasn't the time to be weak.

"He continues to travel east," Gladdic said as they gathered up their gear. "Somewhat to the south as well."

"If he keeps at it much longer, he's going to bump right into the Hell-Painted Hills." Blays' head was so muddled he could feel his heartbeat in his ears, yet the thought that came to him was as crisp and shiny as cut steel. "What if that *is* where he's headed?"

"For what end? To assault it? The Odo Sein could destroy him without suffering a single loss."

"I don't know. But it feels wrong. The White Lich wouldn't send him to the Spires to die. If that's his destination, then they have a plan to undermine it — or to destroy it."

"A plausible suggestion. The Spires represent one of the last threats to the lich's power over Tanar Atain. He may not wish to expand his conquest to other lands until he's secured every corner of his own."

A pit was opening in Blays' stomach. He decided to fill it with hard work. He loaded up the canoe and took up the paddle. It was another warm morning and he soon discovered the mosquitos had been at his legs overnight.

"Sir Bek," Gladdic said once they'd gotten their start-of-the-journey silence out of the way. "Dante Galand is extremely dangerous. Although it would please me if you do not repeat this to him, I believe he may be the most potent nethermancer on the continent. How can we help you to confront him?"

Bek rested his hand on the gunwale. "None of his warlock

tricks will make any difference once he's been bound by the Odo Sein. I can do that at some distance, but I'll need to be closer to restore his soul. You can help me in several ways: by making sure he doesn't run, by stopping anyone else from attacking me as I close on him, and by making sure that there aren't any surprises."

"In that case, I may construct an Andrac or two in order to provide us with more flexibility. When you deploy the Aba Quen, and transfer the part of your remnant to him, how long does the process take? And what does it entail?"

"The process should only take a few seconds. I'll use the Odo Sein to locate Dante's connections to the ether, but rather than using my power to shut down his access, I'll use it to create a link to my own light. Normally, his remnant would be closed to me, sealed away by the strength of the owner's will, but the Aba Quen works as a key to a lock—or a knife to an oyster shell. All I have to do is touch it with the stream to bring it to bear. It will cut through his resistance on its own. This done, I will connect my remnant to his and permit mine to flow forth. At last, I'll stop the flow before too much has left me and I accidentally Blight myself."

"But you've never done this before, have you?" Blays said. "What makes you so sure that you can?"

Bek gazed back at him. "You're worried for your friend. You should be. But don't be afraid of my inexperience. Nearly everyone else who's ever done this was doing it for the first time, too."

"Shouldn't you at least practice? We might only have the one shot at this."

The knight grimaced as if dealing with some visceral pain he knew he could never get rid of. He removed the Aba Quen from his jabat and lowered his head. Within moments, golden splinters swam before his face. He sent them spinning toward Blays. They hit him with the clapping sensation of the Odo Sein, but rather than being cut loose from the nether, his awareness of the shadows expanded as if he'd emerged from a forested hillside onto a clear ridge.

Bek detached a hair-fine thread of stream from what he had remaining and sent it to the Aba Quen. It disappeared into the yellowed ivory of the gecko. A dream-like knife struck the center of Blays' guts, but there was no pain, only the initial shock that precedes it.

"Right now, either of us could open our remnant to the other," Bek said. "All that's needed is to open the barrier. It will feel like a lid or a plug. Can you feel it?"

Blays reached inside himself. He was expecting to grope about blindly and eventually give up, probably while swearing, yet he was drawn toward the ether within himself the same way he was drawn back to earth after jumping in the air. His mind brushed against a tap. He focused on it. His faint touch was enough to begin to pull it loose.

The connection dissipated like a drop of blood in turbid waters. Bek exhaled sharply. "The hard part isn't the ritual. It's finding someone who can do it."

Blays touched his torso in the soft spot just below the breastbone. Cold sweat had sprung up across his body. "Appreciate the demonstration."

Gladdic stirred in the aft of the canoe. "This raises a final point. We have discussed how we will attempt to enact the ritual. But we have not discussed what we'll do if we fail."

Blays shoved the paddle into the water. "Bek just told you that we won't."

"He told us that any failure would not be due to inexperience. But there is the matter of Dante himself. He will fight against us. And he has shown a marked capacity to win."

"If he gets away, then we'll come after him again."

"We remain uncertain that the ritual can even be performed

on a lich. If Bek makes his attempt and learns that it cannot be done, what then?"

"Same as always. We regroup and come up with another plan."

"Such as what?"

"You see, Gladdic, I don't know yet. If I *did* know the solution, I'd skip the whole part where we fail and go right to the success."

"We must allow ourselves to carefully think this through," the old man said. "We learned of this solution through the Odo Sein, an institution which has resisted the Eiden Rane for hundreds of years, and knows his ways better than anyone else in the world. If they don't know how to lift the Blight from a lich, who might we seek to learn from instead?"

"Is the White Lich the only lich who's ever liched? Surely someone, somewhere in the world, can teach us."

"And if we spend months chasing down this ghost, the lich will have time to swallow Mallon, Gask, Narashtovik, and all of the lesser kingdoms. Our new knowledge will be wasted, for by then, our foe will wield the power of a god."

"Then we won't go anywhere! We'll hunt down the other liches, and experiment on them until we work it out!"

"With whose remnant? If Bek expends his experimenting on another lich, who will be left to — "

Blays stopped paddling, twisting about to get a good look at the old man. "What are you trying to convince me of, Gladdic? That sometimes things don't work out the way you planned? Because I feel like that might be the very definition of 'being alive.'"

"You are looking at this from your heart." For once, Gladdic's voice didn't carry any judgment or scorn. "The heart is a brave leader. It inspires us to blaze trails the mind would be too fearful to start down on its own. But if the heart is brave, it is also blind. If we are to avoid the end of all we hold dear, we must turn over command to our minds. Only they have the cold clarity to see a way out from the chasm that opens before us."

They stared at each other. Flies buzzed among the trees. Frogs croaked from the reeds. Some things lived while other things died.

"If the ritual fails, we'll kill him," Blays said. "We'll kill him, and then we'll make our run at the White Lich, and be damned. Is that what you want to hear?"

"It is not a matter of it being what I wish to hear. It is only a matter of what must be said."

Blays' heart wanted to argue, but his mind had already seen what they were facing. He could blind himself to it readily enough. People did that all the time, telling themselves what they wanted to hear, what was easy or flattering or comfortable. That was why kings told themselves their blood made them divine and hence the serfs their slaves; why fathers filled themselves with rum until they found room in their stomach to swallow the idea that it was better to walk away; why children and dogs were beaten for their own good; why so little ever got done and so much was let to fall apart.

He could convince himself it was bound to work out. That even if it didn't work out, they'd find another way. Yes, he could lie to himself easily enough. He, like everyone, had been doing it his whole life.

But he knew that if he did so now, when they met again in the Mists, Dante would curse him for it.

Blays picked up his paddle and carried on.

The next two days were of the worst kind: work and worry in equal measure, with no good cheer or comforts to salve the day's many stings, and the only relief to be had in unrestful sleep. It was enough to make Blays wish that nethermancers had a way to let you excise the memories you didn't want, or to allow you to exist and function for a given period without retaining any memory of that time.

But no, they were too busy playing with their damn rats.

Meanwhile, Gladdic claimed that Dante hadn't moved position. Meaning that he had now spent three full days parked on or near the border of the Hell-Painted Hills. If the White Lich had sent him to destroy the Spires, why would he dawdle there? Awaiting reinforcements? Or had he entered the Hills only to be struck down by their corrosion, and was now lying in a state somewhere between death and undeath, beyond all aid?

For as much paddling as he did that day, Blays found himself almost unable to eat. Even the ripe bananas they'd taken from passing trees felt too dry to be swallowed. He ate anyway, forcing the mush down with the glum drudgery of climbing a mountain—or, for that matter, of paddling for days across an endless swamp.

With the sun ripening to a bloated red, they put in at one of the islands. Gladdic estimated they were still ten to twenty miles away, but there was no talk of lighting a fire that night.

Gladdic seated himself in their bare-bones camp. "He may not be alone. In the morning, I will create an Andrac to see what lies before us. If he is in the company of many Blighted, or the Eiden Rane himself, we will bide our time until an opportunity presents itself."

"Or for us to create one." Blays poked at the ground with a stick. "This still feels strange. Like it might be a trap."

"It might well be. Would that make any difference?"

"To my determination? No. But it probably makes a big difference in our chances of being fed to the fish and subsequently crapped out across several acres of swamp."

"It might well be a ruse. However, the Eiden Rane is typically more sophisticated than that. His every action contains many layers, with contingencies for every reaction that he can foresee. I suspect he has sent Dante to pursue a legitimate goal of some kind, while designing the venture in such a way that it can become a trap if we attempt to interfere."

They talked a while longer, weighing different approaches. Once it became clear they were just rehashing the same tactics over and over, Blays and Gladdic fell into silence, revealing that Bek was snoring and probably had been doing so for some time. The two of them stared into the blank center of camp where a fire ought to have been.

"I have been thinking," Gladdic said. "Is the quantity of ether and nether within the world fixed and finite? Or is more created over time as the mill of the heavens grinds on?"

Blays rubbed his eye. "Interesting question. Let me offer a counter-proposal: who gives a shit?"

"The question has deep implications. If the supply of light and shadow is finite, then as more and more people are born, then more and more ether and nether will be drawn up as their remnants and traces, and hidden away from conventional sorcery when these people die. There would reach a point, then, when it has *all* been converted, and lost in the shadow world, with none remaining in the physical realm. Thus sorcery would pass from the world.

"Whereas if more light and shadow is added to the earth, there will reach a point when everything is utterly saturated by it. Once it is in every particle of our surroundings and ourselves, I think it possible that we may all be born to the talent of magic."

Blays eyed him. "That's what you're thinking about right now? Tomorrow, everything hangs in the balance, and your only concern is what the world's going to be like a million billion years from now?"

"What else should occupy my mind at this time? Worry and regret?"

"That'd be the human response, yeah."

"Regret is the most useless of all human emotions. It does

nothing but fester, and hence should be lanced like the boil on the soul that it is. I have made mistakes, but I do not regret them."

"That's a fine way to pardon yourself for your crimes."

Gladdic smiled, amused. "Perhaps it is. Even so, I will not use this time for regrets. I am old, Blays. Even if we survive the morrow, I only have so many years left to me. Before long, I will die. In the Pastlands, I won't think to ask such questions as whether people like me will eventually become extinct, or if we will become the norm. In the Mists, I'll no longer care about these questions. And in the Worldsea, I will have no need to ask them."

The old man gazed into the night, a thick darkness punctuated by tree-blocked starlight and the fireflies blinking over the water. "The only time to find my answers is now, in this body, on this earth. So that is what I will do."

"Sounds great," Blays said. "While you're answering the mysteries of life, I'm going to sleep my ass off."

He wriggled his blanket into comfortable lumps beneath him. Gladdic didn't lie down for another twenty minutes, yet somehow, the old man fell asleep before Blays did, making the occasional faint whinnying noise, as if he were dreaming of being chased by ghosts, or of meeting his gods and being judged by them.

Blays rolled back and forth, seeking the posture that would allow him to be unconscious for a few nice hours. When he couldn't take it anymore, he got up, slinging one of his sword belts over his shoulder, and walked to the edge of the island. He crouched down, resting his forearms across his knees. The moon was almost full and it glinted on the water in the small patches where it was able to leak through the trees. On most occasions, the swamp felt like a trial to be endured, and occasionally a nightmare to be terrified of. But on that night, it finally felt peaceful.

The day to come felt like a dream he hadn't yet lived. What would he do if they failed? Would he really return to fighting the White Lich? At that point, what would it matter? What if he just went back to Narashtovik?

It would be easy enough. It was early summer and the sailing would be good; he could ask Naran for a trip back on the *Sword of the South*, or make his way to Cavana and book passage from there. A few weeks on the warm seas with a jug of grog didn't sound so bad. He'd make port in Narashtovik and take a stroll over to the Citadel and he didn't think he would even tell them what had happened in the south — not right away, anyway — but he would go straight to Minn, and her jaw would drop and she'd wave her hand in front of her mouth like she did when she was shocked in a good way, a little double-tap as if she was afraid something was going to fall out of it.

And then they'd ride away. Not to Pocket Cove, but to somewhere similarly remote. Gallador Rift, maybe, although that was too central. Somewhere in the foothills of the Woduns, then. A lake within a forest. Together, they'd build a cabin and work the land. A nice little farm. After a year or two, when they were all settled in and didn't have to work quite as hard, they'd start to have children.

Two girls and two boys, he thought. Might take some doing to convince Minn, since at that point, the outside world would likely be coming to an end. But there was always the chance that it would be stopped somewhere, or stall out and take dozens or even hundreds of years for the Blighted to scour every nook and cranny of the land.

And even if the world was all crashing down around them, why not live out the rest of their time together as beautifully as they could?

The more he thought about it, the more he could see it. The trout feeding on the surface of the lake. The screens or filters they'd have to build into the chimney to break up the smoke to stop it from being seen. They'd have to do funny things with the crops, too. Maybe they'd plant their seeds at random in the rich, cool earth beneath the trees, walking the thin line between tending them enough to produce decent yields, but not making the crops so orderly that they could be seen from a miles-distant ridge.

Minn was plenty smart, though. They could make it work. It wouldn't all be work, either. The family could explore together. Stuff a bunch of acorns into a padded cloth and sew it up into a ball and kick it around. Swim across the lake and then sleep in the summer sun. Sing songs to each other, and tell stories in front of the hearth as the snow fell outside and venison stew bubbled on top of the stove. Teach the kids to farm and fish and hunt like his own dad never had.

Blays knew he was indulging himself—that this could never happen, that the White Lich would destroy them much sooner than this, and that Minn would never betray her vows to Pocket Cove by abandoning it—but he let himself fall deeper, allowing himself this one minute to exist in peace.

His oldest son would be named Cal and he'd have blond hair like his father but the serious mind of his mother. Once the boy had a few years behind him and could handle one without hurting himself, Blays would shape a short bow for him and show him to use it, sending him out alone that summer to hunt for small game. Once the boy got good at this, he'd start to pester Blays about when he could go with his father on the deer hunts, and Blays would always tell him the same two things: When you're a little older. When you're a little stronger.

It was the second winter since Cal had started his training. The day before had been their first good storm, leaving four inches of snow that would show every track. Blays got up before dawn to stir up the embers in the stove, then went to Cal's bed and shook him awake.

"Get your bow."

Cal's face, initially a portrait of grumpiness, now shined so brightly Blays was half afraid it'd wake up the others. The boy hurriedly dressed himself in his coats and fur-lined trousers and his boots. They braced one end of their bows between their feet, bending and stringing the weapons, then went outside.

The cold was like a slap to the face. The clouds had gone away, if only for a little while, and the stars twinkled madly, gazing at their own reflection in the lake. The air smelled like wood smoke and snow. Blue shadows painted everything and with the starlight on the snow even the darkness seemed bright, as though they'd stepped out the cabin door and into the nether-world.

"It's cold," Cal whispered.

"That's just the frost demons taking shelter in a warm open mouth." Blays reached down and wrapped the boy's scarf firmly about his mouth and chin so he could barely talk. "Much better."

Blays had his bow with him, along with a sword, but he intended to use neither. He led them over the trail they'd worn through the woods to the east, boots squeaking in the powder. Snow clung heavily to the needles of the pines. Blays kept an eye out for deer, but if he saw any yet, he'd pretend to ignore them. The boy needed to be out of sight of the house, aware of the full vastness of nature and their vulnerability within it.

They topped the eastern ridge and dropped down into the valley below. Two miles from the cabin, Blays grabbed Cal by the shoulder and hunkered down. The boy crouched beside him. Blays pointed through the trees. Two hundred yards away, a deer — either a doe or a young buck — walked slowly through the pines.

Keeping low, Blays circled downwind, Cal sticking to his back like a limpet. The snow muffled their steps. Blays stopped a hundred feet away, which was as close as he dared to creep up on it, but still too far away to make for a good shot, especially with Cal's lighter draw.

But that night, they had luck on their side. The deer, a buck with two points on one side and a spike on the other, wandered straight toward them for ten yards, then started to veer toward their right. Blays nudged Cal and gave him a nod.

The boy gave him a look of half-panic. Blays stomped down a smile. "If you think I'll be mad if you miss, imagine how angry I'll be if you don't take a shot."

Cal's eyes darted to the side in thought—he thought too much, *definitely* his mother's son. At last, he lifted his bow and sighted down the shaft of the arrow. His breath streamed away from his mouth. He loosed his arrow.

It struck the deer with a thud. The animal jerked forward, legs striking at the ground as if it thought the earth had bitten it. Blays hopped to his feet, drawing back his arrow, but the buck went down, sliding in the snow.

He turned to Cal to give him a good word, but the boy's face was so rapt Blays' throat closed. He set his hand on the boy's shoulder.

The vision blurred. Blays tumbled forward, no longer in control of his own mind. The woods and the snow and the night disappeared, replaced by swamp and mangroves and daylight. Two women paddled a canoe through the water, their bodies pale-skinned and long-limbed. Blays could tell at once that they were soldiers. Not from the strength of their shoulders and arms, which was common among Tanarian canoers, but from the dignity of their bearing.

The shape of their noses and angle of their jaws marked them as sisters. Everything else about them marked them as Tanarians, but their clothes were simple hides, and their hair had been worked into basic braids and drawn behind their heads, a fashion Blays hadn't seen in any Tanarian village or city. Everything about them looked to be from an earlier time.

He was in the middle of a Glimpse. The realization was so startling Blays was afraid it'd boot him out of itself, like when you became aware you were dreaming, yet the vision moved on without a hiccup. The two women paddled forward, joking and laughing with each other, keeping a casual eye on the trees and the water.

They spoke and traveled like they were out on a hunt, and they were armed enough for one too, but they made no stops to check for tracks or spoor, and they weren't watching their surroundings with the special attentiveness you'd typically show if you were searching for game.

Before Blays could make sense of that, the Glimpse skipped forward. The sunlight was getting stretched out and the two women were no longer joking or speaking, just paddling steadily, their faces composed in a martial mask. They made for a large island. The woman in the rear set down her paddle and picked up her spear. As the canoe skimmed into the reeds, the first woman took up her weapons, too. She jumped clear as the boat smacked to a stop in the mud. Her sister leaped out beside her.

Ducking low, they advanced through the high grass. Once they'd gained some ground, they ducked behind a tree, switched to their bows, and surveyed the way forward. After a moment, the first woman—who had done most of the joking earlier, and who appeared to be the older of the two, though they were both young—pointed ahead through a lane of trees. The younger woman leaned forward, then nodded.

They crept forward with the stealth of wild cats, entering a shallow ravine. The floor was littered with bones. The two women glanced down at them, jaws hardening. Blays had seen more than enough bones to recognize them as human, but they were much smaller than most of the ones he'd encountered.

The air stank of death. At the end of the ravine, a shelf of rock sheltered a cave of unknown depth. The two sisters spread a few paces apart and advanced on the hole.

They were still thirty feet away when long dark legs unfolded from the cave and grabbed tight to the rock, dragging a nightmarish head and torso behind them. The thing that emerged looked partly human, but its rear legs were spiderish while its front limbs were more supple, practically octopoidal. Its eyes were much too large and its lips were permanently pulled back from its teeth, which looked more like sharp ridges of rock than anything human.

The two women loosed their arrows. With frightening speed, the creature launched itself to the left, the arrows cracking against the rock. The monster jumped from the wall and skittered toward them, scattering bones with its pointed feet. Both women got off another shot, one arrow passing wide while the other struck the creature in the chest. This didn't seem to hurt it too much, but it paused the thing for just long enough for the soldiers to throw aside their bows and ready their spears.

The creature lashed out at them, its arms snapping forward like tentacles, tipped by curved claws. A diagonal line of blood popped across the older woman's stomach. She ignored it, jabbing at the monster's middle. The enemy yanked itself back and the younger woman circled to its right, harrying it with her spear.

The thing moved with supernatural quickness, its claws snapping at them like whips, but the sister soldiers fought like they shared the same mind, one swinging back from an attack while the other pressed in from the flank. The reach of their spears saved them from anything worse than a few shallow cuts. Methodically, they inflicted one stab after another. Nothing mortal, but the creature was bleeding yellow fluid everywhere. It was only a matter of time before they wore it down.

It seemed to realize this, too. It backed toward the crevice it had emerged from. The younger woman lunged forward, looking to impale it. A bone turned under her front foot. Her ankle went out from beneath her, spilling her to the rocky ground.

The beast slung itself forward. Claws tore into the woman's body. A blade-like foot pierced through her chest. The older of the two screamed and charged. The thing tried to back up, but its limbs were embedded and entangled in its victim. It stumbled to the ground, belly exposed.

The soldier stabbed it, then again. It curled on itself, arms flailing. She didn't stop stabbing until it wasn't moving except for the blood oozing from its wounds.

She used the butt of her spear to push the carcass out of range, then kneeled next to her sister. The younger woman was blinking rapidly. Hands clutched to the stab wound to her chest. Blays knew at a glance she wouldn't leave the island.

The older woman tried to pick her up, but she'd been cut up herself and her legs didn't have the oomph. She ran her hand down her face. "Stay here. I'll find something to drag you back with."

"Don't go!" The younger woman grabbed at her sister's ankle. "Don't leave me here with it!"

The action seemed to suck the last strength from her. She fell back, breathing shallowly and quickly.

A ripple of despair passed over the older woman's face. "I'll stay."

The younger soldier died before her sister would have made it to the canoe. The older soldier sat with her head rested on her knees for a while, then stood and went back to the canoe, returning with a flap of canvas. She put the body of the younger woman on the canvas and dragged her back to the boat, lifting her inside. When this was done, she went back to the ravine, used a bone knife to cut off the creature's head, and brought this to the canoe as well.

The Glimpse leaped forward to the woman returning to her village and showing them the severed head of the child-eating beast. Her people cheered. Until she showed them the body of her sister.

Things skipped ahead again to a feast spread across the village dock. The soldier ate a little but mostly drank. One person after another came to talk to and thank her. She began the night stone-faced, but ended it able to laugh, if only a little.

The feast ended. The vision hopped from one moment of time to the next. The woman out on patrol by herself in her canoe, trailing her fingers in the water and yanking them out just as the ziki oko started to arrive. Turning down requests to eat with others at the group table and eventually taking all of her meals alone in her own house. Lying in bed with her back to the door as someone knocked on the other side.

Another feast arrived; somehow, Blays knew it had been one year since the woman had returned to the village with the head of the child-eater. This time, she ate and drank and laughed with the others. One by one, they staggered off to their homes or fell asleep next to each other on the docks.

When she was at last alone, the woman went back to her home. She picked up her spear and her bow and a bag. She placed these in her canoe, climbed in, and shoved off. She paddled into the darkness.

The Glimpse receded, blackening around the edges. Blays strained to hold onto it, but it was gone before he saw what had come of the woman.

He thought he knew, though. He thought that she'd never come back.

He was alone on the banks of the island. The air shimmered like curtains in a gust of wind. A few last specks of stream hung in the air in front of him. He reached for them with his hand.

They faded before he could touch them, yet he knew with un-
canny clarity how they'd delivered him the Glimpse. If all nether
and ether were connected like Ara claimed, then even when a
person died, echoes of them persisted, because the bits of light
and shadow they'd carried with them were still out there, mixed
in with everything else.

You'd never know it, though, because reassembling those
scattered fragments from across the world would be impossible.
So those echoes and memories were lost forever—except for
those who had the Odo Sein, and could tap into everything at
once. Do that, and you got a Glimpse. He didn't know why you
were shown a particular Glimpse, or the full implications of this
knowledge—could you search for specific people? If all nether
was connected, did that mean it was possible to stand in Narashtovik and manipulate the shadows in Bressel?—yet he felt awed,
as if he'd been granted a holy revelation.

Worn out at last, he made his way back to their camp. Bek
snored on. Gladdic's eyes seemed to gleam as if they were open,
but when Blays looked again, they were shut tight.

When he dreamed, he dreamed of the sister sailing away
from the feast in her canoe. When he woke, he still didn't know
where she'd gone.

The day began the same as the others, but they hadn't been on
their way for two hours when Gladdic pulled them off course
and onto an island. He canvassed the ground with his back
hunched, murmuring to himself under his breath.

Failing to find enough traces there, he moved onto the next island. After a minute of hunting around, he took a knee, gesturing in the air. A miniature Andrac unfurled, as small as the one
they'd worked with before.

They returned to the canoe, taking the demon with them.
Gladdic examined each island they passed. Spotting one that

sported crumbling stone foundations, he directed them to it. There, he pieced together a second knee-high Andrac, returning with it to the boat.

"It isn't far now." Gladdic held his fingers to his left temple. "Be on the lookout for Blighted. The last thing we need is for him to know that we are coming."

Blays kept both eyes on the water ahead of them. He was so intent on this task that he was taken by complete surprise when the forest fell away and the Hell-Painted Hills burned before them.

The fiery patterns in the black stone were as subtle as a half-naked woman cartwheeling down the market street, but that day, Blays' eyes were pulled two hundred yards north. There, a straight light brown line extended from the swamps and into the heights, heading directly into the interior.

Blays' mouth fell open. "Lyle's balls, it would have been nice of Ara to tell us they had a *road*! Or were we supposed to figure that out for ourselves, too?"

They'd stopped moving, but Gladdic reached for the gunwale for support. "You have been to the Silent Spires, you buffoon. There is no road to it—at least not yet."

Blays glanced between Gladdic and the strip of clear earth. "That's why he's here, isn't he? To use his earth-moving talents to create an untainted path through the Hills. So the lich and his army can march on the Spires without dying before they get there. Would that even work?"

"The Eiden Rane must believe so. He can easily test his theory by sending a few Blighted along the road. Should they survive, his invasion will follow."

Bek's hand moved to the hilt of his sword. "We have to stop Dante from reaching the Spires. If we can't un-Blight him, then we must destroy him."

"We'll bring him back." Blays could hear the tightness in his own voice. "And then we'll kill the fucking lich."

They retreated a short way into the swamp, bringing the canoe into some shrubs at the edge of an island. Gladdic gestured toward the distant road, nodding to his Andrac. The pair of demons slipped into the water, swimming across it and emerging on the grassy strip bordering the wasteland. As soon as the Star-Eaters set foot on the bare rock, they seemed to blink from sight, the black of their bodies nearly matching the color of the ground beneath them. A slight ripple across the shinier parts of the rock was the only sign they were moving.

The three humans sat in the canoe in silence. Every time a dragonfly buzzed past, Blays' eyes locked to it, watching it for any indication it was under Dante's control.

An hour later, Gladdic lifted his head, gazing into the hills. The two little demons returned to the swamp, surfacing next to the boat.

Gladdic furrowed his brow, silently conversing with them. "Dante is working on the end of the road some two miles from here. He appears to be alone."

Blays took up his paddle. "Shall we?"

"Not yet, I think. Better to wait until later today, when he has exhausted his power extending the road. If he attempts to go elsewhere, I will know of it."

Much as he wanted to rush in then and there, Blays had to agree to the tactical sensibility of the plan. Which did little to make the ensuing wait any less excruciating. Gladdic sent one Andrac back into the wasteland to observe Dante from a distance, assigning the other to patrol the swamps around the canoe to make sure nothing was creeping up on them.

Mid-afternoon, the first Andrac dashed out of the hills and crossed to the canoe. Gladdic nodded as it passed its thoughts or memories to him, or however it was that the priest communicated with his bloodthirsty demons.

"Dante seems to have finished for the day," Gladdic said. "The time is now."

Blays' pulse doubled. "Bek, can I make a request?"

"You may," Bek said.

"While you're connected to him, can you also make him shit himself?"

The knight frowned. "I don't understand. Do you think his condition has filled his bowels with poisons?"

"I *think* we'll never have a chance like this again."

Gladdic clenched his hand in front of his chest. "Before we go forth, remember what will happen if we let ourselves get killed. We will lose Bek, who may be the only Knight of Odo Sein in the country who is able to venture outside of the Spires. We will lose the Aba Quen, delivering it to the hands of the enemy. We will lose our own lives, and with them Tanar Atain will lose one of its few remaining hopes. And when Dante completes his path to the Silent Spires, and the Eiden Rane tears down the towers, the land's last hope will fall with them."

Blays smiled hard. "Do you think I don't understand the cost of failure? I've fought more wars than you've started. And I'm ready for this one."

Gladdic nodded once. Blays brought the canoe in to the boundary of the swamp. Once the others were out, he dragged it into the grass and flipped it upside down. He got a glass jar from his pack. The bearded crab sat in the bottom, resigned to its new lot in life.

Perhaps he should have kept it, just in case. But Blays wasn't sure that he'd be back. And if he did return, one way or another, he wouldn't need it anymore.

Besides, if he was about to die, it would be nice to have done one more act of kindness before the end, however small. He removed the perforated lid, set the jar on its side, and waited for the crab to scuttle out onto the bank. It vanished into the grass.

Blays stepped into the Hell-Painted Hills.

Heat baked from the black rock like a brick oven. A hot breeze blew down to the swamps. Blays had already been sweating, but he was now dripping with it, blasted from below by the stone and above by the sun. Gladdic waved his hand, shading them with a flattened circle of nether. This helped just enough.

Blays made for the road. After the toe-grabbing crags of the warped landscape, walking on the hard-packed earth felt like the difference between swimming in stormy seas and canoeing over placid waters. In the steady wind, some of his sweat began to cool.

As they neared the crown of the first hill, Blays motioned the others down, then crawled forward until he was just past the top. The road continued through the valley and the next hill, so smooth and straight it looked like it'd been painted there by a norren god. He watched the landscape for a full minute, then backed up to the other side of the hill.

"No sign of him yet," he told Gladdic and Bek. "Or of anything else."

Gladdic pushed up his lower lip. "You know him better than anyone. Does this feel correct to you?"

"We've fought before. I'd advise you to assume that we're not going to take him by surprise. But as long as Bek strips the nether from him, all we've got to deal with is a half-decent swordsman."

He crossed the ridgeline again, heading down the slope, one hand resting on the hilt of a sword. Bek whispered to himself steadily, generating a trickle of the stream, which floated along beside him. The road leveled out momentarily, leading them past a snarled twist of rocks that grasped from the ground like broken fingers.

Shadows flashed from the rocks. If the nether had been headed straight for the three of them, Gladdic might have been able to deflect it in time. Instead, the darkness plunged into the soil. The dirt fell away beneath Blays' feet, sinking downward as if it were draining into the center of the world.

They fell.

17

The ground dropped away faster than they fell. Another few seconds, and Dante would stop what he was doing, allowing them to complete the process of what they were doing, and splat all over the solid rock at the bottom of the hole.

"Warlock!" Bek reached out his arm. Splinters of gold streaked upward.

The ground stopped vanishing beneath them. Blays had expected something like that—had been hoping for it, anyway—and landed on his feet, tucking into a roll. The strap snapped on one of his sandals, which flew away to another side of the dark, circular pit.

They were a good twenty feet down. Gladdic was breathing in quick gasps. Ether flared, wrapping around his bloody shin and ankle. Catching a glimpse of bone, Blays was extremely glad to be momentarily blinded as the light did its work.

Gladdic let out a shuddering sigh of relief. The ground beneath them glowed white. He swept his hand to the left as if he were knocking a pile of dishes from a table. Slowly, the earth retook its original shape below them, elevating them back toward the surface.

A face stuck out over the edge of the hole. The long black hair looked the same as ever, but the rest of what Blays saw made his guts clench tight. Dante's face was gaunter than Gladdic's and as eggshell white as the Blighted. The eyes were sunken, switched from a grayish hue to a light and vivid blue. His body somehow looked more brittle yet much tougher, like the trunk of a stunted mountainside tree that would still be clinging to its crag long after everyone alive today was long buried.

"You shouldn't have come here." Even his voice was different: there was a brassy ring to it that made Blays feel like he'd been whacked in the head. "You should have run away."

Blays stepped into his lost sandal, giving the broken straps a hasty knot around his calf. "And *you* should have known I'm much too dumb to act with anything approaching reason."

"You saw that I was watching you," Gladdic said. "You conserved your strength while pretending to spend it. And when the demon withdrew, you moved to ambush us."

"You talk like I've committed treason," Dante said. "But I've acted exactly in line with my orders."

"This brings you joy? Serving the Eiden Rane like a trained dog?"

"Why wouldn't I be happy to perfect the world?"

"I do not see perfect. I see enslavement."

"That's because your eyes are as cloudy as your urine, you gnarled old goat. History is the soil that all fights and wars grow from. That's why we're going to erase it."

"What? History?"

Dante snorted. "Are your ears as weak as your eyes? Yes, we're going to erase history. Along with everything else that divides people from each other. After a while of that, we might even be able to give them their free will back. With everyone united in worship of the Eiden Rane, who will be happy to execute you from a thousand miles away if you ever undermine his law, what's there going to be to fight about?"

"But you would bring the world to the apocalypse for this!

You would destroy everything!"

"No, we'll leave plenty of trees and animals around. Those are more or less fine. It's the people who need a reset. Arawn cursed us when his mill broke and everything's been awful ever since. As for the apocalypse, we only need one of those, after which we get eternal harmony—which doesn't sound as profound as it is, so I want you to take a second to contemplate the meaning of 'eternal.'" Dante paused like the master at a university. "Got it? Now compare that to the current system of nonstop bloodshed and misery that's presently scheduled to go on until the end of time. If you support *that*, then I'll happily suggest that *you* are the real monster."

Something small and frightened reached for Blays' heart. He booted it aside. "Sounds great, except for the part where you murder or Blight every living soul. And the part where you can't guarantee that this glorious eternal paradise will ever come about in the first place. How do you know the White Lich is telling you the truth? Do you really suppose you can trust a fellow who intends to kill literally everyone?"

"I've heard him speak. He believes. He's had hundreds of years to plan this. And in a few more weeks, he'll have the power to achieve it." Dante's eerily blue eyes moved to Bek's sword. It was sheathed, but the swamp dragon horn hilt identified it at once as Odo Sein. "Why exactly did you come out here? To kill me? No, probably not. If you'd worked out a sound method of attacking those like us, you would have used it against the Eiden Rane, both to break the main threat and in the hope that killing him would release me and the others from what he's made of us. It wouldn't, by the way. What's done is done. So if you aren't here to kill me, you're here to rescue me, aren't you? How? Did you think you could simply talk me out of serving the man who'll save the world?"

"We have no such illusions," Gladdic said. "I know that when he takes you, he takes your will as well, much in the way a father would take a knife from a toddler much too young to use it."

"Then you'd have to undo the taking, wouldn't you?" Dante laughed ringingly. "You think you can reverse the will of the Eiden Rane!"

"We can." Blays took half a step forward. Over the course of their talk, Gladdic had used the ether to return the earth to its original state, and they were now at ground level, standing twenty feet away from Dante. "There's a way to un-Blight people. We can do the same for you."

"That's not possible."

"Why don't we try it and find out?"

"Stay where you are." Dante lifted one hand, then slowly lowered it. "How would you do this?"

"Simple. Sort of. The lich has taken something vital from you. All we have to do — "

"Silence!" Gladdic barred his arm across Blays' chest. "You must not tell him the process. He will relay it to his master, who will work to negate it from ever working again."

"What's it matter? We're about to turn him. After that, he won't *want* to tell the lich."

"And if it doesn't work?"

"Then there's no secret to expose to the White Lich, is there?"

"You're lying to me," Dante said. He was the only one among them that wasn't sweating. As unhealthy as he looked, he also looked capable of sitting in the Hell-Painted Hills for thirty years without suffering the slightest discomfort. "If you have no way to undo this, then there's nothing left to talk about."

"He took your remnant from you, didn't he? The bit of ether that's like your trace. That's what turned you into one of his under-liches. By using the Odo Sein, we can transfer a new remnant into you."

"Not if I resist you. Even he has his limits, but the Eiden Rane is the only one who can take a trace or a remnant from the unwilling."

"Unless you have the Aba Quen. Don't worry, your lord will know what it is."

Dante frowned. Gaunt though his face was, it had become ageless, the wrinkles of sun and age wiped smooth. He turned and paced to his right, circling them. "You really can do this, can't you? You found a way. Or at least you think you did."

"Don't act *that* surprised. Now let's get this over with. You'll thank us afterwards."

"I can't believe you actually think you're going to win. If the lich lets you live to serve him, you're going to be so embarrassed about this."

"Have you always been this arrogant? Or did I not notice because it was usually turned against someone else? We're going to bring you back to who you were. You can't stop us and you don't have a choice. Please, go willingly."

"I've given it a lot of thought. And I'm going to tell you to go to hell."

Blays clenched his teeth. "You huge idiot. We can save you!"

"No," Dante said. "You can't."

Still pacing, and without turning toward them, Dante flung out his left hand. Golden splinters cracked from his body and fell to the ground. A storm of nether shot from his palm, roiling toward Gladdic. Gladdic shouted in surprise, throwing himself backwards as he met the darkness with a lightning-shaped prong of ether. The two forces boomed against each other, dispersing into ghostly ash.

Half-hidden behind the cloud, a black blade seared toward Bek. Bek's eyes flew wide. He tried to duck, but the blade swerved to match his motion. It spun through his neck. His head twirled to the dirt road, landing with a puff of dust.

Choking in shock, Gladdic hammered at Dante with paired streams of darkness and light. Dante opened his hand. With a casual gesture, he threw out a barrage of nether, stopping the streams in a sizzling collision.

Blays found his swords in his hands. He couldn't remember drawing them. Nether snapped up and down the black steel. His heart was so loud he couldn't hear Gladdic, who looked to be shouting something. Blays took a step forward.

Dante lifted his hands over his head. "Stop this!"

Gladdic let the nether twist in his hand. Blays halted, swords angled from his waist.

"You killed him." Gladdic's voice was shaky, suddenly old. "How?"

Dante laughed. "While you were racing back and forth across the swamps like such brave heroes, I was studying the Odo Sein. And asking the Eiden Rane for everything he knew about it. Though he was close to an answer, he was missing a few key pieces—but thanks to my training at the Spires, I was able to fill in the gaps. It was challenging, practicing against myself. I wasn't sure it was going to work until the moment I freed myself from the knight's binds."

"That's why Bek couldn't protect us at the Bastion," Blays said. "It wasn't that he screwed up. The lich must have told the sorcerers there how to break through the Odo Sein. But they weren't quite good enough to stop us."

Gladdic opened and closed his left hand. "The Odo Sein has protected these lands against sorcerers for centuries. If it could be broken, someone would have done so long ago."

Dante nudged Bek's head with his toe, rolling it so it faced them. One of the knight's eyes was coated with dust. "I think he'd argue otherwise. The Knights of Odo Sein use the stream to block or sever your connection to the nether. But all they're doing is blocking the connection that's obvious to you. Which means they're undone by their own game, aren't they?"

"I can't even begin to follow that," Blays said.

"You don't have to. You never have. All you've ever had to do is slap together a few ridiculous ideas and occasionally stick a sword in someone."

Gladdic crinkled his brow. "Since all nether is connected, as long as you can access your trace, you can use that to reach out to any other shadows as well."

"That's one way to do it, yes." Dante let his hands hang below his hips, nether swirling around them like a typhoon-stirred sea. "Anyway, your knight's dead. You can't stop me from wielding the shadows, and if you're honest with yourselves, you'll admit that I can murder you both. When the opposite was true, you told me I had no choice, and had to submit to you. So don't be a couple of hypocrites. Bow down to me."

"You have traveled far with me, Galand. You know that I would rather die than serve the Eiden Rane."

"Then it's a good thing he's more open-minded than you are. He's agreed to add you to the ranks of his lieutenants. He told me to kill Blays, but I think if I deliver the both of you to him, he'll change his mind on that."

"I tell you for the last time that I will never serve!"

"Quit your bullshit grandstanding! We're offering you power like no one's ever had. The power to reshape everything. To re-build our world according to a grand plan rather than to watch vain idiots brutalize each other over petty resentments. And if that isn't enough for you, how about this? We'll give you immor-tality. An eternity to learn and study and develop your skills. You know you've always wanted that. I did, and you're ten times as much of an asshole as I ever was."

"I have indeed wanted that. Always." Gladdic's voice came out in a croak. "But I have fought hard these last months to re-gain the pieces of my being that I paid in pursuit of such powers.

I would rather die than walk any further down the path you offer."

"Oh, come on. A hundred years from now, you'll look back at this moment and laugh at yourself." Dante swiveled his icy eyes to Blays. "I know *you* hate the idea. I'm sure you think it's 'immoral.' And that no outcome can justify what we have to do to achieve it."

Blays rested his hand on one of his swords, which he'd sheathed to prevent it from draining his trace. "Revoking the freedom or the lives of everyone currently alive? Yeah, it's a little extreme."

"I'll tell you this: when he converts you, all of those feelings will go away. All of your guilt. Your doubt. Your fears. And you will be grateful to him for his gift."

"Are you saying this because you believe it yourself? Or because he's making you believe it?"

"What difference does it make?"

Blays met Dante's stare. "I want to know who's telling me this. The friend I've had since before we could grow beards? Or the man whose mind has been stolen by a maniac who means to kill everyone you've ever known?"

"It's me. I'm still here."

"Are you? Then do you remember the time Cally sent us to investigate the thefts at Lannovar?"

"The border town. Human merchants were reporting their wares going missing. People were blaming it on the norren. Cally was afraid the whole town was going to erupt into violence."

"Not just violence. Cally suspected King Moddegan was wary that the humans were getting too close to seeing the norren as their equals, which would be trouble for the whole 'hunting norren down and enslaving them' thing. If Moddegan could provoke Lannovar into tossing out its norren—or better yet, massacring them—it'd secure Gaskan policy in the area for another generation."

"We traveled to Lannovar. Interviewed the human merchants, along with the norren trappers and artists who traded with them. Eventually, the trail took us to a fellow named Fanden." Dante chuckled tinnily. "He played dumb, but there was something off about him. So we started keeping tabs on him. A few nights later, he took his dogs out for a walk—he had this entire pack of them, little yappers that couldn't have weighed more than ten pounds apiece, the most useless things you've ever seen —and brought them into the city. While he waited in the old churchyard, his dogs snuck into the merchants' shops and stole everything they could carry in their mouths."

"I still don't believe it. If that fool had put as much effort into honest work as he did into training his dogs, he could've bought half the town." Blays grinned, almost lost in the memory. But the face in front of him wouldn't let him forget. "There's something I've always wondered. After Lira died. We went our separate ways. Lived our own lives. Five years later, I hadn't so much as sent you a letter. But you were still trying to find me. Why? Why keep searching, when at that point we'd spent more time as enemies than we had as friends?"

Dante tipped back his head, gazing into the punishing sun. His face, hardened by the process that had turned him into something less and more than a man, softened with nostalgia. And regret. And pride.

"We'd done great things together. The end of the war destroyed that. Tore us apart. But I wanted to believe that wasn't the end. That any tragedy can be undone, if you can set aside your anger and pain, and reach out in hope."

"We can do that now. Come with us to the Silent Spires. Ara can help you. We will remove this thing from you. It didn't have to end before—and it doesn't have to end now."

"You don't understand," Dante said. He almost sounded sad.

"It ended the instant you refused to kneel to the Eiden Rane."

Shadows erupted from his hands, raging toward them in black malevolence. Gladdic cursed, battering at them with the ether he'd kept close all the while. No one's mouth was open, yet Blays heard screaming in his ears. He reached for his swords. He couldn't seem to draw them. It was like they'd been welded into their sheaths. His vision blurred.

He turned and ran back down the road toward the swamp.

"Coward!" Gladdic shouted. "Deserter!"

If the words were meant to shame him, they'd have to wait in line behind the army currently sieging Blays' conscience. He sprinted onward, knees and elbows pumping, losing himself to the unique euphoria of running as fast as you can. A fine layer of sweat developed across his body.

Footsteps smacked the ground. Gladdic loped down the road after him, his long legs carrying him along the smooth dirt with a speed that seemed impossible for his years. Dante ran in his wake, hunched forward like a wolf before it makes its lunge. Nether shot from his hands. Without looking back, Gladdic countered it with tridents of ether, the glittering dust of their combat falling behind them as they ran on.

Blays crested the hill. The swamp filled the horizons, a humid haze lingering in the air above the trees. There would be no sanctuary there either, would there?

But what else was there to do but keep going in the face of hopelessness? To see if some kindly god or turn of blind chance would take pity on your miserable life?

He thundered down the incline, knees jarring. Two black shapes shot past his shins. The Andrac. They bounded past Gladdic, light shining through their joyous grins, and threw themselves at Dante. Dante stopped and fell back, reaching for his limited supply of ether. Blays thought Gladdic might turn around and join the battle, but the old priest continued toward the swamp.

Ether and nether twirled between Dante and the two little Star-Eaters. The demons were already looking raggedy, but by the time Dante finally put them down, Blays had opened up a lead of a quarter mile. The air was already growing cooler—or at least less scalding—and damper. Trees crowded the edge of the living land. Blays reached the grass, veering south toward the canoe.

He beat Gladdic to the boat by two hundred yards. He flipped it over and shoved it into the water. He stepped in with one foot, then turned around, sighed, and waited.

Gladdic arrived with a face so red it looked like all his skin had left him to seek more pleasant realms. Blays clambered into the canoe and the old man followed. Dante was still a thousand feet away, advancing steadily along his road. The Hell-Painted Hills wavered as the sun baked from their naked slopes.

Blays took up the paddle, giving himself a good splash to calm down his overheated skin, and pushed off into the swamp.

"Why did you run?" Gladdic gasped the words out between breaths.

"To get away from there and over to here."

"And what has this relocation in geography solved? We could have killed him!"

"I'm not so sure. But even if that was true, so what? We kill him and then what do we do? Bek's dead. We can't kill the lich. Killing Dante wouldn't even slow down the advance."

"In what way is running away a superior solution?"

"There *is* no solution, you dogged shithead. We've lost. We might as well get ourselves and our loved ones as far away from here as possible and try to enjoy however long we have left." Blays looked over his shoulder, but the trees and shrubs were already too thick to tell if Dante was still after them. "And if that's inevitable—if it's only a matter of time until the White Lich claims us all — then killing Dante doesn't even make sense. I know I can't let myself be a part of the lich's new world. But if Dante's there, maybe he'll make it slightly less dark."

Gladdic let out a long, slow breath. "You have fallen to despair. I can see this as clearly as I can see my own hand, for I have worn its burden myself."

"I just lost my oldest friend. And, coincidentally, condemned everyone in the world to death or hell. Forgive me if I'm not at my bubbliest."

"Your reaction is natural. But it has blinded you. We have one last chance."

"How's that? Slip a new remnant into Dante's porridge, then all have a big laugh after he eats it?"

"Bek is dead. But you remain alive. Last night, I saw you lost in the Golden Stream. Bek told you exactly what must be done. Let us return, and you will free Dante from his chains."

Blays stopped paddling, twisting around. "We can't. We left the Aba Quen behind."

"*You* left the Aba Quen behind. Others among us have more foresight." Gladdic reached into his jabat and withdrew the ivory carving. The gecko was smudged with blood. "Happy birthday."

Blays took up the idol, certain he was about to fumble it into the water and never see it again. "Even if this damn thing works, I don't know how to lock him out of the nether. He'll rip me to shreds, and then tear the shreds into bits."

"You cannot blame despair for *this* level of stupidity. For surely I had intended to do nothing to help you, observing from afar. However, your petulant whining has convinced me to assist you. I will counter his sorcery while you restore his remnant."

"That could work, but aren't we overlooking something? Like the minor fact I don't know how to use the Odo Sein?"

"You know enough to make the connection Bek described. Do so now, and be quick about it."

"But I still can't reach the stream!"

"I have seen your efforts. You are far closer than you believe. How can it be that I have more faith in you than you have in yourself?"

Blays closed his eyes tight. An ocean of doubts spread before him. He breathed in, relaxing every muscle, then breathed out, tensing them all. Gladdic was scowling like he was working his way through a theological manuscript dense enough to brain a bull with. Blays started the practice of Forest, then broke off, heart rattling, and envisioned the cabin in the Woduns. The snows. The ice on the lake. His boys and girls pelting each other with snowballs—

Golden chips spun about him. The air shimmered, as if he could part it like a pair of curtains and open a view to elsewhere in the world. He swooped toward the fragments of stream, but there was no need: they were already coming to his hand. And they would have the night before, wouldn't they? He'd been too shaken up—first by his reverie, then by the Glimpse of the two sisters—to grab at the stream until it was already fading away.

Before the flecks in front of him could do the same, he sent them toward Gladdic. His motion was clumsy, like trying to throw a plank by the middle instead of the end, but a few of them stuck. Strands and planes of black and white energy extended from all sides of Gladdic's body.

Blays maneuvered between them, fluttering as awkwardly as a fat-bodied moth as he hunted for the connection that would lead him to the remnant. He slipped around a wide plane of nether, then a tangle of white cords. Behind these, a thin pillar of glowing pearl light connected the earth to the heavens. There was no mistaking the remnant. Blays guided the stream to the pearly strand. The golden matter caught fast, binding Blays to the light.

He clapped his hands so hard they stung. "I can do it. I don't know how, or how much, but I can do it!"

"Then we will return now."

"*Right* now? How about I take a few days to practice first?"

"Dante and the Eiden Rane have already learned how to break the Odo Sein's control over the nether. You just told Dante exactly how the Blight is removed. He and the lich will work ceaselessly to learn how to stop this rite as well. We cannot afford to give them a single day, or it might never work again."

"So we have to go now, huh?" This thought should have been terrifying. Instead, Blays was compelled to laugh out loud. "I suppose it's like they always say: when everyone who actually knows what they're doing has been murdered, why not send in the idiots?"

He flipped the canoe nose-for-tail and paddled back toward the Hell-Painted Hills, eyes darting to every movement, which in the lively swamp was nonstop. Gladdic reopened a cut near the end of the stump of his right arm. They broke from the trees, entering a clear patch of water that lapped directly against the Hills.

Dante stood two hundred yards up the shore. He was staring off into the swamp, turned away from them at a quarter profile. It didn't seem as though he should be able to see them, but he swiveled to face them the second their canoe poked from the trees. Despite the distance, Blays caught the blue flash of his eyes.

Blays brought the boat up to land and vaulted into the grass. Gladdic exited in pained stages, as if his legs had already stiffened up following their dash from the wasteland.

Blays felt the nether flow to Gladdic's call. They exchanged a nod. Blays strolled along the bank, keeping one hand near his sword, for what little good it could do against Dante.

Dante watched them come, but didn't budge from his spot. Nether spiraled around his arms. Blays stopped twenty feet away from him.

Dante was smiling. On his new face, it didn't look right. "I never thought I'd see you run away."

Blays tossed his head. "What are you talking about? We've run away from tight spots a thousand different times. I've gone through more shoes than most armies."

"But you've never run away when running meant losing, and the only way to win was to stand and fight."

"I'm here now." He glanced at the swamp, looking thoughtful as he sent a part of his mind to the cabin in the Woduns. "You said you and Daddy Lich figured out how to break the Odo Sein together. But he's been elsewhere all this while, hasn't he? Do you two have a loon-like link between you or something?"

"What does that matter?"

"I want to send him a message."

"Which is?"

"That he should run," Blays said. "Run far away, and never show himself again. Or else the last thing he'll see is my sword—and the last thought he'll have is to wonder what his head is doing so far from his body."

He picked up the stream he'd been generating as they spoke and snapped it at Dante. Dante tried to blast at the golden sparks with nether, but the shadows passed over them without leaving a mark. Showing his teeth, Dante redirected the nether at Blays.

The shadows stormed toward him in sheer fury, ready to rip his body into pieces and chum him across the waters. Heart tumbling like a boulder down a hill, Blays held his position, concentrating on the Golden Stream as it made its ponderous way toward Dante.

The nether closed on Blays. He could duck into the shadows and let it pass by, but he thought if he did that, he'd lose control of the stream. He could probably generate more—assuming he could buy a few seconds to conjure it up without Dante converting him into skewered meat minus the skewers—but he wasn't sure how many more times he could wield it. He was already feeling shakier than when he'd practiced it on Gladdic, and that shakiness wasn't all due to nerves. The only way to come out of it alive was to trust in Gladdic.

The shadows screamed onward, blotting out the sun—and were met with the starry whiteness of ether. The flash dazzled Blays, yet somehow he could still see the pieces of stream as they landed on Dante's transformed skin.

And sank inside him.

A galaxy of nether shot from Dante's body. Blays threw his hands in front of his face, expecting to be annihilated, but the shadows weren't moving. Rather, they were the connections between Dante and the nether exposed by the stream. A few lines of ether extended from him as well, sickly-small in comparison.

None of the ethereal strings looked anything like the column of pearl Blays had seen within Gladdic. He maneuvered around the outermost layers of shadow, groping inward. The darkness surrounded him completely, interrupted here and there by a spindly thread of light. He reached what he knew was the center. And ground to a halt, cold sweat popping across his skin.

"His remnant," Blays choked. "It isn't there!"

Lost in his search, he hadn't noticed that Dante and Gladdic were busy whaling away at each other with everything they had. Nether and ether exploded in constellations of destruction, twinkling away into nothing, only to be replaced by another clash of magic a moment later. Such fights tended to sound like sizzling beef, but this one boomed like winter waves.

"Of course the remnant isn't there, you dung-brained ape," Gladdic sneered. "That is precisely what we are here to fix!"

"Just testing you," Blays said. "Good news. You passed."

He swung back into the surreal vision of the Odo Sein. Black spokes and angled walls jutted from Dante. Blays threaded his way back to the center.

Where a vertical emptiness occupied Dante's core. It was like the shadow of a shadow. Or perhaps more like the gap of a board missing from a fence; even if you'd never seen the fence before, or for that matter knew what a fence *was*, you could still look at it and see at once that something was gone. Blays gathered his remaining stream, which had dwindled as he'd been searching, and sent it to the place where the remnant should be.

Gold shimmered up and down, as though coating a tube of glass so perfectly wrought that it couldn't be seen. A charge ran back to Blays' body with a jolt. He pulled back from the sight of the Odo Sein. Gladdic stood two steps ahead of him, gesturing madly with his one arm as he held off Dante's ceaseless assaults.

Blays had spent the last of his stream connecting himself to Dante, but he needed more to tie himself to the Aba Quen. Feeling quite insane to be daydreaming in the midst of a pitched battle, he closed his eyes, returning to the valley in the mountains. This time, he saw that it was spring, and the children were catching frogs by the pond and making them race each other in the patch of bare dirt behind the house.

Two victories later, one by a bright green frog and the other by a toad named Bumps, a ring of golden chips circled in front of Blays. He opened the front of his jabat and withdrew the Aba Quen. It was slippery with sweat.

The clash of sorcery slowed to a minor skirmish. Dante smiled bleakly, gaze shifting to the swamp behind them. "Took them long enough."

There, the heads and shoulders of the Blighted emerged from the surface. The former people ignored the water streaming down their water-wrinkled faces, gnashing their teeth and splashing forward.

Blays stuffed the statue in his jabat and drew his swords.

"No!" Gladdic showered the foremost of the Blighted with

nether, knocking their corpses back into the water, then spun to deflect Dante's latest attack, which had come so close that the sparks of its negation bounced against Gladdic's face. "You must complete the task!"

Blays backed away from the banks, Gladdic paralleling him. Despite Gladdic's frantic culling, there were already thirty Blighted taking their first steps on shore, with more arising from the swamp behind them. Dante hurled another wave of shadows at Gladdic. The old priest grimaced, laying into the nether with radiant spears. He pushed back the assault, but had no attention left for the coming Blighted.

Blays could hold them off. Probably. But it would stall his progress. The stream he'd just brought forth would vanish. There was no right answer—yet he knew that indecision had killed more people than plague.

He sheathed his swords and withdrew the Aba Quen. Marshaling the stream, he sent a line of it between himself and the ivory statute. The gecko's eyes glowed gold. A pin pricked Blays' core. Dante winced, reaching for his solar plexus. Blays lifted the Aba Quen, waiting for it to do its thing. It rested in his hand like the inert lump of old bone that it was. Blays shook it. Nothing happened. His mouth went dry. Bek had made it sound like—

Dante spun a column of shadows directly at Blays' head. Still retreating from the Blighted, Gladdic countered with an inelegant but equally-sized column of light. As soon as the ether left his hand, Gladdic whirled back toward the Blighted.

The first of them had already launched itself at the old man. It crashed into him, knocking him down and biting at his throat, nails gouging into the side of Gladdic's ribs. Gladdic punched a spike of nether through the Blighted's skull, producing a fountain of brains that were as pale as the Blighted's exteriors.

Gladdic staggered to his feet, de-braining four more of the things before turning to meet Dante's latest attack. The leading edge of the nether pierced Gladdic's chest. He yelled out, clubbing it aside with a truncheon of raw ether.

The Aba Quen still hadn't done anything. Blays stared at it dumbly, ready to bash his own brains out with it. Had he screwed something up? Had Bek left something out? With no other option, he sent the last of his stream into the Aba Quen. This time, as the pin-prick jabbed his middle, he homed in on the feeling.

And found that it brought him straight to the pillar of pearl that resided in his core. There, a golden tether extended from the pillar to Dante.

Blays opened his remnant. Ether poured from him and into Dante.

EDWARD W. ROBERTSON

18

Light streamed between them. Dante watched as the ether entered his body just below his ribs. He looked up and smiled, blue eyes twinkling. "This is how you said the Odo Sein cure the Blight, isn't it? I don't feel a thing. What if your little scheme doesn't work on liches?"

"Then you'll have to excuse us from the remainder of this battle," Blays said, "as we'll need to go register a formal complaint at the Silent Spires for their sorcerous malpractice. What do you say?"

"I think you're trying to distract me from finishing this." Dante shifted his focus to Gladdic, who had seized on the momentary pause to lay waste to the closest Blighted, opening a wide circle around himself.

Dante lifted his hand. Nether coalesced around his fingers, undulating like black fire. Blays' heart collided with his stomach. He'd done everything that he was supposed to — *more* than that; he was only supposed to have provided cover for Bek, not execute the process himself — and he'd still failed.

Then again, there was something comforting in that, wasn't there? He would die knowing that he *had* done everything. And when he emerged from the haze of the Pastlands and into the Mists, there would be nothing left that he'd have to make peace with.

Best of all, he'd be away from the reach of the White Lich, wouldn't he? He could find Minn then. He doubted you could have children in the Mists, but they could still find their mountain valley. Build their cabin in it. And live together until it was time to move on.

The nether sputtered from Dante's fingers. Rather than searing toward Gladdic, it flapped away in confusion. Blays felt Dante calling to the shadows, but the nether stopped a few feet from his outstretched hands, circling him as though it was wary.

"What," Dante said. "Have you done?"

His face writhed as if worms crawled beneath his skin. His head snapped backward. His fingers twisted into claws, bending at impossible angles. The cord of ether running between them brightened steadily. Drool leaked from the corner of Dante's mouth. He staggered to his right, clutching at his heart. Patches of green appeared on his salt-white skin, creeping across his face and arms like living things.

He straightened and faced Blays, jaw hanging slackly, blood and spit spilling from his mouth. "You…"

He convulsed, fell to his knees, and vomited. At first it was red, but the next heaves were green, and the ones after that were as black as nether.

Dante fell to his side. His eyes were open and the pale blue brightness had left them, but his glassy gray eyes didn't seem to see anything at all.

The vision had always been the same.

The city lay beneath him like a map, its silver towers and golden domes gleaming redly as the sun broke from behind the mountain and spilled across all of creation. Snow still rested on the gardens and trees, but there was a note of warmth in the air that suggested it would soon retreat to the heights of the mountain. The people below seemed to sense this, moving about the streets with impatient readiness, smoke chuffing from bakeries and inns, the citizens yearning to return to work on the most beautiful city Dante had ever seen.

Wind gushed over him, rippling his robes. He was flying. This wasn't unusual. In the clean paved streets, those who saw him dropped to their knees and lowered their heads. He banked to his right, gaining elevation, the ether shining upon him just as the sun did while the nether flowed through him like the wind of his flight.

The tower stood against the sky like an upthrust fist. If he'd wanted, the lich could have made it as tall as the mountain, but he'd decided to restrict it to two thousand feet, largely so that human servants and dignitaries could walk about on its terraces and roofs without freezing to death or being flung off by raging winds.

Dante cleared the rooftop, pulled upward, and stalled, lowering gently until his soles touched the silver-veined marble. The Eiden Rane waited impassively, watching the city react to the gift of dawn. In an earlier time, the lich also would have been hurrying off to the day's labor, but he hadn't had to do any serious work in many years. Instead, he passed much of his time there on the roof, watching the people engage in his creation. Dante had never known if he was observing it for flaws, or enjoying the clockwork precision of his work. Knowing the lich, it was probably both.

The lich didn't turn his head. "Sorcerer. Are you ready?"

Dante moved to his side. "It is my honor, my master."

"Walk with me. And receive your destiny."

The portal stood twenty feet high, iron double doors inscribed with blackened runes. There was nothing on the other side. The Eiden Rane lifted his heavy hand. It glowed. Then the runes did, too. With a groan like music, the doors opened. Light of all colors poured forth. For a moment, Dante remembered what it had felt like to be afraid.

The Eiden Rane strode into the light and Dante followed. The light faded. The tower was gone. They stood on a staircase into the stars. They ascended. Everything was perfectly silent except for the rasp of their feet on the treads and a low hum that came from everywhere and nowhere.

With each step Dante took, a memory flashed through his mind. The taking of Tanar Atain. The Battle of the Dundens, when the sorcerers of the northern kingdoms made their great stand, and died to the last. The union of the world that followed as the last human fell and rose again as Blighted. The Long Reward, when the Blighted were given the run of the world for their service. Finally, the death of the last Blighted and the Ceremony of the Second Age, when the lich brought forth the first of his new humans.

The founding of the City of Heavens. The raising of the Thirty -One Towers. The spread of the people across their new home, until every land was filled. The Perfect Peace that knew no struggle nor war. The Final Quest, when the Eiden Rane and each of his under-lords worked to unlock the last secret, and Dante delivered it from the beyond. The crafting of the Starward Gate—and, at last, its opening.

The staircase seemed to go on forever, but Dante now understood that time was an illusion. A platform took shape ahead. The Eiden Rane didn't increase his pace. He didn't need to. Together, they ascended the platform. There, the gods awaited.

Dante lifted his eyes to them. Everything went white.

That was where the vision had always ended.

This time, the whiteness cleared. The platform was empty. The gods were gone. Dante turned to the Eiden Rane. The lich was already half transparent. As he disappeared, he shook his head and turned away.

Nausea spread through Dante's belly. It had been so long since he had felt any pain that the sensation paralyzed him. He retched. The convulsion sent hair-fine cracks racing across his skin. He fell to his knees. Glowing blue-white liquid dripped from the cracks in his body, spattering the platform. As the droplets landed, the light within them dimmed away to nothing.

He whirled and ran toward the stairs to the portal, but as he planted his foot, his ankle snapped. He pitched forward, landing on his elbows and knees, which crunched like chalk. His once-smooth skin dangled from his body in mummified strips. He reached out to the nether. It flickered, drifting toward him, then returned to its crevices, watching in judgment as the gift was stolen from him and his body succumbed to the thousands of years that he'd defied nature's law.

His ears roared. His sight blurred. He thought that was from the intolerable pain, but it was in fact the result of his eyes sinking into their sockets and dehydrating into black lumps. He reached out in agony, leaving a trail of fingers across the platform. His arm shook and fell. He needed to breathe, but he didn't have the strength to expand his chest.

He knew what it was to die—and to be born.

"Dante!"

Blays tried to run toward the prone figure, but his legs wobbled beneath him. He half sat and half fell, laughing dumbly for reasons he couldn't have explained. His head buzzed, the sound vacillating in and out but growing steadily louder. Something white and glowy was extending from his belly, looking like some sort of celestial worm.

Ah. Yes. The channel between them was still open. And it was busy draining ether from himself and feeding it to Dante. He thought that he should shut it off—it seemed to him that if he lost all his remnant, he'd either turn Blighted himself, or maybe just die—but he didn't seem to have any idea in hell how to *do* that.

He decided to sit there and see if any answers appeared. Ten seconds later, with the cord starting to dim, Blays couldn't remember why he was frowning. Or why he was sitting down. Other than the fact that it was very comfortable. That was probably why, wasn't it? That it was so comfy?

A figure swayed in front of him, pale and long-limbed. Its face and chest were slathered in blood. Blays squinted, mouth hanging open. Was he about to get eaten by a Blighted? That didn't seem like the most fun experience in the world. On the other hand, avoiding that fate would require standing up, which he didn't think he'd want to do even if he knew how.

"Blays!" the figure yelled. "The connection remains open! You must close it!"

"But what?"

The figure, who Blays was starting to believe might not be a Blighted after all, drew back its hand and slapped him across the face.

He touched his cheek. "What's that for, you son of a bastard?"

"Close the connection before you lose yourself! Sever the stream!"

The connection? The stream? Blays scowled down at the statue with the lizard and bones that he clutched in his hands. He reached toward the golden thread connecting him to the Aba Quen. This felt like trying to run through chest-deep water. He swore at it, thinking that might help. Either it did or he'd been right about to get to it anyway, because his mind grasped the thread. He yanked as hard as he could. The tie snapped with only the faintest resistance; if he'd been breaking a strand in the physical world rather than within the loony sorcerous one, he would have gone stumbling backwards.

The buzzing faded. Blays glanced about himself, pulse racing, soggy with fresh sweat. Bodies of the Blighted were strewn all over the place. Most had been killed with precision strikes, but others had been knocked into gory pieces, as if they'd gotten too close, requiring Gladdic to hit them with awkward sledgehammers of nether. Which explained why Gladdic was such a great big bloody mess.

Blays scrabbled to his feet, gawking wild-eyed at the old priest. "I was about to lose the last of it. It had me so addle-pated that I didn't even understand what was happening. I think you just saved my life."

Gladdic nodded and tried to say something, but coughed instead, spitting blood down the front of his jabat. Blays rocked back a step, then ran forward just in time to catch him as he fainted.

Gladdic was covered in bites and gashes and awash in blood that Blays had mistaken for the Blighted's. "Gladdic! Wake up, you idiot! Wake up and heal yourself!"

The old man lolled limply. Across from them, Dante lay next to his pools of multi-hued vomit. His eyes were still open. Blays couldn't tell if he was dead, but Gladdic was certainly about to be.

Blays lowered the priest to the ground and ran to Dante. He shook his shoulder, gently at first, then savagely. Just as Blays was about to scream, Dante's eyes popped open.

"Can you hear me?" Blays said. "Are you in there?"

Dante's eyes roved from side to side. "I don't know."

"Do you know who I am? Do you know who *you* are?"

"I don't know."

Blays covered his face with his hands. "You can remember who you are later. Gladdic's about to die unless you get up and heal him!"

Dante looked at him blankly, then at Gladdic and the blood weeping from his wounds into the grass. Dante planted a palm on the ground and shoved himself to his feet. He tottered over to Gladdic, shadows wrapping around his hands. As soon as they touched him, he stopped, taking a deep breath. He rolled his shoulders.

He turned and smiled at Blays. "There I am."

Dante crouched next to Gladdic, steadying himself with one hand. Nether surged to the unconscious priest, eddying over his countless wounds. The bleeding slowed. The worst bite, a chunk taken from the side of Gladdic's neck, filled in layer by layer, until it was replaced with smooth skin much pinker than the tanned parts surrounding it.

One by one, the other wounds followed suit. The nether grew shakier and shakier in Dante's hands. Eventually, he flopped on his rear, back hunched.

Blays stood over Gladdic. "Is he alive?"

"Yeah." Dante gazed down at himself. His jabat was smeared with vomit and blood. "Am I?"

"Yes. Sorry about that."

"There are more Blighted coming. They'll be here any minute and I'm nearly out of nether. We have to get out of here."

Blays sighed. "And I thought I'd finally be able to rest for a while."

He went to the canoe and beached it directly across from Gladdic, stashing the Aba Quen inside. Dante tried to help Blays carry the old man to the boat, but immediately dropped Gladdic's feet and ran off to vomit in the grass. Blays leveraged Gladdic over the gunwale and settled him inside. This done, he gave Dante a hand getting in, then picked up the paddle and headed east-northeast, away from both the Hell-Painted Hills and the direction Dante said the Blighted were coming from.

"If you're going to barf again," Blays said, "please do it over the side, would you? If you add 'scrub the upchuck from the bottom of a canoe' to the list of things I've had to do today, I swear to the gods I'll deliver us straight to the White Lich."

Dante nodded weakly. He was ashen and shaky and Blays wasn't sure if he looked better or worse than when he'd woken up ten minutes earlier.

But he was *human* again. That was what Blays chose to focus on as he conveyed them away from the Hell-Painted Hills and into the overgrown clamor of the swamp. Dante kept glancing behind them. Either he had so little nether left at hand that he didn't want to waste it on his insect scouts, or he was too rattled to think of it.

"So the last couple of weeks were terrible," Blays said once he was reasonably sure they weren't about to be set upon by hidden foes. "Rather than allowing you to simply take my word for it, I'm now going to inflict the experience on you as well."

He launched into a lengthy recap of everything he, Naran, Gladdic, and the late Bek had done since Dante had been taken by the White Lich, deliberately including more detail than was strictly necessary, in part to fill the time, and in part to help re-mind Dante that he was back among them.

He spent a particularly long time on the heist of the Bastion, which had almost been fun, in its way. Despite that, Dante didn't ask a single question or so much as laugh, gazing instead out into the swamp.

"All for a little statue of a lizard," Blays said. "You'd think they'd make a weapon like this more fearsome-looking. I'd have gone with a shark swinging a battle axe."

He paddled along, splashing softly. Behind him, Dante shift-ed his weight. "Then what happened?"

"We headed your way," Blays said. "Personally, I thought it was the perfect opportunity to finally be rid of you, but Gladdic thought it wouldn't be fair if we had to fight the White Lich and you didn't."

He finished up the tale of the last few days of travel between

Dara Bode and the fight at the base of the Hell-Painted Hills. It didn't take much longer. After that, they were both quiet.

"I think we've gone far enough," Dante said once the after-noon had passed its peak heat. "The Blighted would take days to find us on their own."

"If it means I can stop paddling, I'd agree with you if you told me the sky was orange polka dots."

Blays brought them aground on the nearest island that looked large enough to offer concealment. They dragged the canoe to-ward the reeds. Blays picked up Gladdic while Dante grabbed their gear. The old man was still out cold, his skin mottled with the light pink patches where he'd been healed.

Blays found a grassy spot near the center of the island. Dante flapped out a blanket and Blays set Gladdic down. Dante crouched next to the priest, a few shadows flickering around his hand.

Blays moved a step closer. "He all right?"

"He exhausted himself in the battle. He needs sleep, that's all." Dante didn't look up. "Do you still want him dead?"

"Do I *want* him *dead*?"

"You heard me."

"Should I have transferred part of my brain to you as well? I'm the one who woke you up to stop him from bleeding out."

"That's what's confusing me. Because when you threw him off the tower at Aris Osis, I assume it wasn't to give him a dose of fresh air."

Heat prickled over Blays' skin. He'd almost convinced himself that night had been nothing more than a drunken dream. Even now, he wanted to deny it—but when you lied to yourself, you only made yourself weaker. When you came face to face with something about yourself that made you feel weak or scared, you stared it down. And you walked through it. And that was how you made sure you'd never have to face it again.

"How did you know?"

"You were out drinking at the docks," Dante said. "Naran was only a couple of islands away. Almost half a mile closer to the scene than you were. There was no way you could have heard about what happened before he did. Yet the two of you showed up together. Because you didn't *need* to be told."

"Maybe I'd had enough to drink and was on my way back to bed. Then again, I bet you already know that I beat Naran to the tower, and waited for him to arrive before heading upstairs. I thought it'd look less suspicious if I didn't show up alone." Blays plucked a tall blade of grass, tearing it apart piece by piece. "He'd hurt so many people. He'd always gotten away with it. After he hurt Volo, something inside me snapped."

"I know why you did it. I want to know if you still want to see justice done to him."

"If I asked you to, you'd do it? Spike him right now?"

"Yes."

Blays got to his feet, turning his back to them. "Leave him be."

"Why?"

"Because without him, you wouldn't be here."

"This has all been so strange," Dante said. "Typically, pressure like what we've been under breaks people. Warps them into awful shapes. But maybe it can squeeze you into something stronger."

Blays shook his head, then laughed. "I'm too tired to guess. Not if I'm going to take first watch, anyway."

Dante put up a brief fight about handling the watch himself, but Blays rejected each argument. Although there was still plenty of light, Dante fell asleep in less than a minute. Blays waited by the camp for a while longer, then began a small circuit of the island. His head throbbed flatly. It felt like his mind would snap if he tried to think, so he didn't.

He and Dante traded watches every two to three hours. By

the middle of the night, Blays was starting to feel normal again. The next time Dante shook him awake, Gladdic stirred, mumbled blearily, and opened his eyes.

"Told you he'd live," Dante said.

"There goes another ten chucks," Blays said. "I knew I should have smothered him in his sleep."

Gladdic blinked owlishly, then chuckled in wonder. "I am intact?"

"If your definition includes being so old that you season your rocks with dirt, then sure, you are perfectly intact."

"And everyone else is as well?"

"*We're* not old. We are young, or close enough to it to continue to pretend, and one of us has a physique that makes statues gossip jealously to each other in the back garden."

"I can see that *you* are unharmed, and have possibly located a long-lost supply of bottled spirits. Dante? Are you recovered?"

"I've felt better," Dante said. "Including after I've been repeatedly stabbed. But I'm here again."

Gladdic laughed and smacked his knee with his left hand. "Perhaps the gods do not hate us after all. Or perhaps they find the world a more interesting place to observe when you are free to sow chaos across it. Whatever their motives, this is a miracle."

"Blays told me everything you guys had to go through. I suppose I should thank you."

"One might consider our motives entirely selfish, as without your presence, we would be considerably more likely to die at the hands of the Eiden Rane." Gladdic sat up more fully, taking in the warm night and the stars peeping through the boughs. "Life is without any logic at all, is it? Six months ago, I would have given up my right arm voluntarily if it had allowed me the chance to spit on your corpse. And now? Now, I see you are alive, and I appear to be happy."

Blays joined the others in laughing at that. It was still dark out, and would remain so for another two hours, but they'd been sleeping since late afternoon—longer, in Gladdic's case—and seemed awake enough. They ate some dried fish and bananas, which no longer seemed remotely exotic to Blays.

"We don't have anything left, do we?" Dante flipped an empty peel into the brush. "The lich knows how to combat the Odo Sein now. That was the only way we had to get at the prime body without being annihilated."

Blays motioned toward the bag where he'd stashed the statue. "What about the Aba Quen? Can we use that to de-lich him?"

"I spoke with the lich after you ran away. He was utterly un-concerned about the Aba Quen's ability to harm him. He seemed to find the very idea funny."

"So we've lost our only way to hit back at him and he's be-come stronger than ever. Well, that just means the songs they'll wind up singing about us will be even better."

"Before any such songs can be composed," Gladdic said, "what is our next move?"

Dante shrugged. "We go back to the Silent Spires."

"To do what? Complete our education in the Odo Sein? You just said that it was now worthless."

"Against the lich, it is. We're not going there to learn the Odo Sein. We're going there to warn them, and to get Naran and Volo, if she's well. And then we're going to leave Tanar Atain."

Silence hung between them like a dark doorway.

"Er," Blays said. "We are?"

"The Drakebane was right to leave this place. We'll follow his lead."

Gladdic pounded his leg with his fist. "The Drakebane was a coward and a deserter!"

"But he knew this land was doomed. We found an avenue to victory he didn't know about, but we took our shot and we missed. Now, the White Lich has taken Aris Osis. That doubled his army. It likely doubled his personal power, too. It's time to pull out."

"You have spoken with the Eiden Rane many times. You must understand that withdrawing from Tanar Atain does nothing to protect us. Once he consolidates his homeland, he will strike out for the next nation. Perhaps he will go to the south—but perhaps he will come for Alebolgia. And then Collen. Then Mallon. Then everything."

"I know all of that and more. I spent two weeks taking his orders. That's why I'm going to murder him myself."

Gladdic arched his left eyebrow. "Then you do have a plan to defeat him?"

"I don't know have any gods damn idea how to do that. After serving under him, and listening to him talk, I'm not sure it *can* be done. But I know we can't fight him here any longer. Tanar Atain is too wild for us, but it's his home turf, and he's about to control every corner of it. It's time to fall back to somewhere that we can defend."

"There is reason in this. Yet if we cede this land, does it mean we've achieved nothing here?"

"We bought ourselves time. Nethermancers from Narashtovik are already crossing through Mallon. We can meet up with them there. And it isn't just us. We've given places like Mallon and Pocket Cove more time to prepare, too. Without us hampering the lich's every move, he would have swept through Tanar Atain weeks ago. And gone on to overrun Bressel."

"We did more than that," Blays said. "We proved that we can stand against the White Lich and walk away with our lives. We'll do it again—and next time, we'll win."

Gladdic lowered his head. "Then we will return to the Silent Spires. And pray that the gods will forgive us what we do next."

The three of them returned to the spot where they'd arranged to meet the Odo Sein on their return. Dante was scouting the way ahead with his dragonflies, and hence knew before they arrived at the rendezvous that no one from the Spires was waiting for them.

But his scouts had also seen that the Blighted had apparently spotted their boat and were also converging on the rendezvous. Low on options, they ditched their canoe and hiked once again into the Hell-Painted Hills.

Blays spent most of the day's trek bitching about the heat and spitting out ideas about how to harry, slow, wound, hamper, push back, and otherwise resist the White Lich and his forces. He knew that most of his ideas weren't very good, but he lobbed them out there with the express purpose of seeing if anyone else could pick them up and do better, and was disappointed when Dante barely responded to them at all, and in fact seemed irritated that Blays was even trying.

Gladdic picked up and kicked around a few of his suggestions, but Blays quit by afternoon, marching over the uneven ground and wishing for the Spires to appear even though he knew they were more than a day away. *Had* they accomplished anything in Tanar Atain? At best, they'd learned a little about the lich, but they hadn't actually hurt him, had they? Had it been worth it to slow down his progress in exchange for all the lives lost along the way?

Around one that afternoon, a team of lan haba emerged from the hill ahead. In the heat of summer, the oversized goats stank fiercely, but Blays' spirits lifted the instant he took the saddle.

They rode hard, climbing from rock to rock, pushing past sunset, after which Gladdic lit the way with floating globes of ether. Around the same time Blays' stomach was starting to do some serious complaining, they navigated the final ridge and looked down on the green valley of the Silent Spires.

Servants met them at the border between the dead rock and

the living grass. The staff barely exchanged four words with the lan haba-mounted guides before turning around and running back to the towers. Blays and the others came to the plaza and dismounted.

Footsteps dashed across the half-lit square. Ara ran forward, her robe pulling back from one of her legs.

"You're alive!" She rushed forward, embracing Dante. She detached herself and hugged Blays and Gladdic in turn. "Don't look at me like that. When the two of you left, I thought I'd never catch sight of your hides again. Unless the lich used them to skin the hulls of his new kayaks."

"We've avoided such a fate for now," Blays said. "The even better news is we've successfully reduced his army by one."

Ara walked a half-circle around Dante, looking him up and down. "You look fine. A little gross, like you've been sick, but fine. I can see with my own eyes that it worked, so I'll skip right to the meaningful questions: *how* did it work? Did you have to do anything different because he was a lich?"

Blays nodded. "I had to not screw everything up, which was a challenging change of pace. Otherwise, it was the exact same de-Blighting process Bek said it would be."

Her look of curiosity shifted to an unwanted awareness. "Where *is* Bek? Something's happened to him, hasn't it?"

"The White Lich and I worked out a way to break past the Odo Sein," Dante said. "When the three of them came to free me, Bek locked me away from the nether, but only for a moment. I let them get comfortable and believe I was no harm. And then I struck him."

"And you killed him."

"I'm sorry, Bel Ara. I was under the lich's power."

"You don't say? Idiot that I am, I'd completely forgotten that when you were a lich, you weren't yourself. I can still rage at the one controlling you!"

"I know exactly how you feel." Dante curled his hand into a fist, face twisting with an anger Blays had rarely seen on him. "I will kill him for what he's done, Ara. I swear it on my life."

She moved a step closer, examining his face. "I think, at last, you might."

"Where is Naran?" Blays said. "And how is Volo?"

"Naran's asleep. He's an early riser, that one. Likes to beat the sun to rise and help us in the gardens. As for the girl, she's seen no change in her condition. I'm starting to doubt she ever will. During the fighting in Aris Osis, she saw into the depths of the abyss. And it destroyed her. There's something missing inside her now. A spark, a light. I don't think it can be brought back."

Blays had suspected this for some time, but hearing the words from someone else shot a pang of sorrow down his spine. "What do we do, then? Leave her here?"

"We can't travel with her," Dante said. "We need all the speed we can get. If anything, she'll be in *more* danger with us."

Ara nodded to the wasteland surrounding them. "If she stays here much longer, she'll be afflicted with the same thing the rest of us are. She'll never be able to leave."

Blays crossed his arms. "But traveling is her life. It's all she's ever done."

"If she gets stuck here, and comes back to her senses later, we'll do everything we can to free her," Dante said. "But it might be for the best. If the White Lich defeats us, this is one of the last places he'll come to."

"Impressive rationalization," Ara said. "How are you going to come at the lich next, anyway? If he's discovered a way around the Odo Sein, how will you get near him without getting slaughtered?"

"I'm not sure yet. With any luck, we'll figure that out along the way."

"You're going to head for the Eiden Rane without any idea

how you're going to attack him? Remind me why I ever agreed to train you?"

"We aren't going after the lich," Dante said slowly. "We're leaving Tanar Atain."

She blinked, knocked off-kilter for the first time in the conversation. "What are you talking about?"

"The lich and the Monsoon are on the verge of sewing up the entire country. Another few days, and it'll all be theirs. We can't operate a resistance under those conditions. Our only choice is to withdraw, regroup, and put together a force capable of meeting him in the field."

"And leave my country to be devoured? To be murdered and converted into his servants? How can you condemn us to this fate when you just suffered it yourself?"

"Because it's the only way to win."

"No." She advanced on him, eyes locked on his. "You will not leave. I forbid it."

"How are you going to stop us, Ara? By using the Odo Sein to hold me down until I agree to do your bidding?"

"If that's what it takes!"

"Then you'll fail. Because I know how to break the Odo Sein, too."

She flashed her teeth in rage, cheeks mottled red. "Then I renounce my protection of you—and I renounce you. Begone and be damned!"

She turned on her heel and strode back to her tower.

Dante watched her stride away, robes streaming behind her. He was tempted to find Naran, remount the lan haba, and put the entire stupid place behind him, but the anger that had been simmering within him since being released from the White Lich's thrall boiled over. Before he knew what he was doing, he was running across the plaza.

Ara entered her tower, slamming the door behind her. Dante was prepared to knock the door from its hinges, but it was unlocked. He crossed to the stairwell. Her sandals smacked the treads. He ascended after her, his steps as noisy as hers, but she paid them no mind.

He exited the stairwell into the hallway where she kept her quarters just as she was clapping her door shut behind her. He flung it open. She whirled about. The room was so dark her face was little more than shadows, but her eyes burned like forges.

"How dare you?" Dante crossed to her, jabbing his finger at her face. "We've done nothing but struggle for this land!"

"And you're an utter failure, aren't you? So get out before you mess something else up! I order you!"

"And I defy you. What are you going to do about it?"

Face pinched with rage, she lowered her chin. Chains of golden flecks coalesced in a halo above her head. She lashed him with them, ripping the nether away from him. He smiled and envisioned the forest that had once grown across the Hell-Painted Hills. The vision was fleeting, and only produced a few flecks of stream.

But that was all he needed. He picked them up, seeking their connections to all of the other shadows. Her bonds shattered.

"Do you see what I can do?" He gestured east, toward the swamps. "He can do exactly the same. That's why we have to fall back."

"I've already heard you dribble out your stupidities, so you must be here to convince yourself of them, not me. Because *I* know that you promised to preserve my country, and instead, you're forsaking it."

"I've done everything I can! I've bled for it! Lost friends for it! I almost lost my *soul* for it, Ara. We can't fight him here anymore."

"Have you thought through what this means? Without flinching? Without grabbing at every hope you wish to be true while blinding yourself to every flaw that would hurt you?"

"Yes," Dante said. "Over the next few weeks, if not days, the last free Tanarians will be captured, conquered by the Righteous Monsoon or converted into Blighted by the Eiden Rane. At best, the lich will leave the Monsoon to rule themselves as they've been doing, stamping out your ways and replacing them with the unquestioning conformity of their belief. At worst, the lich will turn on them and bind them as his mindless and half-human soldiers. Either way, the Tanar Atain you know will perish."

"That's exactly what will happen." Her voice went husky. "Most of my people will be Blighted. They won't even be able to speak. Most of those who aren't Blighted will be Monsoon loyalists, who want to destroy everything we've stood for. Only a few of the few will remember the culture we once stood for. But anyone who speaks up about it will be put to death by the Monsoon. For those who remain silent, our ways will die with them.

"And that will be the end. Not even the outsiders will remember us, because we didn't let them know us. Even if there comes the day when you cut out the Eiden Rane's heart and burn it to ashes, that won't undo our fate. Tanar Atain is dead."

"You could be right. But you're forgetting something."

"What? That *you* will have known us, and can tell our story for us after we're gone? You don't know us at all, outsider. Even if you mean well, the story you tell of us will be no more than a shadow of what we were. Better to tell no story at all."

"I won't have to tell your story for you. Tanarians are still alive right now in Bressel. I will find the chink in the lich's armor and I'll drive a knife through it with my own hand. Then your people will return to your land. And they will rebuild it."

Her eyes shimmered. "I want that to be true more than anything. But the more we want something to be true, the more we'll lie to ourselves to get it."

Dante almost stopped himself. Instead, seized by impulses that felt like they were coming from outside himself, he took her in his arms and tipped back her head and he kissed her. Her eyes went wide and she pushed against him; but that was only the instinct of surprise. She froze, deciding, before wrapping her arms around him and pressing herself against him.

In time—he wasn't sure quite how long—she drew back.

She touched her mouth. "Why did you do that when you're right about to leave?"

"Because I'm right about to leave."

"You know that I *can't* leave here."

"While I have to. So there's no point, is there? But I'm not sorry."

"I didn't say that I was." Ara regarded him coolly. "What are you going to do now? Against the lich?"

"I imagine that I'll take his life."

"That's as specific as you can get?"

"I don't know how. It doesn't matter. I'm going to do it. And he should be afraid."

"There's something different about you. Something more urgent."

"Is that better? Or worse?"

"Better for leading us where we need to go," she decided. "But worse, I think, for your own peace of mind."

"That might be accurate."

"What was it like?"

He didn't pretend to not know what she was talking about. "I killed people. Lots of them. They hadn't done anything, other than not hand themselves over to the Monsoon or the lich, but that was crime enough for them to die. But most of them? I handed over to become Blighted. That's *worse* than death. They've lost half their soul and most of their mind, and all that's left is hunger and anger.

"I thought I was tilling the field for a new crop to grow. Fixing the mistakes the gods made when they first brought us to this world. You know what's worse than anything I did? That I enjoyed it."

"You literally weren't yourself. Only a fool would blame himself for that."

"I wasn't in a haze of some kind. I remember all of it, Ara. What I did and how good it felt to do it. It feels like it *was* me." He reached for a desk set against the wall, gripping it so hard he thought his hand might break. "That's why I know I'll find a way to end him. It's the only way to dim the screams in my head."

"But there's another way, isn't there? To die fighting him. And you know that." Ara parted her lips. "Come here."

He did so.

Sunlight cut through the open window, shining redly through his eyelids. He opened his eyes. She wasn't there.

Dante rolled from the low-slung bed, picked his wrinkled jabat from the ground, and dropped it over his shoulders. He went to the balcony. Ara wasn't there either, but down in the plaza, Blays and Naran were already loading provisions onto a team of lan haba.

Dante found his sandals and headed down to the plaza. The morning was warming quickly, with an unsteady breeze swirling about them as if it couldn't decide which way to go.

Naran grinned, dropped the pack, and walked over to embrace Dante. "You live! I knew that they would bring you back."

Dante smiled. "That's why you stayed behind, was it? Your raging confidence that I wouldn't kill everyone who opposed me?"

"I'm sorry I wasn't there. I should have been. I didn't believe that I would be of any use."

"You have nothing to apologize for. Anyway, we could sure

use you now. Have you heard our next move?"

"Blays says you intend to leave Tanar Atain. Is that all?"

"Ah, so you do know the plan."

"Until I met the two of you, I didn't know that 'shameless retreat' qualified as a plan of battle."

"Bah," Blays said. "The only people who badmouth it are the ones who don't have the balls to do it themselves."

Dante motioned to the north. "We need to warn everyone halfway friendly about what's happening. Lady Vita in Alebolgia. Those bastards in the Collen Basin. And we might even convince the Drakebane to work with us, or at least not to stab us in the back. Point is it's a lot of travel that I'd really rather not do by foot."

The corners of Naran's mouth twitched. "How can a man employ so many words and still not have enough of them to ask if I can get us on the *Sword of the South*?"

"Can you?"

"When she chose to be, Captain Twill was a smuggler. There were many times when it was feasible that the ship might have to leave port with such haste that some of us would be left behind. She quickly developed a method to unite her ship with her estranged crew."

"Where do we need to go to meet it?"

"Either end of the Hills will work. A few days ago when I spoke with Ara about the matter, she suggested I travel northwest, into Alebolgia. It's no further than the swamps from here, and will be much safer."

"Then that's our plan." Dante clapped Naran on the shoulder, gazing up at the seven quiet towers. "Where's Volo? I should see her before we go."

Naran led him up to the second floor of Ara's tower, showed him to her room, then returned to the plaza. She lay on a thin mattress on the floor. Her eyes were open, but they didn't so much as twitch toward Dante.

"Volo?" He moved beside the mattress. "They say you can't hear us. Is that true?"

She didn't stir. He sent the nether to her, but it showed nothing out of sorts.

"But *I* don't know that you can't hear us," Dante continued. "All we know for sure is that you can't *show* that you can. If you are hearing this, I want to thank you for all your help. Without it, we'd have died or been driven out a long time ago. So I'm sorry that it came to this. Wherever you are, don't give up. And I want you to know that when this is over, I'll come back and I will fix this."

Part of him really thought his words would provoke a response from her—a smile, a flutter of an eyelid—but no part of her moved except for her chest as it rose and fell. Dante gave her a moment, then left the room.

Ara stood in the hall. He moved toward her, but she held up her hand. "No need for that. Just tell me if you'll come back."

"If I live, I will."

She smiled. "Then try to live, will you? Even when we had new knights to train, it was pretty boring around here."

"I'm jealous. At this point, I'd love to be bored."

"Funny, because what I'd love most is to be able to get out into the thick of things and do my best to serve the lich a bowl of his own intestines." She looked him up and down. "But I suppose I'll have to settle for you. Go on and end this, will you? We've lived in his shadow for centuries. We won't last much longer."

Dante nodded. He could have said more, but he didn't and neither did she. She walked downstairs and he followed. Gladdic had arrived in the plaza during Dante's absence, and though Dante's stomach was rumbling, everyone else looked ready to go. He supposed he could eat in the saddle. He swung up onto

THE LIGHT OF LIFE

the back of one of the beasts.

Blays jumped up on his mount and saluted. "Sorry for the ab-breviated stay, but we have heroism to do. I know it might *look* like running away, but that's exactly what we want the lich to think."

Ara held up her hand. Dante waved back. They moved into the trees. Once they emerged from the woods and climbed the ridge beyond, Dante glanced back toward the plaza, but he was much too far away to tell if she was still there.

Mounted on the lan haba, they struck out from the Spires, heading northwest. It was dreadfully hot, obliging Dante and Gladdic to shade them with nether from sunup to sundown. Dante spent most of the day of travel going over everything he and the Eiden Rane had spoken about, sifting through the words and plans for anything that might reveal a weakness in the lich. Yet nothing stuck out.

After a full day of travel, with the very first hints of Blight starting to creep in, they mounted a hill and stopped. Ahead, the fire-streaked black of the Hell-Painted Hills met a brown plain dusted with green shrubs and weeds.

Blays shielded his eyes from the sun. "What are we looking at here? Some kind of dry land? Where's all the muck? The fetid pools?"

"Doubtless the work of a foul sorcerer," Gladdic said. "We should proceed with much caution."

Dante smiled, then curled his fingers into the shaggy fur on the goat's neck. "We've actually done it, haven't we? We've aban-doned the swamps to him. The lucky ones will die. And the rest will serve."

"Do you wish to go back?"

"What would that accomplish?"

"Nothing. In other words, the exact same amount that it accomplishes to sit here and complain about a decision we have already come to terms with."

Dante shook his head, digging for more, but nothing came. "Excuse me for being concerned that we've doomed an entire country."

"The lich doomed it, not us." Gladdic took up his reins. "Now if you have finished displaying your pious compassion for those poor people, shall we proceed?"

Dante dug his heels into his lan haba's flanks. The animals started down the final slope. Frustration swirled in Dante's mind. He *had* already accepted that Tanar Atain would fall. For that matter, most of it was already gone to the lich. Then what was it that bothered him?

The lan haba stepped out of the streaked black rock and onto the dusty reaches of Alebolgia. The four foreigners dismounted, took down their packs and weapons, and thanked the guides, who nodded and rode off to find a safe place to spend the next day recovering before the journey home.

Blays led the way, skirting the Hills as they moved southwest toward the coast. After the closeness of the forests and waterways of Tanar Atain, the openness of the land and the width of the sky was unnerving. The only cover came from low, threadbare grass and the occasional tuft of sagebrush. It had been just as open in the Hills, of course, but that had been different, dead lands where no enemy dared to travel. Now, they were vulnerable again. If something came for them, they'd have nowhere to hide.

Dante jerked up his head. It wasn't the abandoning of the swamp itself that gnawed at his stomach. It was the fact they *had* to abandon the swamp. They'd never been beaten before, had they? Oh, they'd lost scores of battles, but never the war. And perhaps they would still win the greater war against the Eiden Rane.

But they'd certainly lost the war for Tanar Atain. At that very moment, the Blighted were hunting their way across the swamps. Binding people in ropes and carrying them back to the lich to be converted into monsters. And eating one-tenth of their catch alive. For all of their effort, they couldn't stop the cataclysm from swallowing the swamps whole.

As much as Dante hated the lich, and wanted him to die— *needed* him to die—now that they'd lost once, he was no longer so certain that they wouldn't lose again.

The morning wore on. The land ahead shifted from scrubland to low dunes of black sand shot through with grains of red, yellow, and orange. Confused winds poured from the Hills in eddies and dust devils, obliging them to wrap cloths around their noses and mouths. It was a slog and a half, and Dante was more than glad when the sands petered out that afternoon, replaced by gray dirt stubbled with sage and the thorny green spheres of the tumbleweeds that would bounce across the fields in the months of late autumn.

With night coming on, they found a shallow ravine and made camp. Blays poked at the dirt with a stick. "We should light a fire."

"We've spent all day attempting to convert our asses into sweat," Dante said. "And you want to light a fire?"

"The sparking of fire is not only about banishing the cold." Gladdic paced side to side, gesturing like an orator. "It is about establishing a center from which civilization may take its stand against the chaos."

"Precisely," Blays said. "That, and turning dead animals into tasty meat."

"We don't have any meat," Dante said.

"Maybe if we light a fire, some of it will show up in tribute. Gladdic, go get the kindling, would go?"

Gladdic winced and pressed his palm to his back. "I am but

an old man, infirmed by frailty. You should honor your elders by gathering the wood for yourself."

"But I already did the hard part and came up with the idea. You can't expect me to do *everything*."

"The labor will only build your strength, allowing you to be a more able warrior, which will be of the better for everyone."

"Counterpoint: I don't want to."

Naran glanced at Dante and raised a skeptical eyebrow. Dante shrugged.

As the others argued on and on, Dante rolled his eyes and got to his feet. "Stop already. I'd rather do it myself than listen to you two squabble all night."

He headed down the ravine, getting out his torchstone and blowing on it to illuminate the twilit desert. There were virtually no trees and he wasn't likely to find any fallen branches or the like, but he thought it was possible he'd find an old snag that had succumbed to the heat.

After a few minutes, he was starting to think about uprooting some sagebrush instead. Turning toward a reasonably sized clump of it, his light snagged on a coalstick, a short and squat plant found in more arid regions that burned so steadily Dante half suspected they'd been created by some long-dead desert nethermancer. The stalk was no bigger than his forearm. Wouldn't make for much of a cooking fire by itself. Seeing no others around, he cut it near the base with a blade of nether, then sent the shadows back into it, harvesting the stump back to full size.

He repeated this four times in all, then brought his armload back to the camp. "While you fools were arguing, look what I found."

Blays elbowed Gladdic in the ribs. "See? I told you it would work."

Dante's jaw dropped. "You did all that arguing to exasperate me into doing the job for you? Do you have any idea how pathetic that is?"

"Oh, quit complaining. Unless you don't want any of our rabbit." Blays produced two dead rabbits. Judging by the small, precise holes in their foreheads, they'd been brought down by nether.

Gladdic arranged the coalsticks and lit them with a whoomp of shadows. Naran watched as Dante and Blays gutted and cleaned the rabbits.

"The labor involved in this is proof the gods intended us to eat fish," the captain declared. "One cut of the knife and a scoop of the fingers, and they're ready to roast."

He wandered off to trim some sticks to skewer the meat on. By the time Naran got back, the meat was trimmed and seasoned with traveling salt. They arranged it above the fire and seated themselves around it. The smells of the cooking rabbit and the smoke of the coalsticks was hypnotic, lulling the four of them into silence as they watched the fire speak the flickering language that only it understood.

The last few weeks had been ones of setbacks and hardships. Their enemy was stronger than ever, and the only part of the future that was certain was that it would be bleak. Since being freed, a boulder of dread had bent Dante's back.

Yet all it took to shed the weight was to light a fire against the darkness with the help of those you trust.

AUTHOR'S NOTE

If you're getting a kick out of these characters, you can read about their younger exploits in *The Cycle of Arawn* trilogy.

ABOUT THE AUTHOR

Along with *The Cycle of Arawn*, Ed is the author of the post-apocalyptic *Breakers* series. Born in the deserts of Eastern Washington, he's since lived in New York, Idaho, L.A., and Maui, all of which have been thoroughly destroyed in *Breakers*.

He lives with his fiancée and spends most of his time writing on the couch and overseeing the uneasy truce between two dogs and two cats.

He blogs at http://www.edwardwrobertson.com

39970093R00339

Made in the USA
San Bernardino, CA
23 June 2019